Mad Morgan

Mad Morgan

Kerry Newcomb

St. Martin's Press ≋ New York

www.stmartins.com

Design by Nancy Resnick

Library of Congress Cataloging-in-Publication Data

Newcomb, Kerry.
    Mad Morgan / Kerry Newcomb.—1st ed.
      p. cm.
    ISBN 0-312-26197-7
    1. Morgan, Henry, Sir, 1635?–1688—Fiction. 2. Governors—Jamaica—Fiction. 3. Panama (Panama)—Fiction. 4. Caribbean Area—Fiction. 5. Buccaneers—Fiction. I. Title.

PS3564.E875 M33 2000
813'.54—dc 21

                                              00-025936

First Edition: August 2000

10 9 8 7 6 5 4 3 2 1

Patty is my passion and strength.
Amy Rose, Paul Joseph, and Emily Anabel complete my joy.
This book is for them.

Acknowledgments

Thanks be to God for blessing me with life and friends like Aaron Priest, my agent and critic of first line. Thank you, Marc Resnick, for being a wonderful and supportive editor. Thank you, St. Martin's Press, for believing in this humble tale-teller. And here's a tankard of jack iron hoisted in honor of you, my friend, for buying this book and trusting me with a portion of your life. I'll try not to let you down.

This book owes a debt of gratitude to those researchers of pirate lore upon whose literary bounty I have respectfully drawn, to add color to Morgan's story. *The Book of Pirate Songs* by Stuart M. Frank, *Buccaneers and Marooners of America* by Howard Pyle, and *Pirates!* by Angus Konstam, proved to be invaluable resources. These works have been the wind in my sails, and I salute them.

Ho! Henry Morgan sails today
To harry the Spanish Main,
With a pretty bill for the Dons to pay
Ere he comes back again.

—Anonymous, a seventeenth-century sea chant

. . . With a yo heave ho and a fare you well
and a sullen plunge in the sullen swell
Ten fathoms deep on the road to Hell.

—Young Ewing Allison, 1763

Mad Morgan

I. The last night of peace.

Black sky. Black bay. Black rage in the water.
Muscles strained as the swimmer sliced through the stygian sea, sweet smooth, with an economy of effort. Gauging the distance, he saved his strength, a talent learned in the fields where he'd cut cane, slick clean with one swipe of the hooked steel blade. After years of toil, the wicked tool had become an extension of his powerful arm. The plantations took their toll; bone and blood was the price of a hurried harvest. Still, he had refused to die. Years of harsh servitude that broke the spirits of lesser men tempered him. He was lean but powerful, his iron strength had been forged by slavery in the furnace of the Caribbean sun. Ridges of lurid white scar tissue marked his back and shoulders in the pale glare as he broke the sheltering sea, gulped air then dove again, sleek as a watersnake, fanged and deadly on its course. His captors had been liberal in their punishment over the years. A taste of "the cat" was every slave's lot from time to time.

How far now? Not very. Head for the stern. See there, the Jacob's ladder. And the bark is well lit. No doubt the men aboard will be celebrating the birthday of their king, just like the others.

He paused and treaded water and glanced back across the bay to the shore, aglow with lanterns—the streets of Santiago were crowded with a happily inebriated populace. The birthday of the Spanish monarch was cause for celebration. The sounds of music and laughter drifted across the incoming tide, echoed to a lesser degree from the prison ship anchored offshore. He was one man alone, unnoticed, lost in the dark. No alarm preceded him. The carnival had masked his escape. And the watchmen who might have noticed his absence and raised an alert were beyond speaking.

Abelardo Montoya paced the poop deck, his back to the sea and his eyes on the harlots his compadres had brought from shore. The women were willing, obviously, and though plain as planks and broad in the beam, there wasn't one he wouldn't climb if given half a chance. Unfortunately, he had been assigned first watch by Sergeant Salas. Fate had decreed Salas and the other guards would play while Abelardo endured his lonely vigil, with naught but a heavy-bore Spanish musket to clutch in his grudging embrace. The guard stamped his feet and shook his head and tried to look away from the bark's gaily-illuminated quarterdeck. Lanterns hung from the shrouds and along the ship's rail. Rum kegs had been tapped, tankards had been raised to toast the health of Carlos II, and now a solitary piper coaxed a merry tune to dispel the gloom. Abelardo knew he was only punishing himself by watching but he couldn't bring himself to turn his back on the revel below. He sighed, removed his tricorn hat and mopped the perspiration from his forehead and grizzled cheeks upon the sleeve of his faded pea-green coat. The *Dolorosa* wasn't a bad ship, just a prison ship, stripped of its armaments to make room belowdecks for the murderous sea scum they had captured on the island. Guarding prisoners was a boring, tedious job but one that had to be done by someone.

"Hang the lot and be done with it," the Spaniard muttered, his hungry gaze sweeping the quarterdeck below. The ship's company had been raiding the rum stocks for several hours now. Sergeant Salas was roaring drunk and the rest of the crew weren't in any better shape. There wasn't a steady hand aboard, save his own. Curse the sergeant. Salas and the others intended to have their fun till the morning hours. And why not? Captain Gomez would not bring the rest of the crew aboard until tomorrow afternoon, plenty of time to load the whores back into a longboat and point them toward shore. "Not before I sample their wares, I swear," Abelardo scowled. "Short straws," he muttered. "Always choose the damn short straw. That's my luck."

In the middle of his self-pity he heard the Jacob's ladder behind him at the ship's stern rattle against the rail, then something thumped the deck behind him. Abelardo turned, took a step back and stared slack-jawed at the ragged, half-naked apparition that had swung over the side and landed on the poop deck. "*Madre de Dios . . .* what has the sea coughed up? A slave from the cane fields?" Abelardo cocked his weapon. "You had a long swim to hell, amigo." The Spaniard centered the musket on the slave's brow, just below his sodden brown mane.

The slave lunged forward as the guard squeezed the trigger and batted the priming powder from the pan. The flintlock misfired and failed to discharge. Abelardo cursed and clubbed the slave with the gun butt, opening a gash on his cheek. The slave staggered back and dropped his own weapon, a cane-cutter. Abelardo kicked the curved blade out of the way, stepped in close and swung the musket a second time. The slave recovered and dodged the blow, rammed his head into the Spaniard's groin, and forced him back against the rail. Abelardo gasped, dropped the musket, and called out to his compadres in a hoarse voice. The slave wrapped his arms around the guard's legs and dragged him down. On the quarterdeck, the revel continued, its participants heedless of the struggle.

Abelardo slipped a dagger loose from his belt sheath and sliced his opponent's shoulder. The slave ignored the pain, caught the guard's wrist and twisted the weapon in the man's hand, forcing the lethal blade down toward its owner's chest. Abelardo twisted and fought but the slave would not let go. Overhead through a forest of masts, trimmed sails, and rigging, a single star appeared through a rent in the clouds and tried to cast its feeble reflection upon the bay. On the ship below, two men struggled soundlessly for their lives, muscles straining.

Abelardo watched in horror as the knife he held inexorably lowered to his own breast. He once again tried to shout to his companions. Even now they might save him. But the slave covered the Spaniard's mouth with his forearm, then with a violent and overpowering effort thrust the blade deep into the guard's torso. The blade glanced off a rib and sank home. Abelardo twisted and thrashed in one last effort to break loose. But his strength failed him. His killer's gray eyes searched the dying man's features, made a connection; the slave from the sea and his victim bound in silent communion for one last moment.

Gray eyes without mercy, bleak as a thunderhead. Look away. . . . look to the star in the rigging. See how it sparkles briefly, oh, briefly, then fades . . . to black.

The slave rolled onto his side, then lay on his back, gulping air, shoulder to shoulder with the dead man. After a short breather, he crawled across the deck and retrieved his cane-cutter, then, peering over the edge of the poop deck, counted six more guards. Though he ached from his exertions and was near exhausted, thoughts of surrender never entered his mind. His gaze shifted from the blade in his hand to the Spaniards below. *Six to one? Fair enough.*

Loose havoc, harry mercy. Be it now . . . or never. There was blood on the moon tonight, and no turning back.

Welcome the living dead: these men without hope, existing in filth, dying in misery below the quarterdeck of the Spanish bark *Dolorosa.* The prison ship rode at anchor a couple hundred yards off the port of Santiago de Cuba. The imprisoned freebooters crowded in the gun deck were human cargo for the slave pens of Panama. These brethren of the Black Flag would have preferred a cleaner, quicker death. A firing squad, even dancing a jig at the end of a hangman's rope, had to be a better fate than what the Spaniards had in store for them. For men born to the sea, imprisonment and brutal servitude deep in the silver mines south of Panama would be a hellish ordeal.

On this humid, stifling night in the year 1660, the weary denizens belowdecks listened with a mixture of remorse and envy as their captors passed about flagons of rum and lifted their coarse voices in songs of celebration. Someone piped a tune for his drunken comrades. Half a dozen guards, unsteady on their feet, danced to the melody, swilled rum, sang and laughed and good-naturedly vied with one another for the jaded favors of the whores who had been brought across the bay at no small expense to these soldiers.

Sir William Jolly licked his parched lips. His nostrils flared. He could smell the rum despite the stench of unwashed bodies surrounding him. Jolly was a squat, solid-built man. Stringy red hair hung to his shoulders, beads of sweat rolled along his grizzled jaw and brooding brow. At a glance he seemed almost a dullard, a thick-skulled seaman affecting the ragged attire of a gentleman. But even Jolly's captors had noted the deference accorded the disgraced aristocrat by his fellow prisoners. Jolly's past was a mix of conjecture and rumor. It was said the physician had fallen victim to a libertine existence. Drunkenness and gambling may have cost him his heritage, but the forty-year-old physician had found a true calling among the thieves and cutthroats of the Spanish Main.

"Doc?" muttered Israel Goodenough, emerging from the shadows. The tall, rail-thin gunner had to walk stoop-shouldered as he approached. His forehead showed a bruise where he'd recently forgotten his height and clipped the crossbeams with his skull. Israel raised a bony hand and gestured aft where the worse of their number lay in misery upon makeshift pallets of empty grain sacks.

Goodenough dry-swallowed, hoping to coax a little moisture up into his throat. The round knob of his Adam's apple bobbed in the leathery trough of his long neck. "It's Hiram James. The fever's on him again."

"And if he's lucky it will kill him this time," said Jolly, glancing in the direction as a pitiful, almost animalistic wail rose from the shadowy recesses of the ship's stern. The poor soul sounded like some wounded cur left to die in an alley. In contrast, coarse laughter drifted down through the barred grating in the quarterdeck that permitted the only fresh air to reach below. "There's nothing I can do. Without my herbs and tinctures . . ." Jolly shrugged and held up his hands in a gesture of uselessness. Droplets of sweat formed on the bulbous tip of his pocked, pinkish nose.

Listen to the revelry. The bloody curs . . .

Jolly turned his sad brown eyes upward as if he could pierce the oaken beams and observe his captors indulging their debauchery in the lantern light. "They've left but a skeleton crew, I wager," the physician muttered.

"*Sacre bleu*. It might as well be an army for all the good it does us," another of the brethren drily observed. Pierre Voisin was a bastard by birth and a thief by choice. His narrow features were seamed from his perpetual squint and burned dark from a life lived before the mast. "I once was prisoner of the Marathas, south of Bombay. The vizier, old Kanhojii Angria, boiled half our crew in oil. On my honor, he did; then threw 'em to the sharks. I tell you, *mes amis*, be glad these sons of bitches above us at least are Christian."

"Shackles are shackles," said Israel Goodenough. He took no comfort in Voisin's story. "Christians ain't got no lock on mercy. Thomas LeBishop carries the Savior's cross into battle and I never seen such a bloodletter as the Black Cleric." Stooping forward, the gunner kept pace with the physician as Jolly maneuvered his way among his miserable companions. The buccaneers outnumbered the Spaniards. But the iron chains clamped about their ankles and the stout oak door with its heavy iron bolt kept the prisoners from forcing their way topside and commandeering the vessel.

"LeBishop's a hard one," Jolly agreed, shadows and firelight flickering on his coarse features. "Tell us again, Voisin. How did you escape the heathens of Islam?"

"I didn't," the Frenchman replied, flashing a gap-toothed grin. "I got killed!"

Weak laughter filtered through the crowded confines of the gundeck. Bellies growled. The thirst was intolerable. But the last time the freebooters had cried out for water the guards had responded by urinating through the iron grate overhead. A few crusts of mealy bread and a bucket of slops that passed for gruel came infrequently at best. With any luck the men below would starve to death in their shackles before ever setting foot in a silver mine.

"I ain't eaten in so long my gut thinks my throat's been cut," muttered Israel Goodenough.

"That's the only way you'll escape this cursed boat," another man replied, limbs trembling, eyes gaunt, ribs showing through his flesh. "What say you, sawbones?"

William Jolly shook his head and began to pace in a tight circle, his chains rattling with every step. His companions close by growled in discomfort as they moved their shackled limbs out of his path. Jolly stopped and stared at the steps leading up to the bolted door. He raised his clenched fists and shook them at their unseen guards. "Listen to them, dancing on our graves. By heaven . . . if we only had them in our gunsights . . ."

"Heaven?" said Israel. "Your shadow won't ever fall there, William Jolly. It's a mite late to be calling on the angels." The gunner spoke with a sense of grim resolve. He hadn't lost hope quite yet, but the light was dimming fast.

Jolly continued to shake his fists, his mouth drew back in a grimace. This was his fault. Their schooner, *Red Warrant*, had run aground on the coast of Hispaniola, leaving them at the mercy of the Spanish forces. They had avoided capture for several days, but at last, starving and with their captain dead, Jolly had led the men in surrender, hoping to appeal to the mercy of the Spanish authorities. Alas, mercy was in short supply these days. Maybe they should have fought to the death. But he had a daughter in Port Royal. A nine-year-old girl who expected to see him again. He was the only family she had. He must get back to her, somehow, some way. "Nell," he softly whispered to himself. "I swear I shall never leave you again."

He slumped back amid his brethren. In the darkness back toward the stern, poor delirious Hiram James cried out for his sister. The hallucinations shifted: he called out for men to join him at the topgal-lants, he shouted for his comrades to cut away the sailcloth. "Watch yourselves, lads, they're using chain." His breathing grew more labored then rattled deep in his throat and ceased altogether.

"It's all over," someone called out.

"Good for him," Pierre Voisin disconsolately replied. "Should we grieve? *Je ne sais pas.* Why? At least he's free. Hell can be no worse." In the silence that followed the Frenchman's benediction, the bucca-neers gloomily pondered the fate that awaited them all. In sharp con-trast to their mood, the revel above continued unabated. The guards were celebrating as if there were no tomorrow. A scar-faced Spanish sergeant knelt upon the grate overhead, his bulk blocking out the pale moonlight appearing through the tattered clouds. Manuel Salas dragged his pewter tankard across the iron screen, taking care to spill some of the rum. Why not? There was plenty. He enjoyed taunting the prisoners. Animals like these were a constant threat to Spain's colonies in the New World. They deserved to suffer.

"What say you, thieves, murderers, you sons of bitches? The rum is sweet as mother's milk. Are you thirsty, my pretties?" One of the whores joined the sergeant and began to pull on his coat. She was a round, heavyset mulatto, wide-eyed and unsteady on her feet. Salas whispered in her ear. The mulatto nodded and laughed, raised her skirt and presented herself to the prisoners. "Feast your eyes," roared Salas. "For you'll never again enjoy a woman's favor." The sergeant grabbed her ample derriere, turned her about and buried his scarred face beneath the woman's rumpled skirts. The mulatto squealed in delight and rose up on her toes. A few moments later the guard freed himself from her coffee-colored thighs and struggled to his feet. The curses rising from below amused him. He emptied the contents of the tankard onto the upturned faces. "Here you soulless scum, you *bou-caniers.* Drink. Drink." Beneath the grate, several of the freebooters surged forward, struggling to place themselves beneath the trickle of rum. William Jolly bullied his way through the men, with Israel Goodenough and the Frenchman, Voisin, at his side. Sir William put an end to the altercation before it spread throughout the gundeck.

"What is this? Shall we give this jackal the satisfaction of watching us kill one another for a few drops of grog?!"

The prisoners surrounding Jolly grudgingly retreated, chains rat-tling as they shuffled back to their places. Salas hurled the tankard against the iron grate, cursed the physician in the darkness below and, grabbing the whore in his rough embrace, dragged her out of sight.

Jolly and the others could hear him laughing above the din of his companions. Elsewhere on the deck a pistol shot rang out, followed by another. In celebration . . . ?

A few moments later the whore began to scream. The prisoners assumed she was being brutally taken by her paramour. Indeed, there wasn't a guard who seemed to be anything less than mean and dangerous. Suddenly Sergeant Salas landed facedown and covered the grate with his body.

"Has this bastard no shame?" said Israel Goodenough. "Will he go a'romping in bushy park right above us?" Droplets of moisture spattered into the hold.

"More rum," Israel muttered, catching a few droplets on his fingertips. Then he sniffed his fingers and stepped back from the spreading stain. "Blood?" The mulatto continued to scream as she ran across the deck and vaulted over the side of the ship. A mouthful of salt water stilled her cries.

William Jolly dipped his fingers in the moisture and nodded in confirmation. Now one and all recognized the unmistakable clatter of steel on steel. Bootheels drummed across the deck. A door slammed back on its hinges. A musket discharged. The commotion on deck intensified as the guards scrambled about. Someone cried out, *"Quien viené?!"* There were growls and groans, a cry of pain and a litany of curses, all in Spanish. Someone cried out in agony, his voice trailed off. The other prostitutes attempted to raise the alarm but the women were obviously frightened and desperate to be off the prison ship. This far out in the bay there was no one to hear them scream. Even a pistol shot failed to rouse the garrison ashore.

"Sacre bleu. What is happening?" Voisin muttered, echoing the concern of every man. He blessed himself.

Jolly shrugged. "Sounds like hell's come to the dance." He shook his head, stroked his broad rough chin, and moved to the steps leading up to the quarterdeck. The melee raged on. Another guard collapsed, moaning and writhing on the deck until he gagged and died. His companions lost heart and followed the prostitutes over the side of the boat. Their voices grew distant as they splashed and pawed the water, exhorting one another to swim for shore.

Then silence. The seconds crept past. They heard the pad of bare feet upon the quarterdeck as someone made their way past the grate. Upturned eyes followed the sound as it passed overhead then leveled toward the door at the head of the steps leading up from the gundeck.

The iron bolt on the outside of the door shrieked like a banshee as it slid back. Next, the iron hinges offered protest as the door swung open and crashed against the deck. A wiry-looking figure outlined in silvery light appeared on the top step, then started down into the foul chamber. The slave moved with catlike grace; as if stalking prey, watchful . . . dangerous and ready to lash out. William Jolly squinted and rubbed his eyes. The stranger on the top steps brandished a wicked-looking cane-cutter in one hand, a ring of iron keys in the other. He was clad in torn breeches, damp and clinging to his power-ful thighs from the long swim from shore. His torso was burned dark, his belly lean and corded with muscle. The collective gaze of the pris-oners focused on the ring of iron keys dangling from the stranger's fingers.

"I intend to steal this ship," said the man on the steps. He looked to be no more than twenty, young and untried but resolute; he spoke softly, but with conviction, saying exactly what he meant. His gray eyes, tempered like the raw steel of the cruel blade in his fist, cast a spell over this collection of sea rogues. "I shall need a crew."

"Where are the guards?" Israel called out, voicing a question on everyone's mind.

"Some took their chances in the bay. The others . . ." The man on the steps raised his cane-cutter, its hooked blade spattered crimson.

"Who's with you?" another of the freebooters asked suspiciously. "You expect us to believe a jackanapes like yourself captured the *Dolorosa* on your lonesome?"

"Believe what you see," the stranger on the steps replied. Without further explanation, he tossed the keys into the hold. William Jolly made a perfect catch and with trembling hands began to fumble at the padlocks chaining the men to the deck underfoot. At last the ankle clamps fell away and he kicked free of the shackles and passed the keys to the outstretched hands of his companions. Jolly advanced on their benefactor, his great bulk looming over the younger man. This escaped slave was a sight, standing there half-naked, bleeding from several nasty-looking cuts, his shaggy shoulder-length brown hair framing his careworn features—for it was in the hard-edged lines of his face that slavery had marked him the most.

But the young man had single-handedly vanquished the Spaniards, taken the prison ship for his prize, and freed Jolly and his shipmates, one and all. The physician felt the breath of fate tickle his ear. Sir William was standing at the crossroads of all that had gone before, aware that his next decision determined the rest of his life, for better or ill. One thing he suspected: there would be no lack of adventure with this young man.

"By heaven, I'll serve with you. Never let it be said William Jolly forgets a good deed done his way."

"Aye, we're with you," Israel Goodenough exclaimed, rubbing his chafed limbs. He was grateful for a second chance. The newly freed buccaneers surged toward the steps. Jolly halted them with a wave of his hand.

"Lads, here be your captain. What say you?"

"*Mais oui*. I will follow the devil himself if he leads to freedom!" shouted Voisin. And the rough lot joined in with one accord, accepting the physician's decision to give their young benefactor a chance. He had proved a match for the Spaniards, whether he could fly the Black Flag and survive this unruly lot, only time would tell.

The stranger nodded and led the way up into the night air. William Jolly fell into step alongside the younger man. "Tell me, uh, Cap'n, what do you know of sailing a leaky bucket like this?"

"Not a damn thing," the escaped slave retorted. "That's why I need you." A wicked grin split his features. Once on deck, Jolly noted the dead Spaniards sprawled about the ship. Even a jaded old sea dog like himself was impressed. It was as if some terrible force of nature had swept down upon the guards and slayed them where they stood.

"Just who are you?" Sir William quietly asked, a note of unease in his tone. Their benefactor showed no regret for his actions, though he knelt and wiped his blade clean on the baggy coatsleeve of one of his victims.

"Henry Morgan."

Jolly shrugged. The name meant nothing. "You come from plantations ashore?" asked the physician, lighting a lantern. He held up the lamp and quietly appraised his new captain by the lamp's sallow glow.

Morgan nodded. "I was taken from my village in Wales and brought here, a long . . . long time ago." Music and laughter and the sounds of revelry drifted across the black bay. The port was draped in lantern light and the Spanish populace danced in the streets.

"Listen to them," Jolly said. "No one can hold a candle to a Spaniard for celebrating. And when it comes to religion, them's the saintliest sons of bitches I know, that is, when they aren't starving our poor families to death or hanging our kinsmen. Do you be a God-fearin' man, Henry Morgan?"

And for the first time Morgan smiled. But his humor was carved in ice and his storm-gray eyes narrowed and flashed.

"I shall follow only two commandments," said Morgan. " 'Get mad.' " His fierce gaze flared like a lit fuse. " 'Get even.' "

Jolly shivered in the warm, humid sea breeze ruffling the square-rigged sails overhead.

Morgan experienced a flash of memory, his thoughts reached back seven years to Swansea, a settlement on the coast of Wales, a quiet little port engulfed in flames and at the mercy of Spanish raiders. In his mind's eye he watched Welsh men and boys shackled and led away to be chained in the hold of a Spanish raider and carried off to the Caribbean. The rest was a blur of servitude and grueling toil. But Henry Morgan was free now, free to seek his fortune, to roam the Spanish Main. He'd leave Santiago de Cuba far richer than he came, with a ship and a crew. And an unquenchable thirst for retribution.

"What are they celebrating?" Israel asked in a deep voice. He approached from amidships, the tall man folding his arms across his bony chest as he paused to stare off toward shore.

Morgan's ominous reply cut quick as a cutlass, unsheathed from some secret place where the hurt ran deep. "It is the last night of peace."

We are Brethren of Blood,
we are sons of the sea.
We are children of havoc
and born to be free.
Young Morgan was captured and carried away
To far Hispaniola, to slave night and day.
Though he bent to the lash, his heart would not break,
And Morgan swore vengeance, dark vengeance to take.

2. "Kill me if you can."

The "schooner" is swifter but outgunned by the "bark." It is a desperate struggle, a tense game of cat and mouse as these two adversaries—wooden ships with whittled hulls, wooden pegs for masts, and scraps of a mother's apron for sails—maneuver and counter one another upon the dark waters of the rain barrel. The ten-year-old captain of the schooner watches intently. Even in Swansea on the coast of Wales, it pays to be cautious. Henry Morgan glances up at his father who nods approvingly at his son's tactics.

"Well and good, my boy, you did not fall for my feint. I've twenty guns to your twelve and will pound you down to the waterline if you charge on in and trade broadsides." Edward Morgan is no stranger to such duels. Henry's father has never concealed his past from his son, how he had sailed as a privateer under letters of masque permitting him to harass the coasts of France and Spain. To his wife's dismay, Edward has filled his son's head with stories of adventure and peril on the high seas. Priscilla Morgan may disapprove of the stories, but she has been only too happy to spend Edward's prize money on the inn that is their livelihood. And so from time to time, on warm summer afternoons while Priscilla tends the tables in the Sprig and Sparrow, serving platters of her famous mutton roast and flagons of ale to the hungry patrons, Edward and his son often retire to the rain barrel out behind the inn for another lesson in seamanship.

"Next time, Henry, keep the Spanish flag aloft until the last minute.

Then show your true colors. And bare your fangs. We were always out-gunned. Outmanned, too. Trickery is your most important ally. Now, then, ease about. Beware of my twelve-pounders. There's two a'port and two starboard. The rest be eight-pounders. If you drift into my sights I'll blow you out of the water. Remember what I've told you." Edward *glances toward the back door, checking for his quick-tempered wife.* "At close quarters you could have used your grenades." *He reaches into the pouch dangling from a wide, canvas shoulder strap and removes a cast-iron sphere, large as his fist and filled with gunpowder, sealed with an iron plug through which runs a black powder fuse.* "Ten or twenty of these will clear a deck and even the odds. Grenades, then a volley from your marksmen in the rigging while you lower the boarding planks, then charge across with pikes and cutlass and ax."

"Yes sir," *Morgan replies, gray eyes flashing, cheeks flushed with excitement.* "Too late now for hand-to-hand. So it's hard to starboard. I'll use my speed and circle you—see how I tack sharply, here I am. My schooner's rigged with square-sail and fore and aft. I can still use the wind, you cannot keep up with me. Watch when I cross the T and fire a broadside into your stern. My four-pounders will test your merit, Papa."

"Where do you aim?"

"Chain-shot to cut your sails, solid-shot below the waterline. You'll have to send men to work the pumps and it'll slow you even further."

Edward gently mimics the wind and blows on the makeshift sails of the hand-carved boats. "See you trim your sail. Smartly now. Slow down. Give yourself time for a second volley before you clear the stern. Remember, I will be turning also. But you can beat me on the tack. Still, you'll take some damage. The Spaniards will have gunports at the stern. They'll open fire. You'll take damage and nothing to be done for it. Mind your crew, wood splinters are worse than iron. They'll cut a man to ribbons."

"Lord, we thank you for that which we are about to receive," *Morgan solemnly intones as if he is standing amidships, defiant in the face of the enemy guns, his courage setting an example for his men.*

Edward claps his son on the shoulder. "Well said, lad. Well said." *Then his expression turns grave.* "Now you've fought your desperate battle and had your victory, but you've paid a price. You'll have lost men. And your ship will take punishment. Now I'll teach you the most important lesson I ever learned while chasing Spanish gold." *Edward reaches over and collects his son's "schooner" and crushes it in his hand, silencing Henry's protest with a wave of his hand.* "I've taught you to fight when need be, but scouring the seas for a rich prize is more often than not a path to*

debtor's jail. Pay no heed to the tales of iron men and wooden ships duel-
ing upon the deep blue sea." He places the wreckage of the toy ship on the
edge of the rain barrel. "The fox runs and hides by day and strikes at
night where the hens are kept. The tiger stalks the herd then strikes where
least expected. Dying in battle is a fool's game. Let others play it out.
Think first, then fight. But no more than is necessary. If gold is your prey,
then hunt where it is kept." Edward Morgan lifts his eyes to the gray hori-
zon and the rolling tides down below the cliffs at the edge of the village.
"Portobello, Panama, Santiago, Cartagena, Vera Cruz, Maracaibo."
He turns and looks at Henry. "Do you understand, lad?"

"Kill me if you can," Morgan said softly, standing by the starboard rail
on the deck of the *Glenmorran* as the two-masted sloop glided on the
night wings of the wind into Maracaibo Bay. The entrance was narrow here and most ships must chance running aground in the shallows. Not so the *Glenmorran* with its shallow draft and sleek hull.
Nor the *Jericho*, fifty yards behind, with its mercurial-natured captain,
Thomas LeBishop. With soot-smeared sails by pale moonlight, the
pirate ships were all but invisible against the cloudswept stars and distant shore.

Two islands guarded the entrance to the bay and Morgan kept his
eyes on both of them, checking one then the other. Watch Isle, to the
east, was ringed with treacherous sandbars. Pigeon Island to the west
was the larger of the two, a teardrop-shaped knoll rising out of the sea
and crowned with a castle whose seaward ramparts bristled with
enough cannon to batter the fourteen-gun *Glenmorran* and its sister,
Jericho, to kindling.

It was during the waning days of August, it was in the year 1670,
a time when the turquoise waters of the Spanish Main ran red with
blood from Portobello to Port Royal. No treasure ship was safe, no
convoy or guarded port was free from attack.

Morgan's crew watched their captain with pride as he stood
between a pair of eight-pounders and their gun crews, his arms outstretched as if daring the Spanish gunners asleep within the walls of
the castle to awaken and try their luck. One Spaniard or another had
been trying to apprehend and kill Henry Morgan for the past nine
years. Since his escape from Santiago de Cuba, Henry Morgan had
made good his promise. Spanish ports and shipping had known precious little peace. There was no escaping *el Tigre del Caribe*. The
Tiger of the Caribbean was cunning and quick, and though Morgan's

fearlessness inspired his crew, his reckless deeds struck fear in the hearts of the Dons throughout the Americas.

"What say you, Captain Morgan?" one of his men rasped.

Morgan grinned and invited the sleeping Spaniards to try again. "Here I am," he said, presenting himself to those towering black walls. Every fort throughout the Spanish Main had a cage for *el Tigre*, a cage and a short walk to the gallows. But the Dons must catch him first.

"You make a pretty target for a Spanish cannonade," said Nell Jolly. The eighteen-year-old daughter of Sir William Jolly made no attempt to hide the fact that she fancied the dashing pirate captain. Her tone of voice grew warm as a summer breeze whenever she spoke his name. If only Henry Morgan would take the time to notice. Wasn't he a grand sight? It was easy to recall the first time she had ever seen him, the day young Morgan, uncaged and free, swaggered onto the docks of Port Royal, her father following close behind him. Sir William lost no time that day in regaling the populace as to how the brash young man had rescued them from Spanish captivity and accepted their pledge of loyalty on the very decks of the prison ship, slick with the blood of their jailors.

At the time, Henry Morgan had barely noticed this nine-year-old girl with wide, wise sky-blue eyes and a head filled with notions of adventure. Even then, Nell had hungered for a life different from that of the women she knew in port. The fleshpots of the wickedest place on earth had a way of using up a fairer sex, squandering a woman's best years in a brief span of time. No. Nell Jolly wanted more then a life swilled down with bay rum and endless bacchanal.

Still, whatever their faults, at least Port Royal's unsavory lot were free of pretense. Nell found many of its denizens to be more trustworthy than Kingston's landed gentry across the harbor. After her mother's untimely demise, the Brethren of the Coast had assumed her education. Nell Jolly learned to count in the gambling dens. Buccaneers instructed her in seamanship, taught her to climb the rigging like a monkey and to shoot like the very devil.

Nell quietly appraised the captain at the rail. *Patience*, she cautioned herself. *One day you will tire of excess, of blind adventure and endless quests for wealth. One day, Henry Morgan, you will want something more from your life, something of value and meaning. And I will be there.*

The Tiger of the Caribbean was wild as his namesake, but one day he would recognize Nell Jolly for what she was—faithful, loving, and courageous—and in that moment she would tame him. As for now, no bonnier bull's-eye would Spanish gunners have this night than Henry Morgan. His earlier years of servitude had left the buccaneer with a taste for finer things. Long ago, he had exchanged his tattered attire for the colorful trappings of a gentleman. *El Tigre del Caribe* cut a dashing figure in his butternut-brown breeches and linen shirt, his knee-high boots of Spanish leather. He favored a gaudy scarlet waistcoat of silk brocade worn beneath a long burgundy frock coat and a black felt tricorn hat embroidered with gold stitching. His thick brown hair was gathered back and tied with a leather string. The broad black belt circling his waist held a brace of pistols and a throwing dagger sheathed against the small of his back.

"Here, you might need this." Nell Jolly addressed him with casual informality and handed him a cutlass and gold-stitched baldrick, which he draped over his right shoulder. The weapon's yard-long blade was tempered steel, the brass hilt and wrapped leather grip a perfect fit for Morgan's hand.

El Tigre prowled his ship with feline grace, his senses keenly aware of his surroundings, the roll of the ship and the temper of the tides as the bow broke the surface of the silent sea. No patch of fluttering canvas, no creak of mast bearing the weight of the wind escaped his slate-gray eyes.

Now that the game was afoot, and disaster a stone's throw from the deck of the *Glenmorran*, his wiry frame all but crackled with energy. He was never more alive than at such moments of peril. Plucking the whiskers of fate . . . the hazard of risking everything . . . this was his life's blood.

As Pigeon Isle slipped beyond the stern and melted into the night, Morgan turned to his crew. They sensed he was about to speak and began to draw close.

"Gather 'round, lads. I've a question for you."

"Ask it, Cap'n," someone called out.

"Who are you?"

"We are free men."

"What are you?" Morgan continued.

"We are masters of our own fate," the men replied in a rough chorus.

"Aye. Masters of our own fate, beholden to no king or country, and bound only to the whims of our wild hearts and the loyalty to our friends and comrades-at-arms." Morgan's gaze swept over them. He took care to make a connection with each of his crew. "We are Brethren of the Coast, gold and cold steel is our lineage . . . and our

crest, the Jolly Roger fluttering from the mainmast. This be our destiny, to triumph or die. I say this now for every man to hear, and mark
my words. Screw your heart to your backbone, lads, for I am taking
you into harm's way!"

Nell felt a rush of excitement as the crew of the *Glenmorran* nodded and voiced their approval. They were prepared to follow their
captain to hell and back. Hard men and bold, these buccaneers who
trusted "Morgan's cunning" and "Morgan's luck."

"Look there." The buccaneer gestured toward their destination.
The crew scrambled to the shrouds, climbed into the rigging and lined
the rail in an effort to see for themselves. Across the night-shrouded
inlet loomed the coast of Venezuela and the twinkling lights of the
prize Morgan had come for, Maracaibo. Although the prosperous
port lacked the reputation of an impregnable city like Panama, with
its legendary storehouses of silver and gold, rare woods, jewels, and
silks from the Orient. Still, Maracaibo had its own unique treasures.

"Where are the palaces?" Nell complained. "I doubt we'll see much
prize money."

"Listen to you, Toto," Morgan chuckled. The physician's daughter
bristled. How could she command respect among these rogues if they
should overhear her referred to as a "coconut tart"? Morgan relished
the effect the name had on the young woman. She was like a little sister to him. Teasing Nell Jolly was one of life's simple pleasures. "What
do you know of prize money?"

"I know an empty purse and a disgruntled crew when I see one.
And not your own. You'll have to reckon with the Black Cleric if you
fail."

"I can handle Thomas LeBishop," Morgan replied confidently,
glancing over his shoulder in the direction of the *Jericho*, the sloop
that had sailed with him from Jamaica. Was that a hint of doubt in his
voice? Perhaps. LeBishop was as dangerous as a white squall, a cunning, quick-tempered, and ruthless rival, but just the sort of partner
to bring into this Spanish stronghold. After all, they hadn't come to
Maracaibo for a church social.

"The plantations inland will have brought their produce down
from the hills," Morgan continued. "If not, we will harvest them ourselves. I warrant we shall find all manner of tobaccos, cocoa, sugarloaves, cattle, and swine waiting for Spanish cargo fleets. We'll ransom
Maracaibo for its heirlooms, family jewels, and pieces of eight. Prize
money, indeed—they'll pay or burn. Fret not, little sister. Don't knot
your bonnet with such concerns."

"Henry Morgan, we may have lived beneath the same roof when my father brought you home to Port Royal. But I am not your *sister*. And as for bonnets, you'll find no foofaraw here!" She patted the pistols thrust in her belt. A blunderbuss dangled from a sling draped over her right shoulder. A third pistol was tucked neatly away in one of the pockets of her blue frock coat. With her auburn locks hidden beneath her yellow scarf, Jolly's daughter looked like an innocent young lad cast among miscreants. She buttoned the coatflaps across the baggy linen shirt concealing her pert bosom. Brown canvas breeches and buckled shoes completed her disguise.

Nell Jolly asked no favors, but carried her weight as did every man of Morgan's crew. No man had ever complained about her presence aboard ship. Indeed, there were times at sea when her gently lilting voice, raised in song, stilled tempers and soothed this savage lot.

Morgan chucked her beneath the chin and then sauntered back to the stern where Pierre Voisin stood at the ship's wheel and piloted the sloop through the shallows, back into deeper waters and across the bay.

"Steady as she goes," Morgan said, drawing abreast of the Frenchman.

"Aye, Captain," Voisin replied. "Though I swear, any closer to that damn castle and we would have wound up in some Spaniard's lap."

"Or his mistress's. Fortune may yet smile on you, old goat," Morgan chuckled.

"From your lips to God's ears, *mon capitaine.*"

Men near the sloop's bow gauged the depth with a drag line and quietly relayed the information back to the stern. "Just over ten feet," said Sir William Jolly, joining Morgan at the helm. The physician settled his tricorn upon his wide, solid brow. Hours earlier, alone in Morgan's cabin, the physician had made an entry in the ship's log. Struggling by dimmed lantern light, the learned physician had recorded their daring entry into Maracaibo Bay, then, setting his pen aside, hurried up to see how they would fare.

Once they had made it past the guns of Pigeon Isle with its fortress guarding the bay, Jolly breathed a sigh of relief. He glared at the twin islands blocking access to the sea. To his wary eyes they seemed but the jaws of a trap closing on the pirates. How the devil did Morgan plan to run that terrible gauntlet of Spanish artillery once the alarm was given? They'd take heavy casualties among the crew.

"My daughter is too damn anxious to test her mettle," Sir William observed gruffly. His red hair was streaked with silver and thinning rapidly. He was beginning to look like a monk. In another few years, Sir William figured he would be as bald as the Black Cleric.

Morgan nodded, somewhat amused.

"I hear your thoughts," Jolly continued. "I know, a pirate ship is an odd place to behave like an overprotective father. That should have happened back in Port Royal."

"Fear not, sawbones. I shall steer her from distress."

"Nell is a simple, honest lass," her father ruminated. "Plainspoken. Artifice is not in her nature. But she can shoot the eye out of an iguana at ten paces. And I'd hate to cross swords with her. I warrant she can take care of herself."

Sir William watched his daughter move among the crew, walking the length of the sloop, leaning over the rail and then, with too many bodies blocking her line of sight, she vaulted into the shrouds to better study the harbor. The physician had not argued against his daughter coming aboard. At least he could keep an eye on her. Not like in Port Royal with its easy virtue and wicked ways. Better aboard the *Glenmorran* where no man would impugn his daughter's honor for fear of facing the wrath of Morgan himself.

"The *Jericho*'s trying to pull ahead," Voisin reported.

Morgan glanced across the black water. Both sloops were built of Jamaican cedar; their sleek reddish hulls measured seventy feet from bow to stern and were seventeen feet in width. Like the *Glenmorran*, LeBishop's sloop was armed with fourteen eight-pounder cannons. Morgan grinned and climbed the steps to the poop deck and walked to the starboard rail. He produced his spyglass from his coat and focused on the *Jericho*. Overhead the opalescent moon poked through a stream of clouds, a single perfect pearl adrift in the slipstream night. The dappled surface of the bay looked as if it were festooned with shiny pieces of eight. Silvery light outlined the ships and etched in gold the stone and wood houses and the military barracks of Maracaibo.

Morgan adjusted the glass, then steadied his hand until a familiar figure materialized in the eyepiece. "Ahoy, you old pulpit-pounder," he chuckled. Thomas LeBishop's hollow-cheeked features were partly masked by a spyglass of his own as he studied the *Glenmorran*.

LeBishop was older by a decade and, until Morgan's arrival in Jamaica, had lorded over the denizens of Port Royal with a singular presence born of his well-earned reputation as a merciless plunderer. The Black Cleric had been a thorn in Spain's side for many a year. He reveled in his reputation as a brutal and bloodthirsty rogue. Before first setting foot in Jamaica, Morgan remembered how he had been cautioned to cut a wide berth round the Black Cleric and give the man his due. *I didn't then, and I'm not about to start today*, he muttered to himself. *We'll see who's first in Maracaibo.*

Morgan barked out a set of orders for the men aloft to keep the topsails full then snapped instructions to the helmsman.

"Keep a sharp eye, Pierre. Go before the wind."

"Before the wind," Voisin repeated.

A few moments later, the *Glenmorran* slowly, inexorably, began to edge past the *Jericho* and regain the lead. Morgan grinned and hurried back to the rail, where he executed a grandiose bow, sweeping his hat across his chest. He knew goading LeBishop was akin to poking a hungry shark with a bloody stick but that didn't make it any less fun.

Aboard the *Jericho*, the Black Cleric scowled and tossed his spyglass to his quartermaster, the pockmarked Cornishman named Peter Tregoning, a distinctly unpleasant seaman with a fine tenor voice, gnarled features, and a backbone hard as steel. LeBishop issued orders; Tregoning made certain they were carried out. He could read the stars and read men, and had never run from a fight in his life. But even a dangerous freebooter like Tregoning stood aside when the Black Cleric stalked past.

"Beware, you popinjay," the cleric muttered, as if the *Glenmorran*'s colorful captain were standing at his side instead of pulling into the lead. Morgan would precede him into port by a length, though the proud fool might crash his sloop into the docks in the process. " 'Pride goeth before destruction and a haughty spirit before a fall.' "

Taking orders from the likes of Henry Morgan did not sit well with LeBishop. But the offer of a combined raid on Maracaibo had been too tempting to resist. The Black Cleric removed his hat and mopped the perspiration from his bald pate. He had a bald, bony skull and pale pasty flesh that defied the efforts of the sun to burn him dark as the rest of the Brethren. A cross of gold dangled from a ring in his left earlobe.

Though a man of the cloth might have seemed out-of-place in such company, Thomas LeBishop looked every bit the minister in his somber black frock coat, breeches, buckled shoes, and round, broad-brimmed hat; even the wide white collar reflected the service that had been his former calling. It was rumored the slaughter of his unfaithful wife and the murder of her paramour had placed him beyond the company of saints. If such were the case, it wasn't long before he found the devil to his liking. Old Scratch paid well in the coin of the world, gold, silver, whisky, carnal delights, every manner of vice.

The rolling deck of a pirate ship was his pulpit now.

LeBishop gazed down upon his "flock." These battle-hardened cutthroats needed little prompting. They knew what was expected of them and went about their tasks, preparing themselves for battle as the *Jericho* eased itself close to the pier.

One of the buccaneers glanced up at his captain and knuckled his forehead in salute. LeBishop nodded, acknowledging the deference, then, with a hint of brimstone in his bleak blue eyes he addressed his crew.

"For the weapons of our warfare are not worldly, but have divine power to destroy strongholds." A murmer of approval swept through each savage breast. The buccaneers liked the sound of his message. It mattered not whether it came from the pulpit or the ship of the damned.

Morgan turned his back on the *Jericho* and studied the waterfront as the *Glenmorran* eased toward shore. A couple of squat-looking Dutch flutes, square-rigged cargo vessels built for transport, rode easy in their berths. A fore-and-aft–rigged schooner, the sort of vessel favored by those in the slave trade, nestled against the pier a grenade's-throw from the *Santa Rosa*, a three-masted brigantine, almost half again as long as the sloops, and wider amidships.

The brig appeared to be under repair. One mainsail had yet to be hung, and half a dozen lethal-looking twelve-pounders were arranged in an ordered row upon the docks, waiting to be loaded aboard the warship's gundeck. The royal colors of Spain fluttered from the mainmast.

The sloop lost speed as the sails were trimmed and, catching just enough of the sea breeze on the mizzen course and spritsail, crawled the few remaining yards and settled alongside the pier a good fifty yards down the waterfront from the *Santa Rosa* and the Dutch ships. The men aloft finished securing the topsails and then scampered down the shrouds to join their comrades on the deck. A few minutes later the *Jericho* arrived and prepared to discharge its band of raiders.

"Well done, Monsieur Voisin," Morgan said.

"Aye, Captain," the Frenchman called back.

Morgan lost no time in ordering out the gangplank. Goodenough repeated the captain's orders and the freebooters hurried to obey. The walkway was drawn out and allowed to drop with a clatter onto the pier.

For a moment, the buccaneers hesitated, guts tightening, half expecting a first flash of gunfire and the cry of alarm. The silence that greeted them was almost as bad. Beyond the confines of the ship waited the dark unknown. Outnumbered and outgunned, surprise was their only ally.

Triumph or die. . . .

Then, with a wave of his hand and a "devil take the hindmost" grin, Henry Morgan swaggered across the gangplank and led the way into Maracaibo.

3. The tiger in their midst.

E *l commandante ha robado a su mujer,"* Julio Hernandez taunted. "Now that General Vega has brought Cecilia to his apartment at the Inn of the Palms, what will you do? Perhaps you could be posted there as one of his personal guards. That is the only way you will see her."

"Enough," Pablo Morales growled.

"But I think your troubles have only begun. General Vega entertains the new governor of Panama and his bride-to-be. As much as Cecilia fancies el commandante, no doubt Don Alonso del Campo has piqued her interest. Though why any man would favor a *puta* when he will soon be married to such a beautiful woman as Señorita Elena Maria de Saucedo is beyond my understanding. But who can ever fathom the destinies of kings and whores?"

The soldier's voice echoed along the section of waterfront he and his compadre had been ordered to patrol. "*Sí.* First, General Vega, and maybe even the new governor if the repairs on the *Santa Rosa* are delayed and Cecilia can catch him apart from the señorita. I warned you—forget her; now she belongs to General Vega. His treasures are beyond your reach, my friend."

Pablo Morales, a handsome young corporal, took another drink of rum and managed to slosh a few droplets onto his disheveled white breeches and pea-green coat. He adjusted the musket strap slung over his shoulder. He stared down at the bottle of rum dangling from his right hand as if expecting emotional support, then glowered at his friend. "Cecilia loves me alone. One day I will take her for my wife."

"Unless Don Alonso del Campo fancies her enough to steal her from Vega and bring her with him to Panama," Julio replied. He shook his head and sighed. "But if I had a woman like Señorita Elena Maria to marry, I would never lie with a whore again. A woman with wealth and beauty, mmm. . . ."

"Julio. . . . we grew up together. As children we ran wild through the streets of Aguilas, played in the shadow of the walls of San Juan Castle. We ate our fill of lobsters and prawns we stole from the nets of fishermen. The warm sea eased our hurts, the warm sands were our bed. We shared the same willing girls, drank kisses and sweet wine, and when we became men, together you and I entered the service of King Carlos and came to the Americas." Pablo frowned, having lost his train of thought for a moment, then nodded and continued. "If anyone else had talked about Cecilia Tulero as you have done, I would have slit his throat from ear to ear."

The corporal ran a thumb across his throat for emphasis. Even with his good friend, young Pablo was hard-pressed to control his temper. But then he was a poor man in love, a mere corporal. And what chance did he have compared to men like General Vega, the military commandante of Maracaibo, or, worse, the newly appointed governor of Panama?

"Don Alonso shall take the señorita Elena to wife when they reach Panama." Morales cursed the trade winds that had brought the newly appointed governor to Maracaibo. "Why should he need to amuse himself with Cecilia?" Pablo grumbled, bemoaning his fate.

"Because the governor is a man like General Vega and Cecilia has breasts like ripe round melons," said Juan Hernandez. "But don't worry, my friend. The *Santa Rosa* will soon be repaired and Don Alonso will continue on his way to Panama, leaving your woman here for el commandante, and none the worse for wear, except perhaps for her tired back."

Pablo cursed and made an awkward, halfhearted grab for his comrade, who escaped his grasp. The two soldiers were flush in their youth—dark-skinned, immortal, handsome; both were fancied by the tavern wenches whenever there was time and a few extra *escudos* to spend. But Cecilia Tulero was no common prostitute. She serviced only the upper class, the landed gentry and men of quality who patronized the Inn of the Palms, kept apartments there, and made its owner, Miguel Gonzales, a wealthy man, but still a pig. Of course, what Cecilia did in el commandante's bedroom was work and, in her mind, wholly separate from the secluded trysts she enjoyed with the handsome corporal. Perhaps she even loved Pablo. But love would never be enough.

The two soldiers continued to struggle, neither opponent able to best the other and both of them feeling the effects of the "jack iron" they had swilled. The dark, potent Jamaican rum had claimed better men than these. Then Pablo lost his grip on the bottle. It fell, glanced off his shin, and shattered in the street, staining the bricks underfoot. Their altercation set off a round of barking; packs of wild mongrels bestirred themselves in the alleys behind the warehouses and began to bay and howl.

The docks were crowded with trade goods not yet loaded aboard the Dutch flutes. Mounds of tanned hides, sacks of cocoa piled high as a man could reach, and stacks of fresh-cut lumber blocked the occasional breeze. The air was heavy with a salt sea-smell. Pablo paused to catch his breath and stare glumly at the shattered bottle. "Idiot. See what you have made me do. Now what will we drink?"

"Perhaps the bitter brew of surrender, señor." The reply drifted out of the darkness just ahead.

Pablo Morales raised his lantern. "*Quien va alli?* Who goes there?"

"I am Morgan," said the buccaneer, stepping out from behind the cocoa and into the pool of yellow light.

"*El Tigre del Caribe!*" Morales gasped. The two Spaniards struggled to bring their muskets to bear on the pirate. Before they could open fire, Morgan raised his hands as if summoning the angels. In this case, there appeared an armed host, without a single celestial spirit among them. More than two hundred freebooters emerged from the shadows. The Brethren were armed to the teeth with pistols and musketoons, axes and cutlasses; a crowd fierce enough to turn any man's backbone to jelly.

The two soldiers spun on their heels and attempted to make a run for it. The dark and terrible silhouette of the Black Cleric rose up before them. His cutlass flashed in the moonlight. LeBishop slashed Hernandez from shoulder to navel. The Spaniard staggered back, his musket clattering to the cobblestone street.

"Well done, señor," Hernandez gasped. He held up his hands in an attitude of surrender.

Morgan hurried forward, recognizing the wounded man's peril. "LeBishop, we want them alive!" He hoped the soldiers might be able to provide some useful information.

"I can do better," LeBishop replied, closing in on the mortally wounded Spaniard. The Black Cleric grinned mirthlessly.

"No!" Morgan hoarsely called out. Too late. LeBishop skewered the man with his cutlass, yanked the blade free, and started after Pablo who retreated in horror from the cutthroat.

"But you are a man of God," Morales exclaimed, as the Black Cleric closed in for the kill.

Julio Hernandez groaned as he sagged to his knees, his features bunched with fear and pain. He reached out to Pablo, called his childhood friend by name, the words garbled by the blood and bile welling up into his throat; and in his final moments, while he was still unable to comprehend that his life was ending . . . the breath caught in his chest and he slumped forward.

"Now then, let the fear of the Lord be upon you," LeBishop intoned, quoting from Chronicles as he continued to advance on Morales. Moonlight glinted off the gold cross dangling from his ear. Pablo tore his gaze from Julio's corpse and backed away from the Black Cleric. LeBishop's cutlass sawed the air between them, his naked blade slick with the blood of this night's first victim.

Morales shrank back toward Morgan. The Spaniard tossed aside his musket and fell to his knees before the notorious buccaneer. "Spare my life, señor!"

LeBishop moved in to finish the task at hand but Morgan placed himself at sword's-point. For a brief moment it appeared to the raiding party that LeBishop was going to run Morgan through.

Tension swept through the ranks of the Brethren. They hadn't come all this way to kill one another off. Nell, standing shoulder-to-shoulder with the men, held her breath, fearing the worst. At her side, Sir William cocked the pistol in his hand. He was prepared to interfere in case LeBishop failed to listen to reason.

"No," Morgan calmly ordered, his angry gray eyes searching LeBishop's features. "He is of no use to us dead."

The Black Cleric considered his options and, after what seemed an eternity, shrugged and stepped back from the cringing soldier and lowered his sword. He knew Morgan had a plan in mind to get their ships safely past the fort out on Pigeon Island. They'd not be able to sneak past them again. Escape seemed impossible. But Morgan always had a trick up his sleeve. No, it wouldn't do to jeopardize the raid. "And *you* are of no use to *me* dead," said the Black Cleric.

"Naturally," Morgan said with a chuckle. "It is the basis for our friendship." He glanced over his shoulder at the physician. "Sir

William . . . take a dozen men and secure the governor's brig. Take Nell with you."

The young woman started to offer a protest but her father shooed her away. They chose their men and headed down along the dock toward the Spanish ship.

"*Gracias,*" said Pablo, warily watching LeBishop.

"*Sí,*" Morgan nodded. "You have heard of me?"

"*Sí.* Everyone knows of *el Tigre del Caribe.*"

"Then you know my word is good. If I say you live, you will live. And if I say you die . . ." Morgan ran his hand across his throat. "Whose brig is being repaired?"

"It belongs to Don Alonso del Campo, the new governor of Panama."

"And what is he doing here in Maracaibo?" There were no secrets in such a port.

"He is returning to Panama from Spain in the company of his intended bride, the señorita Elena Maria de Saucedo. Her father, Don Bernardo Saucedo, sent her to Madrid, to be educated at the court of the King. Now, upon his death, she returns to Panama to claim her inheritance—a fine house, the family plantation, even gold mines, I am told. Not hers for long, though. Such a dowry would make any woman a suitable bride, even a *criollos* like Elena Maria. So Don Alonso is only too happy to take her to wife." Pablo made the sign of the cross and searched the stony faces of the men gathered around him. He hoped such gossip would win him his life. "The *Santa Rosa* was damaged by fire and put into port for repairs. Don Alonso and the señorita are the guests of General Vega. They have taken an apartment here in town."

"And the soldiers like yourself?" asked Morgan, intrigued.

"Most are stationed on the island. There are troops in town, but asleep in the barracks at the base of the hills. A few of us patrol the streets."

"We'll need the commandante," Israel Goodenough suggested, towering over Morgan and his prisoner.

LeBishop had grown weary of so much talk. He was a man of action, and began to pace among the trade goods, impatient to be off through the town. If the Black Cleric had his way, the streets would run red with blood by morning. But Morgan knew of another way. He hoped to avoid a pitched battle with the populace and the militia, unless all else failed.

"General Vega is quartered at the Inn of the Palms on the Calle de

Hermanos. The apartments there are only for the *peninsulares.*" It was only yesterday that Pablo had observed the general in the company of the beautiful Cecilia on the balcony of his apartment overlooking the palm-lined courtyard. It was an unpleasant image, one Pablo could not forget: the way Cecilia laughed and flirted and pretended not to notice the lovesick corporal standing in the dust of the street—helpless, bitter, his heart aching, his sad features framed by the wrought-iron gate. Why should he protect the likes of General Juan Paolo Vega? Why should he care about any of the rich and the powerful?

Morgan dragged the Spaniard to his feet. "The Inn of The Palms? Then you will lead the way. Betray me and I will hand you over to the Black Cleric."

"I should like to meet this señorita," said Thomas LeBishop. "I might turn Elena Maria from her papist ways, if not with my sword, then my rod." His suggestion was greeted with coarse laughter among the cutthroats who followed his flag. A few of them grudgingly stepped aside, allowing Pierre Voisin to join Israel Goodenough and Morgan at the head of the column. The little thief leaned in toward his captain.

"You should quit making a target of yourself," the Frenchman suggested. "A wise man would do well not to tempt the Black Cleric. The milk o' human kindness curdled in him a long time ago."

"Listen to him, Captain," Goodenough concurred, but kept his voice low. The gunner had no wish to make an enemy of LeBishop.

Morgan ignored their warning. "Did you hear, lads? Maracaibo has already given up two of its treasures. I warrant Spain would pay a pretty ransom for the likes of the governor and his bride-to-be." He waved his men forward, a self-satisfied smile splitting his clean-shaven features. Despite the Black Cleric's reluctance to curb his ruthless tendencies, this raid might still prove to be a success.

Morgan stepped over the body of the slain soldier who seemed to stare at something beyond the grasp of living men. The pirates filed past, ignoring the dead man for fear of seeing their reflections captured in his sightless eyes.

A few scattered lights along the shore beckoned, although most of the settlement was shrouded in shadows while its inhabitants slept soundly in their beds, taking comfort in gently wafting breezes, secure in the knowledge they were safe, protected . . . and wholly oblivious to the tiger in their midst.

4. "Welcome to Maracaibo!"

The Inn of the Palms was a large two-story apartment house fronting the Calle de Hermanos, a tree-lined avenue of shops and houses whose windows were shuttered against the night. A faint breeze stirred the branches of the palm trees. A pair of frigate birds, disturbed from their rest by an unseen predator, soared above the clay tile rooftops. Parakeets piped and trilled then quieted again. At the Inn of the Palms, music drifted down into the courtyard from the balcony of one of the apartments, an incongruous Irish jig played upon an Irish harp.

Elena Maria allowed her skilled fingers to perform a carefree run across the strings. The melody rose from her spirit—oh, it was a tilting tumbling phrase that brought a smile to the lips of the two men who comprised her audience. A river of Gaelic melodies went a' coursing from the French doors, flowed down to the courtyard and through the gate to mingle with the whirr of rushing wings, the tinkling tones of a shell windcatcher, and a sibilant sea breeze.

The harp grew still. Elena Maria lowered her cheek onto the bogwood frame and placed the palm of her hand upon the strings as if in supplication, then General Vega and Don Alonso—her betrothed—began to enthusiastically applaud.

Twenty-three-year-old Elena Maria de Saucedo, already a spinster by everyone's standards but her own, rested the instrument upon its stand. It was a handsome piece, with its dark sounding board and forepillar capped with the carved head of a cockatrice.

Unlike some women, Elena Maria was at ease being alone with the general and Don Alonso in the drawing room. She could read the desire in their eyes. The señorita took a sip of wine and acknowledged the compliments of her audience.

Look at them. They think they know my heart. Men are like harps, waiting for the right hand to coax sweet melodies from them. Leave such men their fantasy, but the proof is in the player.

Elena Maria considered herself a virtuoso.

"Bravo, Señorita," said General Juan Paolo Vega, a portly little man who mopped the perspiration from his florid cheeks with a cotton kerchief he kept tucked in the sleeve of his coat. His features crinkled as he smiled and helped himself to another *torta de jojoto*. The corn cake was a kitchen staple, a hearty dessert whose batter was rich with sugar, crushed vanilla, and heavy cream.

"You find the cake to your liking?" said Elena. It was the general's third.

Vega nodded, and without the least bit of self-consciousness wolfed down the confection and brushed the crumbs from his waistcoat. The officer looked disapprovingly at his crystal wineglass; its emptiness was an affront.

"As I said, she has the hands of an angel," Don Alonso added. "One of her tutors at court was an Irishman. It was he that taught the señorita to play. I shall be forever in his debt." The newly appointed governor of Panama, ten years her senior, stroked his close-trimmed black beard; his brown eyes sparkled as he appraised his bride-to-be. *Beauty and wealth, God bless Don Bernardo de Saucedo.*

The old landowner had known that his daughter, despite being educated in Madrid, would never be accorded the same influence as one of Spanish birth. Elena Maria, though a clever and enchanting creature, was still a *criollos*, one born in the New World. By this marriage, the señorita's father had ensured his daughter's welfare. Elena Maria would be under the protection of someone with lineage and breeding, someone born in Spain, a *peninsulares*, whose family had a place at the Spanish court and enjoyed the favor of the king.

Elena Maria met the governor's stare for a moment, then demurely lowered her gaze. Her beauty captivated him. She was fair of skin, with a long, aquiline nose, prominent cheekbones, and darkly intelligent eyes. A wealth of black hair, lustrous as a raven's wing, framed her strong features. When she looked at him again, her moist lips parted with a come-hither smile.

Don Alonso del Campo rose from the overstuffed chair, patted the wrinkles from his ruffled shirt and royal-blue waistcoat. He favored a gold-stitched sash drawn tightly about the waist of his rust-red breeches, as if to slenderize his appearance.

"My dear sir, it seems the general's banquet table agrees with you, perhaps overly so," Elena observed drily.

"I have a robust appetite," Don Alonso admitted, patting his growing paunch. "But I am still fit, as I shall prove on our wedding night." His silver-streaked hair glistened in the firelight as he roared with laughter. Don Alonso clapped Vega on the shoulder, who chimed in with good humor. But the general's laughter seemed a bit forced, even vague, as if his thoughts were elsewhere, no doubt lost in imagining the señorita among the tousled sheets of her four-poster bed, her ankles in the air, her moist sheath waiting for her lover's lance. The general gulped and mopped his brow. It was suddenly hotter in the drawing room than ever before.

Don Alonso moved with an air of confidence that came from being born to a family who, despite their chronic debts, had the favor of the court. Vega's blatant interest in the señorita excited the governor. Don Alonso placed a hand on Elena's bare shoulder, his fingers caressed her soft flesh.

"When we are married, my pretty . . . you shall play nothing but sweet ballads, the joys of love, eh?"

"Love ballads are often melancholy," Elena replied. Light and shadows played upon the emerald taffeta folds of her dress. She tilted her chin, brushed her long hair back from her face, her dark eyes a guarded, calculating, lustrous green; the mysteries of her heart were like the waters of a hidden grotto, undiscovered and beyond the reach of men.

"The hour is late," said General Vega. It was a struggle to drag his hungry stare from the swell of her breasts and smooth shoulders.

"One last glass of wine before you go," Don Alonso said. "Where is your servant, Elena? The witch is too slow. Consuelo, a drink for el commandante, and be quick!"

A woman emerged from Elena's bedroom. The servant, a half-breed *Kuna* with skin the color of fired clay, had just turned down the covers on her mistress's bed. Consuelo was a small-boned, quiet woman who kept her own counsel and was devoted to Elena. Don Alonso knew her as an unfriendly, close-mouthed creature, someone to be viewed with suspicion. He placed no confidence in her claim to be able to see beyond seeing. Despite Elena's assurances, Don Alonso scoffed at the Kuna woman's bewitchments.

Consuelo did not care a whit for the governor's opinion of her. In earlier days the half-breed servant had wet-nursed more babies than she could remember. Her breasts were flat, leathery pouches now, her spare frame was all but lost beneath her faded blue dress and lace smock. A few brushy strands of dull gray hair escaped the confines of her lace cap. Her right eye, the "witch-eye," was masked by a milky-white film.

Consuelo concealed her disapproval of Elena's guests behind a mask of indifference as she served the two men from a recently decanted Madeira. She refilled their wineglasses, then cautiously approached Elena, who dismissed the servant.

"That will be all, Consuelo. Wait for me in my bedroom. Attend me there. I will be along directly."

"Sí, señorita." Consuelo nodded and set the tray and crystal carafe on an end table. The nurse trundled off through the bedroom door. She cast a brief glance toward the governor, then departed, drawing the warmth from the room and leaving in her wake a chilly peace.

The Madeira was cloyingly sweet to the taste buds of one who had been raised on the bitter, fermented nectar of the agave; still, the señorita joined in the toast to her impending marriage to the governor. Elena Maria performed her social rituals to perfection.

At last, protocol dictated General Vega should extricate himself from one of the drawing room's overstuffed chairs. Bathed in the moonlight pouring in through the French doors, Vega stood at attention and unsteadily raised his glass in the woman's honor.

"Señorita, if Don Alonso changes his mind, come back to Maracaibo and I will marry you myself."

"And what will your wife and your mistresses have to say about that?" asked Elena Maria.

The general frowned and stammered a protest that did more harm than good as he sought to reassure the woman of his fidelity.

Don Alonso seemed amused by el commandante's discomfort. The governor was becoming accustomed to Elena's outspoken nature.

General Vega blushed like a schoolboy despite his fifty years, and turned away in surrender. "Hmm, yes, perhaps, well now, uh, hmm, I see my reputation precedes me," he said, his cherubic features souring. "Anyway, do not begrudge me my few pleasures. My wife and I are joined in name only. She keeps to our plantation, back in the hills, and I remain here at the Inn of the Palms. It is an arrangement that suits us both." Vega coughed and then adjusted his military coat, taking care to pat the wrinkles from his sleeve. "The hour is late, my friends, and I must bid you *buenos noches.* Duty awaits."

"No doubt exhausting 'responsibilities.' I commend you, Señor," Don Alonso added with a chuckle. He had been introduced to the general's mistress, an earthy, well-proportioned little tart. "It is reassuring to witness such a hardworking commandante. I only hope my own officers in Panama are as diligent. If you need any help tonight, I am certain I can rise to the occasion."

"Many thanks, Gobernador. But I can manage. Besides, I have no wish to deprive you of the companionship of such a delightful lady."

"You are most kind," Elena told him. "But Don Alonso must accompany you. I am sorely in need of rest."

Don Alonso could not conceal his disappointment. "But my dear . . ."

"Of course, you would not have me compromise my chastity before our marriage vows were spoken in Panama." Elena's eyes were wide and innocent as she spoke.

Don Alonso's shoulders sagged. Clearly his thoughts were less on propriety and more on lust. Still, there was nothing for a gentleman to do but withdraw. "Never," he lied. "Sleep well. *Sueños dulces, mi señorita.*"

The governor kissed her hand, then followed General Vega into the dimly lit hall. A soldier stationed near the top of the stairs scrambled to attention as the officer and the visiting dignitary appeared in the corridor. Vega dismissed the man with a wave of his hand. The soldier slumped back into his chair, his rumpled uniform receding into the shadows as he resumed his half-dozing state.

Most of the apartments were empty this night. The landed gentry who kept them for their own assignations with their spouses or paramours had yet to arrive in town.

"You are a stronger man than I, my friend," said Vega. "Elena Maria is a very beautiful woman. Yes, I am a brute and would have her if she were mine."

"But she is not . . . yours," Don Alonso icily replied.

Vega took no notice of the governor's tone, and prattled on. "Fortunately for me, I have a woman waiting for me. *Mucha mujer*—much woman. I will not sleep alone this night. Perhaps I will not sleep at all."

"Yes, well . . ." Don Alonso replied, staring at the door to the apartment the general had provided for him. It adjoined Elena Maria's quarters. "I have a purse of doubloons and daresay I shall not want for companionship."

"*Sí*. I understand. A man has needs. Miguel downstairs will bring you a woman. Someone tempting as a honey cake, I warrant."

"That might not be wise, with the señorita de Saucedo on the other side of the wall," said Don Alonso.

"There is a back stairway that exits through the kitchen. And if a man were discreet, he could come and go unnoticed even by his intended bride." General Vega described the lay of the streets, and the whereabouts of a brothel where a gentleman might find someone warm and willing, the kind of woman who would never, ever say she was "sorely in need of rest."

"What is it? Speak your mind—you know you will eventually," Elena told her nurse.

"I do not like these men," Consuelo said.

"Of course you do not," Elena replied, sitting patiently on the bench seat at the foot of the bed while the mulatto brushed her hair. "But do not fear. I will never allow Don Alonso to take you away from me."

"I worry that he will take you away from yourself," the nurse countered, the milky orb that was her right eye peering at and through Elena's reflection in the mirror.

"What do you see, old mother?"

"That you do not hold the governor in your heart."

"Of course not," Elena Maria admitted in a matter-of-fact tone. "Why would anyone wish to marry for love?" She smiled, amused at her nurse's candid observation.

Consuelo shook her head and sighed. Behind her a breeze stirred the curtains over the window, ruffling the fabric. She could hear the distant crash of tides, imagined the sea rising and falling, like some great beast making love to the earth beneath a blanket of stars.

The Kuna half-breed was nervous. She who often counseled Elena had never felt so helpless. The tingling in her limbs served as a warning; she had a premonition that disastrous events were about to be set into motion.

"I have served the house of Saucedo nearly as long as I can remember. I was born within the walls of the hacienda. When I was a child your father sent me to the priests. They baptized me, taught me about the Christian god. And now I walk the path. But the Old Ones still speak in my soul. Spirits of earth and fire and wind warn me against what is to come. But what can I say to one so strong and willful? You must be wary of these men."

"No matter what you think of Don Alonso del Campo, this marriage is a contract now between two families. Land . . . wealth is not enough. I must have the name to be secure. But do not worry. No one shall ever take my inheritance. Not even the governor." Elena patted Consuelo's arm. "You are correct, though. An old nurse's advice is powerless in the face of politics."

Consuelo shook her head and sighed. The señorita's remarks did not sit well with her. But she could not put a name on her fears. If only the *Santa Rosa* had not been damaged by fire. If only they had not put into port, but been able to continue on home . . .

"Last night I dreamt of the road leading past the graveyard in Panama," Elena said, staring dreamily into the mirror.

"*Sí.* The path of tears," Consuelo nodded. She blessed herself with the sign of the cross, then placed a hand on the stone talisman she wore about her neck to ward off evil.

"In my dream," Elena continued, "I saw the road was covered with a pink cloth and set with platters of food, glasses of wine, plates of fruits and cakes. There were people in the ditches beside the road, all the nobles and their ladies, squatting in the dirt, feasting on the banquet I had almost ridden over in my carriage. They were finely dressed, all of them *peninsulares*, eating and drinking. Some of them recognized my carriage, they welcomed me and bid me join them, in the ditch, in the shadows of the tombstones." She gazed frankly at the nurse. "What does it mean, mamacita?"

Consuelo Navarro ceased brushing the woman's hair. The breeze in the window died. After a long pause, the nurse resumed her labors. Then she spoke.

"*Pequeña niña* . . . every banquet has its price."

Pablo Morales stood aside and with trembling hand indicated the wrought-iron gate that opened into the walled courtyard. Morgan brushed past the Spaniard and forced the gate open, begrudging the way it creaked on its hinges. He stalked through the entrance, his sharp eyes scouring the shadows and the apartment balconies that ringed the courtyard on three sides.

Morgan scrutinized the walled garden, his muscles poised, every sense heightened. It was impossible to move quietly along the pathway of crushed conch shells. The debris crunching underfoot seemed deafening to Morgan as he led his shipmates along the footpath and cautiously approached the brass-trimmed front door. Thank heaven for the music of the harp. He took note of the lamplight shining from behind the drawn curtains. Harps? Perhaps the angels were welcoming them into a trap.

He glanced toward the windows where a faint trickle of illumination filtered into the yard. Something stirred near his foot. He dropped a hand to one of the pistols jutting from his belt, heard purring, and relaxed as a calico cat emerged from beneath a cane-backed chair. The animal was accustomed to visitors and hungry for attention. It arched its back and brushed the pirate's trouser leg, rubbing its ears and whiskers against Morgan's boot.

"What do we have here?" Henry chuckled. He knelt and stroked the animal's back. The feline continued to purr, and after a few more caresses allowed the buccaneer to scoop the creature up into the crook of his arm. It was a large, well-fed cat, too fat and lazy to be bothered chasing the rodents that infested the back alleys. It was accustomed to being handled and accepted the well-armed stranger in the garden without suspicion.

"I hope the women are as willing," Pierre Voisin said, observing the affectionate feline. "But then, I am Voisin, so how can they refuse, eh?" The Frenchman studied the darkened windows, the innocent-looking balconies happily devoid of marksmen. He clapped young Morales on the shoulder. "Well done, *mon ami*. I am in your debt—you are Pierre's good friend, unless, of course, this is a trap, and then I will gut you like a fish."

Behind the Frenchman and his prisoner, Thomas LeBishop and a dozen freebooters crowded through the entrance. The rest waited in the street. They were a salty lot, eager to explore the pleasures Maracaibo had to offer. The Inn of the Palms looked as good a place to start as any.

A stone pool flanked by mango trees dominated the center of the courtyard, and water lilies drifted on the still surface of the water. Fished darted and splashed among the moss and lily pads. Up ahead, winged beetles, mayflies, and ashen-colored moths whirred and fluttered in suicidal formations about the lanterns hung to either side of the front door. Firelight played upon wall carvings that depicted buxom maids frolicking by moonlight amid finely-wrought vines and flowers.

Tregoning, Thomas LeBishop's first mate, tripped over a clay jug, stumbled and skinned his knees on the cobblestones. Several of the men behind him laughed at the fallen man's antics. The column brought up sharply. Cutlasses clattered as two men collided with one another. Morgan glanced around at his company of rogues and freebooters, brought his finger to his lips, his expression stern. After a last moment of jostling for position, the men grew quiet.

When had the harp ceased to play?

Morgan turned his back on them and tried the iron knocker on the door. He rapped three times, waited, then repeated the process. The cat in his arms began to meow. He pressed his ear to the door panel and managed to hear a woman issue orders, apparently to her husband. Morgan cringed at the sound of her brassy voice. *Lord spare me from such a fate.* The woman continued to admonish her husband until the poor sod acknowledged defeat and agreed to answer the door. Morgan could hear the man muttering to himself, a litany of complaints that increased in volume as he approached from the opposite side of the door.

"Miguel Gonzales and his wife Rita," Pablo whispered. After identifying the cantankerous couple, the Spaniard retreated and tried to lose himself among the pirates.

"The hour is late," Gonzales growled from the other side of the door. The proprietor was prepared to take his displeasure out on whomever had disturbed his sleep.

"And my purse is heavy with doubloons, señor," Morgan replied. "I have been at sea since leaving Cadiz and endured the rough company of common seamen for lo these many weeks. I am Don Medino Escutia, secretary to His Majesty King Carlos II. Do you deny me comfort and the solace of a warm fire and a bottle of your finest Madeira? I am inclined to be generous, but perhaps my gold will spend easier elsewhere." The cat in Morgan's arms grew nervous and began to struggle and escape the pirate's grasp, but Morgan caught the cat behind the neck and managed to bring the nervous feline under control. The truce was illusory—the animal began to howl in protest.

"No! No, Don Estéban. Your pardon, I beg you." Gonzales was awake now and loath to offend any man of rank. The inn depended on the patronage of the landed gentry and the occasional titled visitor who preferred not to associate with common soldiers and seamen. "Only, the hour is late. Pardon, I say! A warm fire you shall have, and my wine cellar is well-stocked. And if you wish, I can provide you the company of some of the most beautiful women in all of Maracaibo: Nubian temptresses, Kuna native girls, taut and tight to the touch; *criollos* with skin like silk and wishing only to please . . . Curse this catch. Just a minute. One minute, señor, *por favor*." The innkeeper continued to fumble with the latch.

Voisin, peering through a crack in one of the shutters along the front of the inn, suddenly abandoned his post and hurried back to Morgan's side. "There are soldiers within—I counted three but there may be more."

Morgan glanced back at the Spanish sentry. "You did not say anything about soldiers here."

Pablo gulped and took a step backward, only to be brought up sharply by a line of cutthroats who were not about to let him pass. The Spaniard gulped and glanced around at the hardened faces of the men surrounding him. He reluctantly faced Morgan yet again.

"General Vega's personal guard," he confessed. "Usually four musketeers. But Don Alonso may have his own escort."

"If you are lying or have not told me all you know, I swear it will not go well for you," Morgan said, his storm-gray eyes narrowing.

"No, señor, on my oath, I have told you everything." Pablo eyed the cat that Morgan continued to calm. The prisoner was confused by the man's behavior. "Señor Morgan, if the governor or General Vega are elsewhere it is not my fault," Morales protested. "I do not know which rooms Don Alonso or the señorita have taken. But el commandante's quarters are at the top of the stairs, the fifth door down. I know, though I have never visited there. General Vega has taken my woman to his bed." The young man's features tightened, his voice turning bitter. "I have watched them from the street, on the balcony. I tell you true, el commandante is the last man I would protect."

The latch slid back at last. The door opened. "Welcome, Señor Estéban Escutia! Consider my house as your own." A swarthy little man with pockmarked skin, the scrawl of his lips hidden beneath a thick black moustache, appeared in the doorway.

Morgan kicked him in the chest and sent him flying backward into the spacious foyer. He followed the man into the foyer and in a matter of seconds assessed the situation. A broad staircase lay before him. To his left lay the dining room and beyond it, the kitchen, where Rita Gonzales shrieked in horror at the sight of the pirates. In the long, open sitting room to the right, a pair of surprised Spanish soldiers fumbled for their muskets and attempted to bring the weapons to bear on the intruder.

Morgan gave the cat's tail a savage tug. The animal howled, bared its claws. Morgan tossed the animal at the soldiers. The terrified creature landed on the first man and raked his face and neck, then leaped onto the second man and caused him to fire his musket into the ceiling, blowing away a chunk of the wood. Morgan picked up an end table and knocked the closest man senseless. Another pirate brushed past him, leaped a brocaded couch, and took the second soldier down.

Morgan reversed his course and ran to the stairway. He took the first few steps in stride, glanced up, and saw a soldier draw a bead on him. "Strike your colors, lad, I offer you quarter." The soldier hesitated. Some inner sense caused Morgan to fling himself to the stairway. The soldier pulled the trigger, loosing a blossom of fire and a deafening boom in the confines of the house. The slug whirred past the pirate chieftain. Morgan heard a man groan, and looked over his shoulder. LeBishop was a few paces back. He had dragged the innkeeper in front of him, using the smaller man as a human shield. Gonzales clutched at the bloodstain spreading across his chest. His legs went slack as the Black Cleric tossed him aside.

Morgan charged up the remaining flight of the stairs.

"Mercy, señor," the soldier called out. "I surrender."

Morgan rounded the corner, ducked back as a second shot lit the darkness. It was a wild shot, taken as the soldier retreated down the hall. Henry Morgan cursed. "That's twice, on my oath!" He drew one of his pistols, stepped into the hall, and advanced on the Spaniard who was attempting to reload for the second time. Seeing the pirate bearing down on him, and having no time for a third try, the soldier tossed his musket aside.

"I accept your quarter, señor."

"Too late," Morgan snarled, and shot the man through the heart.

The door to Elena's apartment crashed back against the door. Morgan entered the drawing room, saw the bedroom door slightly ajar. He crossed the room, knocked upon the wooden panel, and stepped aside. Gunshots followed. A pair of holes appeared in the center of the door. Wooden splinters littered the ground at his feet. Morgan peered through one of the holes and grinned at the sight of the women. The half-breed nurse looked to be a hag, but the señorita kneeling on her bed, smoking pistol in her hand, made his blood boil.

Morgan kicked the door open, stepped in and bowed, sweeping his hat before his chest.

"Elena Maria de Saucedo, permit me to introduce myself. I am Henry Morgan, a privateer and captain of the *Glenmorran*. And you, my dear lady, are my guest."

Elena Maria studied the dashing figure before her with a certain amount of incredulity. He seemed wholly oblivious to the shouting, the pistol shots, the crash of doors echoing throughout the Inn of the Palms. He behaved like a suitor, as if presenting himself to her for the first time. She was surprised he knew her by name. But then he must also be aware of Don Alonso.

"Your *prisoner*, don't you mean?"

"I know the difference even if you do not," Morgan said. He approached the two women, gently removed the pistols from their hands. "You will have no need of these as long as you are under my protection. I would suggest you find more suitable attire." Morgan swung about and returned to the drawing room. He heard a rustle of cloth and sensed movement. But the apartment had another guest by this time; Thomas LeBishop stepped forward and intercepted Elena as she charged with drawn dagger, a slender, razor-sharp blade with a jeweled hilt. She altered her course and slashed the Black Cleric across the cheek, opening a gash from cheekbone to jawline. Blood flowed down LeBishop's face and spattered his shirt. The wound had to be painful, yet he did not react with even so much as a wince. The man merely caught her wrist and twisted the weapon from her grasp. He licked the blood from the blade, then, catching her by the neck, drew her soft flesh toward the point of the blade.

"There'll be no ransom for a corpse, LeBishop," Morgan said.

LeBishop heard. His eyes undressed the woman in his grasp. "Look at you," he told her. "She's a brave one," he said to Morgan. "Rigged for battle. But not for long. I'll trim her shrouds." He touched the knife to her throat then released his hold and tucked the dagger in his belt. "One day I shall return it to you," he said, the promise fraught with meaning. He frowned, his eyes narrowing, two slits filled with menace.

Elena stepped back and gathered the folds of her dressing gown about her. Her gaze shifted between the two men, assessing both of the buccaneers. She forced back the fear rising in her throat; it came with the daunting realization that she was at the precarious mercy of the Black Cleric and Morgan the pirate—*el Tigre del Caribe!* She would need more than pistols and daggers to stay alive. This situation, however intolerable, clearly required other, more effective weapons.

Morgan ran his hand along the strings of the Celtic harp. Elena, startled at the sound, moved forward to protect the instrument. The notes reverberated in the room.

"Please, sir, I accept your protection." Her features softened. She searched his gray eyes, connected with something storm-tossed, impetuous, as dangerous as his namesake, and, disturbingly, as exciting. A tall, lanky cutthroat appeared in the apartment doorway and called Morgan over. The pirate excused himself and crossed the room to Israel Goodenough, who leaned forward and softly relayed his report.

Elena waited, pretending to ignore the way the Black Cleric stared at her. He wasn't fooled by her indifference. The commotion in the inn had for the most part subsided, but Elena could not overhear what was being said. She did not have long to wait, however. Morgan returned to her side.

"It seems the governor is nowhere to be found," Henry announced. "Hardly gallant of the gentleman. I must say I am disappointed. Were you my lady, I would carve a path to your side."

"But I am not your lady," Elena pointedly observed.

"No. And I am certainly no gentleman," said Morgan. He bowed and took his leave, whispering for Israel to remain in the room until LeBishop left. The stench of powdersmoke lingered in the hall as Morgan made his way to Genreal Vega's apartment. The dead man at the end of the corridor continued to bleed into the woven rug.

The freebooters outside the door stood aside and allowed Morgan to enter and confront el commandante. The officer struggled to maintain his dignity under the circumstances, despite being naked from the waist up and clad only in his undergarments. Watery-brown rolls of fat curled over his waistband. His round, fleshy features glistened with sweat. Voices carried from the general's bedroom, where the Spanish sentry, Pablo Morales, exchanged heated accusations with a buxom young woman who refused to hear him. Suddenly Morales slapped her across the face. She sank to the floor weeping.

Voisin shook his head in despair. He excused himself, left Morgan's side, and ambled into the bedroom. He slapped Morales across the skull with butt of a pistol. The man dropped like a sack of yams. Then, with a twinkle in his eye, the Frenchman offered his hand to the woman. His voice lowered, he all but purred in a mixture of French and Spanish as he closed the door and led the woman to bed.

Morgan grinned and turned his attention to General Vega. "Señor, you will dress and take us to the barracks where you will order your soldiers to surrender their arms. In the morning you will inform the elders of the town not to resist us." The grin left his face; Morgan's gray eyes turned cold as dead winter ice. "Any man who lifts a hand against us, I will hang him and his wife and his neighbors and burn their houses, and their children I will carry off and sell to the slavers so that all their miserable days they shall curse their father for valuing his trifles more than their lives." Morgan lowered his voice. "And that will be a kindness compared to what the Black Cleric will do."

Vega gulped—summoning his failing courage, gathering what was left of his dignity—and stiffened his spine and folded his arms across his bare chest. If his people suffered, so be it. "Never! Do you understand? This port is under my protection. Never will I assist you in any way!"

Morgan nodded. The pirates to either side of the general grabbed his arms. Morgan drew a pistol from his belt, cocked the weapon, and stuffed the cold gray barrel down the front of the general's long underwear. Vega's eyes grew wide as saucers as the large-bore iron muzzle jabbed into his scrotum.

"Never?" Morgan asked, his finger curled around the trigger.

"Señor, por favor," Vega said changing his tune. His features went slack. "What was I thinking, my friends? Welcome to Maracaibo!"

5. "We will meet again."

Three days after the capture of Maracaibo, a skiff flying a white flag of truce from its single mast left the protection of the fortress on Pigeon Island and skimmed across the bay toward the port. The occupants of the skiff—three soldiers, a boatswain, and Don Alonso del Campo—hardly spoke during the crossing. The boatswain was busy with line and rudder; Don Alonso was lost in his own sour thoughts; and the soldiers rode in glum silence with no wish to share their opinions of the governor who they were forced to accompany on this damnable excursion beyond the safety of the castle walls.

The boatswain brought the skiff smartly about and trimmed the sail, allowing them to drift with the tide approximately a hundred yards from the waterfront. Knowing full well they were under the scrutiny of the cutthroats in the town, the Spaniards waited for the buccaneers to respond in kind.

They didn't have to wait long. Henry Morgan, with Sir William Jolly and half a dozen buccaneers, scrambled aboard a johnnyboat and rowed away from the pier. His crew put their backs into the work, plunged their oars into the tranquil surface of the bay. In the distance, a school of striped mullet broke their watery bonds and shot upward, gleamed silver in the sun, then landed with a slap and a splash, returning to the aquamarine sea. Morgan reveled at the sight, finding kinship with any animal yearning to be free.

"Keep your eyes wide and your powder dry," he cautioned.

"Pull, you beauties. If the work be too hard for you, perhaps you should have stayed back in Jamaica. I am sure Sir Richard Purselley could find you some suitable duties, swabbing out the governor's chamber pots or tending to milady's combs and ribbons!" Sir William exhorted. "Pull on them oars. Sure, and you've had enough practice pulling on 'em when the women weren't about."

"Come and give us a tug, you old bilge rat," one of the buccaneers retorted. "After the *puta* I bedded last night, you look pretty good." Rafiki Kogi was a strong, rangy African, an escaped slave who years earlier had found emancipation among the Brethren. Naked to the waist, he displayed ebony flesh that glistened with sweat.

"There now, Mister Kogi, she was no doubt comely enough for the likes of you," Morgan said with a chuckle. He was burned almost as dark as the African. The captain of this rough crew was simply dressed now, in butternut-brown breeches and a blousy shirt open to the wide leather belt circling his waist. He was armed with a pistol and a wicked-looking dagger whose curved blade resembled a steel claw, a weapon befitting the man called *el Tigre*.

"Comely . . . *Mtu huyu ana wazimu*—I swear she had a face like a barnacle!"

Morgan and the others dissolved into laughter at Kogi's expense. The African glared at them, finding not a trace of sympathy for his plight. Then he grinned broadly and shook his head in mock dismay.

"*Ku-tosha!* Enough!" Kogi raised a hand to the heavens. "I am among jackals," he added with a sigh, hoping the spirits of his distant people might come and rescue him. Not that he would have left. He cupped a handful of water and splashed his face and shaved skull. Droplets rolled down the ridges of scar tissue that furrowed his back like freshly tilled fields. He wore the marks proudly now, as did many of the Brethren, including Henry Morgan, who had vowed: *Never again.*

Never.

At last the two boats pulled abreast of one another. The soldiers glared warily at the pirates as if in the presence of savage beasts. The buccaneers drew in their oars and kept their weapons within easy reach.

"I am Don Alonso del Campo, governor of Panama, champion of the Church, and defender of the faithful in the Americas and personal emissary of his most Christian majesty, King Carlos of Spain."

"I'm Morgan."

"Ah . . . *el Tigre del Caribe*. I thought you would be larger. And have fangs and claws. You don't seem so menacing."

"You're the one who got chased out of Maracaibo," Morgan remarked offhandedly.

"An act of piracy for which you will hang," Don Alonso said.

"Pirate? Hardly, sir. I carry letters of marque. My actions are sanctioned by King James under the statutes of war."

"But we are at peace. You fool, the treaty was signed and presented months ago. Your own English governor, Sir Richard Purselley, probably has word of the treaty. You are committing an act of war, a deed for which you will no doubt be punished by your own magistrate. Now, you will depart Maricaibo and return all provisions and goods stolen from the Spanish citizens, or find both Spain and England turned against you."

Sir William blanched at the news. But Morgan only laughed. "What? Shall I trust the silken tongue of a courtier, and a Spaniard at that! No . . . I will keep your port until I am through with it."

Don Alonso scowled. The uniform he had borrowed from the captain of the garrison on Pigeon Island was ill-fitting and had begun to chafe his neck. Sweat soaked into the heavy material. Now, to add to his discomfort, Morgan was proving far more difficult than the governor had hoped.

"Do what you will, then, but know—the longer you remain in port, the better I shall like it. I am not here by chance. There are two frigates due any day now. You may have entered unnoticed, but do not think you will be so lucky again. The guns of Pigeon Island will send you to the bottom, night or day." Don Alonso gestured toward the fortress across the bay. "Surrender now and I will spare your life and the lives of your men."

"And make us your guests in Panama. I have sampled Spanish hospitality," Morgan replied.

"Then you have sealed your fate. The gunners lining those high walls will have no mercy." He waved toward the fort. The fortress blossomed flame and smoke as the heavy cannons roared along the length of its walls. The passage between the two islands erupted in a forest of geysers, spewing water and foam into the air. The thunder of the guns reverberated throughout the bay. It was an impressive sight and had the desired effect on the men in the boat. Only Morgan feigned indifference. He stroked his chin as he contemplated the fortress.

"What was built by men can be torn down," he said.

"Then the blood of your crew will be on your hands. But if you have any honor you will send out the señorita Elena Maria de Saucedo and permit me to escort her back to the safety and comfort of the castle."

"She is there," Morgan said. He glanced over his shoulder as Israel Goodenough and Pierre Voisin arrived at the dockside, escorting the governor's bride-to-be. Behind them shuffled an undulating column of the town's populace, impressed into service, carrying plunder to the boats. "You can come and get her"—the governor immediately ordered the boatswain to put into port—"in Jamaica. And bring fifty thousand gold doubloons. I shall await your pleasure in Port Royal."

Don Alonso's expression fell. He gasped and sputtered, looked from the woman on the pier to the pirate. "You would ransom the señorita? How dare you!"

"It's a fair price. A woman like that can turn a boy into a man and make an old man feel like *un amante* again." A murmur of agreement swept through the ranks of the buccaneers.

For a moment Morgan thought the governor was going to forget his flag of truce and order his men to fire on the johnnyboat.

Indeed, Don Alonso considered just such an action before coming to his senses. Exchanging a volley at close range would be suicidal and serve no purpose. Morgan the pirate had thrown down the gauntlet. So be it. Don Alonso snapped an order to the boatswain and took his seat beneath the boom. He dare not look in Elena Maria's direction for fear of meeting her gaze and being shamed by her expression. "We will meet again," he said.

Don Alonso continued to glare at Morgan as the boatswain lowered the gaff-rigged sail and brought the skiff about. The buccaneers returned to their oars. The warm air fairly crackled with the tension as Morgan and the governor sought to stare one another down in a subtle contest of will that only distance resolved.

A weighty silence followed the johnnyboat on its return to the pier. Eventually the boat glanced off the wooden brace and the men climbed out and disappeared toward the waterfront cantinas. Sir William lingered at the edge of the pier, slow to join the others waiting on the dock.

"Go ahead, sawbones. Have your say. What's gnawing on your insides?"

"I am troubled by what the governor said. Do you think he was telling the truth, about the treaty?" Sir William muttered.

"Since when have you known a Spaniard to tell the truth?" Morgan replied. He clapped his friend on the shoulder. "See here, William Jolly, don't turn into an old woman on me."

Sir William shrugged and tried to appear consoled. But he had his misgivings. Morgan had never steered them wrong. For many a year they had enjoyed remarkable success. Perhaps he was being overly concerned; then again, the careless man wound up on the gibbet.

Israel and Voisin were waiting on the waterfront. Elena Maria stood between them, washed in golden light, black tresses trailing in the sweet, salt breeze.

"What did he want, Captain?" asked Goodenough, a hint of worry in his melancholy features. He was never comfortable on land, but preferred the roll of a deck beneath his feet and the crack of whipcord and canvas in the wind.

"Our surrender."

"He says we're trapped," Sir William added.

"*Mon dieu*, so we are at his mercy . . . ?" The Frenchman stood aside as Morgan took Elena by the arm, relieving the man of his charge. The little thief continued his harangue. ". . . While we sleep in his bed and drink his wine and gorge ourselves on his Christian cheese? Ha! You tell me who is trapped?"

"We are," said Morgan.

Morgan offered his arm but Elena ignored the gesture. The pirate captain clasped his hands behind the small of his back and walked alongside his captive. It was difficult not to look at her. No doubt she was accustomed to attention. Women like her always were. Each soft curve and budding swell was swathed in lace or amber-and-cream taffeta. She smelled of rosewater and lilac. Her every movement seemed fluid and sensual.

They ambled past a column of Vega's soldiers, unarmed and each man shouldering sacks of wheat, bales of tobacco, barrels of salt pork, and sugarloaves. Vega's men were a glum lot, humiliated by their fate, betrayed by their commander who had ordered them to surrender. They worked in silence; now and then a man would pause to look at the distant fortress guarding the mouth of the bay. There was some satisfaction in knowing the pirates would have to run through a hail of blistering cannon fire before reaching the open sea. And Morgan's ships would no longer have the element of surprise to protect them.

Morgan felt he could read their thoughts—that his own days were numbered, and so the soldiers and townsmen saw no reason to resist the buccaneer's demands. Morgan was as much a captive as they were. It was only a matter of time. And they might be right.

"Where are you taking me?" Elena asked, redirecting his attention back to her.

"To my brig. You'll be safe there. My men obey my word, but I travel in hard company. And you have made an enemy of the Black Cleric."

"The *Santa Rosa* belongs to me," she corrected.

"Yours . . . mine—what do words matter as long as it takes us safely to Port Royal?"

She paused and looked out across the bay. Seeing Don Alonso in the skiff stirred her emotions, and they weren't of romance; he had made good his escape and abandoned her to thieves and cutthroats.

"Don't worry. He'll pay your ransom. I have seen his kind before. Men like him would rather pay than fight."

"You are a common brigand." Elena said, turning on him, bitterness in her voice. But she saw the desire in his eyes. Of course he wanted her. After all, he was a man. "What do you know of Spanish nobility?"

Morgan seemed lost in thought as they continued in stony silence down along the dock to the *Santa Rosa*. Morgan gestured for her to continue up the gangplank where Consuelo awaited her mistress on the main deck. But Elena Maria refused to move. She wanted her answer.

"What do I know of Spanish nobility? I could show you the marks on my back, the track of the cat that cuts to the bone . . ." Morgan spoke as he walked, and the woman fell in step with him, as if the force of his presence was like an undertow, sweeping her along despite her efforts to resist. "I could describe years of servitude and captivity—except the nights and days are a blur now. It is as if I had died then, only to be born again one night in the harbor off Santiago de Cuba."

Morgan and the señorita might as well have been a lady and her suitor on a Sunday stroll in the plaza. In this case, however, the place of rendezvous was beneath the skull and crossbones; the man at her side was hardly a gentleman suitor, but one of the most notorious buccaneers to plague the Spanish Main. Morgan led her beneath the shadows of the masts, down the shadowed steps, and into the captain's cabin at the stern of the ship. These would remain her quarters during the crossing to Jamaica.

Consuelo tried to follow the couple into the cabin, but Morgan closed the door in her face and latched it as an afterthought. The last thing he saw of the half-breed woman was her oval brown face and its look of surprise.

The interior of the great cabin was the width of the ship, with windows across the stern. A feather bed had been built into an alcove against the starboard wall. Chairs and a walnut table for dining dominated the center of the room. A rolltop desk and chair had been shoved near the window to make room for Consuelo's cot. The room smelled of leather and sea salt, tobacco and rum, rosewater and French powders.

"Señorita? Are you safe?" the servant called out.

Elena's emerald eyes studied her captor's face. It was a good face, a mixture of cunning and reckless enthusiasm—somewhere, a hidden hurt—but not the face of a man driven mad with a need for revenge. Vengeance might be a part of his character, but it did not rule him. And if not that, then what could she use? Where was his weakness? Perhaps the answer was the simple fact that they were alone in the cabin, out of sight of everyone, the two of them alone, and anything could happen.

"Well, am I?" she asked.

"What?" he replied, his eyes drawn to her lips—moist . . . pink as a first blush.

"Am I safe?"

"Not hardly," he said, and took her in his arms. His kiss was bruising at first. His mouth was hungry for her. The second kiss was tender and deep. She did not fight him.

"Señor . . . Wait, I must attend my lady! Doña Elena, are you all right? Please!"

Elena Maria leaned back in his arms, felt the heat between them, knew where it would take them, considered giving her desire free rein, to cast off the bonds of propriety. It felt good to be hidden away. For a brief moment, all that she was and wished to be, paled before the moment, the very instant when passion vied with her own common sense. She was Elena Maria de Saucedo. She was her father's daughter, a *criollos* woman in a world forged by men, yet determined to survive. No, survival wasn't near enough. Don Alonso would find that out.

Morgan hadn't expected her to be so willing: black hair, green eyes, hot blood; his throat tight now, burning, she had drunk the strength out of him. He wanted her. But she was more than a lady, she was a woman. He would be more than a pirate, something . . . *more*—the word escaped him—someone to aspire to be with. Once they had set sail and were under way, there would be no time for such matters, no clandestine visits to the great cabin, not one improper word or glance. His mates would be watching. And a sea voyage was no place for conflict among his crew. Things would be different in Jamaica. He could wait.

Morgan started toward the door, hesitated, turned to look at her. She was standing before the window, outlined in sunlight and the deep blue beyond. "I can save you."

"Save me—from what?" she asked, and was tempted to chide him for his impertinence.

"You asked what I knew of Spanish nobility. Behind their wigs and gold brocade, the Dons are but thieves who rob the land and its people." Morgan shook his head in disgust. "But they do it in the name of God and King. The nobles see themselves as the chosen few, given to rule and oppress the rest of us." He drew close to her again, this time wary of the heat. His gray eyes were like twin stormclouds. Now it was Elena's turn to tremble. "The governor and his kind . . . *your* kind . . . hate me not for what I have done, but for who I am: a *free* man."

6. Morgan's walk.

Captain Gregorio Muñez, commanding in General Vega's absence, knew he would find Don Alonso atop the limestone parapet, alone with the sunwashed sea breeze and the governor's own dark thoughts. Don Alonso heard the rattle of pebbles on the stone steps as Muñez climbed the wall to the gun emplacement. The artillery crew, lounging beneath the makeshift shade of a piece of sail-cloth held aloft by bayonets and a ramrod, attempted to look busy as the officer reached the ledge.

Don Alonso, his back to the gunners, shifted his stance and braced his elbows on the limestone wall. He appeared to ignore the officer. The port across the bay held his interest to the detriment of anything and anyone else. The nobleman's features were tightly drawn; he chewed unconsciously on his lower lip as he peered through his spyglass. From his vantage point on the seawall, Don Alonso had a clear view of Maracaibo. He need only elevate his spyglass above the tall fronds, vines, and the thicket of palm trees concealing the tapered western tip of Pigeon Island, for the piers and waterfront and conchshell streets to fill the lens. The governor had kept this vigil every day since his encounter with Henry Morgan out in the bay.

Maracaibo was always on his mind. His frantic escape from the Inn of the Palms and his cowardly flight from the besieged town, abandoning Elena Maria in his haste, proved to be a bitter pill for such a proud man to swallow. Every time Don Alonso focused the spyglass on the distant shore, a great sense of shame welled in his breast.

Captain Muñez, the untried officer General Vega had left in command of the fortress guarding the Maracaibo straits, would not soon forget the morning his unwanted guest ran his stolen skiff ashore on the wooded tip of the island, stumbled and crawled the half-mile to the landward walls, and staggered up to the practically unguarded front gate. Immediately upon entering the castle, Don Alonso was brought to young Muñez, to whom he delivered the news that Maracaibo had fallen to Morgan the pirate.

Not a day went by that Don Alonso didn't contemplate the port, scrutinize the waterfront with its collection of warehouses and cantinas, fume in silence at the sight of the freebooters swaggering through the streets while columns of townspeople and soldiers, impressed into service along with the slaves, loaded plunder aboard the ships. The *Glenmorran* and the *Jericho* were two ships whose names were synonymous with skullduggery. Morgan and the Black Cleric, a rogue and a butcher, both kin to the devil.

Don Alonso del Campo straightened and wiped the moisture from his face. Sweat blurred his vision. He dabbed at his eyelids then returned to the spyglass. He could just make out the alley where he had remained in hiding amid the rubbish and discarded crates and nets. Through a twist of fate, the governor had departed the Inn of the Palms through the rear door off the kitchen even as the pirates entered the courtyard and forced their way inside. Hearing the commotion and suspecting the worst, Don Alonso had briefly considered returning for his intended bride. It was an idea he promptly dismissed. He was of no use to Elena Maria or anyone else dead. The governor had kept to the alleys and waited until the wee hours of the morning before creeping out to steal the skiff. It took him well past daybreak to fight the tide and cross the bay to the castle on Pigeon Island. The palms of his hands were still blistered from the ropes and rudder.

Muñez cleared his throat and waited to be acknowledged. The young officer resented the governor's presence in the fort. Don Alonso, by virtue of his age and station, had a habit of countermanding the captain's orders whenever it suited him. As Muñez marshaled his troops for an assault on the town, Don Alonso exerted his authority and insisted the garrison remain intact. Don Alonso saw no reason to endanger the Spanish garrison. Let the buccaneers try to escape. Their prize-laden ships had too deep a draft, and the waters around

Watch Island were too shallow and cut with sandbars and coral reef for pirates to sail out of range of a Spanish cannonade.

No, Morgan and his men would have to keep to the channel and that would bring them within easy range of the Spanish guns. The fortress's seawalls bristled with enough twelve-pounders to blow the cutthroats out of the water. Morgan had to realize escape was futile. The pirate would have to surrender. The longer the brigands remained in Maracaibo, the more they risked an encounter with one or more of the Spanish warships that frequented the port. Muñez had assured him the frigate *San Bartolomeo* was due any day now.

"You sent for me, Governor?" Muñez asked, growing weary of being ignored. The captain stared out across the bay. Osprey, gulls, kites, and kingfishers glided on the thermal winds. Now and then one dropped like a bolt from a crossbow, stabbed the sun—kissed sea, and soared aloft with its wriggling prize. Hunters and the hunted, predator and prey, they soared and darted and dove, made their kill and retreated . . . like the very cutthroats who had sailed into Maracaibo past the fort's silent guns. Muñez's features reddened at the thought. He had his own cross of shame to bear.

Well, the guns would not be silent on Captain Morgan's return. The Tiger of the Caribbean had sailed into a trap. The garrison was on alert now, all two hundred men. Just let Morgan's freebooters try to escape. The captain brushed the limestone dust from his sleeve. His stomach growled. The officer ruefully reminded himself that he ought to have been enjoying a hearty breakfast and not running to the whims of a some dignitary.

"Our hour is at hand," Don Alonso said. "For days I have watched those cutthroats loot the town. Well, their sloops are riding low in the water, the townsmen have been cleared from the docks. Yesterday they finished the repairs on the *Santa Rosa* and trimmed her sails. They mean to sail her back to Jamaica. I'll see her at the bottom of the harbor first." He handed the spyglass to Muñez. "See for yourself."

The officer obeyed, adjusting the eyepiece until the distant shore defined itself in the glass. He wanted to ask about Elena Maria and if the governor intended to see her at the bottom of the bay as well, but some questions were best left unasked. He studied the port, took note that preparations were indeed being made to get the ships under way. For some reason many of the brigands were congregating along the waterfront as if waiting for a final command from the one who had brought them this far.

No farther, Muñez thought. He had to agree with the governor for the first time since Don Alonso staggered out of the sea. The officer barked an order to one of the gunners, who leaped to his feet and scurried off to relay the message to the bugler. Within minutes a call to arms echoed throughout the compound. Soldiers in various stages of dress scurried from the barracks built along the base of the walls and up the ramps and limestone steps to take their places behind the massive stone ramparts.

A baleful sun climbed the fearful lemon sky, the temperature began to rise with the lengthening day. Buckets of water were brought up from the wells and left for the gun crews sweating in the steamy heat.

Killing men was always a thirsty business.

At dockside, the combined crews of the *Glenmorran*, the *Jericho*, and now the *Santa Rosa* waited for Henry Morgan. Sir William Jolly, Israel Goodenough, Voisin, and the others were accustomed to the ritual. Thomas LeBishop fumed and paced the pier and complained about the waste of a decent wind, though in truth he was reticent about running a gauntlet of hidden bars and channel guns.

As for the *Santa Rosa*'s most unwilling passenger, Elena Maria de Saucedo seemed confused by the behavior of these brigands. Flanked by her guards, assigned to ensure the señorita's presence on the brigantine, Elena stood with hands clasped, frowning as she observed the freebooters aboard their ships and clustered along the waterfront.

She sensed another's eyes upon her and saw Thomas LeBishop watching her from where he stood near the gangplank. For a moment Elena thought the pirate intended to board the brigantine and carry her back to the *Jericho*. The Black Cleric's lips curled back and he held up his Bible. An unusual bookmark jutted from the leather binding. Elena recognized the ornately carved, obsidian hilt of the dagger she had wielded against him. His ravaged cheek bore a lurid scab of encrusted blood that ran the length of his face. LeBishop patted the Bible and then bowed deeply, a gesture more menacing then gracious, and then seemed to dismiss her from his thoughts as he hurried back along the waterfront, anxious to board his sloop. As far as the Black Cleric was concerned, as long as the señorita was worth money, retribution could wait.

For the past week and a half, Elena had expected Don Alonso to emerge from hiding and rescue her. That likelihood seemed to grow more distant with every passing moment. And yet she did not despair. Indeed, she was more determined then ever to turn this capture to her own advantage. She had never met a man like Henry Morgan. The way he wielded power excited her. She had seen something in his eyes from the moment he had burst into her apartment and confronted her. There was a reckless energy lurking beneath his demeanor, a quality of purpose akin to the predatory beast that was his namesake. All this, and chaos in the twinkling of his eyes. One thing the woman knew for certain: Thank heavens her knife had missed him. The Tiger of the Caribbean was the only thing standing between her, and LeBishop's vengeance.

"Where is your Captain Morgan?" Elena asked of the young lad standing alongside her.

"Morgan's walk. It is his way." To the lady's astonishment, her companion replied in a young woman's voice.

"But you are . . ."

"Nell Jolly," said Nell, tilting back her cap to reveal her curly hair. "And I'm as much a woman as you, señorita. Maybe more." Nell's tone made it clear she had no use for the Spanish noblewoman.

They were a pair as diverse in appearance as in personality: Nell in her short coat, linen shirt, broad belt breeches, and buckled shoes; Elena Maria in a long-waisted travel gown, the pale blue overskirt pulled back like the curtains of a proscenium stage to reveal a cream underskirt. And where Nell Jolly walked unattended, Elena had her shadow. Consuelo stood a few paces behind the *criollos*, in the shadow of the shrouds, her brown hands clasped before her and resting upon the small lace apron over her skirt.

Nell was armed with pistol and cutlass.

Elena had only her wiles.

"I do not understand. Where does he walk?" the Spanish woman asked.

"Not 'where' so much but 'how.' Curse him. Bless him, the glorious fool, but he'll do himself in one day, I swear. And I'll not weep for him, not shed one tear, on my oath."

"Ah, I see." Elena Maria said.

"You see nothing!" Nell snapped. She turned her back on the woman. "Be still or I will have you locked in your cabin until we put out to sea." But for all her gruff talk, it was Nell's silence that betrayed her.

Morgan walked unarmed through the streets of Maracaibo. The town was his now, his until he sailed away, and afterward, his still, in the collective memory of the populace, then in legend long after the bitter legacy of his visit had faded. With the surrender of the troops stationed in town, the settlement had fallen into line. At first the populace proved slow to cooperate. The inhabitants hoarded their wealth in hidden cupboards, woodpiles, and beneath floorboards. The Dons changed their minds after Morgan burned half a dozen homes and a plantation on the edge of town. Suddenly the streets were full of Spaniards hauling out their heirlooms and buried coffers of coins and jewelry.

Morgan's law was simple. He held his men on a tight rein, permitting no abuse or cruelty toward the townspeople as long as they obeyed his every edict. Defiance would be met with swift and brutal retaliation.

He prowled past shuttered windows, along narrow streets where he passed several groups of shopkeepers, landowners, venerable seamen, any of whom might have been able to overwhelm this solitary figure by sheer force of number. One group in particular, a trio of prosperous-looking merchants, appeared to be seriously considering the opportunity the pirate captain was presenting to them. All they had to do was rush him en masse. They had numbers on their side.

But Morgan seemed to read their thoughts. He faced them, climbing up onto a low wall, and opened his arms as if preparing himself for sacrifice.

He waited, presented a perfect target. All they had to do was come and take him.

"Do it," he softly challenged.

One of the men, a heavyset townsman with a solid jaw and swarthy complexion, dropped a hand to his coat pocket. Was that a knife or a pistol?

"Come on," Morgan purred. His willingness unnerved them. The townsman's companions suddenly lost their courage. Dire images of their own deaths, horrible fantasies of their families sold into slavery, were too much to bear. And when they failed to act, he turned his back on them. "I thought not," he said. Once Henry Morgan had been a slave to men like these. Now he walked among them like a lord. Fear ruled them, fear he had placed in their hearts and minds.

Down through the green streets, past painted shops and shuttered stalls, past children hiding in alleys and behind the lush foliage, past courtesans in their brothels and mixed-breed slaves, many of whom had already abandoned their captivity and cast their lot with the buccaneers . . .

All eyes were upon him, no hand against him, a man invincible through his own daring. Sweat seeped into his linen shirt. A fair wind tugged at his long brown locks, ruffled his loose sleeves. A stray dog barked to protest his passing. The shadow of a hawk passed over him. A shutter creaked listlessly on its hinges, swaying to and fro.

An old blind man sat in the shade of a lemon tree, singing to himself, his leathery features bobbing up and down with the refrain. The song died on his lips as he heard Morgan approach.

"Be off with you," the old one snarled, batting the empty air with his walking stick.

Morgan knelt by the blind man and placed a gold doubloon in the palm of his hand.

"Take this, *viejo*."

"What for?"

"Tribute for your courage."

The blind man bit the coin and, satisfied it was the real thing, tucked it in his pocket. He cackled as if he had just bested the pirate in a trade. Morgan grinned and, dodging a final thrust of the cane, continued through the town, up one street and down the next, working his way to the sea.

When Morgan arrived on the waterfront, Sir William, Israel, Nell, and the rest of freebooters breathed a sigh of relief and scrambled aboard the ships. Sir William took a skeleton crew aboard the *Glenmorran*. Morgan led the rest to the *Santa Rosa*. LeBishop and the *Jericho* had already cast off. Oars poked through the ports on the lower deck and dug into the bay. The sloop pulled away from shore. The *Glenmorran* soon followed. Then it was the *Santa Rosa*'s turn.

Morgan crossed the gangplank and swaggered amidships, bowed to Elena Maria.

"You would do well to retire to your cabin, señorita."

"I shall remain here," Elena replied.

"You may be dodging chain-shot before the morning is through."

"The señorita is not afraid," Nell interjected, her tone thick with sarcasm.

"So be it," said Morgan. "Voisin . . . can you sail this bucket?"

"To perdition, if need be, *mon capitaine*." The Frenchman removed his cap and scratched his head, obviously concerned about attempting to escape in broad daylight.

"Put your backs into the oars, lads," Morgan called down through an open hatch, where his rowers labored in the stifling heat. The brigantine eased away from the pier and when she caught the wind in her mainsails, the oars were drawn in and the guns were rolled back into the ports.

Morgan leaped onto the ship's railing and caught a hand in the shroud as he leaned forward over the glassy surface of the bay for an unobstructed view of the port. He watched its whitewashed buildings recede into the swampy coastline.

Farewell, Maracaibo. It was a nice place to pillage, but he wouldn't want to live here.

7. "The way it was once . . . the way it is now."

As the recently appointed governor of Jamaica, Don Alonso del Campo had no business crouching in the thicket of *monstera* ferns, wild ginger, tangled vines, and flowering lobster-claw. The path before him wound off through a thicket of fishtail palms clustered tightly together like an ancient phalanx defending the wooded shore from attack. Tiny gnats, like swirling ashes, whirred about his sweat-streaked features, alighted on his eyelids, and invaded his nostrils. He wasn't alone in his discomfort. The bothersome insects tormented the skirmishers Don Alonso had brought out from the safety of the fortress. While the soldiers around him cursed and grumbled, the governor concealed his discomfort behind a mask of pretense and bravado. Of course, the Spanish aristocrat had some help. Where does a man look for bravery if he cannot find it in himself? Don Alonso hunched forward and, shielding his actions, slipped a small silver flask from his shot-pouch and took a couple of swallows of bay rum. The warm spring spreading through his limbs fueled his false courage. Now he could slay giants.

Captain Muñez had argued against the governor's decision to lead the foray. But Don Alonso had insisted. He was determined to demonstrate to one and all that he was no coward and that his escape from Maracaibo, however disgraceful it seemed on the surface, had been the act of a rational man.

Something bit the back of his neck. He slapped. The sound seemed louder than he had expected in the leafy thicket. His hand came away bloody. He wiped the palm clean on his trouser leg and then transferred the musket back to his right hand. He motioned for the skirmishers, thirty soldiers in faded white uniforms and cockade hats, to ready their weapons and follow his lead. The Spaniards eyed one another, their misgivings plainly evident. They had no confidence in the man leading them into the unknown. And if what they had seen earlier in the morning was any indication, this patrol was going to be clearly outnumbered by an overwhelming force of buccaneers disembarking on the shore beyond the palms.

The same thought had crossed the governor's mind.

Earlier that morning he had watched with great anticipation as the two sloops and the *Santa Rosa*, at quarter sail, left the safety of the harbor and eased across the glassy waters of the bay. Their approach was tentative at best, as if the crews dreaded what was to come. The Spanish gunners were prepared to give the men beneath the Black Flag the welcome they deserved.

But to the amazement and consternation of Don Alonso and the garrison, the pirate ships weighed anchor well nigh of the entrance to the bay. As Captain Muñez, Don Alonso, and the troops looked on in puzzled silence from the fortress walls, a stately procession of longboats bearing a well-armed contingent of cutthroats pulled out from the brigantine and headed toward the island. The longboats disappeared beyond the dense barrier of broadleaf ferns and palm trees screening the far shore from view. A few minutes later the longboats made a return crossing, with only a pair of oarsmen dutifully rowing back to the brigantine. Then, after a few moments, as long as it took to take on more brigands, the longboats made a return trip to shore, with another armed party of buccaneers sitting two abreast. Somewhere on the leeward side of the island, beyond the woods, these pirates joined their brethren already ashore. The process repeated itself for the better part of the morning.

"What was built by men can be torn down."

With a slip of the tongue, Morgan had sown the seeds of his own destruction. Don Alonso was convinced the buccaneers intended to storm the landward walls of the fortress, the very battlements the Spaniards had chosen not to protect. Don Alonso was certain of it. But Muñez was not so easily convinced. The continuing procession of longboats, ferrying the brigands to shore, caused the governor to order the gun crews to strip the cannons from the seaward walls and bring them around the perimeter of the castle and mount the twelve-pounders along the ramparts facing the woods. While the gun crews labored to bring the guns about, Don Alonso had chosen his thirty men and instructed them to volunteer to follow him into the undergrowth to get a better read on Morgan's intentions. If the pirates were ashore in any great number, Don Alonso intended to discover where and how many and bring this information back to the fortress.

He caught a glimpse of movement through the trees and halted in his tracks and brought up his musket. He managed to catch himself in time and ease his finger off the trigger before he blasted a round at a pair of enormous grackles. The black birds exploded from the undergrowth and swooped past the startled patrol. The soldiers heaved a collective sigh of relief and followed the governor into the gloom beneath the fishtail palms. They made slow, tedious progress. Within a matter of minutes the fortress was obscured by the dense foliage. It had proved impossible to keep in formation. The very nature of the terrain broke their ranks and divided the skirmishers into smaller clusters of anxious men, muskets ready, nerves on edge, regretting each and every step that took them farther from the main gate and the safety of those stout walls, soon to be bristling with a heavy complement of cannon and grapeshot. Any assault was going to be met with a murderous fire once the guns were in place along the landward walls.

Perhaps there was a better way to prove his courage. Don Alonso began to reconsider his options, hoping to curb his fears by finding a less precarious adventure with which to rescue his reputation. He slapped his cheek, his neck, and brushed the gnats from his eyes. He paused to take a breather and to listen for any suspicious sound. Suddenly he experienced a burning, prickling sensation that spread from his calf to his knee. He glanced down and discovered he had chosen to squat next to an ant bed. The nasty little insects, hardly more than brown dots no bigger than a pinprick, had a bite that burned like fire. And worse, they attacked not singly but in battalions. A couple of the men around him found themselves assailed by a similar colony of pests.

The governor's subordinate, a corporal named Jesus Simone, dropped his musket and stripped off his pants. His legs were covered with red welts from the bites he had received. The corporal began to slap feverishly at his thighs and calves. Don Alonso chose what he thought was the more dignified approach. He rested his own musket against a nearby tree trunk and began to crush the insects between his flesh and trouser leg. Only when the determined survivors made a dash for his crotch did he shed his pants and finish the task, brushing the last insects away with short quick strokes. The look in the governor's eyes dared any man to crack a smile. He shook out his trousers until they were free of unwanted visitors, quickly dressed, and slung his powder flask and shot-pouch across his shoulder. Then he reached for his musket but miscalculated the distance and struck the weapon with his fingertips. He made an attempt to correct his mistake, but the musket slipped from his grasp and fell to the ground, discharging on impact. The shot rang out and shattered the stillness. A swirling flight of emerald-winged parrots swarmed skyward. As the gunshot faded in the distance, the line of trees ahead of the skirmishers erupted in thunder and flame.

Hell broke loose from the thicket of vines and palm trees barring the path. Don Alonso flattened himself against the first patch of ant-free ground he could find. Fire and black smoke, whirring lead slugs and sudden death, roared all around him. Don Alonso hit the dirt alongside Jesus Simone. The corporal began to thrash and moan as he clutched at the blood spurting from his throat.

"*Mierda!*" the governor exclaimed. He met the corporal's dying gaze and in that horrible event found the strength to stand and drag his pistols from his belt. "To me. To me!" he shouted, exhorting his men to form a line of defense at his side. The skirmishers returned fire but could not tell whether their aim had any effect.

Half a dozen grenades came sailing over a cluster of ferns, fuses sputtering as the flames disappeared into the round black spheres. The ground shuddered with each detonation. Iron splinters shredded plants, punctured flesh. A soldier was tossed into the air like a rag doll and landed upside down and draped over a stack of deadwood. Another poor soul staggered backward, bleeding from a dozen wounds, then sank out of sight in the pall of gunsmoke.

"Close ranks!"

Don Alonso emptied his pistols in the direction of the pirates. Some of the skirmishers struggled to hold their ground, but too many of the patrol had no stomach for annihilation. They turned and ran for their lives.

A third of the skirmishers were dead or dying; others had fled. His command was obviously about to be overrun and captured or killed. Don Alonso had seen enough. He was certain Henry Morgan and his brigands were planning to storm the gate. Let them come. Don Alonso would welcome them in kind. He barked an order to the men around him, ordering the soldiers to depart the field in an orderly fashion. The soldiers tried. But their resolve wilted before the constant heat of the gunfire the pirates continued to pour into their ranks. At last, the governor broke into a run, keeping low, and with him, the soldiers departed the field and beat a hasty retreat back to the fortress.

As the last of the gunshots reverberated in the distance, Henry Morgan returned to the wooded shore, followed by the dozen hardy seamen who had helped him create the illusion of an armed host. A longboat with Rafiki Kogi, another oarsman, and eight pirates pulled into the shallows. Once out of sight of the Spaniards on the battlements, the eight buccaneers reclined on the floor of the longboat so that it would appear they had disembarked for the shore, further swelling the ranks of the attackers. Another boat rounded the point, bobbing on the breeze-driven waves.

Morgan hailed Rafiki then glanced around him. Twenty-two men were all that had come over from the brigantine. Hardly an army. But the Spaniards didn't know that. And his men had put on a good show, firing and shouting, hurling grenades, and giving the impression of a force three times their number. Pierre Voisin drew abreast of the captain. The Frenchman finished reloading his pistols and thrust them in his belt. Behind him, clouds of acrid black gunsmoke began to drift past the trees and out toward the water.

"Reckon we convinced them, Captain?"

"We'll find that out soon enough. I shall return to the *Santa Rosa*. See that the rest of you quit the island within the hour. I should not like to waste a good wind."

Morgan waved for the African to bring the longboat closer in to shore. Then he waded into the shallows and climbed into the boat.

"*Jambo*, Captain. We heard the gunfire. Sounded like a whole war be breaking out."

"The Dons started the ball but lost their stomach for the dance," Henry chuckled. "Lucky for us."

The men crowded together on the floor of the longboat managed to create just enough room for Morgan to squeeze down among them for the uncomfortable trip back to the brig.

"Easy now, my beauties," he told Kogi and the other the oarsman. "Don't work so hard. The Dons must think the boat's empty, remember? Just an easy pull back across the bay. Only the two of you aboard. Nothing to it."

"*Wako uongo.* Tell that to my aching back," Rafiki grumbled. The African continued to mutter and grumble until the fortress eased into view. Then he began to sing in a low voice, a song of a distant people, a distant land. And the oars dipped and swung in an arc, dipped again into the dappled sea; he rowed to the rhythm of his cadence and the quick, clipped phrases of his native tongue. He sang of luck and misfortune, of courage and cunning.

" '*Ninavyooona. Fania yokuambia.* As I am seeing. As I am telling you, of a time of battle and daring deeds.' " Tribal memories stirred deep in his soul. The vestige of an ancient culture, old as the veldt and the mountains of the moon. Times changed. But he was still among warriors. " 'The way it was once,' " he sang. " 'The way it is now.' "

"Where are they?" Captain Muñez complained, pacing the length of the parapet to siphon off some of his youthful impatience. Conscious of the men around him, and sensing their anxiety, he struck a position of defiance, legs planted firm, stern-faced, a man ready for anything. But this waiting was worse than any torture he could imagine. "All morning, all afternoon, we work, we wait, move the cannons, break our backs. Well, I say come and let us kill you, Señor Morgan. We are ready, my men and I."

And the soldiers who heard him nodded sagely to one another. Here was an officer worth following. He would let the pirates make the first move, then crush them. There would be a great victory, one to tell their grandchildren.

"Where are they?" Don Alonso said, arriving on the wall and unaware he had echoed the captain's sentiments. "Come taste what we have in store for you. Not even the claws of *el Tigre* are a match for these twelve-pounders." Morgan was clever. A land attack was a brilliant gambit, but doomed to failure. The cannons were loaded with enough grapeshot to cut his forces to ribbons. "What was the last count, Paloma?" Don Alonso asked one of his aides, a bookish, weary-looking corporal the governor had impressed into his own service. The corporal had been only to happy to oblige the governor, after all; duty with Don Alonso exempted Estéban Paloma from the grueling task of shifting the majority of the cannons from the bay to the land approach.

Paloma stirred from his drowsy state on hearing his name spoken. The wind's warm breath fanned the corporal's grizzled features as he unfolded a piece of paper he had been making marks on throughout the day. Corporal Paloma cleared his throat and then checked his totals. "I counted two hundred and thirty-six men crossed from Morgan's ships to the shore. None returned."

"Then what are they waiting for?" Don Alonso grumbled. The sooner he taught this brigand a lesson, the better.

"What are we waiting for, *mon ami*?" said Voisin, crouched on the steps leading to the upper deck. Most of the crew waited in the stifling heat below, having retired to the gundeck to keep themselves out of sight. The few dozen men Morgan had used in his ruse, after hours of crossing and recrossing the bay, had finished their task. Concealed in the longboats, they had returned from shore and scurried like rats up ropes lowered to them from the open ports on the gundeck.

Morgan moved among his crew. Quarrels died when he passed. Men took courage from him though he seemed unaware of the pirates crowding the deck. He offered no words of comfort to stiffen their spines and prepare them for the fact that he was gambling with their lives. Yet there was a stillness about him, a calm at the center of a storm. And on this ship of iron men, all eyes were upon him. Voisin spoke for them all. What was he waiting for? When were they going to make a break for the open sea? When?

Morgan took no notice of the crew. He was listening to the ship. It spoke to him in the creak of timber head and deck beam, in the way she settled in the water and drifted on the oncoming waves. He paused by the door to the captain's cabin, placed his hand upon the latch, then hesitated. Within the cabin itself, Elena Maria brought her finger to her lips. Consuelo fumed and fidgeted but held her counsel. Elena placed the palm of her hand upon the door. The wood felt warm to the touch, as if a fire raged close by. She trembled, not out of fear, but excitement. Another woman might have bemoaned her fate. Elena Maria intended to make the most of her present predicament. A man as resourceful and daring as Henry Morgan did not come along every day of the week. There had to be a way to turn this encounter with *el Tigre* to her advantage.

Morgan knew she was close by. And he might have succumbed to his baser instincts. But now was hardly the time or place. There would be other opportunities, providing the Spanish gunners didn't send them all to the bottom of the bay. He continued across the deck, nudged Voisin aside, and climbed the steps. There, on the fringe of sunlight and shadow he waited, his soul reaching out to the ship and the sea and the good wind. And when the men below did not think they could endure another moment he turned to them, eyes ablaze, his limbs poised like a cat about to pounce. Then he grinned and bounded out onto the upper deck and with arms outstretched to embrace this moment of truth, exclaimed, "Now!"

A ragged volley erupted from the seaward ramparts. The sound startled the defenders manning the walls to either side of the main gate. Don Alonso grabbed up his musket and sword and prepared to repulse the brigands as they charged from the underbrush. He peered over the battlements as Captain Muñez was in the process of leading a force of skirmishers into the woods to determine the state of Morgan's buccaneers. The roar of the cannons sent the captain and his men scurrying back to the safety of the fortress. Don Alonso searched the underbrush, expecting to find a full-scale assault under way.

Then came the daunting realization that the ragged fire hailed from the ramparts overlooking the bay. Sweat glistened in his close-trimmed beard; above that bristly line of salt-and-pepper hairs, the governor's cheeks paled. He stared down at Muñez, who had reached the same conclusion. The few remaining twelve-pounders on the seaward walls kept up their pitiful barrage—too few, too late.

"No," Don Alonso muttered. "No!" It was impossible! They had seen with their own eyes, boat after boat of pirates ferried to shore. Morgan wouldn't leave his men behind. What was happening? Perhaps a feint to draw attention from the gate. Maybe . . . yes . . .

Muñez left his men by the gate and dashed across the compound, past a stone magazine, barrack, a smithy, el commandante's quarters during his infrequent visits to the island. Don Alonso tersely instructed the gun crew to continue to prepare for an assault on the gate. Then the governor quit his post and began to make his way around the perimeter of the fortress. He kept to the walkways, the longer route, for the walls were irregular and built at angles to themselves to facilitate a crossfire on an attacking force. His borrowed clothes, ill-fitting at best, were patched with sweat by the time he reached an empty gun emplacement where Captain Muñez stood leaning on the battlement, dumbstruck, a spyglass gripped loosely in his hand. He turned as Don Alonso approached. The younger man was almost in tears. His lower lip quivered. For a moment Don Alonso thought the officer was about to strike out at him.

"What have you done, *Gobernador?*" He held out the spyglass.

Don Alonso took the instrument. The sun was a molten orange ornament balanced on a riff of rose-tinted cloud and sinking toward the low hills beyond Maracaibo. The air smelled of salt, of decaying seaweed, of defeat. The two sloops were already through the entrance to the bay. The *Santa Rosa* was still within range; unfortunately, the guns that could have been brought to bear on the brig had been loaded with grapeshot and hauled across the fort to defend against an attack by land that didn't exist.

The governor peered through the spyglass at the brig. He could see Elena Maria, standing on deck, bound for Jamaica, and there was nothing to do but watch helplessly. She was looking at him. He could imagine the accusation in her eyes. The governor shifted his stance, swept the deck, then came to rest on Henry Morgan himself.

The pirate was standing on the rail in full view of the defenders, an easy target for a twelve-pounder. But the angle was wrong. And Morgan knew it. He made a pretty target, with his shirt open to the waist and his bronze chest naked to the sun, his long hair streaming in the wind like the mane of a great beast.

"I am *el Tigre del Caribe*, the scourge of the Dons, beholden to none, a brethren of the Black Flag. The sea calls me by name. Gold is my destiny. *Adiós,* Señor del Campo. I will wait for you and your gold in Port Royal!"

And with that the pirate captain bowed courteously, swept an imaginary hat across his chest, flashed a broad grin, then bounded to the deck and began to issue orders to his crew.

The governor turned livid. This would not end here. As soon as one of the overdue warships put into port, Don Alonso vowed, he would take up the pursuit. *I will bring this brigand back in chains or see him die by my hand.*

He smashed the spyglass across the corner of the parapet; the impact shattered the lenses and bent the brass casing. He glared at the young captain, squared his shoulders, drew himself upright, and assumed the dignity of his station. The brash young officer retreated from the aristocrat's cold, emasculating glare.

"What have I done?" said Don Alonso. "On the contrary. What have *you* done, Captain Muñez? It appears you have allowed Henry Morgan to escape."

We are Brethren of Blood,
we are sons of the sea.
We are children of havoc
and born to be free.
Morgan sailed from the bay on the wings of the wind.
Fare you well, Maracaibo, should he ne'er come again.
Too late for your pistols and swords that are keen
For he's stolen your treasures and captured your queen.

8. " ' . . . so that death passed upon all men.' "

From his perch astraddle the fore topgallant, on a yardarm sixty feet above the deck, Henry Morgan opened his arms to the crossbreeze swelling the canvas sail beneath him. The brig swayed and trembled, connecting him to the pulse of the mysterious deep. No man was his master, no fate held him bound. His future was now, and that was enough. Every raid was like being plunged into the depths of darkness, every return was like being born anew. He lived by his courage and his cunning and, of course, his luck. Morgan's luck. He vowed to never get so old that regrets outnumbered his dreams.

Thomas LeBishop, standing amidships on the upper deck of the *Jericho*, looked back at the Spanish brig and the captain in the rigging. The Black Cleric scowled and grumbled, "Reckless fool," beneath his breath. He could only hope Morgan would make a misstep and fall and break his blasted neck.

"Look at him, Mister Tregoning. Ever since that damn Welshman arrived in Port Royal . . ." LeBishop scowled, leaving the statement unfinished. For the past ten years he'd watched his own influence erode while Morgan flourished, returning time and time again with the hold of his sloop filled to the gunwales with plunder. Well, no more. Morgan had served his purpose, LeBishop told himself, the wind fluttering the hem of his black coat as he drew a worn leather-bound Bible from the same coat pocket in which he kept a heavy-bore pistol with a cut-down barrel for close-in killing.

" 'As by one man sin entered into the world, and death by sin . . .' " he read aloud. The Black Cleric glanced around at the hardened rogues who sailed beneath his flag. Every man jack of them was eager to squander his ill-gotten gain in the fleshpots of Port Royal. LeBishop continued to read. " ' . . . so that death passed upon all men.' "

"What does it mean, Cap'n?" asked Tregoning. The quartermaster's flinty gaze never left the crew as they tended to the sailing of the ship. The *Jericho* was running with full sail to the wind, slicing through the gnarled sea.

"That is for me to know, old friend, and Henry Morgan to find out." LeBishop returned his Bible to his coat pocket and exchanged it for a small glass flask of brandy from his waistcoat pocket. He took a drink. It would be the first of many.

At the *Glenmorran*'s stern, Sir William leaned his elbows on the rail, lit his pipe from a length of burning hemp, and contented himself to watch the brig churning across the wake of the sure, swift sloop. Israel Goodenough made his way aft to join his friend. The sea was choppy and hammered against the hull and the helmsman kept the *Glenmorran* leaning into the wind.

"Is that Henry on the foremast?" Goodenough asked, fishing in his pocket for his own clay pipe. He removed his hand and stared at the trace of tobacco on his fingertips and frowned, trying to remember where he had last set it down.

"Who else?" Sir William grumbled. He straightened, pursed his lips, clasped his hands behind his back, and shook his head, muttering a sigh of disapproval, as if he were a schoolmaster watching the perilous antics of a favorite pupil.

"Let the younkers risk their necks, I tell him. He's too old for climbing around the rigging like a powder monkey. It's easy enough for a young man to lose his purchase. One careless move and what would our captain do then?"

"Fly," the gunner chuckled, "I have no doubt." He wiped his mouth on the sleeve of his shirt, dabbed the perspiration from his brow. He stared down at his callused, scarred hands disfigured by brawls and powder burns. Two of his fingers were crooked where the recoil of a nine-pounder had slammed into his fist. "But old? That's us, friend. Getting too old for boarding parties and duels and out-running Spanish gunships."

"But not for a homecoming. There'll be a carnival tonight in Port Royal," Sir William observed with a wink and a nod.

"And a time for serious sinning. But Henry would do well to watch himself. I seen how he looks at the señorita. And, I imagine, so has Nell," said Goodenough.

"My daughter has had a quick fuse since she set her sights on Henry Morgan."

"Gunsights, if he ain't careful," Goodenough retorted. He made his way over to one of the swivel guns mounted astern. It was a Span-ish piece, forged in the ironworks of Seville. The gunner appreciated the craftsmanship that went into the two-foot-long barrel and forked mount. The Spaniards made fine weapons. They were a pleasure to steal.

He loaded the swivel gun with gunpowder and cloth wadding then dusted the fire-hole with fine-grain priming. He took the length of smoldering hemp from Sir William and touched the glowing tip to the gunpowder. The fire-hole ignited, flared, the swivel gun roared its salute in the direction of the brig. All hands on the deck of the *Glen-morran* bolted upright, startled from their labors by the blast and the cloud of black smoke billowing from the stern gun.

Morgan heard the swivel gun boom, and swung down to the shrouds, caught hold on the whipcord rigging, and leaned out to wave in the direction of the *Glenmorran*. He shouted down to his crew and gave orders to return the salute. The gunners were only too happy to com-ply, and loosed a volley that thundered across the bay.

"Take that, Israel Goodenough!" Morgan shouted, although he knew his friend could not hear him. Morgan seemed immune to the precariousness of his position. With his dark brown hair streaming in the wind, his features washed in the burnished light, the captain wel-comed this journey's end. A great sense of accomplishment and ela-tion welled in his heart. He looked beyond the sloop and his spirit soared as the island of Jamaica rose like the first glimpse of paradise over the horizon. Lush forests, jagged hills, waterfalls spilling down from alabaster bluffs, a pearl-white shore bathed in the light of after-noon. Here was refuge for the weary buccaneer, a safe port for the Brethren of the Black Flag, and the lair of *el Tigre del Caribe*.

After eight days and nights spent constantly on their guard, searching the horizon for pursuing Spanish frigates, the jumble of houses, taverns, shops, and brothels of Port Royal were a sweet sight. Even the threatening line of thunderheads building behind the Blue Mountains failed to mar the island's welcome beauty.

"Shall I call out, Captain?" asked Rafiki Kogi, leaning over the edge of the crow's nest that capped the main mast. Like Morgan, the African was stripped to the waist. His ebony flesh soaked in the warmth of the afternoon. He tossed a spyglass to Morgan.

"By all means, Mister Kogi," said Henry Morgan. He more closely resembled a common seaman then the master of a ship. He'd exchanged his finery for a pair of breeches cut from a rough red nap; about his waist was a broad leather belt from which dangled a satchel of silver coins stamped with the likeness of the Spanish crown. He maneuvered, sleek and nimble-footed as a cat, through the intricate tangle of whipcord and brass grommets and panels of extra sail.

"Land ho!" the African bellowed.

A cry of enthusiasm drifted up to them from below. Hatches were opened and the men on the gundeck scrambled up into the sunlight to catch a sight of home and hearth. The crew of the *Santa Rosa* cheered and slapped one another on the back, shouted a salute to Morgan. Blue glass bottles of rum were passed around and everyone had a chance to drink a toast to the gods of sea and sky who had brought them safely to Port Royal. As the *Santa Rosa* entered the bay, a flotilla of outriggers, johnnyboats, and skiffs pulled away from shore. Most of the craft were piloted by the local youth, the bastard offspring of buccaneers who called Port Royal home. They came on in every manner of craft, young hellions to a fault, eager to prove their worth, born with the sea in their blood and a thirst for youthful adventure— boys and girls together, all of them eager to be first to reach the ships before they docked. At first the youth started for the *Glenmorran*, but then someone noticed Morgan atop the rigging of the *Santa Rosa*, and the makeshift flotilla altered its course for the brig.

Morgan waved to the throng. And yet even as the smaller boats narrowed the gap between their crafts and the oncoming brig, an innate sense of caution caused the freebooter to make a quick appraisal of the ships in the bay, the redoubts and batteries whose guns protected the entrance to the harbor and the waterfront with its familiar conglomeration of shops, taverns, brothels, and rooming houses that the civilized world had dubbed "the wickedest place on earth." Among these narrow winding crowded streets, anything could be had for a price, every desire fulfilled, every thirst slaked. Its populace was free to fight or run, buy or sell, be drunk or sober, however they pleased. A revel could be counted on to last round-the-clock. But these weren't mere free souls celebrating an innocent way of life that placed them outside the stranglehold of kings and courts and decrees: violence had become a way of life; the night-shrouded alleys were often sites of last resort, and home to the quick and the dead.

Port Royal was wild and untamed, a place of sin, beyond the rule of law, where rum flowed free, where every man was master of his fate, and the women were as good as gold . . . or pieces of eight, or pearls, emeralds, rubies, or bartered bolts of silk, sacks of sugar, bales of tobacco, kegs of cocoa . . .

The island's hidden valleys and forest-covered mountain ranges were bordered by limestone cliffs whose base the tides had eroded into a white sandy shore. The bay's dark sapphire surface lightened in hue the closer one came to land, until the shallows were all but translucent and sunlight plunged to the seafloor. The sky was filled with a swirl of gulls and terns flashing white against the sky. Brown pelicans in flocks and alone dove into the sea, then, with their great wings pummeling the air, emerged from the surf with the catch of the day wriggling in their beaks.

Morgan satisfied himself that all was well. He looped a length of rope around his wrist, then, once secured to the yardarm, leaned out until he could see the Frenchman at the helm. He noticed the women had also arrived on deck. Doña Elena cut a fine figure even from this height.

"Monsieur Voisin! See you follow the *Glenmorran* into the bay—ease past the ships of our good brothers. This brig carries a deep draft. Best we anchor offshore. Bring us in past the *Sea Witch*. Take care we don't crowd Calico Jack. That tub of his needs a good bit of room to come about."

"With pleasure, *mon capitaine*," Voisin shouted back. He knew the shallows and reefs like the back of his hand, and pointed the bow of the *Santa Rosa* toward the southern shore at a point about fifty yards out from the dockside where the stonewalled warehouses crowded the waterfront.

Port Royal and its helter-skelter maze of narrow streets dominated the peninsula bordering the south side of the bay. The infamous stronghold, with its brightly painted limestone-and-wood buildings, was awash with activity. As the great sea bell on the tip of the peninsula began to peal, signaling the return of Morgan and his crew, the denizens of Port Royal crowded into the narrow streets. Not even the menacing sky could dim the enthusiasm that greeted Morgan's arrival. His return called for a festival. The prodigal town was eager to welcome *el Tigre del Caribe*, for he was one of their own.

Sir Richard Purselley, governor of Jamaica, whom the gods favored with warm eyes, an aquiline nose, a generous smile, and a heart as cold as the gold he coveted, paced the terrace in front of the governor's house, paused to adjust his periwig, brushed a curious bee from the cup of bloodred Bordeaux his Maroon servant had set out for him, and then took a seat upon the high-backed wooden throne built to his specifications by a local artisan.

"Well, Captain, do you hear that?" He tilted his wineglass in the direction of the peninsula and the pealing bell. The bells atop the church of St. Bernard in Kingston took up the call. "Sounds like a bloody coronation. Do you think it's Morgan?" He glanced over at the English officer standing close at hand.

"We'll know soon enough." Alan Hastiler—his square-jawed, honest features wearing a mask of seriousness—leaned his yeoman's hands upon the stone railing as he studied the bay. A Northumberland childhood had little prepared the British marine for the Caribbean. At first he had dreaded this placement. But it hadn't taken long for the island to work its magic on him. The warm trade winds, the music, the exotic foods, the sunlight and hills and heady perfume from the flowers that seemed always in bloom and pervaded every aspect of life, had tempered his rigid English upbringing.

It had become a daily struggle to remind himself that he and his marines were charged with enforcing English law and ensuring order and the English way of life in Jamaica. Granted, paradise may have rounded some of his 'edges', but he was still the same servant of King and Country.

Captain Hastiler stared at the wineglass in the governor's hand and its companion on the tray and licked his lips. It was rumored the governor kept a fine cellar. But Hastiler knew hell would have to freeze over before the foppish aristocrat, seated on his "throne," offered him a taste of his wine. Until that time or the world should end, the governor of Jamaica imbibed alone.

A formation of black-and-yellow orioles erupted from the wooded slope below, swooped over the terrace, and dove and darted across the sky, past the circular drive where Hastiler's carriage waited to take the officer back down to the blockhouse, barracks, and redoubts that guarded the approach to Kingston and protected the good citizens from the incursion of Spanish gunboats, or the errant pirate vessel that chanced an unwelcome approach.

Protection. Now there was the galling truth. Since his appointment as governor, Sir Richard Purselley had borne the indignity of knowing that the presence of these freebooters had been the island's chief defense against an attack by Spain. By legalizing the antics of men like Morgan with letters of marque, England had assured Jamaica would remain a stronghold of British sovereignty in the heart of the Spanish Main. The Brethren had been a necessary evil, up until now. But the winds of change were blowing. The governor had received a dispatch informing him that English vessels were on the way and the island would soon be properly garrisoned. And just in time. Henry Morgan had become far too popular among the island's miscreants. Already, the freebooter considered himself above the governor's authority; and that could not be tolerated.

Hastiler and his marines were here for the good citizens of Kingston, the planters and merchants who lived in elegant limestone manors, kept shops and taverns and the very presence of "merry olde England" alive in the Caribbean. Port Royal, on the opposite side of the bay, could take care of itself. The freebooters and cutthroats who called it home needed no arm of British might to protect them. A decent Englishman went among them at his own risk. A Spaniard would fare even worse. So had it been, so would it always be. Old hatreds, like habits, died hard.

Purselley considered this state of affairs as he watched the orioles sweep up past the two-storied facade of the governor's estate and then vanish over the clay tile roof, losing themselves among the trees and gardens beyond the manor. Purselley noticed the lowering sky and considered the possibility of a storm. Not that it would curtail an evening of drunken excess. He had never known inclement weather to dampen a celebration in Port Royal. A streamer-tailed hummingbird suddenly hovered near the table, attracted by the sweet odor of wine. Its twin tail feathers were twice as long as its black-and-green body as it flashed back and forth, inspecting the governor's table. Then, with a flash of its iridescent chest feathers, the bird disappeared.

"There, sir, it's the *Jericho*. And the *Glenmorran*," Hastiler called out. Unlike Port Royal, no one in Kingston ran down to the docks to await the buccaneer's return, although the presence of his booty-laden ships would no doubt have a keen effect on the local economies of both ports. Now that a truce existed with Spain, the well-to-do residents of the island were fearful Morgan's antics might have placed them all in peril.

"Wait . . . there's another ship," Hastiler blurted. Purselley stood, waited anxiously as Hastiler slipped a spyglass from his coat and used it to study the brig as the vessel rounded the peninsula and headed toward the far cay. "It is a Spanish ship, the *Santa Rosa*," the marine announced. "Captain Morgan's aboard. By heavens, it appears to be a prize ship."

"Excellent," Purselley said. "Then Morgan has indeed committed acts of piracy against our new allies." The governor stood and held out his glass of wine to the oncoming brig. "Well done, Henry Morgan." Sir Richard emptied the glass then hurled it against the rail, shattering the crystal into a thousand pieces. "I have you now."

Soon after the guns of the *Santa Rosa* fired their salute and announced their arrival, Elena Maria, against Consuelo's stern advice to the contrary, had appeared on deck to catch her first glimpse of the notorious haven for pirates and cutthroats. The entire tableau of wind and sky, of the island and the stormclouds, the smell of the sea, the mixture of colors—stark white, emerald, sapphire, and aquamarine—the excitement that swept through the crew, the coarse voices and the activity of the men as they prepared to make the final approach through the shallows toward home . . . all of it permeated her being, thrilled her in ways she could not explain. Consuelo would have been horrified to learn Elena Maria sensed a kinship with this unruly lot. It was a secret the *criollos* intended to keep to herself.

"Look, Consuelo, what do you see?"

"Danger waters, señorita," the half-breed replied, eyeing Nell Jolly who approached them from where she had been standing near the ship's wheel. Nell had been watching Morgan in the rigging. Every time he altered his position along the spar she would catch her breath and will him to control his boyish antics. The arrival of Doña Elena and her half-breed servant on the upper deck was a signal for Nell to abandon her place and approach the señorita.

Sir William's daughter had made a point of intruding on Elena Maria de Saucedo throughout the journey from Maracaibo, taking care to prevent Morgan from ever having the opportunity to be completely alone with the señorita. Nell Jolly suspected there was more to Don Alonso's intended bride than met the eye. Morgan was a romantic, albeit a misdirected one. Nell intended to nip this infatuation in the bud.

"That's Kingston, across the bay," said Nell. "The governor's residence is next to that blockhouse on the north side of town. Sir Richard Purselley will no doubt invite you to be his guest." Nell hoped Elena Maria would insist on being escorted to the governor's manor the minute they dropped anchor. The señorita's silence was infuriating.

If Elena Maria resented Nell's presence, she hid her feelings behind a mask of civility. She made a quick study of the tidy, well-ordered community of farms, the whitewashed houses of well-to-do merchants and the port's landed gentry, and, lastly, the hillside above Kingston with its ostentatious English manor and the blockhouse built for the English governor and his contingent of Royal Marines. The limestone walls of the manor and fort gleamed stark white against the dark, craggy backdrop of the Blue Mountains. Along Kingston's waterfront, a squat trio of merchant ships and an English fore-and-aft–rigged schooner nestled against the pier.

"Best you stay close to me—I'll see you safely to the governor," Nell suggested.

"And miss the celebration?" The question came from overhead. The women looked up in time to see Morgan dangling from a hoist line above their heads. He relaxed his grip and dropped to the deck, assuming a complacent air about the acrobatics that had dropped him practically at their feet. "What kind of hosts would we be?" He raised his tone of voice so that his remarks carried to the Frenchman at the wheel. "The señorita has been confined aboard the *Santa Rosa* for much too long. She needs to stretch her legs. What better place than at carnival? Am I right, Monsieur Voisin?"

"Mais oui, mon capitaine."

"Sir Richard will be displeased that you delayed presenting her to him," Nell said, her eyes flashing daggers at the Frenchman for agreeing with Morgan.

"The governor is always displeased," Voisin replied, without meeting the young woman's searing stare. He avoided her gaze, glanced up at the gray clouds building above the mountains, and willed the storm to hold off until the morning. "And besides, he knows nothing of our guest. Who's to tell him?"

"The señorita will be safer . . ."

Morgan ended her argument with a wave of his hand. "Enough, Toto. There is no safer place to be in all of Port Royal than on the arm of Henry Morgan."

"I would see your 'carnival,' Señor," Elena said, smiling in Nell's direction; a sea breeze ruffled the lime-green folds of her taffeta dress. "It is the least I can do, since my husband-to-be, Don Alonso, will one day hang you for the privilege of my company."

"If that is my destiny, then I shall demand more from you than a stroll through the streets, señorita—and die a happy man, I warrant."

The cries of the boys and girls in their skiffs, canoes, outriggers, and johnnyboats, drifted to them on the sea breeze. "Your pardon, ladies." Morgan trotted off to the starboard side and leaped into the shrouds. A hue and cry went up as he revealed himself to the boats below. His name rang out in the stillness. He was a hero to them, a figure of legend whom almost everyone respected, and many feared. The cheers from those youthful throats was music to his ears. Morgan laughed and swept his hand before him as if he held an imaginary hat. He bowed most graciously to the offspring of the Brethren.

"They love him," Elena Maria observed.

"Of course," Nell remarked.

Even as she spoke, Morgan reached into his pouch and brought out a handful of silver coins and hurled them into the air. The coins plopped into the shallows and the boys and girls dove from their boats into the crystal-clear aquamarine waters to retrieve the treasure he had sown upon the sea. He repeated the process—much to the delight of the young people bobbing on the surface, who dove down into the shallows in search of the gleaming pieces of eight.

"And why not?" Nell added as the young people swarmed to the starboard side of the brig, their boats crashing harmlessly into one another and glancing off the hull of the *Santa Rosa* as Morgan emptied the contents of his pouch upon the sea. "He is a river to his people."

9. Bluffed!

Heaven save us," Consuelo muttered. But heaven had no place in Port Royal. "Doña Elena!" she shouted, trying to keep up with the kidnapped bride-to-be. But her cry was drowned out in a sea of voices.

Shops and taverns and gambling dens and inns crowded the peninsula. Bacchus ruled the streets. Elena Maria had never seen such a diversity of people crammed into such a small area as the pirate lair. Women of every shape and hue—Maroons, mulattos, women from Dublin and Burma and Malaysia and Normandy—were draped in silks and satins, their rouged cheeks and curious ways a mockery of the aristocrats they pretended to be. The streets teemed with swaggering scalawags attired in the finest garments money couldn't buy: fine linens from the Orient, intricately stitched waistcoats, shirts and silk breeches fit for nobility—and no doubt stolen from the same. A dozen dialects filled the air—and music, shouting, haggling over bartered goods . . . Someone danced, someone argued, someone fought and cursed and died. Always more and more, always too much of sight and sound and smell: woodsmoke and tobacco and frying meat and swilled rum and liberally sprinkled perfumes stolen from the locked trunks of irate Spanish ladies. Elena's senses could not handle it all. It made her dizzy.

Half a dozen brigands jostled past. They were a salty lot, half-drunk and glad to be ashore, although envious of the recent arrivals. First came a pair of rawboned Irishmen fit for brawling and debauchery. Their captain followed along, behind the Irish seamen. This gentleman rogue wore a calico waistcoat and velvet breeches, walked arm in arm with a coarse-looking, heavyset woman in coat and breeches and half-opened shirt; the mounds of her breasts threatened to escape the confines of her bodice, bulged over the pair of pistols tucked in her belt. These hell-bound brigands jostled and shoved past the half-breed woman, almost knocking her off her feet. Consuelo heard the couple addressed as "Calico Jack" and "Anne Bonney" by the men who followed them. She knew the names, for the pair were infamous throughout the Spanish Main.

Anne Bonney kept up a bold chorus, which she sang in Gaelic at the top of her lungs. Calico Jack was a man of average height, but lofty ambitions. The dashing, debonair pirate captain had never met a church coffer he didn't love to pilfer. Bonney, and the rest of Calico's crew, were rogues to be reckoned with, and no man offered to block their passage as they headed for the great bonfire by the signal bell on the tip of the peninsula. Suddenly Calico Jack altered his course, turned, and grabbed Consuelo and swung her about in his arms while the gray-haired woman yelped her protest. Another of his companions cut in and danced a reel with the unwilling half-breed woman. Then Anne Bonney took her turn, grabbing the old woman by the arms and spinning her about until the servant lost her balance and stumbled.

"Come, come, you old hen, where's that pretty little chick you serve?" asked Jack.

"The señorita's a sweet hatchling, all right. But beware her talons," offered his paramour. Anne Bonney drew a cutlass from her belt and sawed the air with its yard of cold steel. "Captain LeBishop didn't keep his distance, and look what happened to him."

The two Irishmen in the lead erupted into laughter: a mean-spirited, coarse display at the old woman's expense.

"Come along, you horny bastard," said Anne Bonney, shifting the blade she held until the point touched Jack's coat, over his heart. "I warrant I am woman enough for you." Bonney was a thickset woman with blunt features and a gruff disposition who, despite her affection for Calico Jack, had been known to entertain a lady or two in her boudoir whenever Jack lay drunk and unable to service her needs.

"Now, my love, my heart beats true, and only for you," Jack said.

"Be careful how you cast your net or it won't beat at all."

Calico Jack patted the blade aside and leaned into the woman, grabbed her about the waist and fondled one of her breasts. Then he laughed and patted the seat of her baggy breeches and continued on down the street. One had the impression her threats excited him more than kept him in line. By the time Jack and his mistress had tired of their antics and gone merrily on their way, Morgan and Elena Maria were well out of sight.

Consuelo sighed with relief and sagged against a smoke-filled stall whose owner was selling bammy and fried fish to passersby. The proprietor—a balding *boucanier* with gold rings in his ears, a face as wrinkled as an old war map, close-set eyes, and a forehead that crinkled when he smiled—handed the smallboned woman one of the delicacies from his grill, a deep-fried, pancake-shaped slab of cassava bread folded around a chunk of fried fish.

"Ain't no bammy better than mine," the old man cackled. Then, as an afterthought, added, "Calico Jack and Anne Bonney are a bad lot, and you best give them a wide berth."

Consuelo had already come to that conclusion on her own.

He gestured for her to eat, and Consuelo, unable to think of anything better to do, nodded her thanks and devoured the meal with gusto. Before she had finished, the stallkeeper produced a flask of sorrel and, afterward, a clay pipe packed with ganja. Consuelo knew she should be trying to catch up to her mistress, but after cup or two of sorrel and a few puffs on the stallkeeper's pipe, Consuelo had to struggle to remember just what it was she had been so concerned about.

The ganja quickly took effect, although before the drug took complete control, she learned her benefactor's name was Harry. And Harry had been a rake and rover for many a year until the seas became too rough and his bones too bruised. But the old relic still had some life left in him and he was full of suggestions as to how he might give Doña Elena's servant a "proper welcome" to Jamaica.

The Brethren of the Black Flag gathered on the tip of the peninsula, oblivious to the threatening elements. The signal bell summoned one and all for the Grand Reckoning—as it was now, had been, and always would be. This was the night of homecoming after a raid, when the ships returned with their plunder. It was the moment each man lived for. And not just the crews who sailed with Morgan or the Black Cleric—friends and rivals, wives and whores, and bastard children gathered for the lighting of the council pyre and the distribution of the plunder. Here with the black sea on three sides of them, here beneath the rumbling stormclouds that blotted out the moon, here with fire and sword, the crews were dissolved, quarrels resolved, and the lists detailing the spoils of Maracaibo were produced. After settling each man's claim, the crews of the *Glenmorran* and the *Jericho* would be dispatched to the warehouses where the quartermasters would distribute each man's rightful share.

Henry Morgan looked the part now, in his sapphire-blue velvet jacket with shiny brass buttons, a silk shirt the color of clotted cream, and rust-colored breeches. His long brown hair was concealed beneath a knotted scarlet scarf. The broad black belt around his waist bristled with a brace of pistols and a double-edged dagger. He paced around the bonfire, cajoling with the populace, bestowing a trinket or two upon the older women, and indulging in some good-natured bragging about his exploits, for this was at least part of the reason so many of the Brethren had come to the shore: for the drama of it all.

Thomas LeBishop did not care a whit for drama. The longer Morgan took to prowl the beach, the more impatient his rival became. The Black Cleric finished off the brandy and then looked around at his crew as if suspecting them of holding out on him. The Black Cleric was a figure of gloom and smoldering resentment in his preacher's garb; his scarred cheek added a note of sinister appeal to his appearance, as if the pirate had been blasted by the heavenly powers he so often invoked for his own vile ends. LeBishop rocked unsteadily on his feet. He swayed, shook his head, tried to concentrate on the proceedings. The liquor he had consumed dulled his senses. He blinked and rubbed his dull blue eyes, and tried to suppress the effects of all he had consumed.

He surveyed the crowd that had come to the Great Reckoning, his bleak gaze swept over the familiar firelit faces of the cutthroats and freebooters. They were a salty lot, every man jack of them had a date with the gallows in England or France, Spain or the Colonies.

His own crew was nervous. They had seen him like this before, and slowly began to drift away by twos and threes. Only Tregoning, that able seaman and a clever assassin in his own right, remained at his captain's side. The Cornishman recognized the storm stewing in LeBishop's soul. It was clear as the rumbling overhead. He didn't envy the object of LeBishop's wrath. No man was a match for the Black Cleric—with blade or pistol, drunk or sober, he was the Grim Reaper.

Tregoning noticed that LeBishop had fixed his sights on the captive señorita standing among the crowd, flanked by Israel Goodenough and the African, Rafiki Kogi. Suddenly the Black Cleric stepped back into the crowd, melting among them like a living shadow. Tregoning watched LeBishop maneuver his way through the throng and come up behind Morgan's men. There was going to be trouble. Tregoning could hardly wait.

Every Great Reckoning began in the same fashion: with the reading of the Articles—for such a reading had begun the journey and it was customary that the same Articles should end it. Morgan paced the cleared circle around the bonfire, the strong cut of his countenance etched in the fire light. Flames leaped and danced against the night, timber split and cracked and exploded into flame and raged against the approaching storm. Embers were sucked skyward in an updraft to compete with the shimmering shades of blue lightning. Bolts of electricity glimmered and rippled along the clouds, then split the sky with a thunderous crash, and repeated themselves until it seemed as if devils were dueling behind those terrible battlements of black wind and water vapor.

"These are the Articles. Any man who places his mark upon this paper sails under these same laws," said Morgan. He glanced around at the faces turned toward him.

"Read on, dearie. Then come and have a romp," a comely wench called out. "Your friends have missed you." She cupped her enormous breasts, their pink crowns barely concealed by her low-slung bodice. She grinned and tossed her head like a sassy filly attracting her stud.

Morgan grinned as the crowd laughed at his expense. "Well now, Sadie Palantine, I need but one pillow. Who is the other for?"

"Sir William Jolly," Sadie retorted. "If the poor sod could only manage to find his way. At his age he needs more than a map to find my treasures." A pack of ten-year-old boys, like angels with dirty faces, crawled to the fore. Wide-eyed and anxious to be a part of a forbidden world, they peered out from behind the frock coats and aprons of the adult men and women just as Sadie Palantine lifted the magenta hem of her dress and flashed a glimpse of her alabaster thighs in Sir William's direction. The crowd roared its approval.

The physician coughed and cleared his throat and refused to dignify her remarks with a comment. He remained seated at a table, a ledger before him. He looked up on hearing his name, then realized who was doing the talking and returned to his lists and his ciphering.

Jolly knew any gibe spoken by the likes of Madame Palantine was bound to cost him a measure of his dignity.

Morgan glanced over at Elena Maria, who appeared somewhat awed by the press of humanity that had followed the Welsh buccaneer to the Reckoning. It was obvious to her that here in Port Royal, there was no ambivalence toward Henry Morgan: he had his enemies; she could tell them by the way they skulked on the fringes—men like the Black Cleric and his cronies, whose eyes burned with a dark jealousy, whose expressions betrayed the malice in their hearts.

Come to think of it, where *was* LeBishop?

She could not locate him. But she knew he was watching her. She felt his touch of evil tingle along the back of her neck. Unsettled, the señorita returned her attention to the crowd around her. Henry Morgan was held in high esteem among most of these cutthroats and freebooters: men of every color and creed, freed slaves, thieves, fugitives, deserters, everything from the detritus of society to ne'er-do-well aristocrats, and all of them standing equal around the fire, equal before the other Brethren and by the Articles to which they swore.

In a way it was exhilarating. Elena Maria had never experienced such a gathering of free souls. These men and women, outcasts of the world, had created their own society devoid of caste and birthrights, where one man or woman was the equal of any other. They rose and fell on their merits, by their wits, on the strength of their swords, by trick or trade. If her own world were like this, she would have no need of Don Alonso or his place in court.

Too bad.

She could not imagine such rabble being able to resist the might of Spain. No doubt they were destined to wear out their welcome among the English as well. What monarchy could afford to allow such freedoms to go unchecked?

Elena Maria looked up at the sky as the lightning shimmered along the base of the clouds and wondered how long the elements would hold themselves at bay. She had brought nothing to protect herself from the rain and did not want to consider what might happen if the clouds finally unleashed their downpour. Her dress was cut from bolts of pale green Indian cotton, soft and supple and trimmed with French lace about the bodice which barely clung to her ample bosom. Heaven help her in a cloudburst. Of course the other women would fare no better, and many of them, although harlots and tavern wenches, were more finely dressed than she, in unpatterned taffetas, silks, and satins, and velvet cloths embroidered with spangles and lace.

As Morgan prepared to recite the Articles and distribute the plunder, he glanced around until he caught a glimpse of Nell Jolly in the shadows, just beyond the fringe of light. In her breeches, blouse, and baldrick she looked ready for a fight, a strange attitude, seeing as they were among friends—dangerous friends to be certain, but not here by the pyre, not on the night of Reckoning and the distribution of the spoils. He nodded in her direction and she started to wave on reflex, but the gesture was brief and lacked warmth. She glanced in Elena Maria's direction, scowled, and retreated into the darkness.

" 'Article One,' " said Morgan, puzzled by her behavior. " 'Every man has a vote in affairs of moment and equal title to the fresh provisions, or strong liquors, and may use them at pleasure unless for the good of all there is a vote for retrenchment.' "

"Well said," shouted one of the freebooters, a red-cheeked, dissolute scalawag with a peg leg and pocked face. "I'll drink to that." He drained the last of a bottle of rum and tossed the empty vessel into the black tides.

" 'Every man is to be fairly called in turn, by list, on board of prizes. To desert your ship or your mates in battle is punishable by death or marooning.' "

"*Ninavyoona*. As I see it, keelhauling is too good for such a man," Rafiki Kogi blurted out. "We 'hang' together or let him hang alone." And again the crowd concurred. Morgan continued to read from the parchment in his hand, describing the conduct of the crew concerning women, and that any drinking past eight o'clock in the evening was to be done in the open, above deck, and that every man should keep his pistols and cutlass clean. At last he came to the passage they had been waiting for.

" 'The captain and the quartermaster are to receive two shares of a prize, the master and boatswain and gunner, one and a half shares, and the remainder of the crew, a half share.' "

"Then hurry up, Captain Morgan. I'll make my mark and be done with it," another man called out. Many of the crew voiced their consent to this suggestion. But Morgan continued on to the last point.

" 'Every man's quarrels are to be ended onshore, at sword and pistol.' "

"You have said it!" LeBishop shouted, advancing into the circle of light. He had caught Elena Maria by the arm and forced her from the protection of Morgan's men. Israel Goodenough and Rafiki Kogi glared at one another, each man blaming his companion for a lapse in judgment.

Morgan's expression grew dark and threatening. He dropped the articles in the sand, crunched them underfoot and approached the Black Cleric. "Let her go," he warned.

Elena Maria struggled against his iron grasp, but the churchman's strength was surprising. One moment she had been a mere spectator, one of many, yet standing apart, separated from the throng by an aura of nobility. Then suddenly she had felt LeBishop's talons dig into her arms, his forward motion sweeping her into the circle of firelight.

"Certainly I will let her go. But not before I carve my name in her. The señorita may be a queen in Panama, but here she's only a pawn in Port Royal, to be used as a man sees fit."

"My word is upon her," Morgan said.

"Mind you, Henry," Calico Jack called out. "The Cleric has God on his side." The pirate chuckled at his own cleverness. Anne Bonney nudged her way forward; she seemed excited by the prospect of a duel between the two captains. LeBishop was without peer. She doubted any man could best him. But then, Henry Morgan was unique in his own right. Although he never looked for trouble, she had never known him to run from a fight. He did have a golden tongue . . . *El Tigre del Caribe*? A fox, more likely.

"I am not some piece of property—" Elena Maria snapped. The crowd laughed. Their amusement was most disconcerting, as if they knew something she did not. "How dare you lay hand on me!"

"Avast there, señorita. Stow your pretty speeches. None fear you here. Say no more or I'll lay more than than my hand on you, by my oath." LeBishop looked at Morgan. "Your word, do you say? I put my mark on the Articles, same as you." The Black Cleric released his hold on his captive and flung aside the flaps of his coat to free the hilt of his cutlass. "And I am entitled to my share. Unless you want to split her in two, then we must settle this thing, right here and now. I will take my share in the woman and claim her as my own. If you do the same, then so be it. We shall see which one of us leaves the circle." He held out a fragment of a page torn from his Bible and placed it in Morgan's outstretched hand, then caught hold of his cutlass and prepared to free the weapon.

"Blasphemer," said Morgan, ignoring the threat. "Gone and torn a page from a Bible, have you? What manner of ill fortune have you called down upon us?"

Thunder crashed and lightning carved a jagged wound across the sky. LeBishop, startled, inadvertently glanced up toward the heavens. When he looked back, Morgan was holding a brace of pistols pointed at his belly. The crowd tensed, expecting the worst, a cold-blooded killing. LeBishop relaxed his grip on the cutlass.

"Then we'll settle this my way, as you have called me out," Morgan replied. "I shall choose the weapons and the particulars as is my right."

"It will not save you. No man is my equal with sword or pistol."

"We'll see," Morgan replied. "Sir William!"

The physician made his way forward from the crowd. He could not hide his displeasure. "Gentlemen . . . May I call you gentlemen?"

"No!" Both men growled.

Sir William gulped and went pale. He didn't need the likes of these two men after him. "How may I be of service?"

"Count to five. Then drop your hat. When it hits the ground, we fire."

"I shall need a pistol," LeBishop said.

"You will have one of mine," Morgan said.

"And how many paces until we turn and fire?"

"This will do," Morgan grinned. "I'll take a walk afterward." He held out the pistols. "Take your pick."

LeBishop grudgingly chose the one in Morgan's left hand. "Mad. You're mad. We cannot fight at such a distance. It is suicide."

"Nonsense. One of the pistols isn't loaded. We won't know which until we pull the trigger." Morgan glanced over at the physician. The crowd fell silent. One could hear the churning tides and the crackle of split timbers amid the dancing flames. No one spoke.

"Count," Morgan told his friend.

"But this is madness."

"No. It's an affair of honor. LeBishop has called me out. Only he can end it."

The Black Cleric stared down at the flintlock in his hand. It was a sleek, beautiful weapon with a dark walnut grip and a large bore. At this range the weapon would blow Morgan in half. That is, if it was the loaded gun.

"One."

LeBishop hefted the pistol, tried to judge by the feel and the weight if the gun he held was loaded or not.

"Two."

Did Morgan know? He must know. Yet he had allowed the Black

Cleric to choose. He struggled to clear the brandy-soaked haze from his brain.

"Three."

Didn't help. The pistol began to waver in his hand. He stared at the gun muzzle pointed at his belly. The bore looked big enough to hide in. And, he noted, Morgan's hand was steady. The man must know something.

"Four." Sir William Jolly retreated out of harm's way. All eyes were on the men in the firelight: Henry Morgan the younger, whose daring and wiles had won him the loyalty of most of the populace, and Thomas LeBishop, a man of dark deeds and unpredictable nature. Men feared him. And wisely so.

Fear . . . LeBishop stared into Morgan's calm gray eyes and caught a glimpse of death, and knew right then and there what had to be done. This was neither the time nor place for a confrontation. Morgan was reckless to a fault. But this was not a game to the Cleric's liking. Better to lose the battle and wait for better odds.

"Hold!" said LeBishop, and tossed the pistol at Morgan's feet. "Another day. Another time. The señorita isn't worth it."

"A lady is always worth it," Morgan replied.

Thomas LeBishop shrugged and turned on his heels and started back across the clearing. He paused alongside Elena Maria, touched his scarred cheek, as if to indicate the same might be in store for her. But the señorita refused to be intimidated.

"Would it had been your throat," she whispered.

"LeBishop!" Morgan called out. The Black Cleric turned and his eyes widened as Morgan raised the weapon in his hand and pulled the trigger. Fire flashed in the pan. LeBishop winced, expecting the impact to follow. But the gun did not fire. He stared at the pistol in the sand, realizing he had held the loaded one. Nervous laughter filtered through the crowd.

Bluffed!

Before LeBishop had a chanced to react, someone began to play a fiddle, another man a fife, another, a walking drum. The crowd broke ranks and closed round the fire. Rafiki and Israel Goodenough hurried up to Morgan, to clap him on the back and congratulate him on surviving a second confrontation with the notorious Black Cleric. Morgan worked his way clear of his crewmen and caught up to Elena Maria. He took her hand in his hand as the celebration got under way. He avoided Madame Palantine, maneuvered out of the clutches of half a dozen other women, none of whom were strangers. It was time for all the Brethren to claim their spoils and then dance by the fire, dance by the bay, drink and dance in the streets until the storm came to sweep them all away.

10. "Every sunset is mine."

The governor of Jamaica sat before the cheerful blaze in his fireplace, dozing, dreaming. The slumped shadow of Sir Richard Purselley in his wingbacked chair flitted across the neatly arranged books of his library. Purselley's head, with wig slightly askew, rested against the cushioned backrest, rising and falling as he inhaled and exhaled. Now and then, his lips pursed, he muttered in his sleep, stirred, once almost reached out, then repositioned himself, never quite escaping the hold of his dreams, not quite waking yet never sinking into deep slumber. The droning downpour provided the perfect accompaniment to lull the mind. Echoes of distant thunder, the steady *drip drip drip* from the eaves of the house, the patter of droplets striking the shutters, soothed his nerves, conspired to prevent him from waking up.

Sir Richard had begun the evening with the best of intentions, settling down with a glass of cream sherry, his lap desk, and the collection of notes and half-scribbled pages that comprised his work-in-progress, a manuscript entitled *Marooners of the Cay*, being an account of a dashing young English officer's adventures after being shipwrecked on a Caribbean island. He'd finished a preface. The rest of the book consisted of chapter headings followed by the beginnings of scenes that went nowhere, and trailed off into unfinished phrases, all of which bore mute testimony to the author's lack of discipline and inability to nurture a paragraph after the first blush had faded off the bloom of a well-thought opening sentence.

His lap desk was balanced precariously upon one knee and the arm of the chair. Half a dozen pages littered the floor at his feet, a quill pen had come to rest upon his purple velvet dressing coat, leaving a circular black stain where the ink had leached into the cloth. Sir Richard grumbled and shook his head as his manservant Joseph, a white-haired old figure in a brocade waistcoat, fine cotton breeches, hose, and buckled shoes, appeared in the doorway to the study and considered whether or not to "let sleeping dogs lie." His wrinkled, dusky features furrowed as he considered his options.

"Sir Richard does not like to be disturbed when he is working," the manservant said. He glanced around at the English officer standing behind him.

Captain Alan Hastiler nodded and gently forced the old man to stand aside. "I think the governor will want to grant our visitor an audience even at this unseemly hour." Hastiler shrugged out of his cloak and handed the rain-soaked garment to Joseph. "Don't go far, old man. I shall require it again—too soon, I dare say."

"And the . . . uh . . . young woman?" Joseph asked, lowering his voice. He shifted his stance and looked down the hall toward the front wing of the house. Just inside the foyer, a pair of double doors opened into a broad, high-ceilinged councilroom where Purselley held court much like some regent of old. Here in this room, Pursel-ley presided every afternoon during the week, granting audience and resolving disputes, exerting the authority of the Crown over all Jamaica, including Port Royal.

"Yes, quite so, the young woman," Hastiler said, stroking his square chin. His brown hair was close-cropped into tight ringlets lying flat against his skull. "Attend her. Bid her remain in the councilroom. The governor will address her soon."

"As you wish, sir. But His Worship . . ." The old man was clearly fearful of upsetting the governor.

"Everything will be fine," Hastiler said, and shooed the manservant back down the hall. The English officer continued into the study, gingerly crossed the room until he stood before the hearth. Despite the brisk storm and howling gusts of wind, it was still too bloody warm for a fire fit for a midwinter's night in the Orkneys, although it gave him the opportunity to dry his uniform. The captain quietly appraised the governor for a moment. The man was young, willful, disdainful of others. Hastiler suspected Sir Richard was better suited to the life of the court, with its intrigues and romances. The Spanish Main was no place for brittle men.

Hastiler sighed and shook his head and wondered, whispering, "Well now, young Hotspur, whose mistress did you take a'romping in bushy park for you to have been so banished? Your courtiers here are brigands and cutthroats. Fortunately for us, they'd rather whore and drink and carve one another—heaven help us if they ever come together." Morgan came to mind. Hastiler had a grudging respect for the man. But the officer also knew the brash privateer was probably the most dangerous man on the island.

Time was wasting. It was an hour before midnight and there was much to do. He cleared his throat. The governor did not seem to notice. The captain tried the tactic again to no avail.

"Sir Richard," he said—and repeated the name yet again. The rain droned on, restful, constant, and nearly worked its seduction on him. The captain shrugged off his lethargy and leaned over and placed his hand on the governor's shoulder. "Sir Richard."

Purselley came awake with a start and raised his hands before his face in horror; round-eyed, terror-filled, he thrashed as if attempting to ward off some dreadful image, the awful vestige of his dreams. Papers went everywhere, the lap desk crashed to the floor.

"No! No! Be off, I say, and plague me no more!" His vision cleared and he recognized the Englishman standing before the hearth, recognized his blessed room, blessed stout walls, thrice-blessed port. He grabbed the cup and swilled the liquid like a man dragged from the sea and dying of thirst. He poured another measure. "It is the good captain," he said, as if reassuring himself he was among his own kind, back in a familiar world. He dabbed the perspiration from his forehead. "There was an enormous raven, with wings black as the pit of hell, and it came soaring out of the darkness like some horrid bird of prey, and its talons were long and curved and cruel-looking. And it came for me. For me!" He managed a deep breath. "But it was only a dream, no doubt conjured by the curried chicken and pepperpot soup I had for supper." He glanced around.

"Where is Joseph? What are you doing here?"

"I brought you a guest."

"At this hour? Are you mad?"

"She awaits us in the councilroom."

" 'She'?"

"A young woman, yes. Perhaps you have seen her before."

"Appealing?" The officer had piqued Sir Richard's interest.

"As a dagger with a keen edge."

Sir Richard patted the folds of his coat, oblivious to the ink stain. The room with thick limestone walls pressed in on him like a tomb tonight. He was anxious to quit the place.

The governor led the way down the hall, taking time to light a few extra oil lamps on his way. The hall was devoid of ornamentation, merely a clean, direct passageway, passing alongside the stairway to the rooms above. Out of habit he checked each room he passed along the way: the dining room, a sitting room, a room crowded with wooden cabinets containing assortments of silver settings, dinnerware, and cutlery. A room cleared of furniture save for music stands and an arrangement of chairs left for a quintet of musicians from Kingston. At last he rounded the corner, stepped into the foyer, took a right turn and entered a long wide room built off the front of the house to serve as an assembly chamber. A massive mahogany desk and high-backed chair dominated the far end of the room. The rest of the space was given over to an assortment of benches. The tall windows were shuttered against the storm but the wood panels rattled on their hinges whenever the thunder rumbled.

Joseph was standing near the entrance. Despite his years, the old man stood erect as a ramrod as he bowed slightly and stood aside. The councilroom was draped with shadows, though a cluster of candles illuminated the portion of the meeting room near a door that opened into a public garden and walkway, thus permitting the residents of Kingston and Port Royal to enter by some other way than traipsing through the governor's house.

Sir Richard did not see anyone at first. Lightning flashed and pierced the patches of darkness within the room. He caught a glimpse of a slender figure watching him from the far corner. The governor glanced over his shoulder at Hastiler. "Well?"

"Two of my men stopped her carriage as it turned past the barracks and started up the hill road. They brought her to me. She has . . . news . . . concerning the exploits of our Welsh friend, Captain Henry Morgan."

"Indeed," said Sir Richard. Now his interest went beyond desire. He folded his hands behind his back and strode into the center of light near the front door. He tried to sound older and wise beyond his years. "Well then, I dare say this is a subject that interests me." He squinted at the figure in the shadows. "Come, come. Introduce yourself. You will find I can be a most appreciative friend."

"Sir Richard . . ." Captain Hastiler motioned for the figure in the shadows to step forward into the light. "May I present Miss Nell Jolly."

The storm failed to discourage the festival. The denizens of Port Royal enjoyed themselves despite the elements. If a man or woman drank enough, danced long enough, and loved to excess, a little rain didn't matter at all. Elena Maria had participated in carnivals in Panama and was no stranger to spontaneous celebrations, but she had never witnessed anything quite so given over to abandonment as what began in the streets of Port Royal and ended in Morgan's carriage along the shore road.

These Brethren were no shirkers when it came to libertine behavior. Henry Morgan had driven her through crowded streets peopled with all manner of celebrants. Men and women wearing animal masks howled, grunted, laughed at one another, danced and kissed and fondled, enjoyed a careless regard for clothing. There were no heroes here, but rogues and villains and daredevils of the Spanish Main, jostling for entrance to a dozen taverns or brothels or milady's boudoir.

Tempers flared. She saw these buccaneers and the women who loved them circle each other, knives flashing in the glare of lightning, mud-drenched torsos wrestling and twisting while crowds of onlookers cheered them on. Everywhere were music and cries, curses and song, the thick sweet aroma of rum and tobacco mingling with the stench of fire, of lightning-fused air, of sex-slick flesh, burned rice and peas, and the spicy pungent scent of Mannish water, a pepper-laced stew made from boiling a variety of vegetables, fruit, and a goat's head in an iron pot. But this night, the wanton abandonment he had once enjoyed and actively participated in held no appeal for Henry Morgan.

The señorita's presence left him hungry for more than the carnival had to offer. So he led Elena Maria to his carriage and drove away from the town and followed a winding road that stretched between sand dunes and clumps of palm trees and wound its way up from the peninsula to a secluded house built on hillside in a thicket of golden palms and frangipani and flame of the forest, a tulip tree which bloomed in scarlet cups and permeated the air with a dazzling scent that almost made the woman swoon.

Morgan called out for the mare in its harness to whoa, and pulled back on the reins until he brought the carriage to a halt about a hundred yards from his house. He turned and watched the storm as it broke around them. Forked lightning lit the night. The oncoming waves were capped with iridescent blue foam, the sea itself swelling and falling, crashing against the far cliffs. In the glare Morgan pointed to a precipice beyond his house.

"Two Tainos lovers plunged to their deaths from that point. Rather than submit to Spanish slavery and risk separation, they embraced, bound their hands, and flung themselves to the rocks below."

"Why are you telling me this?" Elena Maria asked, huddled beneath a blanket. Raindrops splattered on the leather roof of the carriage. She wondered as to the whereabouts of Consuelo. It wasn't like her nurse to leave her alone. And yet she was secretly glad. Whatever happened this night, at least there would be only two witnesses, herself and Morgan the pirate. They were lost in the storm. "Can people really love that much?"

"There is no other way to love," said Morgan. He had discarded his coat now and placed it over her lap. His shirt was drenched and plastered to his muscled torso. Elena Maria's bodice had also suffered from the elements and clung to her bosom in such a way as to reveal each breast and taut pink crown beneath the sheer lace fabric.

"Don Alonso would not understand such passion, I think," Elena Maria said. "But do not think he is immune to other emotions. He will ransom me and then exact his revenge. His hatred runs deep. He will never rest until he repays you for your misdeeds."

"And what have I done?"

"Sir, you are a thief."

"I have only stolen that which did not belong to Spain in the first place. The Dons loot an entire culture and then complain when a man like me relieves them of their ill-gotten gains." Morgan laughed and slapped his knee. "By heaven, who is the greater thief?" He gave the horse its lead. The animal started forward.

"You'll know when Don Alonso comes sailing into Kingston Bay."

"With a ransom I warrant, or . . ."

"Or what?"

"I'll slit your pretty throat," Morgan chuckled and ran his finger along her neck, then cupped her face and kissed her full moist lips. Thunder crashed. The earth trembled beneath them. The very air crackled. By the time the kiss ended, the carriage was well on its way to the house by the cay. At last Morgan released her, sat back, and gulped a lungful of air. By heaven, he had to wonder just which of them was the prisoner. She might be a fine lady, this *criollos*, but she was also a woman of fire and beauty just waiting for the right man to unleash her passions. *He* was the right man, the only man.

"I built my house to catch the last light of day. Every sunset is mine." He climbed out of the carriage, held out his arms to her, helped her down, and then the two of them sloshed through the rain and mud.

The house was built upon a pole-and-beam construction and set partway up the hillside, well away from the shore, so that even during a monsoon, if the floods came, the house would still be above the surging sea. He took her hand and together they climbed the steps to the porch whose thatch roof shielded them from the rain. Droplets battered the woven fronds overhead and cascaded down the steps and poured from the eaves.

Elena Maria paused there, to look back toward the town, its lights hidden now; the storm had drawn a curtain of rain across the peninsula, obscuring Port Royal and the bay. *We could be the last two people on earth.* They were alone. And anything could happen.

Morgan opened the door and brought the señorita into the large front room that dominated the entire front of the house. He felt his way along the wall to a lantern, raised the glass chamber, struck a spark until he lit a taper, and then touched that single flame to the lantern wick.

The wick, soaked with whale oil, burst into flame and illuminated a portion of the room, a wall hung with muskets and swords and pistols, a long table littered with maps and journals, an opened chest of books at one end. A doorway opened onto a bedroom where the lantern light reached all the way to a large feather bed mounded atop a mahogany four-poster frame.

It was a rustic palace made of thatch and wood, as if the house itself had sprouted from the hillside and been formed by a quirk of nature. And it would have been all the more inviting if Captain Hastiler had not appeared in the doorway and blocked the view of the bed.

Morgan drew back in surprise. But he quickly recognized the uniform and the officer's blunt, honest features, and refrained from reaching for his own weapon. Elena Maria gasped and pulled Morgan's coat about her shoulders for modesty's sake.

"Alan Hastiler," said Morgan.

"One and the same, Captain Morgan."

"You're a long way from the barracks." Morgan checked the other doorway that led off into a dining area that he seldom used, for he took his meals on his porch or in town. As far as he could tell, Hastiler was alone. But he could be wrong. "Come all this way to welcome me home?"

"To bring you to the governor. And your guest." Hastiler nodded toward Elena Maria. "Your pardon, Doña Elena, but I assure you that you are among friends. Sir Richard has prepared a place for you in the governor's house."

"We'll pay our respects in the morning—late," Morgan said.

"Not good enough," the officer said.

"It will have to do." Morgan walked to the front door and shoved it open. Lightning shimmered, revealing a pair of disgruntled-looking English marines standing on the porch, muskets leveled at the free-booter.

From the looks of their muddy trouser legs and sodden red cloaks it appeared they must have been hiding in the crisscross of timber-and-beam scaffolding beneath the house. The marines kept their muskets pointed in his direction and slowly advanced. They looked wet and miserable, and judging by the look of their scowling expressions, the English soldiers blamed the buccaneer for all their discomfort. Morgan heard the unmistakable sound of a gun being cocked behind him and turned to face Hastiler yet again.

The officer leveled a horse pistol at Morgan's chest.

"The governor insists."

11. "If only someone would rid me of this meddlesome rogue."

It is a poor welcome, Doña Elena," Sir Richard Purselley said, crossing around from behind his desk and hurrying across the councilroom to personally extend his regrets. He wore a floor-length velvet robe over his ruffled shirt, waistcoat, and cotton breeches. The strain of the long hours had taken their toll, left pouches under his eyes, and added a nervous twitch to one corner of his mouth. "I am Sir Richard Purselley, governor of Jamaica by appointment of His most Royal Majesty, Charles the Second."

He glared at Morgan. The buccaneer returned the stare, his slate-gray eyes wary, his expression inscrutable. Morgan knew this clandestine visit could hardly bode well. He took stock of the meeting room, noting the two soldiers lounging to either side of the entrance hall that led off into the governor's house. Another couple of marines had been rousted from sleep and stationed behind the governor's desk and chair at the opposite end of the room. Then there was Hastiler and the two soldiers positioned to either side of the buccaneer. Six . . . no, seven well-armed men. *Purselley is expecting trouble*, Morgan thought; then he remembered: *Oh, that's right . . . me.*

"I only just now discovered your presence among these brigands," Purselley said, addressing the woman. "But once I learned of Captain Morgan's perfidy, I alerted the entire garrison and dispatched them to rescue you."

"Captain Hastiler's was a most timely arrival," Elena Maria replied, unable to bring herself to look at Morgan. The world had intruded on them, plucked her from the unreality of the storm and the house by the sea, and brought her into the light. She was once more the kidnapped bride-to-be, and had better be on her guard. A single rumor in the wrong ear could ruin a señorita's best-laid plans.

"Joseph!" Sir Richard bellowed. It took an immense effort on the English governor's part to keep from ogling the glimpses of firm round flesh visible beneath the sodden lace that no longer adequately covered Elena Maria's bosom. The Maroon servant appeared in the hall doorway. "Wake Rebecca. Have her attend Doña Elena until we can recover her own servant. Prepare a room for our esteemed guest."

The old man bowed and hastily departed. Thunder rumbled overhead, foreshadowing unpleasant things to come. Outside, the storm's intensity increased, bending the branches of the blue mahoe and mimosa trees lining the drive; wind gusts assaulted the hillside, rippling the ferns and mosses and sweeping up the governor's road to rattle the door and moan about the walls.

"And you will ransom me?" Elena Maria asked.

"Heavens no, my dear lady. England and Spain are no longer at war. I tried to warn Captain Morgan about that fact before he set sail. Indeed, I had heard rumors from other merchant ships and forbade him to leave Port Royal until news of the treaty could be confirmed. Word arrived soon after he departed, against my expressed orders."

"I sail where and when I please," Morgan said, unable to endure the youthful governor's tirade in silence. A youth spent in captivity and servitude was not an easy thing to forget. "I signed no treaty with the Dons."

"You signed no—!" Sir Richard sputtered. His cheeks reddened as a patchwork of spidery veins engorged themselves with blood. "Your raid on Maracaibo was an act of piracy. And the dastardly abduction of this woman who is to be married to Don Alonso del Campo, the governor of Panama, could well jeopardize the newly signed treaty."

"I sailed under letters of marque," Morgan retorted, realization dawning that Sir Richard knew far more about Elena Maria and Maracaibo then he ought to. Such information could have only come from someone in Port Royal—LeBishop? Perhaps . . . "I am authorized as a privateer and enjoy the protection of the Crown."

"Your letters of marque were revoked the minute you disobeyed my orders and left Port Royal. And you shall be held accountable." Sir Richard stiffened and folded his arms across his bony chest.

Morgan did not like the sound of that. He glanced around the councilroom, weighed his options, pondered whether or not he could overpower the soldiers flanking him. But then there was Hastiler, who could be a capable opponent . . . and the other two soldiers by the side door.

"You and the merchants and the good citizens of Kingston have enjoyed our protection against the Spaniards for many years now. Our presence has ensured Kingston's prosperity as an English colony. Do you think Captain Hastiler and his marines, a single ship, and a few cannons and redoubts overlooking the harbor would protect you if the Spaniards came in force? It is the Black Flag they fear."

"But now there is a peace. And I have received dispatches assuring me that Jamaica will received a proper garrison of men and ships. The rule of Law is coming to the island . . . to all the islands, including Port Royal."

"We are the Brethren of the Coast. We are free men."

"No longer."

"Two hundred men sailed with me to Maracaibo. You cannot jail us all, Sir Richard."

"No, but I can begin with you," Purselley said. "Captain Hastiler, escort Captain Morgan to the keep. We will bind him over and dispatch him to England for trial and proper punishment."

Morgan tensed. Anger flashed in his gray eyes. He took a step toward Purselley, who recoiled in surprise. The soldiers brought up their muskets, Hastiler jammed his smoothbore pistol into the small of his prisoner's back.

"Mind you, the woman, Captain Morgan."

Elena Maria would be in harm's way if a melee ensued. Morgan saw his chances shrink from slim to none. He could not endanger her. And besides, Sir Richard's charges would never stand.

"I'll play your game, Sir Richard," Morgan said. "But know this: one word from me and the Brethren would storm your gates. But this is our home. Treaty or no, Spain will not tolerate an English presence for long. The Dons covet this island and will one day come to drive you out. Then you will have need of us to help you stop them."

Morgan turned and bowed to Elena Maria. "I regret this evening's untimely end. But there will be another." He grinned and winked. Then he returned his attention to the governor of the island. "Take me to England, Sir Richard. But don't hang your hopes on my swinging from the gallows. All the plunder I have delivered to the English court has bought me the influence of a great many friends. There are magistrates of the Admiralty who have grown quite fond of the gold

I've sent them. Indeed, they've gorged themselves on the fruits of my labors. I doubt they will think kindly of the man who shooed them away from the trough."

"Be off with him," Purselley ordered.

"I might even return with a governorship of my own."

"I said take him away!" Sir Richard's eyes seemed to bulge in his head as if they were about to explode from his skull.

Elena Maria watched in silence, uncertain what to make of her changing fortunes but determined to use the situation to her advantage. "Señor?"

"Yes. You must forgive my outburst." Purselley sighed and took a lace-trimmed kerchief from his waistcoat pocket and mopped the perspiration from his face. He waved a hand toward his fragile-looking manservant, who arrived with a sleepy-eyed scullery maid. Rebecca was a slim-hipped dusky young girl, she curtsied, announced a bed was drawn back for the señorita, and then waited off to the side.

"There is a Dutchman setting sail tomorrow," Sir Richard said. "I will see that it brings a dispatch to Don Alonso, informing him of your safety, and that I have placed Morgan under arrest. Until the governor comes to escort you home, you shall be my treasured guest. You will want for nothing."

Elena Maria lowered her eyes demurely. "You are most kind."

Sir Richard swallowed the lump in his throat. Even bedraggled, the señorita was an enchanting creature: those dark eyes, the long tresses, her full, inviting lips. "Then I bid you good-night. I am certain your own servant will be returned to you in the morning."

Sir Richard bowed and kept smiling until Joseph, Rebecca, and the señorita were out of sight. Thunder cracked like an artillery barrage outside his window, causing him to jump. The smile faded, to be replaced by a scowl, as if he had bitten into a sea grape and choked on the bitter juice. *Curse Morgan,* he thought, and ambled over to the desk and wearily sagged into the thronelike chair.

"Señor . . . you look troubled. You have been so kind to me, is there something I can do to help?"

Purselley was surprised to see Elena Maria standing in the doorway to the hall. She seemed so small and delicate, standing there in the flickering lamplight.

"Doña Elena. You are most kind. Ah, but I fear my troubles are beyond your gentle powers to correct. The damnable pirate was right. No doubt Morgan does indeed have friends at the Admiralty. For almost ten years now, he has been enriching their coffers as well as his own."

Sir Richard had begun to see the weak link in his plan. Morgan might well return from England more powerful then ever. But backing down and setting him free could also be a problem. That would only further strengthen Morgan's reputation. Sir Richard said as much to the woman.

". . . So you see, I dare not keep him, I dare not set him free." The English governor winced, as if he had plucked a rose only to be skewered by a hidden thorn. "If only someone would rid me of this meddlesome rogue."

"But Señor Purselley, I might be able to help after all," said Elena Maria. The rain droned on. Her voice, soft and seductive, carried to him from across the large open space, from where she stood, half in light, half in shadow.

"You, milady?"

"And my future husband."

12. A snake in the garden.

Kingston jail was a small blockhouse that had been built on the edge of the limestone promontory during Spain's occupation of the island. The place had served as a watchtower before the advent of Port Royal, for it overlooked the turquoise sea, and from its height a man could track the approach to the bay. But no one kept vigil over the bay this night. The half dozen soldiers Captain Hastiler had left in charge to guard the prisoner in the blockhouse sprawled around a blazing campfire, enjoying cuts of fresh roast pork, sliced mangoes, and baked breadfruit washed down with bottles of fine French wine from Henry Morgan's private reserve, a cache of stolen spirits the buccaneer kept locked away in a warehouse in Port Royal.

"Guard duty ain't half bad, if you asks me," one of the marines muttered, uncorking another bottle. "Cut me off another strip of that hog, will you, Sergeant McCready?"

A barrel-chested Scot kneeling by the spit glanced over his shoulder at the underling who had spoken, considered the request, shook his head, declining, then carved a portion of roast pork onto his own plate. "The last time I looked you had two arms and two legs, Mister Blackthaw. Serve yourself unless someone's gone and put a 'Your Worship' after your name."

Robert McCready finished filling his plate with half a mango, stood and started toward the blockhouse. Grease from the carcass sizzled and popped as it dripped into the fire.

"If that's for our prisoner, best save your steps," another of the men remarked as the sergeant walked past. Ethelred Plummer was a hatchet-faced son of a fishmonger who had joined the Royal Marines to escape from the monotony of life in the tiny coastal town of Mousehole. "I checked in on him. Looks like the Captain Morgan's gone and drunk himself to sleep. There's a bottle of rum, better'n half empty, by his bed. I doubt the man will stir a lick till morning."

McCready glanced toward the front of the blockhouse, shrugged and returned to the circle of men around the fire. The lot of them were under his command, and when out of the public eye or the scrutiny of officers, treated McCready with a degree of familiarity unthinkable in everyday life. He had risen from their ranks, several times, and twice been returned after committing some drunken offense.

"Fair enough," Blackthaw said, holding out his hand. "Since the pirate's indisposed I'll take the plate for you, Sergeant."

"The devil you say," McCready replied, and speared a chunk of pork with his knife. He stuffed the morsel in his mouth and wiped the drippings on the sleeve of the coat Blackthaw had draped over the stacked muskets.

"Hey now! On my oath, Sergeant . . ." Blackthaw exclaimed, his bunched, homely features plainly revealing his indignation. He tried to stand and confront the Scot but the ground seemed so soft and mushy, he settled back on his buttocks and held his head. "Damn Frog wine. At least with jack iron a man can feel his drunk coming on and has the time to get ready for it. This here brew is as sneaky as a damn Maroon."

"Them savages will steal the coins off a dead man's eyes," another of the men remarked, and the others nodded in accord, sharing a common opinion of the Jamaican natives who had fled Spanish occupation and forged an uneasy alliance with the British.

A breeze gusted up and over the edge of the bluff, bringing with it the smells of the sea and the sound of distant drums. It was the third night in a row that the ceremonial cadence filled the summer's night, summoning the Maroons to a lonely stretch of shoreline south of Kingston below the Hellshire hills.

"Listen to them. Will they never stop?," said Plummer.

"Aye, when the last of their blood wine's been drunk and the last of their women impregnated," McCready said, absentmindedly passing his plate of food over into Blackthaw's outstretched hands.

The Maroons, the descendants of runaway slaves who had intermarried with the local Caribe inhabitants, lived in the mountains in the center of the island and came down from their secreted villages to trade with the English and to renew themselves in a ceremony by the sea. Three days of chanting and ritualistic dancing and sacrifice that culminated in a frenzy of heightened copulation appeased the Elder Gods and assured the fertility of the fields, the propagation of each family, and the prosperity of the village.

"I could help them there," another of the men spoke up. The rest chuckled. They were far from home and the Maroon women were often exotic and appealing to even the most faithful of husbands. "You've seen 'em, eh, McCready?"

"I have," the sergeant replied. But he said no more and the men knew better than to ask. So they sat in silence, listening to the crackling embers while the drums played on. The hypnotic rhythms stirred the fire in their eyes.

The warm wind swirled about them, set the flames dancing. It gusted past the men, rattled the shutters on Morgan's prison, moaned through the chinks in the log walls, tugged at the loose shutters on the roof, and disturbed the knotted rope hanging from the upstairs window at the rear of the blockhouse . . . the rope down which Morgan had made good his escape.

Elena Maria could not sleep. Three days in the company of Sir Richard Purselley had nearly driven her to distraction. And now the drums, the cadence of distant fertility rights, the sighing wind, it was more than she could endure. And then there was the memory of what might have been, how the heat from Morgan's body had warmed her through her clothes there in his house by the sea, he had held her in his arms, she had wanted him, with no thought of the consequences, wanting him, and the drums . . . the drums . . .

She rose from her bed and walked out onto the balcony overlooking the front drive. The wind tugged at her dressing gown, caught the folds and lifted them from her body, sent them streaming out like vapors. It was too warm. She undid the lace bows and shrugged free of the silken cotton dressing gown and allowed it to settle around her ankles. She stepped out of the clothes and stood naked in the night, arched her back, her breasts taut as the sea breeze caressed her. She ran her fingers through the thick strands of her hair, across her naked shoulders, then outstretched her arms to the starlit sky.

She shuddered, gripped the rail until her fingers turned white and bloodless, till they cramped. And only then did she release her hold on the iron and turn back to her room and walk across the cool palm wood floor and fling herself upon the four-poster bed. Her breathing was ragged at first then gradually settled. She tried to think of Don Alonso and realized she would never feel for him the primal urges coursing through her veins this night. *But I will pretend and it will be enough.* She ran her hand across her breasts, down across her flat belly, and lower still. She closed her eyes and gave herself to distant rituals played out unseen by a people she did not know.

And then she was no longer alone.

Elena Maria gasped and opened her eyes and looked toward the window as if drawn by some force too powerful to resist. She gasped. Henry Morgan stood on the balcony, filled the doorway, stepped into her bedroom. He shrugged out of his loose-fitting shirt. She made no effort to cover herself but remained supine. He knelt on the bed, one knee, his gray eyes burning with an animal lust as they ranged her body.

"How?"

"A rolled-up blanket on the cot in the blockhouse, a makeshift rope ladder discreetly lowered from a back window," he said. He made no mention of the horse he had stolen, the clandestine ride through the deserted streets of Kingston. None of it mattered. Only the unfinished business between them.

The sight of her took his breath away, her perfect breasts, the pink crowns like ripe berries . . . he lowered his mouth to her, tasted her, rolled his tongue around her flesh. She inhaled sharply, her belly concave as he nibbled between her breasts and down below her rib cage, his lips and tongue enticing every curve and nook until her body began to spasm. She cried out and dug her fingers into his back and surrendered herself to the throbbing of the drums.

Morgan rose, looked toward the door leading off into the hall, waited, listening for footsteps in the hall, heard only the throbbing drumbeats in the dark. Elena Maria, lost in the passion of the moment, helped him strip away his clothes until he stood naked. Her teeth and tongue raked his flesh until he could no longer do anything else but have her.

"*Ahorita,*" she moaned. "*Ahorita!*" Then she drew him down and he covered her body with his.

And they were one.

* * *

Near midnight, two horsemen approached one another along the shore road, a U-shaped trail that led out from Port Royal and wound past Morgan's house on the hillside above the bay, swept up from the peninsula, and cut through a thicket of royal palms and a grove of coconut trees at the base of the limestone bluffs midway between the Brethren's stronghold and Kingston proper.

"No good can come of endeavors done in the dead of night," Sir Richard muttered to himself, recalling the words his grandfather, the Earl of Shrewsbury, once had told him. But now was not the time for a man's conscience to get the better of him. If there is a snake in the garden, kill it.

Purselley shifted nervously in the saddle; the distant drums unnerved him, made him jump at shadows. He gave his saddle pistols a reassuring pat. He chose to wait on horseback and allow the other man to approach through the slanted moonlight. The governor of Jamaica took a moment to peruse the bluff, hoping to catch a glimpse of the blockhouse on the promontory, but the trees obscured the sky-line. No matter. Morgan was up there, imprisoned, but still danger-ous. Three days had passed since his imprisonment, such as it was. Time and patience were wearing thin. Sooner or later Sir Richard must send Morgan to England to stand trial, release him back to the Brethren, or risk an all-out uprising among the denizens of Port Royal loyal to the pirate. The two men were playing a waiting game. And up until now Morgan had had the upper hand.

The second horseman walked his mount into the clearing, drew up and quickly appraised the situation, then cautiously approached. Thomas LeBishop tilted his wide-brimmed black hat back from his features. A sea breeze ruffled the black cloak draping the man's spare frame. His lace collar and sober visage were white as bleached bones.

Something stirred near the water's edge. The thicket seemed to pulse from a chorus of tree frogs whose incessant chirruping filled the night. Palm fronds rustled in the sea breeze, accompanied by the rhythm of the eternal tides.

"Well met, Sir Richard, though I would have preferred a measure of rum or perhaps a taste of the fruits of your wine cellar."

"The governor's house is too public a place for what I have in mind."

"Ah, then you have not invited me for tea and biscuits," LeBishop chuckled. He eased back in the saddle and rested a hand upon one of the pistols in his belt. It was not a threatening gesture but the pirate thought he heard a brace of muskets answer from somewhere off in the shadows. "Speak your piece, Sir Richard. Speak lively now. There's none to hear it save the sea . . . and she is one mistress who can keep a secret."

The Black Cleric had seethed with curiosity ever since one of the governor's aides had delivered Purselley's request that the two of them should meet. This most unusual hour and place had been the governor's choosing. LeBishop had no wish to experience Morgan's fate, and said as much to Purselley.

"If you intend to charge me with piracy, be warned, I shall not go quietly."

"I have the man I want. The problem is keeping him."

"The problem is the man."

"I am told you have no love for Henry Morgan."

"He casts a long shadow. It could do with some trimming."

Purselley nodded. "Yes, I agree." He stroked his chin, pausing to choose his words, then tugged at his waistcoat and shifted his weight.

"What else have you learned?"

"That your loyalty can be bought and there is nothing you wouldn't do for the right price."

LeBishop chuckled. "You've been talking to my mother," he chided. Then his humor faded and his tone grew solemn. "Every man has his price, be he lord or commoner." And he quoted from Romans. " 'As it is written, there is none righteous, no, not one.' "

Now, with the word of the Lord out of the way, it was time to make a deal.

Elena Maria reached out and felt the warm empty space alongside her and realized she was alone in the bed. The woman rose up on one elbow, saw Henry Morgan dressed but sitting on the edge of the bed. He had been watching her sleep.

"Your pardon, señorita—by your leave, I must return to prison." He grinned. "I'd hate for the soldiers Sir Richard has posted to keep me under guard to get into trouble on my account."

"You are going back?" Something else was different. The drums had stopped. The ritual was at an end. "You could stay with me a while longer."

"And be discovered by that one-eyed witch who guards you? She'd cast an evil spell and rot my manhood. I'd hate to lose my staff now when I've finally found such a proper use for it."

"I agree," Elena Maria giggled as he leaned down and kissed her hip.

"Then I must return to Purselley's jail."

"And there you will remain."

"Until tomorrow night. I shall not wait for Sir Richard to act. I'll plead my case before the court when I reach England, on my oath. I shall see Purselley removed no matter what the cost. And I'll buy me a proper title. Then I'll go no more a'roaming, but return to live a quiet life here."

"And plague my people no longer?"

"Only every chance I get. After all, your Don Alonso will not rest until he has avenged himself."

"You hardly know him."

"Vengeance is a subject I am well versed in." Morgan stood and walked to the window. She disturbed him. Up until now, the Dons had been a faceless lot, each of them guilty for what had befallen young Henry Morgan long ago. But Elena Maria was different. She was the enemy, or at least she was supposed to be. But this woman had awakened a fire in his blood. Being with her made him see beyond his days of raids and plunder and the careless life of a freebooter. A man ought to aspire to more.

"Meet me aboard the *Santa Rita* tomorrow night. I will take you away with me. You have no love for Don Alonso."

"No . . ." she agreed. "Still I have my duty."

"Duty is nothing but a set of shackles. Come and be free."

"You don't know what you ask, Señor."

"Be with me."

"I cannot."

"Your eyes say yes." He kissed her again and then walked to the window. "Tomorrow night," he said, and disappeared over the balcony. He landed catlike in a bed of hibiscus blossoms. He heard the sound of approaching horsemen and crouched in the shadows and waited, biding his time.

The minutes crept past, then, out of the gloom, Sir Richard Purselley arrived, walking his mount along the drive and across the front of the house, and then vanished behind the estate, no doubt on his way to the stable. He was followed by a pair of soldiers who rode slumped in the saddle, half asleep and blindly following the governor's lead.

Morgan wondered what Sir Richard was up to and decided it had to be nothing good. He waited for the drive to clear, then scrambled out from cover and trotted across the driveway and worked his way into the trees below the terrace where he had ground-tethered the mount he had stolen from a pen in town. Before dropping out of sight he turned to look back at the front of the governor's estate and the dark opening that was the doorway out onto the balcony.

Was she watching him?

"Henry Morgan," he said beneath his breath, "she's turned you into Jack-pudding. Ah well . . . I suppose someone had to prick the chart and set me on my way."

Being with Elena Maria was like sailing through a storm and emerging unscathed only to find oneself on an entirely different course and longing to dare the elements again.

Where would it lead?

For now, back to jail.

13. "Will you gamble with your life?"

Except for the half dozen Royal Marines loitering about the perimeter of the blockhouse beneath the noonday sun, Morgan had the place to himself. *El Tigre* was caged, but at least he had room to prowl. Sir William and the other members of his crew who had made the climb to the blockhouse marveled at their captain's continued good spirits.

"I've rarely seen such long faces," Morgan chuckled. He looked well fed and rested and somewhat bemused by his situation.

"And I think you've gone and taken leave of your senses. Best I brew you up some medicinals. I dare say a pot of soursop tea will bring you back," Sir William said. He began searching in his leather pouch for the proper ingredients, an oilskin packet of dried leaves.

Voisin and Israel Goodenough, with his already morose features, nodded sagely. The two men concurred with the physician. They were still puzzled by Morgan's behavior. Oddly enough, as far as Morgan was concerned, Nell Jolly seemed the most distraught. This was the first time she had accompanied the others. The woman acted embarrassed to be here, and seemed ill-at-ease.

"This is a bad thing. I like none of it," said Rafiki Kogi where he stood at the windows, peering through a crack in the shutters. When he was certain the two guards were otherwise disposed, he turned back and removed a brace of pistols from under his shirt. "C'mon, Captain, *mnataka niwasaidie*—let us help you."

"Put those away, my friend. I am not going anywhere, at least not until tonight." Morgan propped his feet on the edge of the long oaken table that dominated the center of the room, and sagged in his chair. The rest of the furnishings consisted of eight cots, several sea chests whose contents were unknown, a barrel of salt fish and another of water, and a scattering of chairs and stools. A couple of basins had been left on a long table at one end of the room, iron pots hung above a hearth for preparing the meals. Pots and pans and wooden bowls and plates lined a nearby shelf. The front door opened and a rotund, red-haired Scot entered the room. "Besides," said Morgan. "I've grown fond of Sergeant McCready's cooking. I'd hate to miss dinner."

Robert McCready glanced up on hearing his name and, stepping out of the sunlight, paused a moment to allow his eyes to adjust to the interior. McCready carried a basket under one arm, a musket was slung across the other. He looked over at Morgan, touched a knuckle to his forehead as a salute and then paused by the door, taking note of Rafiki's pistols. He frowned and then continued over to the table where he set the basket down in front of Morgan. "Here now, you wouldn't be plotting mischief, Captain Morgan? You gave your word about escaping."

"Not in the slightest," Morgan grinned. "Mister Kogi is just showing off this fine set of pistols he took off one of the Dons in Maracaibo." He leaned forward in his chair, lifted the cloth that covered the contents of McCready's basket. The marvelous aroma of spices and fresh-baked bread wafted into the air.

Morgan sighed in satisfaction. "Never fear, I'll not run off unless I take you with me. I dare say I've grown accustomed to a hot pasty with my tea." He removed a pocket-shaped loaf of bread the size of his fist. The pasty was stuffed with roast pork, squash, plantain, and sugary yams. Golden-brown juices seeped from a pinprick in the crust.

Morgan took a bite, closed his eyes, and savored the experience, the meat and its juices, the peppery sauce, and vegetables blended together in a most delicious marriage of flavors. He nodded approval to the sergeant, who beamed with pride, then the buccaneer slid the basket over toward his companions.

Voisin hurried forward, his stomach growling, and helped himself to one of the delicacies. The Frenchman hesitated halfway through a mouthful and saw Sir William and the others glowering at him.

"What is it?" Voisin asked.

"Little thief. We came to free Captain Morgan, not dine with him!" Nell blurted out.

So far, no one knew who had betrayed Henry Morgan although some suspected the Black Cleric might have had a hand in it; Sir William's daughter encouraged such gossip all she could. "And if none of you will join me in this, then I shall face the English on my own." She glowered at the sergeant. McCready squirmed beneath her cutting glare and shifted his stance.

Guilt fueled her indignation. Curse her foolish heart. How could this have happened? She knew her actions were beyond forgiveness. She had only intended to alert Sir Richard so that he would bring Elena Maria de Saucedo across the bay to Kingston, removing her from the proximity of Port Royal and Captain Henry Morgan. Pursel-ley's actions had caught Nell completely by surprise. Morgan's imprisonment left her shaken. She parted her coat and dropped a hand to the knife and pistol tucked in her belt. "Henry Morgan shall not hang."

"I don't intend to," Morgan said. He stood and clapped McCready on the shoulder and led the sergeant to the front door before things got out of control. "Now, 'Mother' McCready, on your next visit, a few more bananas and some mangoes would be nice." Morgan clapped the sergeant on the shoulder and placed a gold doubloon in the palm of his hand. "I'll have another supply of spirits for you and the lads tonight." The soldier's objections died aborning as his hand closed around what was enough to keep him running whores for a month.

"As you wish, Captain Morgan," McCready said, and slipped through the open door into the sunlit yard. Morgan waved to the other guards then closed and secured the door with a makeshift barricade consisting of a length of strong rope and an oaken bench. With the final knot tied, he continued on over to one of the windows overlooking the sea and leaned his elbows on the sill, allowing the sunlight and sea breeze to wash over his sun-bronzed features. Below him, a straight drop of a couple of hundred feet to the rocky coast prevented a man from crawling out and making good his escape.

"Nell's right," Sir William said, acknowledging his daughter as he addressed Morgan. "I never thought you'd let Purselley have his way. For the past few days me and the lads here have been climbing this bloody hill, checking on you, waiting for your orders to storm the place and bring you back to Port Royal. All we need is a word from you. But you never give it." The physician scratched his jaw. "What's your plan, Captain? Surely you don't aim for the likes of Sir Richard Purselley to keep you here till you rot."

"Not hardly," Morgan soberly replied. "And if he starts building a gallows before nightfall, then you beauties come a'running." He lingered at the window to watch the rolling tides, the azure sky dotted with gulls and terns, and off to the north, the pristine arrangement of streets and houses, shops and gardens, the port Jamaica's landed gentry called home. *Kingston, look at her*, he thought, *she sits astride the hill, genteel and gracious as a lady and across the bay, her wanton sister—disreputable, aye, and dangerous, but far more fun*. But of late, the reckless existence he had known and freely followed was not enough. His encounter with Doña Elena Maria had disturbed all his plans. For the first time in his life he had begun to think of something beyond the next raid against the Spanish, beyond a future defined by a freebooter's unholy trinity: a warm bed, a willing lass, and rum aplenty. He wanted something more.

"Tell us, then, what would you have us do?" Nell said, biting her lower lip. She wanted to confess her treachery, to bare her soul before them all, but could not bring herself to do it.

"Keep the lads in check," Morgan told them. "Port Royal is our home. Ours. We must not jeopardize this by an attack on the English troops. I will not see us hounded from one cay to another throughout the Caribbean." Morgan turned his back to the blue horizon and faced them. "Sir Richard cannot afford to free me. And now I suspect he may have second thoughts about taking me to England. So I shall go without him. Will Jolly, get me twenty good men. Meet me aboard the *Santa Rita*. We'll steal her tonight and take her around the point to the mouth of the Black River. We'll provision her there then set sail for England. I shall stand before the court of King Charles and answer these charges of piracy."

"I am told it's a bleak ride across the Thames from Newgate Prison to Execution Dock," Sir William muttered. "The way is salted with many a brave man's tears."

"They say you can hear the poor blokes wailing for mercy all the way to Hampton Court," Israel glumly added. He did not relish placing himself within a rope's reach of an English noose.

"I'll not share their fate." Morgan folded his arms across his chest. His gaze was sure and steady, his voice filled with conviction. "But I say Sir Richard has outsmarted himself this time. Blood is thicker than water, but gold is thicker still. I am not without influence. I filled the pouches of the English lords and helped them drape their wives with jewels. Peace or no peace, they know I can make them even richer. No. There will be no gallows for me. Indeed, I plan to petition to have Sir Richard Purselley recalled from his posting and replaced with a governor who will unite this island and secure it from the Spaniards forevermore."

"A tall order. And since you have the ear of the King, just who did you have in mind for the governor's post?" Sir William asked, somewhat astounded by the scope of the privateer's ambition.

"Why, myself, of course," said Morgan. He turned and looked out across the bay. Was that a sail on the horizon or a white cloud lifting like a dream over the edge of the world? A butterfly landed on the sill, slowly fanned its wings, bright yellow, black, and radiant orange, before taking flight again.

Henry Morgan breathed in the warm sweet fragrance of blue-and-white plumbago flowers, purple periwinkles, and the bold sea air. He checked the horizon yet again. Yes, they were sails; a ship was making good time as it approached the Jamaican coastline.

Nell Jolly stepped forward, her pert, pretty features unable to mask her worried state. She was clearly more distraught than any of the men. She struggled to find the words to make him change his mind, knowing all along she would not succeed. "Henry Morgan . . . will you gamble with your life?"

It was an honest question, one he had asked himself many times over the past couple of weeks, and one for which Morgan had an honest answer.

"But Toto, I've done nothing else since first we met."

Thomas LeBishop had already bloodied his sword. Two men faced him on the sea strand near the alarm bell. One of the men, a grizzled cutthroat named Barnabas Sims, nursed a gash across his right biceps. Blood seeped down his arm and threatened to cause him to lose his grip on his cutlass. His companion, Square John Pettibone, was half the man and twice as fearful of the Black Cleric. Square John was only eighteen and wished he could take back the offhand remark that LeBishop was never supposed to have heard.

"Say it again," the Black Cleric purred as he sawed the air with his blade. Overhead the gulls were wheeling, spinning like angels in a whirlwind. Below, the blue tide encroached upon the shore, spilling seaweed, starfish, and bits of broken coral. A crab, dislodged from one lair, scuttled out of harm's way and hid beneath a length of driftwood, anxious to avoid contact with humankind.

"Go to hell," said Barnabas Sims.

"We never said you was afraid of Morgan," Pettibone exclaimed, "I swear."

"Don't beg," Sims growled. "Show your backbone."

"It was Barnabas claimed you'd met your match in Henry Morgan. I was just saying that it sure looked like you backed down. But I didn't know for sure. And 'twas no fault of your own. I warrant it was a smart play. Your pistol could have been empty."

" 'For God hath not given us the spirit of fear; but of power,' " said the Black Cleric. He stepped in and aimed a strike at the younger man. Pettibone yelped as the blade sawed a chunk of flesh from his thigh. He screeched and backed into the surf. Sims lunged forward. LeBishop whirled about and caught the man's blade on his own, disarmed him with a twist of his wrist and sent his cutlass spinning across the sand. Sims darted out of harm's way and broke for his sword with LeBishop hot on his heels.

" 'For day and night thy hand was heavy upon me,' " LeBishop proclaimed, and with an overhand blow opened up the man's back from the base of his neck to his waist. Barnabas Sims arched his spine and outstretched his arms. His mouth drew back in a silent scream and he sank to his knees in the sand. The muscles along his neck stood out in stark relief. And still no sound escaped his throat. His eyes rolled back in his head and he sank backward onto his bootheels.

"Oh, sweet mercy!" Pettibone moaned. LeBishop turned to face him. "Well then, if you must have me, then by heaven you shall." The fear in his throat made him sound shrill. But at the last he summoned a kind of courage born of desperation—the will to fight because there is no place to run. He charged out of the sea. LeBishop waited, his cutlass poised, the blade gently swinging back and forth; then up it swept to flash in the sunlight. Steel rang upon steel.

"As for you, you were dead in your transgressions and sins," said LeBishop. He stuck out a leg and tripped the younger man as he blundered past. Square John fell forward onto the mud and sand, rolled over on his back and tried to stand, but the Black Cleric held him back with a well-placed boot to the chest. He stood over his vanquished foe, arm raised, the steel blade inches from his chest.

"Why me?" Pettibone said, his voice a hoarse rasp.

"Because you're here," said LeBishop, and pinned the man's heart to the sand. Pettibone gasped and clawed at the cutlass blade jutting from his chest. He groaned, his features contorted, and his hands outstretched, reaching for the life that was beyond his grasp, then dropped loose as a rag doll's. His head turned to the side.

It took a healthy tug to drag the weapon free. By then Pettibone had quit wriggling.

LeBishop heard footsteps behind him in the sand and he whirled about, weapon ready, only to confront his quartermaster, Peter Tregoning. The gnarled little Cornishman brought up sharply a few paces from the red-stained tip. Tregoning had no use for a cutlass. Pistols were his weapon of choice and he carried a half dozen on his person at all times. But he wisely kept his hands clear of the weapons and held them palms upward and empty. His cheeks were red and he was breathing heavy from the run up the beach; his eyes seemed to bulge as he fought to catch his breath.

"Captain LeBishop, see you there. The Dons are sailing into Kingston bay."

LeBishop scanned the approach from the sea and blanched at the sight of a Spanish frigate, the *San Bartolomeo*, bearing down on the peninsula. The frigate had chased him from a prize ship on more than one occasion. He looked back toward Port Royal. The ramparts protecting the waterfront were completely unmanned.

"Blast your eyes, where's the alarm?" LeBishop exclaimed. "Who is tending the signal bell?"

"Begging your pardon, Captain, but you've gone and killed them," said Tregoning.

The Black Cleric glanced at the two corpses, then at the great brass bell on its scaffold and carriage erected a few yards back from the water's edge. "The devil, you say." LeBishop trotted over to the bell; his speed increased as the three-masted warship swung toward them, revealing an impressive array of guns along the length of its solid-looking hull. The Black Cleric climbed the scaffolding hand over foot, and gaining the platform, grabbed the pull rope and gave a mighty tug. The bell began to swing on its housing, gained momentum, and finally began to ring out its warning.

Behind them, farther up the shore in Port Royal, buccaneers stumbled from taverns and crib houses and inns and made their way to the battlements. Despite the fact that the frigate was flying a flag of truce, the Brethren of the Coast hastily swabbed out their batteries of twelve-pounders, loaded them with roundshot, and replaced the fuses as the colors of Spain rounded the point and entered the harbor.

"Here comes a grand marquessa," Tregoning called out, striving to be heard above the bell. The *San Bartolomeo* was rigged with a variety of fore-and-aft and square sails. It plunged through the green-blue waters with a sense of purpose that dared defiance. "And see, she flies a flag of peace."

"That may be," said LeBishop, eyeing the frigate whose decks bristled with hardened seamen and troops of well-disciplined musketeers. Its gunports were open to reveal a lethal array of twelve- and fourteen-pounder cannons. "But she's dressed for war."

Elena Maria basked in the warm sunlight that washed the second-floor balcony fronting the English governor's estate. She leaned upon the wrought-iron railing overlooking the circular drive, relishing this last moment of calm, this last opportunity to be herself. Soon she must drape herself in pretense, like a well-worn shawl. But at least Don Alonso had made a timely entrance. Now she would not have to depend solely on an incompetent English governor to keep her plans alive.

An hour earlier Consuelo had roused her charge from a late-morning nap and alerted the señorita about the arrival of the *San Bartolomeo* in the harbor. Anticipating a visit from Don Alonso, Elena Maria had quickly dressed, choosing a flowery-print dress, sewn from brown-dyed bolts of Indian cotton. Its broad-lace–trimmed bodice was simply embellished with tiny pearls, while the accompanying cream-colored apron and mantilla were embroidered with pastel blue silk thread. She wanted to appear both chaste and elegant for the governor of Panama.

Consuelo joined her mistress on the balcony outside the guest bedroom. From the front of the house the two women could watch the road, the circular drive, and the sun-dappled bay. Elena Maria could watch the well-ordered streets of Kingston. She had walked them all during the past four days, escorted more often than not by Sir Richard himself, who kept up a constant chatter about the burdens of authority and the bright future he envisioned for himself after a successful tenure as the governor of the island. Sir Richard's wife had returned to England some time ago. Elena Maria assumed Purselley's lady had no stomach for adventure.

Elena Maria was quite the opposite: Life in Spain at the court of King Carlos would be a dreary fate. It was a trait she shared with the buccaneers of Port Royal who preferred their freedom to the comforts and constraints of the Old World. She glanced aside at the nurse, who seemed preoccupied with her own thoughts.

"What do you see, old woman?"

Sunlight and memories had drawn Consuelo out to the balcony. She steadied herself against the railing, turned her weathered countenance with its blind right eye toward the bay and Port Royal. She did not answer at first, but continued to study the peninsula, the wind tugging at her cloth bonnet, lost in her thoughts or visions. It was hard to tell, for when the mood came upon her, it was as if the woman withdrew from the world. Something in the distance distracted her—perhaps the Spanish frigate in the harbor—or had she divined that Elena Maria had not spent last night alone?

"Tell me, Consuelo, do you look to what-will-be? Perhaps your thoughts lie in Port Royal, perhaps in the bed of your recent paramour?" Elena Maria grinned as the servant swung about to protest: *that* got the old woman's mind off her mistress's affairs!

"But Señorita, I promise you, I never so much as even . . ."

Elena Maria stilled her with a glance and an upturned hand. "Nurse, you have never lied to me. I should hate to think you would deceive me now." Elena Maria shooed a hovering dragonfly from her face. "I remember when that pair of handsome young English soldiers returned with you that first morning on the island. I had never seen you in such a state. Bedraggled as a lost puppy brought in from a storm. I could not understand where you had been or what you had seen. You made no sense."

"I was lost and confused," Consuelo tried to explain.

"Evidently you have been lost and confused for the past four days." The Kuna half-breed had made a clandestine visit to the buccaneer stronghold each afternoon.

Elena Maria decided not to mention the curiously satisfied smile she had glimpsed on the old woman's face, a look of *amor* that she knowingly recognized. The servant immediately began to try to explain her absences and offer a litany of apologies, but her protests and shaky indignation only fueled Elena Maria's desire to tease her servant all the more.

"It is a day of joy. You will be reunited with Don Alonso del Campo," Consuelo observed, changing the subject. From their vantage point they could see a column of men make its way from the frigate to the pier and down along the waterfront. The distance was too great to identify the men but she was certain Elena Maria's intended groom was among them.

"Yes, a day of joy," the señorita echoed pensively. She turned and, leaning out over the railing, tried to catch a glimpse of the blockhouse on the point overlooking the sea. She could see the path to the jail winding off through the pineapple trees and the blockhouse itself rising just beyond a bluff fringed with almond trees and blue mahoe.

She pictured the man imprisoned within its sturdy walls, dangerous as caged heat, clever and ruthless if pushed to the point of no return. But he was still a man. And like all men, his vision was clouded by the fire in his loins. Still, she had to be careful, to choose her course with care. Morgan was nothing like Thomas LeBishop. The Black Cleric was predictable and had shown he would back down before an overwhelming force or a well-played bluff. Henry Morgan was different. He was fierce and determined, and his pride ran deep. She thought back to his surrender in Purselley's councilroom. *El Tigre* went along willingly with the English soldiers. He had avoided a melee, kept her safe from injury, and lured Sir Richard into a trap of the governor's own devising. Now Henry Morgan intended to place himself beyond Purselley's reach. Presenting his cause to an English court was certainly putting his life on the line. It was a life Doña Elena Maria intended to put to better use.

She heard the carriage approaching from the hillside; the rattle of harness and clatter of iron-rimmed wheels telegraphed its impending arrival. Elena Maria felt her pulse quicken. The wait seemed interminable here on the balcony, where the sun melted down like sweet amber honey and drenched the verdant hills. The world about her was an eruption of color, flowers of every hue and shade opened their petals like seductive maidens, revealing their intimate treasures to a worldly paradise rampant with a natural joy.

Elena Maria hid her gloom, buried her misgivings and the truth of her feelings deep within herself as she awaited Don Alonso, trusting he would make a grand show to impress the English. No doubt he paraded through the streets of Kingston with a detachment of well-armed Spanish musketeers in his wake. He would want to impress the locals, to present a show of force to keep the inhabitants of the island in their place.

"Señorita, why so glum?" Consuelo asked. She was deeply troubled by the woman's moodiness. Elena Maria had always been such a happy child. Her father's death had changed all that. No. The servant corrected herself, her memory sharpened. Everything had changed when Elena Maria had realized she needed to seek a husband of noble birth among the courtiers in Spain to give legitimacy to her inherited holdings in the New World.

Elena Maria was intensely aware that she and Morgan had at least one thing in common. She glanced at the rumpled conforters covering her feather bed and remembered the previous night's lusty interlude. *Well, more than one thing.* Whatever pleasures they had stolen could only be temporary. They were both prisoners. The constraints of Spanish society were as confining and unjust as Purselley's prison. Morgan had his ship and his guns and a crew of hardened rogues. Such a man could always fight his way to freedom. She had to use the weapons at her disposal, her wits, her courage, and the fire in men's eyes.

The carriage rolled into view. Don Alonso stood in the carriage as it rolled to a stop before the governor's estate. His scarlet coat and gold-trimmed waistcoat were resplendent, his white breeches and hose immaculate. He removed his plumed tricorn hat and swept it before him in a bow that almost dislodged him from the carriage. Sir Richard Purselley, seated next to the visiting dignitary, was pleased to see Joseph and the remainder of his servants emerge from the front door and present themselves as the carriage rolled to a stop. But Don Alonso only had eyes for the woman on the balcony. He rushed forward with Sir Richard at his side, leaving the carriage, servants, and a dozen musketeers in green and white to await their liege's pleasure.

Joseph snapped an order and Purselley's household staff instantly went to work, scurrying back into the estate like so many insects. Elena Maria took a deep breath, filled her lungs with the perfumed air and held it until the warmth filtered into her bloodstream and went coursing through her body. Now she was ready.

Elena Maria reentered the bedroom, stood in the center of the floor, her hands clasped together. She heard voices in the hall, then a soft knock at the door. She turned and summoned her servant.

"Consuelo," she said, with a nod toward the door.

"Sí Señorita."

"I think while you were visiting Port Royal yesterday, you learned from a 'friend' that Henry Morgan intends to steal the *Santa Rita* tonight and sail for England. At least that is what I will tell Don Alonso."

"Mistress? You wish me to lie?"

"Just do as you are told, old nurse. Or it will be the worse for both of us."

The half-breed nodded and hurried across the room. The latch creaked beneath her hand and the door swung open. She stepped back to permit the governor of Panama to make his way into the room. He appeared none the worse for his ordeal in Maracaibo. Indeed, his brooding gaze burned with a singular purpose. But his expression revealed a mixture of delight and relief at finding the daughter of the house of Saucedo alive and well.

Elena Maria curtsied, sank to her knees and took his hand in hers and pressed her lips to his fingers. "I prayed you would rescue me. I never lost faith in you." There was a slight flutter in her voice, as if she were attempting to hold back a torrent of tears.

"Señorita, I came as soon as the *San Bartolomeo* arrived in Maracaibo. A day earlier and we would have closed the trap on Henry Morgan. Sir Richard informs me that he has the situation in hand. But rest assured I would have sailed to the ends of the earth to bring you home." Don Alonso was taken back by Elena Maria's heartfelt remarks. He had worried she might accuse him of betraying her into the hands of Morgan and his brigands. Evidently her experiences had left her a chastened woman. He liked the change. "There, there, *pobrecita*," he added in a paternal tone of voice, stroking her hair beneath the lace mantilla. He helped her to stand. "I came for you, *mi amor*," he told her tenderly. Then his voice turned cold. "And for one other."

"Then you had best hurry," Elena Maria replied. She looked past her betrothed as Sir Richard Purselley appeared outside in the hall. He nervously cleared his throat and entered the room, holding his tricorn hat in his hand.

"Good, you are here, Sir Richard," said the woman. "What I have learned from my nurse is for the both of you."

14. "The sea always wins."

The chairs within the councilroom had been cleared from the main floor and removed to the side walls to afford space for those dignitaries and their ladies who chose to dance to the strains of the Military Consort; the repertoire included a number of pavannes and ballads that tested the artistry of the musicians. Thankfully, the guests were of a forgiving nature, their charity plied with copious quantities of Madeira and several fine bottles of port.

Sir Richard Purselley had invited every plantation owner, merchant, and town official from Kingston to the ball. A goodly number, despite their reticence to socialize with the Spaniards, had already made the trek up the road to the governor's estate. However distasteful it might be to kowtow to the likes of Don Alonso del Campo, the local dignitaries were loath to insult Sir Richard, who could be counted on to hold a grudge the next time he sat in judgment over some dispute involving those same islanders.

Captain Hastiler gingerly made his way through the crowd, skirting several couples who had taken to the center of the hall and were stepping off the intricate patterns of a dance to a lover's canticle. Servants milled about in the dining room, each with his or her own appointed task. Joseph, Purselley's manservant, personally oversaw the appearance of the banquet table. He had directed the servants under his charge to arrange a formidable feast: platters of curried goat served with dasheen, a yamlike root boiled and mashed with fiery little peppers guaranteed to send the unwary gasping for ale or wine. The guests would be free to gorge themselves on mounds of sweet banana fritters, bowls of rice and peas, along with the gossip of the day—what of this truce between the two great powers? would it last? and what would life be like without the benefits of having access to the wealth of stolen goods provided by Morgan and his buccaneers?

Captain Hastiler found one of the servants in the outer foyer, inquired as to the whereabouts of Purselley and was told the governor had stepped outside and could be found at his favorite spot, the terrace overlooking the bay. Hastiler proceeded out into the fading light and approached the English governor, only too aware the man did not wish to be disturbed. But Hastiler had a right to know what was going on. Events had been set in motion that were beyond his ken.

Sir Richard Purselley watched the horizon deepen in hue to burnished gold while blushing clouds billowed above the rim of the earth, turned crimson as the sun set beyond the Hellshire hills and the Santa Cruz Mountains and the Cockpit Country where the way was harsh and spiny plants erupted from the broken land. He considered the shadows as they crept through the streets of Kingston, seeped across the bay, blanketed the Spanish frigate and the English bark, painting the waters indigo, until at last the edge of night engulfed Port Royal. But among those ragged streets, the taverns and gambling halls unshuttered their windows and hurled back the night with an onslaught of lantern light and song.

Hastiler nervously cleared his throat as if to announce himself.

Sir Richard frowned, dragged from his reverie by the officer's presence. "Yes, Captain?" he said with a glance to the side. "Did you sample the curried goat? I daresay Joseph takes a hand in the preparation."

"No, sir," the captain said, "though you set a fine table. But that is not why I have come."

"Ah, then, pray tell what is your reason for this intrusion?" Sir Richard folded his hands behind his back. He was handsome in his magenta-colored coat and ruffled shirt, tight cream-colored pants and hose and buckled shoes. A small ceremonial dagger in a jeweled sheath dangled from the red sash circling his waist.

"It concerns your guests," Hastiler said. "Word has reached me that the *San Bartolomeo* has already taken on fresh water and sacks of fruit. And Don Alonso del Campo and the señorita are nowhere to be found. They are not within the hall or anywhere on the estate. Earlier today one of the servants remembers seeing them depart in the company of musketeers. Evidently, no one really knows where they have gone."

"Indeed," said Purselley, peculiarly composed. "Well, I feel certain they will turn up." Sir Richard returned his attention to the sunset and the bay. If the governor was concerned that his guests of honor were absent from the ball, he certainly did not show it. "Relax, Captain. All is well."

Hastiler stared at Purselley in bewildered silence. The officer had been fighting the Spaniards too long to change. He trusted the Spaniards as long as he could see them. And that was the problem. Where was Don Alonso and what was he up to?

For the better part of that same afternoon Henry Morgan had watched the sea as it rolled onto the shore, changing the shape of the land, forming and reforming the strand. Men went to the sea in wooden ships, iron men willing to brave the elements, to toss high great swaths of sail and catch the wind.

"Plough the waves, plunder and harry, follow the trade winds, be brave, be quick and shrewd, and riches can be yours. But remember, Henry"—his father's ghost stood next to him at the window; a diaphanous memory Morgan saw or imagined he saw, heard or imagined he heard—*"at the end of the day, the sea always wins."*

He had been young then, and hadn't understood. But now he knew. The sea was a harsh mistress, both cruel and kind, deceptive, then deadly. He had seen his fair share of good men vanish beneath the blue-green waves, seen white squalls engulf ships and drag them under in a matter of seconds, with all hands struggling and screaming and crying out for salvation to an unforgiving God.

"Yes, Papa," he muttered, a sense of loss washing over him. The past was growing dim now, Edward Morgan's ghostly visits were rare, arriving unannounced but never unwelcome, to haunt his son. Henry glanced toward the front door and imagined the detail of marines sent to guard him, Sergeant McCready, and the others, with plenty of fine claret, enough for each man to drink his fill. Soon now, it would be time. But he wanted no confrontation with Royal Marines when he departed. The few drops of juice extracted from the forbidden fruits of the machineel trees that grew near the shore at the base of the Hellshires would render the men unconscious and leave them sleeping till dawn.

He craned his head around the sill and studied the frigate anchored off the Kingston cay. He never thought he would see the day when a Spanish warship would sail unchallenged into the bay. Where were the gunners manning the fortifications protecting Port Royal? Truce or no truce, a few warning shots should have been in order, just to keep the Spaniards honest. The presence of the *San Bartolomeo* gave him cause to worry. He suspected Don Alonso had been aboard the vessel. All the more reason for Henry Morgan to take leave of Sir Richard's hospitality.

But what of Doña Elena? Would she be able to escape? If he closed his eyes he could still feel her warmth. All that grace and breeding underscored by a fiery passion. Now, there was a woman worth fighting for. But she deserved more than just a common freebooter. Henry Morgan had wealth. It was time he had privilege. And the power that came with it.

"I shall be more," he said, his attention returning to the peninsula and Port Royal, in all its squalid glory. "I shall be more."

He turned from the window and finished dressing, his movements slow and measured, like a knight donning armor or a matador his suit of light: first the baldric and cutlass, then a brace of pistols, large-bore weapons capable of stopping a charging bull; next, a rust-colored coat with gold stitching around the edges, a long cravat about the throat; the yellow silk bandana about his head to hold his unruly mane in check completed his attire—proper dress for defying English governors and stealing both the ship and the bride of a Spanish Don.

Morgan stalked across the room, hoping he wouldn't have to lower himself out of an upstairs window. Throughout his confinement, McCready had proved lax about bolting the front door from the outside. It was worth a try. He placed a hand upon the rough panel, gently pressed, and was rewarded with what seemed a deafening squeak. He hesitated, expecting shouts of alarm, then continued to shove. The door swung ajar and Henry Morgan emerged into the dying light to be greeted by half a dozen of the island's finest soldiers: McCready and his men lay in various attitudes of disarray about a campfire. They had barely begun their evening meal before succumbing to the drugged wine. Uncorked bottles of claret lay where they'd been dropped, flies buzzed about the congealed juices seeping from a wooden platter of meat pies. The marines looked like rag dolls left over from a child's play.

Morgan checked the soldiers; they were alive. However, they'd probably regret it come morning. The aftereffects of their drugged sleep would be raging headaches for one and all. Morgan knelt by the sergeant, rearranged him into a more comfortable position, and then patted his shoulder.

"G'night, mother," said Morgan.

The *Santa Rosa* rode easy in the harbor, just as Henry Morgan had left it but a few days ago. Moonlight played upon the shrouds where the knotted cords glistened with sea spray. Someone, probably Pierre Voisin, had hung a lantern near the bow to signal all was ready and the ship and its spartan crew awaited their captain.

But Henry Morgan remained ashore, a solitary figure standing aloof from the gathering of his peers who waited to see him off. The minutes crawled past until even his friends began to wonder among themselves what had brought this mood upon him. Was he having his own misgivings about the course he had chosen? There was not a one of the Brethren who would risk life and limb before the English courts.

Only one suspected the true reason for his reluctance to depart. And she was the only one who dared approach him. The waterfront was deserted this night; for the most part, the spirit of revelry was quartered in the center of Port Royal, where the taverns, brothels, and gaming houses were clustered together like harlots in a hurricane. Morgan heard the footsteps behind him and swung about with a look of expectation on his face that faded when he recognized Nell Jolly. In that moment her heart broke. But she hid it well.

"Leave me," Morgan grumbled, and dug his hands into his coat and glared at the shore road as if blaming it for all his troubles.

"No," Nell said.

"Do not vex me, Toto."

"It's my lot in life," she said. "Pierre and Israel are aboard the boat with several of the lads. How long will you keep them waiting?"

"As long as I choose."

"And you will risk alerting the Spaniards aboard the *San Bartolomeo*? You will never have a better opportunity. See you how the governor's house is ablaze with lights? Sir Richard holds a great ball and all of Kingston's bluebloods are in attendance—all this to honor Don Alonso del Campo and his would-be bride."

"What's this?" Morgan asked, staring off across the bay toward the estate on the hillside, curious as to the activity surrounding the governor's house. So Sir Richard was entertaining the Dons. One heavily armed frigate and Sir Richard was prepared to grovel before Don Alonso.

"She isn't coming."

Morgan turned to protest, then stared angrily at the young woman. "What you are talking about?" He scowled and moved away from her. Nell followed.

"She will be here," he said.

"No she won't," Nell told him.

"How can you tell? Do you read the future now?"

"No," she said. "Only the present." Nell stared down at her coat and breeches and the weapons she carried. She had done a good job of concealing her womanhood but it didn't change who she was. "Beneath this baldric and coat I am as much a woman as Doña Elena Maria. I can see into her heart."

"And what have you learned?"

"That which you already know. She loves you not."

Morgan stiffened as if struck. He fixed his cold gray eyes upon her until Nell was forced to look away. She reached out to place a hand upon his arm but he brushed her aside and started down the pier toward the johnnyboat that would take him out to the brig.

A small crowd had gathered at the middle of the pier. Word had spread of Morgan's impending departure. His actions did not sit well with the Brethren. Morgan was leaving and they wondered why, and when would he return.

Sir William Jolly wore a grave expression as he greeted his friend. But if the physician had his doubts about Morgan's decision to present himself before the English courts, the old sea wolf kept such counsel to himself. He could not fail but notice how, even now, Morgan continued to search the waterfront as if he was expecting someone in particular.

Calico Jack and Anne Bonney were there. And more of the Brethren, swaggering rogues with names as colorful as their reputations: Dutch Hannah Lee and Cockade Tom Penmerry and Six Toes Yaquereño—the Portugee Devil. Morgan knew them all. They were thieves like him, rebellious and hard-living and full of spirit.

"See here, Henry, we've just learned what you're about. It seems a poor time to leave, with the Dons among us," Calico Jack complained.

"If I didn't know you better, I'd think you were running away," said Six Toes. The squat, heavyset buccaneer sensed a chill as Morgan turned his gray eyes toward the man and fixed him in a bleak stare. "But then, of course . . . uh . . . I do know you better."

"Portugee don't mean any harm," Dutch Hannah spoke up. She was a thick-featured woman, born large-boned, and like Anne Bonney, Dutch Hannah was as tough as any man who sailed beneath the Black Flag. She tilted back her floppy-brimmed hat and hooked a thumb in her wide leather belt. "We stand ready to follow you against the Dons or Purselley and his lot."

"I've a crew of fifty men who'll come running, you just give the word," Cockade Tom Penmerry added, dabbing at his lip with a silk kerchief. He was a slim, finely dressed, foppish individual, dangerous when angered, ruthless in battle. Of the captains, only Thomas LeBishop was absent. Morgan figured the Black Cleric would be glad to be rid of him for a time. As for the others, standing in the dark among this hard lot, Morgan could think of no finer band of fallen angels with whom to cast his fate.

Penmerry's remarks elicited a murmur of agreement from the group, and each captain offered to summon their crews and oust both the English and Spanish from the island. Hands dropped to sword hilts, coat flaps pulled back from pistol grips. They were going to talk themselves into a war if he didn't stop them. Morgan held up his hand and called for them to hear him.

"No trouble now. I've already spoke my piece to Will Jolly. But here it is, aboveboard and full to the wind. Jamaica is ours and we will not be driven from it. But we can never prevail against the might of England and Spain. This truce will not last. But I shall seize this momentary peace to address the English court. I have friends there and intend to oust Sir Richard Purselley without firing a shot or turning a friend into an enemy. We can be loyal to the Crown and still be free. But we shall not kiss the hem of Spain's coat."

"More like the seat of the Don's britches, if you ask me," said Anne Bonney. A chorus of laughter followed her remark. Morgan passed among them, feeling the camaraderie of these wayward souls. He reached the end of the pier and climbed down into the johnnyboat where two night-shrouded figures waited at the oars, reserved and ready to ferry him out to the *Santa Rosa*.

"I should be going with you," Sir William said, restating a quarrel they had already punished themselves with.

"Stay with your daughter," Morgan said, taking his seat at the bow. "She will have a greater need than I."

"See here, you young roister—" the physician began.

Morgan cut him short with a wave of farewell. At his command the oarsmen leaned into their work. The johnnyboat pulled away from the pier. Morgan continued to search the landing, hoping that at the last minute he might spy Elena Maria coming to join him, calling his name.

The oars rose and dipped beneath the ebony surface of the bay, rippling the mirrored moonlight. An ominous silence closed around them. Morgan leaned forward, elbows on his knees, and tried to avoid looking at the distant hills and the brightly lit governor's house.

"Hail you there, the *Santa Rosa*!" Morgan called out, cupping his hands to his mouth and trying keep his voice from carrying across the bay to the *San Bartolomeo* at the Kingston docks. On a night as still as this, anything was possible.

No reply came forth.

"Voisin, you little thief, bring the lantern around amidships. I'll climb the Jacob's ladder."

No answer. Nothing. Morgan didn't like this.

He glanced over his shoulder at the oarsmen. "Draw up there, lads. Something's amiss. And until I get an answer, we're close enough to suit me."

"But not enough to suit me," one of the oarsmen replied. Morgan recognized the voice of Thomas LeBishop, thick with menace and directly behind him. Morgan reached inside his coat for one of his pistols as he turned to confront the Black Cleric.

"Rest easy now, Captain Morgan," LeBishop said, and cocked the blunderbuss he had just lifted from beneath his feet. He'd concealed the weapon with a swath of sackcloth. The weapon was loaded with a lethal mix of roundshot; at close range the blast would cut Morgan in half.

"Appears 'his high and mighty' is at a loss for words," said Peter Tregoning, revealing himself to be the other oarsman. He chuckled and tilted back his tricorn hat then put his back into the oars, his strong arms pulling them across the water to the *Santa Rosa*. "*El Tigre* don't look like much right now."

"And take that hand from your coat, Henry, nice and easy now," LeBishop ordered. "If I see anything more than your empty fingers I'll blow a hole through your backbone."

"What are you about, Tom?" Morgan glowered, folding his arms across his chest.

"Sir Richard's business," LeBishop replied, jabbing the business end of the blunderbuss between Morgan's shoulder blades as he reached around to retrieve the buccaneer's brace of pistols from beneath the flaps of his coat and drop them over the side. The flint-locks disappeared—*plunk . . . plunk*—beneath the stygian surface.

"You've made some low enemies in high places, Captain Morgan," Peter Tregoning chuckled, relieved he wouldn't have to continue the pretense. The freebooter had feared discovery back at the pier.

"Sorry, Captain, this is nothing personal," said the Black Cleric.

"It's always personal," Morgan said.

"No. This night, I am merely a hireling," LeBishop continued. "You are a threat to Sir Richard. So he has arranged to have you removed from the island. I daresay he has paid me most handsomely to place you beyond the reach of English justice. Though I shall not grieve for you, it troubles me to see you end this way. You and I should have settled our differences with cutlass and ax. But I can forgo the satisfaction of spilling your entrails."

"Then to whom has Purselley delivered me?" Morgan knew the answer even as he asked it. "Would he betray his own countryman to Spain?" The buccaneer shook his head in disgust, then looked over the side of the boat at the water, his muscles tensed as he considered his options. There weren't many.

"I don't like what you're thinking," LeBishop said. "Don't try it. One wrong move and we'll end it right here."

"It will end," Morgan said. "But not the way you think, by my oath."

Tregoning pulled in the oars as the johnnyboat scraped the side of the brig below the gunports and eased beneath the rope ladder dangling close to the waterline. Something large with skin like silver chain mail splashed in the moonlight. Mysteries lurked beneath the tides, and men's hearts. "Up that ladder," said LeBishop. "Climb, you proper bastard. Climb."

Morgan stood and considered leaping over the side of the johnny-boat. But he had friends aboard the *Santa Rosa* and must learn their fate. He reached up and caught hold of the first rung and hauled himself out of the boat. "Another time . . ." he promised, looking over his shoulder at LeBishop.

"Another place?" LeBishop finished, and waved at the ladder. "Not so. 'It is appointed unto men, once to die . . . ' "

Morgan heard the johnnyboat pull away as he climbed up to the ship's rail. He could feel LeBishop's blunderbuss trained on his back. Morgan scrambled up the final rungs of the rope ladder and reached the railing without incident, then dragged himself over the side and stood, unharmed, his pulse racing as he confronted a dozen Spanish musketeers. The Spaniards trained their long-barreled muskets in his direction. The welcoming detail parted to allow Don Alonso del Campo to saunter forward and confront the buccaneer. The governor of Panama stroked his close-cropped beard with one hand; in the other he held a short-barreled pistol.

"Well now, it would seem we have a guest."

"Where are my men?"

"I have no use for them. I have everything I came for." He motioned for Morgan to follow him. "I am not without a charitable nature." The musketeers closed in; one of them immediately brought out a pair of shackles. Morgan pulled back, lashed out, caught one man by the throat and hurled him aside, but another soldier clubbed him in the small of the back with the butt of his musket, knocking the wind out of him. Morgan sank to his knees, gasping. Pain shot along his lower ribs. By the time he managed to catch his breath and regain his footing, the shackles had been fastened about his ankles.

Morgan glared at the chains, reached down and tugged at them. Don Alonso's crew hurried about the deck. He saw that the sails had been unfurled and the anchor weighed. The same could be said for the *San Bartolomeo.*

Sir Richard's party was a ruse—Morgan surmised, disgusted with himself—*designed to trick me into thinking the Spaniards were being feted by the English governor while in reality Don Alonso and his crew were preparing to leave the same day as they arrived.*

"I am told you have a friend in Sir Richard Purselley," Morgan grumbled aloud, adding the governor's name to a mental list he kept in his mind's eye.

"Well now, I think we have something in common when it comes to Sir Richard Purselley—contempt." Don Alonso opened a snuffbox, pinched a few grains of the contents and placed them in his nose and then sneezed. The sensation evidently pleased him. "But he serves a purpose. My purpose. Now, as for your men, do they come with us or do I leave them here? They could swim to shore. The decision is yours."

At the governor's command, Morgan was brought before his shipmates. He was relieved to see them relatively unharmed. Israel Goodenough and Pierre Voisin and the remainder of their companions staggered toward the buccaneer.

"Captain Morgan, they were on us before we knew it," the Frenchman said. Voisin's gritty countenance was a welcome sight in a bad circumstance. "*Mon ami*, I swear we fought them tooth and nail."

"Let them go," Morgan told Don Alonso. "If it is me you are after, then so be it."

"Very well." Don Alonso nodded and barked an order to the musketeers, who fell upon the buccaneers and began to bind their wrists before forcing them over the side. Several of the men tried to resist and were bayoneted for their troubles.

Morgan was momentarily caught off guard by Don Alonso's random brutality. Men he knew and had sailed with and fought alongside lay writhing on the deck, bleeding to death; others were bound and hurled into the bay, their cries ringing on the dead of the night as they kicked and twisted and tried to keep themselves afloat, only to inevitably sink beneath the still waters. The Spaniards laughed among themselves—they enjoyed their work and were amused by the antics of the drowning men.

As the musketeers attempted to deal with Israel Goodenough, Voisin, and the last of buccaneers, Morgan broke free and despite his shackles hurled himself upon the guards with enough force to drive several of the Spaniards back against their companions.

"Israel . . . Pierre . . . over the side, you beauties!" Before the Frenchman could protest, Morgan literally shoved the little thief over the railing. Israel caught Morgan by the arm and tried to pull him along as the Spaniards descended on them. Morgan twisted free and flung himself upon the musketeers coming to the aid of their *compañeros*. "Avast, you rum-humpers! I'll slit your throats and carry off your skulls!"

His efforts bought a precious few seconds, long enough for the rest of the freebooters to leap over the side of the *Santa Rosa*, dragging Israel with them. As they splashed into the sea, Spanish musketeers swarmed over Morgan and rushed forward to fire down at the men in the water. The stench of powdersmoke filled the air.

Morgan was hoisted to his feet and dragged before the governor. Don Alonso slapped his prisoner across the face. But Morgan would not look away. He continued to stare at the Spaniard, his head unbowed.

"You vex me," Don Alonso said. He watched his soldiers blast away at the escaping freebooters. The musketeers were excellent marksmen, but the night was dark and the black waters hindered their aim. His soldiers fired and reloaded and fired again at the desperate targets bobbing on the surface of the bay. "But no longer. I shall have no more trouble from you," Don Alonso replied. "We must get under way," he said, snapping at a gruff-looking boatswain who saluted and began to harangue the crew. "Prepare the rope for *Señor* Morgan. Toss the line over the yardarm. As soon as we clear the harbor we shall have him dance for us."

A cheer rose from the throats of the *Santa Rosa*'s crew. The breeze that filled the sail tugged at the hem of Purselley's dark purple coat and ruffled his wig. Across the bay, the frigate was under way as well, the *San Bartolomeo* angled about and ran up a full complement of sails as her crew followed the *Santa Rosa* out of the bay.

"How did you know I intended to take the *Santa Rosa* tonight?" Morgan said, driven to ask and yet not certain he wanted to know. The timbers underfoot began to creak and groan, the sails above slapped and grew taut as they captured the wind. The ship trembled as if with a life of her own.

"A little bird told me," Don Alonso beamed. He was delighted by this turn of events. The shame of Maracaibo had been expunged from his soul. Don Alonso del Campo had captured *el Tigre del Caribe*. But the punishment this miscreant deserved had only begun. Upon the governor's order, a crewman at the stern of the ship signaled the *San Bartolomeo*, waving a hurricane lantern from side to side then up and down.

The frigate had also caught the wind and was gathering momentum. The warship tacked across the bay and picked up speed. As the vessel passed within a hundred yards of Port Royal, the *San Bartolomeo*'s array of twelve- and fourteen-pound guns loosed a vicious broadside, belching smoke and tongues of fire from its gunports. The thunderous discharge reverberated throughout the bay. The effects were horrible to witness.

Lead shot brought down the rigging on the *Glenmorran*, severed the mainmast on the *Jericho*, crippled another pair of schooners. A second broadside of explosive shot hammered the waterfront, blasting the gun redoubts and starting numerous fires throughout the port.

Warehouses burst into flame. Men and women poured into the streets, their silhouettes a blur as they stumbled about in confusion or hurried to man the port's defenses. In the glare of the explosions, Morgan noticed Thomas LeBishop and Tregoning in their johnny-boat.

LeBishop frantically waved his hands in an attempt to ward off a second volley. Geysers erupted around the johnnyboat. Behind them on the pier a gun redoubt exploded with enough impact to knock the Black Cleric off balance and capsize his small craft, pitching both men into the bay. Another redoubt exploded. Bodies were hurled into the air, arms and legs flailing against the firelight.

"You were under a flag of truce," Morgan exclaimed.

"There can be no truce with the likes of thieves and kidnappers and murderers!" The governor bellowed for all his men to hear and approve. A cheer rose from the throats of his musketeers. The waterfront was ablaze now. A few of Port Royal's guns opened fire but their sights were off, the elevation too high, and the iron shot did little more than rip a few holes in the sails.

Morgan could no longer tolerate the carnage and tried to make a grab for the Spanish governor. He tripped on the shackles and landed humiliatingly, facedown at Don Alonso's feet. Don Alonso ordered him dragged upright and a pair of soldiers roughly hauled him to his feet, keeping a tight grip on his arms.

"Ah, my dear, I think we have redeemed your honor," said the governor, looking past Morgan. Elena Maria emerged from the captain's cabin below. "My little bird, she sang the song, sweet to my ears."

Don Alonso moved his hands as if conducting a piece of music, as if hearing a melody everyone else was deaf to. "Can you not hear it? What a sweet melody." He sang: "All is lost, *Señor Morgan*." Don Alonso walked over to Elena Maria and kissed her hand then turned back to his prisoner. "Listen well: All is lost."

Morgan stared at Elena Maria. Her part in this was impossible to deny. She had set the stage and he had played the fool. No man could have performed the part any better, bowing and scraping to her passion, her desires, and treacherous beauty. She met his gaze but showed no emotion. The glare of the fires ashore played upon her well-turned features as Morgan was led amidships to the knotted rope that dangled above an open hatch.

His hands were quickly bound and the noose slipped over his head. The rough hemp dug into his throat. Morgan stared down into the black opening. The rope was assurance he wouldn't have far to fall.

Father . . . bless me now.

The crew in the rigging halted their labors to stare down at the execution. The musketeers gathered around, hoping to see their prisoner break and beg for mercy. But none of them really expected him to. Elena Maria folded her hands upon her apron and waited. And watched. She glanced in the direction of her future husband. Something unspoken seemed to pass between them, for he nodded then ambled forward.

"So it is come to this, Señor Morgan. Make your peace with God."

"I have never been at odds with God," Morgan replied. "Only bastards like yourself. A pox be on you and your kind. And cursed be faithless love." He looked up at the stars, took a last breath, stepped forward.

And dropped like a rock.

We are Brethren of Blood,
we are sons of the sea.
We are children of havoc
and born to be free.
Betrayed by a passion, he will live to regret,
The power of a woman, the traps she can set.
But beware *el Tigre* who prowls in his cage,
What you sow with betrayal, you shall reap with red rage.

15. The city of gold.

It had taken ten long days for the *Santa Rosa* to make the journey from Jamaica to Portobello on the Caribbean coast of Panama. Arriving in the Spanish-held port, in the shadow of the fortress that protected the settlement, Henry Morgan emerged from the ship's hold, filthy, hungry, but unbroken. Thrown in with a band of Kuna slaves recently captured during a raid on the Portobello piers, Morgan was forced to labor alongside the sullen natives and unload the trade goods from the *Santa Rosa* and *San Bartolomeo* onto large, oxen-drawn freight wagons.

Don Alonso was anxious to reach his governor's estate in Panama City, and ordered the wagon train to set out from the port the following morning. Morgan and the Indians marched at the rear of the column, choking on the dust, driven along by whip and the occasional prodding of the lancers escorting the governor and his intended bride.

Three of the Kuna raiders died trying to escape during the four-day march across the isthmus. The wagon train kept to the heavily patrolled military road and avoided the Indian-infested jungles that were home to the rebellious remnants of the rebellious natives. Morgan could sense the dread the Spaniards felt toward the impenetrable vastness of swamps and vine-choked forest that stretched off to either side of the narrow line of ridges, highbacked hills, and plateaus the road followed.

Not a day went by that Morgan didn't see Doña Elena Maria de Saucedo, always from a distance. Only once, Elena met his gaze when none were watching and she flashed him a brave smile of encouragement that puzzled Morgan all the more. Sympathy from the woman who had so skillfully betrayed him to his enemies?

On a warm and cloudy afternoon in late September, the wagon train bearing Don Alonso del Campo arrived at the walls of the fabled city on the Pacific. Soldiers at the gates cheered and waved their tricorn hats. Messengers were dispatched throughout the city to proclaim the arrival of the new governor.

Panama City was a glorious sight. But standing in the dust churned by the wagons, Morgan took note of its sparsely defended walls and the practically unattended redoubts. So, the Spaniards considered themselves secure from a landward attack. It made sense. Any force larger than a Kuna war party would have to approach over the mountain roads and be forced to battle its way past a number of fortified outposts before reaching the city and by then Panama's defenders would have been alerted and prepared a nasty welcome for their enemies.

Of course, there were always the swamps and the jungle, but then, only a madman would attempt to lead a force along such a route. Yes, a jungle approach was suicidal. Still, throughout the trek from the Caribbean coast, Morgan had studied the dense rain forest choking the valley floor below the mountain road. An army could hide down there. But beneath the forest's emerald canopy, the undergrowth defied the unwary trespasser. No one could live in the jungle for long, and keeping one's bearings down in that forbidding terrain had to be next to impossible.

Church bells shattered the buccaneer's moment of introspection. The first set of bells begat another, then another, until they pealed throughout the city, welcoming Don Alonso and his entourage. The wagons started forward with the new governor taking the lead. He wanted to make a positive first impression. Then came a detachment of lancers, next the beautiful Elena Maria de Saucedo, the city's own "princess," and behind her coach, a column of Spanish dragoons, then the freight wagons hauling trade goods from the opposite coast. On entering the city, it was Don Alonso who received the bulk of the attention. No one paid attention to the prisoners at the rear of the column, the impassive, sole surviving Kuna warrior and with him, Henry Morgan, the Tiger of the Caribbean, a legend in the dust.

*   *   *

"Welcome to Panama City," said the hangman, his gruff though morbid humor brightened by a day of perfect sunshine. Clad only in coarse cotton breeches and well-worn black boots, the Spanish executioner was a burly fellow, with hairy shoulders and long arms, his legs slightly bowed. The black hood he wore did little to conceal his features. The man's thick lips, bulbous nose, and close-set eyes were clearly visible through the ragged openings in the cloth.

Henry Morgan looked around at the crowd of people who had come to watch him die. His first day in the city promised to be a short one, unless Don Alonso had once more ordered the rope to be only loosely secured. Was this a ruse or the real execution? He steeled himself for the inevitable discovery. It was hard for Morgan to feel confident with a rope around his neck; still, he doubted the governor would wish to be rid of him so easily.

Morgan searched the upturned faces in the compound for Elena Maria. Then he lifted his eyes to the haciendas atop the rolling hills that defined the northernmost reaches of the city. Was she there on a balcony, watching from a distance, afraid to meet his accusing stare, to see what her betrayal had wrought? The question remained—what part was she playing? Her passion for him had been real. He could have loved her. But she had taken his emotions and used them against him; he had made it easy for her. Nell Jolly had warned him. Lord, but he hated it when Toto was right. He wondered how Elena Maria had revealed his plans to Purselley and Don Alonso without incriminating herself. Anything was possible with her.

She had played him like that damn harp. And though it galled him, he had to stand somewhat in awe of her mercurial affections, a caress in one hand and a dagger in the other. What did the señorita have in store for the governor, a man that she was being compelled to marry though it was against her own wishes? Here was a man she did not love and who would, by right of marriage, receive control of all her father's wealth. *I may be getting off lightly.* Morgan winced as the hemp noose chafed his flesh. *Then again, maybe not.*

"Make your peace, señor," the executioner whispered.

From the scaffold, Henry Morgan could see beyond the barracks walls. He had a surprisingly clear view of Castillo del Oro. The City of Gold.

The crowd thought he was praying. Morgan looked to the

sparkling blue bay and the spacious waterfront with its warehouses and guarded vaults. It was common knowledge among the Brethren that through this port passed the plunder of the world: gold ingots and bars of silver stolen from the mines of Mexico and throughout South America; pearls and silks, jewels and dyes and rare woods from the Orient and East Indies; and from the local plantations along the coast, sugar, tobacco, coffee, and cacao, all of it stored and awaiting transport across the isthmus for the yearly departure of the treasure fleet bound for Spain.

A forest of masts and sails crowded the harbor, merchant ships from Portugal and Holland, Spain and Genoa and Morocco, bringing in goods and slaves from along the coast and across the vast ocean. No force of freebooters on earth could challenge the might of a Spanish Gold Fleet with its escort of Spanish frigates and brigs. But here in the vaults and warehouses of Panama, the fortune of a lifetime waited. Emeralds and rubies and delicately carved jade had a siren call all their own.

Henry Morgan, standing on the gallows, on the brink of death, inhaled the warm fragrant air and smelled . . . treasure. And his mind was filled with possibilities. He had not been born to die at the hands of a Spanish executioner or dance a fatal jig at the end of a hangman's rope. Morgan was determined to live.

Then the hangman tugged on the latch. The gallows trapdoor fell open and Morgan dropped through the opening beneath his feet. He saw the patch of dirt race toward him. He experienced a momentary rush, a brutal tensing of his muscles as he awaited the tightening of the noose, a flash of pain to be followed by the pop of his neck, one last breath, then strangling, his limbs numb, legs kicking.

But the rope, as aboard the *Santa Rosa*, had not been secured. Morgan plummeted through the gallows floor and landed on the hard-packed earth beneath. His knees buckled on impact and he rolled onto his back and lay there in a patch of sunlight, looking up into a painfully bright blue sky.

It was noon and the bells of *Santa Maria* began to toll the hour. The invocation from one belfry was quickly taken up by the bells of San Francisco Cathedral on Bolivar Plaza and Las Mercedes, joined by those of Cathedral de Santa Ana and San Domingo and San Felipe. The pealing of the bells drifted across the city where more than fifteen hundred residences—from fine estates built of brick and stone, to thatched-roof *jacals* with mud floors—covered a stretch of rolling hills and grasslands nestled between mangrove swamps, and farther inland, impenetrable jungle.

The city formed a crescent overlooking the bay of Panama, a place of sheltered harbors protected by walled battlements and island forts. The governor's hacienda and the military barracks dominated the north side of the city. It was here in the Plaza de los Armas that prisoners were brought for public execution.

The presence of Henry Morgan had ensured a good crowd this day. But the men, women, and children who made up the onlookers had not been informed of the governor's ruse. A collective gasp had risen from the throng when the trapdoor had sprung open, dropping the pirate to the ground below. For a brief moment, the crowd had thought Morgan's head had been severed by the weight of his body against the resistance of the hangman's rope—such grisly occurrences were not unheard-of. Then the people in the plaza realized the rope itself had slipped from the crossbeam and lay coiled on the pirate sprawled beneath the scaffold.

The soldiers surrounding the gallows had a merry laugh at Morgan's expense. They appreciated the show. Don Alonso, in all his finery, dressed in a scarlet coat and white breeches and gold-buckled shoes, swaggered forward, acknowledging the applause of his compatriots. The governor had made a good impression.

Don Alonso issued an order and a pair of burly soldiers scrambled under the gallows and dragged Morgan back into the daylight. The Plaza de los Armas outside the main barracks in the heart of the city was crowded with soldiers and civilians alike. They had turned out to see the dreaded Captain Morgan, *el Tigre del Caribe*. Here was the persecutor of the Church, the widowmaker, the despoiler of cities. Here was Morgan, the prisoner, the former slave returned to the servitude from which he had escaped so many years ago. Slaves did not need leg irons, nor even shackles. There was no place to run. The city was ringed by a wall and beyond the wall was the sea on one side, the treacherous swamp and the Darien jungle on the other, where war parties of the hated Kuna waited to kill and mutilate the unwary intruder.

"Not today," said the governor, stroking his close-cropped beard. "But one day perhaps. First, however, I will see you broken, the great Henry Morgan humbled, a slave laboring once more for the glory of Spain. You shall load our ships, you shall haul and sweat in the warehouses and on the docks. The treasures of an empire you will bear upon your back, and you will do this until you die."

He reached up and tightened the noose until the rough hemp rope cut into his neck, until Morgan's breath came in ragged gasps. It appeared the governor intended to strangle him here and now, despite his flowery threats. Then Don Alonso released his hold and loosened the knot, dragged the noose over the man's head, and dropped the rope in the dirt at his feet. "Now, what do you have to say to that?"

"You had better kill me now," Morgan hoarsely replied, struggling to maintain his balance.

"Of course," said Don Alonso. "Elena Maria said you would prefer death. It was she who convinced me that slavery was crueler than death. No, I shall not help you escape your fate. Better to see you bend to the lash, to work and strain, to be humbled before all the people of Panama. She was right. That is the fate you dread more than the gallows itself."

Henry Morgan grinned. His eyes were red-rimmed, his once fine clothes were ragged remnants of his former glory. His scraggly beard and hair were matted with dirt and his neck was chafed raw from the mock hanging he had endured aboard the *Santa Rosa*. But he laughed. And the soft sound of his voice sent a chill up the spines of his enemies. Citizen and soldier alike, both men and women, heard that voice on the warm wind and shuddered. It was like something unnatural, fearfully strong, as if fate had reversed itself and the people in the plaza were at Morgan's mercy.

"Take him to the stockade!" Don Alonso exclaimed gruffly, breaking the freebooter's hold on the crowd. Half a dozen dragoons rushed forward and surrounded the buccaneer and dragged him off toward the slave compounds down near the waterfront. It seemed the rabble issued a communal sigh of relief once *el Tigre* had been led off to his cage.

16. "Can anyone deny you?"

Night and shadows and rain upon the shuttered windows, rain leaked in through gaps in the roof, rain blown in through the broken windows and doorless facade of the warehouse, left puddles and rivulets on the floor of the warehouse where nearly a hundred raggedy men sprawled on pallets of straw. The downpour had driven all the prisoners inside from the adjoining compound. Upon the hard clay floors they'd built fires and arranged themselves for another evening of fitful sleep. The air within this makeshift prison was thick with the stench of sweat and dirt, of woodsmoke, and the fear of desperate men for whom imprisonment was a living hell.

The sights and smells opened an old wound in Morgan's psyche. Years of plunder and piracy had failed to exorcise the demons of his youth, purge the memories of a night long ago when his world had come to an end—the night when the Spanish raiders came and attacked his Welsh village and carried him off into captivity.

He struggled in his sleep, warred with the shadows of evil on this restless night in Panama City. It was difficult to rest while bruised and lost in the confines of Panama City, with the press of the bodies around him, where hopelessness permeated every grunt and groan. Despite his every wish to the contrary, an old nightmare was reborn.

*   *   *

He is running for his life, his lungs burn from the effort, he is running to warn his parents and the rest of the village that a ship flying the colors of Spain has anchored just offshore, and several longboats are unloading well-armed raiding parties on the coast of Wales. Morgan's village, in the moonlight, is just ahead; in his dream he can see his father's tavern. But the harder he tries to reach the door, the more the image drifts beyond the reach of his fingertips, receding beyond his grasp. He tries to shout a warning but his voice is little more than a whisper. Then the tavern bursts into flames, and the night reverberates with gunshots and the cries of the raiders, the clash of swords, someone knocks him to the ground and the last thing he hears is the splintering of timbers and the roar of the flames. He'll awaken in the hold of a prison ship to find his world has ended. But all this happened long ago. Things are different now.

Aren't they?

A few days had passed since his mock execution before the populace of the city, time passed in a hot blur of hard labor and harsh treatment. The Spanish guards had no use for slackers, and zealously applied the whip and gun butt to each and every unfortunate soul who paused in his labors or dallied too long by the water trough. Morgan escaped the worst of it; he kept his head down, avoided eye contact, and dutifully did as he was told.

Beans and rice were the staples of life, with a chunk of gristly meat thrown in for good measure. The slaves on the waterfront worked from dawn to dusk, ferrying the cargo from the piers to the warehouses. Filing through the city streets, they passed unnoticed among the good people of Panama City, who considered these unfortunate wretches nothing more than beasts of burden or worse, mere vermin to be put to use if possible, or shipped off to the inland mines.

In the stockade, among the prisoners themselves there was a pecking order, with the city's common criminals having the most power. Drunkards, brawlers, murderers, thieves, and rapists, no matter how heinous their crimes, were loyal subjects of King Carlos at least, and shown favoritism by the guards. Henry Morgan was considered a bloodthirsty brigand akin to the devil himself and was treated accordingly. Likewise, to their captors the Africans were black-skinned heathens capable of being trained to perform the most menial of tasks. Not even the good padres came to visit. The rebellious Kuna Indians fared even worse.

During the trek from Portobello, the captive natives were continually threatened and struck with riding crops and makeshift switches. The implacable warriors of the jungle were regarded as savage brutes, responsible for the deaths and maiming of many a Spanish wayfarer crossing the isthmus. From what Morgan could gather, the plantations were always under harassment by the natives. No one was ever truly safe. Overseers and slaves were found dead in the fields. Family members had been carried off by war parties who emerged from the jungle, struck quickly, and disappeared back into the rain forest. Occasionally, a military patrol ventured into the mangrove swamps east of Panama City; some never returned.

Morgan began to gain a healthy respect for the Kuna. Despite Spain's overwhelming military presence, these inscrutable redskinned devils refused to be conquered, and continued to defy those who had stolen their lands and driven them into the deadly wilds of the Panamanian jungle. The buccaneer felt a kinship for anyone who hated the Spanish as much as he did. As far as Henry Morgan was concerned, the heathen rascals couldn't be all bad.

"Henry . . ."

"Let me rest, Father. Or send me dreams of roast suckling pig, fry bread, and a tankard of bay rum."

"Rest can wait. You'll have eternal sleep if you aren't careful. You'll leave your bones here."

"No. I shall find a way to escape. Though it will gall me to leave empty-handed."

"Gold, you've seen it?"

"The ransom of kings. I've borne it on my back. Silks and gold ingots, jars of spices and chests of jewels and jade."

"Blood ransom," cautioned the ghost. *"Blood ransom."*

"The best kind," Morgan muttered in his sleep.

"Henry!"

The voice reverberated in his skull. Morgan bolted awake. Perspiration trickled down his cheeks. His brown hair was slick and wet with sweat. He lay in the dark corner of the warehouse, removed from the mass of prisoners, his back to the wall and near a barred doorway.

The hour was late. The rain droned on, masking the snores of the men scattered about the lower reaches of the great room. Something had awakened him, and not just the ghost of his father. His senses reached out; instincts that his years as a privateer had honed razor-sharp gave him an edge over most ordinary men. He waited and watched, and in the distance the thunder rolled out of the sodden sky and rippled across the city, a faint wind haunted the narrow streets and alleys and made a welcome entry through the barred entrance. Beyond a row of shops and seashore cottages with red clay tile roofs, the streets of the waterfront were tantalizingly close.

Someone splashed through a mud puddle, an unwary step that gave them away. Morgan eased over on his side, peered through a larger open entrance and spied a pair of sentries walking abreast, crossing the compound through the slanted downpour. But the soldiers weren't the menace. Morgan shifted his position, turned on his side and froze. A number of prisoners, he counted five, had risen from their crude beds across the room and begun to warily pick their way among the slaves. From what he could tell, they looked to be a dangerous pack in the faint light; he caught a glimpse of makeshift clubs and the gleam of broken bottles.

Morgan glanced around, prepared to attract the attention of the guards, only to see the gate to the compound slowly shut behind the sentries as they entered their quarters. Nothing good was going to come of this. He returned his attention to the five men. Were they coming for him? If this was another of Don Alonso's little torments, Morgan figured he'd find out the painful truth soon enough.

Three of the men were of average height and wore coarse cotton shirts and ragged knee-breeches, their hair plastered to their heads, eyes ablaze in the shimmering glare of sheet lightning that filtered in from the prison yard. The other two were men of size, one especially was a big, hulking brute with bearded features who made no effort to conceal his approach.

None of the men wore shackles. Escape was impossible. With the sea on both coasts, the mountain road continually patrolled, and all around the city the unforgiving jungle and swamps infested with serpents and alligators and the warlike Kuna, where would the prisoners escape to?

The Africans watched impassively, their dull faces turning as the Spaniards moved among them. One of the five tripped over a three-legged stool, cursed and kicked it aside, making enough noise to wake the rest of the unfortunates. Being the lone Englishman, and cast among his mortal enemies, Morgan steeled himself for what was to come. He expected no help, and was bold enough to think he didn't need any.

The five Spaniards paused, exchanged glances, muttered among themselves as if they had momentarily become lost, then resumed their progress, attempting to move with caution as men will do when they are about a dark purpose. They quietly reached the midpoint of the room and then altered their course yet again and turned away from Morgan.

If not me, then who? the buccaneer wondered. One of the five provided the answer. The lumbering brute Morgan knew as Tonio gestured toward the last of the Kuna prisoners who had survived the march across the isthmus. The tribesman's companions had been left behind, shot dead along the military road as they attempted to escape. This prisoner alone had been recaptured alive, despite his efforts to join his comrades in death. Imprisonment was the worst punishment imaginable for one who had lived his life free beneath the jungle's canopy of the trees and the stars.

The Kuna warrior opened his eyes. Instinct warned him. His feral gaze swept across the men advancing on him. He snarled as they approached.

Morgan saw the warrior rise to a crouching position, balance on the balls of his feet, muscles poised. He was smaller than Morgan or any of the five Spaniards confronting him. And though slight of build, the warrior looked as tough as whipcord. Still, he was sorely outnumbered: none of the Africans was going to lift a hand to help him; those of his tribe who had suffered capture were either dead or had been dragged off to the mines. One last warrior remained, and like *el Tigre del Caribe*, it was rumored he had a date with the hangman.

"*Sí,* it is him," one of the Spaniards muttered. "I was right. This is Kintana."

The warrior bristled at the sound of his name on the lips of his enemies.

"I am Kintana," he hissed in Spanish. A warrior, yes, but a man without honor because he had been taken alive.

There was a time long ago, before the deaths of his children, when he had vowed to make the Spanish oppressors who had stolen his mountains and forests and sweet flowing streams regret their deeds and tremble at the sound of his name. For two decades he had raided and burned the outlying farms, threatened the plantations, ambushed the patrols sent to apprehend him, and left the severed heads of his enemies at the city gate.

But his foray against Portobello had proved a costly blunder. Kintana and handful of men had survived that raid, to his shame. He almost welcomed the prisoners advancing on him. Death was preferable to the dishonor he felt.

One of the five reached for him. Kintana lunged and darted under the man's grasp, took a knee in the jaw, swung, and was borne back by the press of his attackers and forced against the stone wall. A fist slammed into the side of his jaw and sent a white hot flash of searing pain behind his eyes. He bit a hand, heard a yowl, a broken bottle gouged his thigh, a section of stool cracked his shin then his shoulder blade. Kintana grunted in pain.

Tonio lifted the warrior off the floor by his throat. The smaller man kicked and struggled to break the Spaniard's hold. He drove both feet into Tonio's belly. The big man grinned and tightened his hold on the warrior's throat. Kintana clawed at the viselike grip until he drew blood.

"Bastard," Tonio cursed as his victim continued to struggle. The other four attackers attempted to get in a blow or two.

"Wring his neck," another of the men chuckled.

"Twist his head off," a third called out, and began to mock Kintana by mimicking a chicken. Suddenly the man ceased his taunt, groaned, and dropped to the floor, unconscious. Morgan stepped up and clubbed big Tonio across the back of the neck. The Spaniard shook off the blow.

The other three men turned to meet this new threat. Morgan ignored them and leaped astride Tonio's back and brought his forearm across the Spaniard's throat and closed off the big man's windpipe. Tonio slammed back against the wall, driving the man on his back into the stone. Morgan held on. Tonio clawed over his shoulder, flailed wildly. His friends attempted to drag the man from his back but were sent sprawling as Kintana leaped among them, scattering his attackers. He dodged a broken bottle and, snarling like a panther, fell upon the Spaniard closest to him and slashed him open with a jagged shard of glass. The man howled and retreated, cradling his right forearm..

"Tonio!" the other two called out, unsure of themselves.

But their companion had troubles of his own. The big man, unable to draw a breath, slowly sank to his knees. Morgan, still astride Tonio, used his leverage to drive the Spaniard face-first into the hard floor. The buccaneer rolled free of his opponent and jumped to his feet as Tonio struggled to prop himself up off the floor on his knees and fists.

Morgan kicked the brute in the side of the head. The big man grunted, flopped over onto his side and stayed down.

The two remaining Spaniards called out to their comrades and managed to shame several other men into joining the fray. Half a dozen shadowy figures rose from their blankets and started across the warehouse floor toward Morgan and the Indian. The Spaniards grudgingly trusted in their overwhelming numbers to prevail.

Kintana held his ground, fists opening and closing as he crouched, preparing to spring. He began to chant softly in the language of his people, a tongue that was older than the Spanish empire. Morgan stepped past the Kuna warrior and confronted the prisoners.

"Enough! I am Morgan the pirate. Trim your sails and come about, or prepare for bloodshed, you milk-livered skalawags!"

"We know you English. Stand with the savage. So be it," someone called out. "There are but two of you and many of us."

"Aye. And I have no doubt you will prevail. But I will not go quietly." Morgan paused to allow his words to sink in. Then he continued in a voice most grave. "There will be blood on the moon before you drag me under. How many will I take with me? Four, five . . . ? How many will I blind or cripple? For the rage is coming upon me, and woe to the poor devil who stands in my way. Come, then, you briny dogfish." Morgan advanced on his would-be attackers, a move that startled them. He addressed them calmly, with the detachment of a man who didn't care whether he lived or died. "Come and die for your master's pleasure—them that put us in irons will delight in all our suffering. For in the end, there is no country here, no flag within these walls; we are not enemies, but brothers, bound to one another by our common misery. The choice is yours, mates. Endure together or damn ourselves for the governor's sport."

His words had the desired effect and struck a chord with the men around him. The Spanish prisoners hesitated and began to argue among themselves. They considered the wisdom in what he was saying. No one wished to be the first of Morgan's victims. Who wanted to lose an eye or wind up lame? In the end, the Spaniards did an about-face and shuffled back to their places.

Morgan inwardly sighed in relief. He turned and caught Kintana scrutinizing him, a puzzled expression on the warrior's dark face. The Kuna Indian did not utter a word, but with a detached air slowly swung about and returned to his corner of the room, stepping around Tonio's fallen form.

"No need to thank me," Morgan said with a shrug, and crossed back to his straw pallet. He settled back against the wall and gingerly eased into an upright position. His back was bruised and his shoulder throbbed from where the big man had clawed at him. He sighed and closed his eyes and must have drifted off, because suddenly he was nudged awake by a guard slapping the butt of his musket against the buccaneer's feet.

Morgan reacted with a start. He blinked and took a moment to get his bearings. It was still night, still raining. He couldn't have been asleep much longer than an hour. He looked up into the leveled muskets of a pair of guards and between them, the flat brown features of Major Gilberto Barba, the officer assigned to oversee the prisoners on the docks. Barba was a man of average height, with a massive girth and sloping, powerful shoulders. From what Morgan could tell in the time he had spent on the waterfront, the major was a man who cared only that his charges delivered a hard day's work for their squalid bed and plate of food.

Barba was not a vindictive man, and though his ways were harsh, he tried not to be unfair. What went on within the walls of the abandoned warehouse stockade was none of his concern. Let the animals prey upon themselves, let the strongest survive. Come sunrise, he expected the prisoners to be prepared to work, and work hard.

"*Ven conmigo,*" he said. He tugged a double-barreled pistol from his belt and cocked the weapon. "You will come with me." Morgan saw no reason to argue with the man.

The coach arrived at the rear of a gaily lit two-storied hacienda fronting the Avenida Balboa, on a hillside a few blocks from the governor's palace in the center of the city. The hacienda was ringed with an intricate maze of gardens and narrow covered walkways; the patterns of the rocks underfoot were indistinguishable through the rain and the gloom. Major Barba issued an order in a clipped tone and the driver continued past the hacienda, circled the block and brought the team of horses past a carriage house and stable, through a wide gate, along a drive that wound beneath a grove of willows. The carriage came to a halt near a picturesque stone garden-house just inside the walls of the hacienda.

The major ordered his escort to remain beneath the trees, and brought Morgan up onto the covered porch. The rain kept up a syncopated beat on the red clay tile roof. While the soldiers remained outside, shielded from the elements beneath the draping branches, Barba and Morgan entered the garden house. In the relative quiet of the anteroom Barba motioned for Morgan to continue inside.

"Be warned, señor, do not give me cause. I will not hesitate to kill you." He gestured toward another doorway.

Morgan nodded and continued into the garden house. He entered a warm, well-lit interior, furnished with two comfortable high-backed chairs before a hearth. A large, comfortable-looking four-poster feather bed filled an alcove; another set of ladder-backed chairs had been set before a table groaning beneath platters of baked chicken, a tureen of black-bean soup, and a bottle of Madeira.

Morgan started across the room and headed straight for the table. Something moved out of the corner of his eye, a stranger, keeping abreast of him. He glanced around in alarm before realizing he had seen his reflection in a nearby mirror hung upon the wall and sandwiched between two stained-glass windows depicting a pair of bleak-looking saints with chipped glass eyes upturned toward heaven.

Morgan approached the mirror, confronted his image—bearded, shaggy hair, eyes pouched and deep-set from lack of sleep. He was thinner, but not yet gaunt. The flesh around his neck was ruptured and scarred from the mock executions he had endured. One day Don Alonso would forget his pretense or grow tired of his cruel game and end Morgan's plight.

Morgan heard the rustle of a grown. He glanced across the room and noticed the woman in the chair by the fire. Elena Maria rose from the chair and stood with her back to the hearth. The firelight shining through her "*robe à la Française*," a simple sack dress falling loosely from just below her shoulders to the floor, outlined her body's supple curves. The raindrops made a merry noise, spattering against the windows and pouring from the eaves. Seeing her—illuminated, even radiant—made Morgan feel dirty and almost ashamed to be in the same room. Then he remembered who had helped put him here.

He spun around and stalked across the room. Elena gasped at the unexpected suddenness of his advance, and tried to retreat but found herself between the hearth and the pirate—a painful burn or a broken neck. She was about to call out to the major when Morgan altered his course and stopped at the table. He began to gorge himself on the food, ripping off chunks of chicken, treating tureen as his own private soup bowl, using the ladle for a spoon. He made no apology for his lack of manners though he did pause a moment to offer the ladle to the lady. She declined. He shrugged and dug into his meal.

"Gilberto Barba is an old family friend. His loyalty has always been first and foremost to my father and to me and the house of Saucedo. I can count on his discretion."

"He won't save you."

"What do you mean?"

"The fat major won't keep me from snapping your neck," Morgan told her. "But, first things first." He poured a tankard of Madeira, passing the cup below his nostrils and inhaling the bouquet. Then he swilled it down, spilling a trickle out of the corner of his mouth and wiping his face with his forearm.

"This is how you would repay me for saving your life?" she asked, nervously eyeing the door. Perhaps she had overestimated her beauty and the power of the passion they had shared.

"For betraying me into Don Alonso's 'care'?"

"Let's not dwell on the past," she purred. "I shall help you to escape."

Morgan looked up at her, tossed a well-gnawed chicken quarter aside, wiped his hands on his filthy shirt and crossed around the table to stand before the woman at the hearth. She smelled of rosewater, her lustrous black hair spilled over her bare shoulders. He reached up and brushed the tresses away from the swell of her breasts, her soft flesh barely concealed beneath a cream-colored silk bodice. Then his hands closed round her throat. She did not cry out. He pulled her to him, crushed her lips with his in a bruising kiss. Then he released her. She staggered back a step, wrinkling her nose at his sodden stench, her shoulders bruised by his rough embrace.

He laughed at her discomfort. "One gets used to the smell," he said, "the perfume of slavery." He returned to the table. No matter what, Morgan intended to leave this room with a full belly. He tore another roasted hen in half. "So, now you will save me, eh?"

"Yes. And all I ask in return is one small favor."

"Very well, my lady, and what must I do for you in return?"

"Kill the governor."

Morgan's eyes widened. "Your husband?"

"Not yet. But soon. We will be married a week from today in the Cathedral de Santa Maria. That night, Major Barba will bring you to this garden house. He will provide you with weapons, a uniform, everything you need." Elena Maria sat in the chair before the fire and focused on the dancing flames, a miniature vision of hell. All that was needed were the poor souls in torment.

She had suffered enough—the loss of her father, a marriage of convenience to establish her ties to the Spanish court—but she would not lose her birthright to any man. "Don Alonso wishes to return to my father's house on our wedding night. Gilberto will bring you to the rear entrance. I will bring Don Alonso to the garden house when we arrive. I shall remind him of the bed and my desire to consummate our union apart from the house and the servants. He will be anxious to please me. Wait for us here. And kill him when he enters."

"With gun or knife?"

"With whatever it takes—both, if you must. No doubt he will be unarmed. I can see to that. You can count on me."

"Of that I am certain. And then what? There will be patrols searching for me once he is discovered."

"Most of the troops are garrisoned in the forts. By the time they have been brought over to the city you will be beyond their grasp. Gilberto will take you to the waterfront and place you aboard the *Castille*, a bark that I shall dispatch to the Caribbean. It will sail with the dawn wind. I will personally guarantee your safe passage around the cape to Jamaica. I won't raise an alarm until the *Castille* has sailed. You see, we can both have our freedom."

"You will be Doña Elena Maria de Saucedo del Alonso, a woman of wealth and title," Morgan remarked coolly.

"A woman blessed with independence. A rare thing in a world that favors men."

"And yet, for all your struggles, I don't think you will ever be free. To steal the wind, to call the thunder, to stand before the breaking dawn and watch the sun rise golden over the edge of the world like the eye of God Almighty and know you can go anywhere and be anything you wish, if only you have the courage to dare the devil."

"Will you do it?" Elena Maria squirmed impatiently. "One day the governor will grow weary of his sport and the noose will tighten around your neck for the last time."

"You planned this. From that first night in Maracaibo. You played us all like cards and charted my course to this very moment."

"Will you kill my husband?" she repeated.

"Yes."

Elena Maria appeared visibly relieved. "You must remain with the prisoners. But the major assures me you will not be mistreated. And there will be extra food. I do not want you to become weak or infirm."

"You are most kind." Morgan quietly watched her, noticing how the firelight flickered and danced upon her sultry countenance, concealing her face in patterns of shadow and light. Even now, Elena stirred him; knowing she was poison, he was still tempted. They stared at one another in uncomfortable silence—they might have been two people who had woke from a night of passion to find themselves standing on opposite shores, surprised to discover an ocean lay between them.

Elena Maria called out, "Gilberto." The rotund officer immediately entered the room. He frowned at Morgan's proximity to Doña Elena. But she did not seem any worse off. Barba grudgingly appraised Morgan, the officer absentmindedly twirling the tips of the thick moustache covering his upper lip. The buccaneer had lost some weight, but his gray eyes were clear and bold, and there remained an aura of danger. "Return Señor Morgan to the compound," the woman said.

Morgan, on hearing his name, shoved another half of chicken inside his shirt and started toward the door. On impulse, he altered his course, brushed past the major, made his way to the woman's side, moved in close, leaned over the chair and whispered in her ear.

"Once I could have loved you, señorita."

"Love?" She responded to him, despite his unkempt features. There was something wild and animalistic and dangerous that drew her to him. Unfortunately, now was hardly the time or place. He would need a bath first, a change of clothes, but even then, she had a greater need for his more-lethal talents then she did for lust. Alas, and alas. "And now, Señor?"

"Now I think you will give the governor a wedding night he will remember till the day he he dies." He straightened, winked at the major, who gruffly escorted him from the room and out into the rain. Leaving his prisoner in the coach under guard, Barba hurried back inside. Alone with the daughter of his oldest and most trusted friend, the major could not prevail against his curiosity.

"Well, Señorita?" he said.

"He will do as I ask."

"Ah, can anyone deny you, Elena Maria?"

"Not for long." The señorita's coquettish smile warmed the major's heart as she made her way to his side and kissed him on the cheek. Gilberto turned red from his neck to his scalp. "It is an injustice that you should be relieved of your post as commandante and placed in charge of prisoners, simply because Don Alonso wishes to appoint his own man to that post. My father never would have allowed it."

"Don Alonso is the governor. He can do as he wishes," Barba grumbled.

"Not for long. Señor Morgan will see to that."

"And what then, after Morgan has struck?"

Elena Maria touched a finger to her lips, her brow furrowed as she pondered the situation. "I think my husband's murderer ought to die while trying to escape. And you shall be the heroic officer responsible. What say you, old friend?"

"It is only justice," the major replied. "A man should answer for his crimes."

Barba returned his prisoner to a side gate, a small opening in the compound wall barely large enough for a man to slip through. Morgan hesitated in the rain as Barba reached out and touched his arm. The rain had stopped, though the air was heavy with moisture. Barab took no chances but kept the double-barreled pistol trained on the buccaneer.

"There is nothing I would not do for the señorita," the major told him. "I watched her grow from infancy to the beautiful woman she has become."

Morgan started to make a comment about what he considered to be Elena's somewhat tarnished soul, but decided to keep his opinions to himself. After all, Morgan knew what it meant to be desperate. In a way, he could not blame her. What was a woman to do but use the only weapons at her command?

"On the day of Doña Elena's wedding, every bell in every tower throughout the city will proclaim the marriage. There will be a great fiesta to honor the governor and his new bride."

"I should like to attend."

The major ignored the buccaneer's remarks. "When you hear the bells and night falls, make your way to this gate and wait for me. I will come for you. Take care you do not alert the other slaves."

"Be prompt," Morgan said. "I hate to be late to a party." He swung about and continued on through the gate, skirting a deep puddle of muddy water. Two musketeers materialized out of the night, and unbarred and then bolted the wrought-iron door as Morgan recentered the compound. Barba leaned out of the coach. Droplets glisten along the trim of his tricorn hat as he silently studied the man in the arched little entranceway. Then Morgan surreptitiously waved and vanished from sight.

"You'll have your freedom," Barba muttered, easing his backside onto the bench seat and closing the door. He tapped on the ceiling

and the driver touched his whip to his team of matched sorrel geld-
ings. The coach sped away from the warehouse and prison compound
with such a quick burst of speed, the major was thrown back against
the seat. He cursed and held on for a rough ride.

Morgan ambled across the empty prison yard and returned to his
meager straw pallet, where he stretched out and tried to digest all that
had happened. Unable to rest, he propped himself against the wall
and listened to the sounds of the snoring men. He wished he could
sleep but his mind was racing.

Elena Maria plagued his thoughts—the smell of her hair, the taste
of her lips. Then he grinned; the food wasn't bad, either. Suddenly
Morgan realized he was being watched. He searched the shadows;
sheet lightning shimmered, reflecting a cold blue light in the warrior's
eyes. Kintana stood and stalked over to the buccaneer, then squatted
as if by a campfire.

"Who are you? Why did you stand with me, Anglais?"

"Because you were outnumbered. They might have killed you."

"We are both dead men, you and I. What does it matter when or
where? You should have stayed out of it. When the rope closes off my
neck, my spirit will not be able to escape. Fool Anglais. I would have
chosen to die in battle."

"But would you choose not to die at all?"

"What are you saying?" Kintana's eyes were like coals smoldering
beneath the ashes of a spent fire.

"I have an idea that just may save both our lives. Or get us killed.
But then, why worry? Like you said, amigo. We are dead already."

17. And Morgan, her beloved.

"*Gloria Patri, et Filio, et Spiritui Sancto.*
"*Sicut erat in principio, et nunc, et semper, et in
sæcula sæculorum. Amen.*"

By the decree of el gobernador, all prisoners and slaves were allowed a day of rest in honor of the governor's marriage. For the past week, Panama City had prepared for a wonderful celebration. Don Alonso let it be known he wished one and all to share in his happiness. A great fiesta had been planned. Streets were festooned with lanterns and ribbons. Smokehouses were raided and supplies of smoked ham and sausage and *cabrito* were confiscated; kitchens were put to good use and the cooks within saddled with countless demands for pies and custards and breads, and immense iron pots of stews.

On the morning of the wedding, while the governor and the nobles crowded the Cathedral de Santa Maria, a mass execution of chickens was under way to provide platters of roasted hens for the afternoon feasting. Planters and their families had drifted in from outlying farms and mining estates to partake in the festivities, curry the favor of the new governor, and to laud the wedding of Elena Maria de Saucedo.

"*Otende nobis, Domine, misericordiam tuam.*
"*Et salutare tuum da nobis.*

"Domine, exaudi orationem meam.
"Et clamor meus ad to veniat."

The celebrant, Father Estéban Pinzón, sneaked a surreptitious peek at the bowed heads of the congregation that filled the Cathedral de Santa Maria. He was the shepherd and they were his flock, the bright and beautiful, these families of wealth and station, *criollos*, citizens of the New World who a lifetime ago came with their slaves and their empty ships, to claim the land, dig the hills and mountains, reap fortunes, and found dynasties on the backs of the native tribes.

Father Estéban knew it was the plunder of a dozen kingdoms— gold, silver, rare woods, coffee, and cacao—that built Panama City. But the lure of wealth also brought the message of Christianity and salvation to the heathens, and saving souls for Christ was a good thing. So the priest had chosen not to concern himself with the necessary evils of civilization, trusting in God to understand. Father Estéban genuflected at the foot of the alter and continued to recite the order of the liturgy. His acolytes turned toward the white-haired priest, whose craggy features and blazing eyes were to the populace the very image of the Divine, and responded.

"Introibo ad altare Dei.
"Ad Deum qui laetificat juventutem meam."

The words were far older than the fabled city, protected by its walls and a bay bristling with redoubts and breastworks and enough cannons to sink any pirate fleet foolish enough to enter the bay. Don Alonso, kneeling at the bottom of the steps below the altar, was top-heavy for all the medals attached to the front of his coat. His silver-streaked hair was hidden beneath a periwig, a bead of sweat escaped from his scalp and stung his brown eyes, he blinked and tried to will away the discomfort. His coat was too tight. Now was not the time or place to fidget. He had to think of something else to take his mind off the perspiration and the oppressive heat.

The records in the library!

Don Alonso had spent many an afternoon poring over the ledgers and accounting books, detailing the enormity of wealth that was about to come under his direction. Before the week was out and the marriage bed grew cold, he intended to begin drafting instructions transferring significant portions of the gold and silver into his family's coffers. For too long, Don Alonso had watched his own father depend on the kindness of the court of King Carlos. Things were going to change after today. His father's house would be financially restored.

Don Alonso glanced aside at the señorita kneeling beside him. He had never seen a woman look so radiant and desirable; she was the epitome of grace and beauty in her lace dress and shell comb and a mantilla of white silk to cover the wealth of her black tresses that the half-breed, Consuelo, had taken all morning to arrange. At least Old Witch-Eye was good for something.

Hurry up, priest! Look at my bride. Was there ever a man so fortunate? She filled his eyes. His heart beat wildly with renewed passion for this woman. What more could he ask for . . . a woman of beauty, wealth, with the voice of an angel.

"Adjutorum nostrum in nomine domini.
"Qui fecit cælum at terram."

Elena Maria pretended to pray and plotted the governor's death. The Lord had always helped those who made the most of the opportunities presented to them. That's all she was doing, securing the house of Saucedo and all that was rightfully hers. She looked at him and smiled. Every night he had been at her hacienda, forsaking the governor's estate and the duties of his office. Responsibility would come if he were given the chance. But Elena Maria didn't have the time. She was not about to dally and see her birthright looted just so Don Alonso could return his own family to prosperity.

The children were singing, their melodic, high sweet voices floating above the distinguished gathering. They sounded like cherubs. It was like listening to sunlight, as if the glory of the morning and the warmth of the summer sun could be put into words and sung.

Her father had made many friends throughout his life and they had all come to wish her well and share her joy. Come the morrow and they'd be offering condolences. First she must endure the liturgy, then the binding of the marriage covenant; next, the fiesta, and an afternoon spent traveling throughout the city to be received by the populace. The celebration would last throughout the afternoon, but come nightfall Don Alonso had already promised to have his carriage whisk them away and back to the house of Saucedo. The governor's own estate was not as large or ostentatious. Don Alonso had already informed her the house of Saucedo would do nicely for their wedding night.

Elena Maria vowed the consummation of this marriage would never happen. She had seen to that. She glanced aside at the governor, his gold-embroidered tunic taut across his belly. Sweat glistened in his beard, trickled along his cheek and neck.

Suddenly she realized the priest had addressed her. What? She was supposed to respond. But what had he said? Father Estéban was staring at her.

"Amen," she meekly tried. No one else had heard her. But her reply was obviously wrong, judging by the look on Father Estéban's face. He frowned and continued to recite the liturgy. She looked ahead to what was to come, the consecration and Eucharist and the solemn blessing of their union. And afterward a cage of doves would be set free to signal to the city that the ritual was concluded.

Then let the music begin, send the strolling troubadours along the boulevards. The mercado *shall be given over to the musicians and the dancers and of course, the bride and groom. And elsewhere in the city, as night approaches, she would direct Major Gilberto Barba to pay a clandestine visit to the prison compound down by the waterfront and set the final act of this drama into motion.*

The children began to sing anew, shattering her fantasy, and returning her to the solemn invocation of the Holy Liturgy. And now there was incense. The fumes wafted above the heads of the bride and groom, drifted over the congregation in the cathedral, to gather in thick sooty strands, binding the ankles of the carved saints.

The bride could feel her old nurse watching her with disapproval. *My dear Consuelo, rest, easy. Be assured. All is well.* Elena Maria vowed she would endure the day. Come tonight, when Don Alonso came to her bed, roused and eager for a romp, he'd get more than he bargained for.

Martyrdom.

And Morgan, her beloved. Now, this was a bitter pill, for she really did care for him. His death would lie heavy on her heart—and be her cross to bravely bear.

"Kyrie eleison. Christe eleison. Kyrie eleison."

"Lord have mercy."

"Christ have mercy."

"Lord have mercy."

18. Acts born of desperation and greed.

Major Gilberto Barba made his way along the limestone wall of the slave compound, keeping to the shadows, pausing every few paces to search his obscured surroundings. If he hadn't lived in Panama City for most of his life, he would have been hopelessly lost. Barba was grateful for the fog that had rolled in from the bay during the night, blanketing the city in a ghostly gray shroud.

Although it failed to dampen the celebration, the mist served to drive the festivities inside. The grounds and ballroom of the governor's estate, as well as the taverns and crib houses near the waterfront, were crowded with men and women whose saturnalian excess was a match for any Roman bacchanal.

Earlier in the day, at the conclusion of the marriage rites, church bells had pealed throughout the city and continued unabated until sundown out of deference to the new governor. His marriage to Doña Elena Maria, Panama City's favored daughter, was the catalyst for a fete that promised to last from dusk till dawn.

Gilberto Barba thought of himself as an honorable man and yet this night had he had agreed to commit murder. Call it retribution. Don Bernardo de Saucedo, Elena's father, had been his friend and benefactor. Years ago, with Don Bernardo's blessing, Gilberto had assumed command of Panama City's entire garrison. His had been a position of power and responsibility.

The new governor, Don Alonso del Campo, had changed all that.

Barba scowled, finding in his anger the fuel to hold his course. He had been relegated to being little more than a glorified overseer by Don Alonso. This would not stand. Barba had served too long and too well to be shunted aside, cast off like an unwanted barnacle.

He paused to check his bearings, took a moment to catch his breath. This damp air was taking its toll on him. His chest was tight and he was struggling to breathe. He heard the trudge of bootheels as a pair of sentries made their rounds, patrolling the perimeter of the warehouse and compound that housed a volatile assortment of slaves and prisoners assigned to labor on the waterfront.

What if they discovered him, crouching in the shadows? Gilberto struggled to swallow, his throat was suddenly dry as a brick. He held his breath, heard the familiar murmur of a trio of men in conversation; voices he recognized were complaining about not being allowed to participate in the fiesta. However, the two men were going to be relieved from their post as soon as they returned to the guardhouse from their excursion around the block. There was still time for them to partake in the governor's good fortune and drown themselves in rivers of rum.

The footsteps halted momentarily and Gilberto overheard the sentries discussing the carriage and gelding he had left tethered to a post near an apothecary shop. But the hour was late and the men were tired. The waterfront was a lonely place to be with only the lapping of the waves against the piers and the creak of anchored vessels for company. Where was the man who would not prefer the gaily-lit fleshpots, the songs and bawdy laughter and the music of the strolling troubadours, to guarding a couple hundred slaves and prisoners?

The sounds of celebration that drifted on the mist-blanketed night kept their queries brief, and in the end led the soldiers off into the fog to finish their patrol without incident and return to the comforts of their post: a cheery blaze, a well-lit room, a jug of rum, and the easy camaraderie of friends.

That a slave might escape was of little concern to the patrol. Pity the poor miscreant who attempted an escape. The sea blocked one route, the well-patrolled mountain road held little chance for success, and the swamp and jungle-choked lowlands where the Kuna headhunters prowled provided a deadly deterrent.

Barba breathed a sigh of relief, listening to the sound of the receding footsteps. He did not relish a confrontation with the sentries, nor would it do for them to connect his presence with Morgan's impending escape from the compound. The major grinned, considering

Elena Maria's elaborate scheme. Her father would have been proud. The old Don had not achieved his wealth by being a choirboy. He had fought and clawed his way to power over the backs of his enemies. He had been born with a sense of his own righteous destiny, was unflaggingly loyal to his friends, and up until his death was determined to hold on to every gain.

Gilberto recognized much of the old Don in Elena Maria. They were two sides of the same coin. Like her father, the daughter was manipulative, clever as a fox, and utterly ruthless—any man worth the red blood flowing in his veins was at her mercy, including the notorious Henry Morgan. The buccaneer was going to prove useful indeed, far more so than he would have been, dangling from the gallows in the plaza.

With the new governor out of the way, rank and power would be Barba's again, of that the major was certain, especially after he apprehended and killed the notorious *Tigre del Caribe*, avenging the pirate's despicable murder of Don Alonso on his wedding night. There had been a time when a man like Gilberto Barba would have balked at the notion of what he was about to do for Doña Elena. But ambition has a way of changing some men. Acts born of desperation and greed become palatable.

Gilberto reached the bolted iron door that permitted entrance to the walled yard outside the warehouse that served as shelter for the imprisoned. Barba pressed his cheek against the iron panel and listened, heard nothing, took his pistol and tapped the twin gun barrels against the door. His three short taps were answered in kind.

Barba glanced around, a useless gesture, as the fog had thickened to the point that it concealed most of the street. The air was heavy with the smell of algae and rotting vegetation carried ashore and deposited by the tides. The palms of his hands were moist, his mouth was dry. *You'd think it would be the other way around.*

The Spaniard leaned into the bolt. He gritted his teeth, doubled his efforts. The rusted metal slowly gave in under pressure, iron groaned, then the bolt began to slide back. Gilberto finished with the first bolt and started on the second, which was even more rusted than the first: the going wasn't any easier. He was thankful for the elements that cloaked the streets in the forgetful fog that seemed to absorb noise.

With the second bolt clear, the major thumbed back both hammers on his double-barreled flintlock, leaned his broad shoulder and well-padded physique into the door. The hinges protested every inch as it swung open.

Morgan slipped through.

"Be quick, I have a—"

Gilberto never finished his sentence. Morgan's fist caught him flush in the throat. The officer sank to his knees, gasping for breath. The buccaneer snatched the pistol from the major's hand and tapped the man across the skull with the gun butt. Gilberto moaned and curled over on his side.

Morgan helped himself to the rest of Gilberto's weapons, a second double-barreled gun and a small-bore *miqulet* pistol the major had tucked away inside his coat pocket. Morgan glanced over his shoulder as Kintana emerged from the prison yard. The Kuna native warily checked his surroundings, his flat features vaguely discernible in the mist. His nostrils flared. He looked at Morgan, still uncertain whether the buccaneer was a friend or just some new kind of enemy. Years of persecution and warfare had taught him to regard all white men with suspicion.

Kintana noted the pistol in Morgan's hand and the others he had tucked in his belt. The buccaneer offered one of his weapons to the warrior. Kintana knelt by the unconscious major and removed a bayonet from man's belt, leaving the leather scabbard behind. The Kuna straightened, his primal senses searching through the gloom. He silently appraised the direction of the breeze, then with a nod in Morgan's direction, turned and loped off into the murky night.

"Be careful, Anglais," drifted back through the gloom.

Morgan shrugged, closed the side door to the prison yard and bolted it shut before the other prisoners discovered it and a citywide alarm was raised. He managed to half drag, half carry the major's rotund frame back to his carriage, where he deposited the unconscious figure on the seat. Morgan discovered a change of clothes and a blunderbuss and a particularly nasty-looking hatchet.

Elena Maria had wanted to be certain Morgan had the tools to dispatch the governor. A mirthless smile split the buccaneer's haggard countenance. Capture and imprisonment had taken a lot out of him, sapped his reserve of strength. But he could still think, still reason, still observe. While laboring on the waterfront he had become acutely aware of the many ships anchored in the harbor, including those belonging to Elena Maria, none of which was in any condition to sail. He had enough sense left to read a trap when one was set for him, and just enough strength to effect his escape. Retribution would have to wait.

But he could just imagine the look on Elena's face . . .

* * *

Don Alonso and his new bride left the governor's estate with the cries of well-wishers ringing in their ears. Elena Maria's husband helped her into the carriage and pointed the gelding away from the fortresslike "governor's palace" and the lingering line of merchants and mine-owners and planters, whose names the new governor could hardly recall.

"A wonderful idea, *mi amor*," said Don Alonso, flicking the reins with his right hand, and with his left, unbuttoning the green-and-white tunic he had worn for the wedding ceremony. The heavy woolen material was weighted down with row after row of medals reflecting the light from the lanterns hung on either side of the carriage. He sighed as each brass button came undone, permitting his growing paunch to expand. "The governor's palace is a poor cousin to the house your father built. We shall live there until the palace is made suitable for us. I'll have a work detail adding rooms and several gardens."

Elena Maria looked demurely at him, playing the part of a nervous young bride as the carriage clattered down the Via España and turned onto the Via Mercado and on to the Avenida Balboa. Elena tried to listen and react to what her husband was saying, but her thoughts raced ahead to what they might find in the garden house. Major Barba had been dispatched hours earlier. Gilberto would have had ample time to free Morgan and prepare a proper reception for the governor.

Consuela suspected, Elena Maria was sure of it. The old woman had approached her earlier in the morning, while Elena was being dressed by half a dozen servants who laboriously fitted her into a lace wedding gown. The *criollos* had become furious with her nurse's innuendos and exploded in a tantrum, ordering everyone from the room but Consuelo. The half-breed had held her ground.

"Well, old nurse, speak what is in your heart."

"I see what I see."

"With one good eye and one blind. Tell me, then."

"I see what I see." Her eyes, nose, mouth, cheeks look sculpted out of clay dug from the hills. She looked for all the world like a carved deity come to life.

"I do not want your counsel. I am my father's daughter, I am the house of Saucedo, and it will stand. And none will divide or despoil my birthright."

Consuelo shakes her head. "You choose the shadow way, it changes you. You can never come back to the light."

"You are a foolish old woman today, but I forgive you."

"A foolish old woman?" Don Alonso said, guiding the carriage down the narrow drive that led past the barn out behind *la casa de Saucedo.* He applied the carriage brake when they pulled abreast of the garden gate. "What are you saying?"

"Consuelo," Elena Maria explained, blushing. Caught in the act of reliving a memory she had not meant to speak aloud, the young bride was forced to defend herself. "She could not understand why I wished for us to pass this evening alone in the garden house."

"The old witch, we should be rid of her. I find your idea rather exciting. And we will need no servants for what I have in mind," Don Alonso chuckled.

"Mi madre!"

"Have no fear. I shall be tender as the rain. Now, out of this cursed mist before we grow ill from these vapors."

"The gloom fills me with dread. See that the door is unlocked and the lamps lit within. I will follow."

"As you wish, Señora," said the governor. He had waited for this woman long enough. Tonight she was his, and the vast wealth that was her birthright. All his . . .

Elena Maria watched him enter the garden, heard the door to the garden house creak open. She waited, expecting a gunshot. Nothing. But Morgan had to be within. A knife, then, yes; of course, he was accustomed to close-in fighting. She climbed out of the carriage, stood alone in the dark, searched the mist for some sign of Gilberto Barba. But no, he would be within the garden house to finish what Morgan started. She felt a pang of regret, a secret, searing pain that tore through her. But she had done what needed to be done. And there would always be other lovers.

She walked through the garden, caught the scent of roses and lilacs and freshly turned earth. It was done, had to be by now. That made her a grieving widow. She practiced a suitable expression. She would need to wear widow's rags for at least six months. Then slowly abandon her mourning garb, allow her "grief" to subside while she went about her family's business.

Elena Maria cautiously approached the door. She took a deep breath, cleared her throat, steeled herself for the bloodbath within.

Blood and bones were the price of freedom. So be it. She had done what had to be done.

The door opened at her touch and she entered the garden house, continued through the anteroom and stepped into the lamplit chamber. She froze in her tracks, her mind struggling to take in the scene: the fire cheerfully ablaze in the hearth, the oaken table set with platters of *pan dulce*, marzipan truffles, honey-spice tarts, and a china teapot.

No! No! Where are they? Morgan?

There should have been signs of a struggle, a pool of blood, the air reeking of powdersmoke, Gilberto Barba standing over the bodies of both men. That had been there plan.

Don Alonso del Campo sat on the edge of the four-poster bed, his tunic and shirt and waistcoat tossed across a nearby chair along with his waist sash. He drained a glass of wine, spilling some of the vermilion droplets onto his naked chest. Elena Maria reached out to steady herself. The room reeled for a moment and she almost fainted. The color drained from her features. Her limbs went rigid.

He betrayed me! No! It isn't possible. Morgan betrayed me. How did he know? Damn his eyes. But it couldn't be.

And yet, anything was possible.

"Well met, *mi amor*," Don Alonso said in his most seductive tone of voice. Rising from the bed, he ambled across the room toward the benumbed young woman, his new bride. "I promise you a night to remember."

And reaching out, he took her in his arms and led her to bed.

19. It is easy to take a life.

"You are a mad animal," Gilberto said, his speech slurred. The lump on his skull resembled a miniature volcano. Blood clotted the swollen knob like a dried lava flow. The major held up his bound wrists. "You have tied this too tight. It hurts. And my hands are numb."

"Quiet," Morgan snapped, and yanked the man's bound hands down and out of sight. Though he had discarded his prison rags for the green coat, white trousers, and calf-high boots of a Spanish grenadier, the bound officer behind him might attract unwanted attention.

"If you are caught you will be hanged as a spy," Barba warned.

Morgan laughed and gingerly touched the raw, puckered scar tissue on his neck. "Really? Now I *am* afraid." He flicked the reins and continued his survey of the city, proceeding along a shrouded avenue and past the third cathedral he had seen that night. This church was smaller than the Cathedral de Santa Maria and less ornate which seemed to befit the fact it was dedicated to St. Francis of Assisi.

Since his escape, Morgan had avoided a direct flight from the city. With Barba slumped unconscious beside him in the carriage, Morgan risked capture for the opportunity to study the port's defenses. For the better part of an hour he had guided the carriage through the gloom, noting how the warehouses containing most of the fabled wealth of the city seemed concentrated near a massive redoubt bristling with cannon and, from the glow of the coals in the braziers, well-manned by Spanish troops.

Driving back through the center of town he followed the line of battlements, rock walls eight to ten feet in height, that protected the city from a landward assault, although any approach from Portobello over the military road would involve constant skirmishes with the troops stationed throughout the route, rendering a surprise attack on the city nigh impossible.

The southeastward approach across the densely wooded San Blas Mountains and down through the swamp and bayou country seemed the least defended, and with good reason. Only a fool would attempt to bring a force through an impenetrable jungle. From what Morgan had seen on entering the city, the bayous provided precious little solid ground on which to mass an assault and, should an attack fail, the swampland was a deathtrap with no room to make a quick and orderly retreat.

When Barba regained his senses he assumed the buccaneer was lost and, keenly aware of the pirate's reputation as a murderous villain, immediately began to pray for an opportunity to escape. However, Morgan didn't miss much, and kept a pistol handy. So Gilberto watched the familiar sights of the city roll by, all the shops and taverns and even the well-lit estates where the perhaps the new governor had made a brief visit with his new bride and received the accolades of the gentry and enjoyed a toast to the happy couple's health and prosperity; yet the major dared not call out, aware the first word would also be his last.

Growing anxious now to depart the city, Morgan took a shortcut across a spacious plaza which during the day would be crowded with merchant stalls and their customers. The iron-rimmed wheels clattered on the cobblestones as the carriage sped toward the *mercado*. A guard hailed him from the darkness. Morgan jabbed the twin gun barrels into Barba's side.

"Answer him."

"No," Gilberto muttered.

"Suit yourself," Morgan said with shrug. "When you get right down to it, I don't give a damn. Here and now, or face it later—it's all the same. But I'll die hard. And I won't die alone."

Gilberto Barba didn't like the sound of that. He considered his options, found he had none, then shouted out his name and told the sentry he was about the governor's business. The sentry called back that he would also like his turn with "the governor's business" this night. Both men had a hearty laugh.

And the carriage rolled on—down the Via España, past an armory and barracks, past a detachment of drunken lancers on their way from one brothel to the next, skirted another plaza and the gallows where Morgan had endured the terrible pretense of his own execution and the derision of the crowd—winding through the mist-cloaked streets until they came at last to the main gate, two great oaken doors secured with a timber and a pulley system to raise and lower the massive wooden beam that barred the entrance.

Morgan braked a few yards from the gate, and waited as two weary-looking figures shambled out of the shadows, rubbed their eyes and shouldered their muskets and peered at the occupants of the carriage.

"*Abra las puertas,*" Barba called out.

"Is that you, Major?"

"*Sí.* Open the gates."

"But the hour is late, Señor."

Gilberto winced as a pistol barrel dug into his side. "Do you question me?"

"No, no, Major, never," one of the men blurted out.

"Then be quick about it."

"*Sí,* as you wish," the other gatekeeper replied, awake now and hoping to defuse the situation before he and his compadre both wound up in trouble. He grabbed a nearby rope and dug in his heels and gave a hearty downward tug. The wooden timber barring the doors rose on its iron hinge and settled into an upright position. Then each man trotted out to a door and walked them open. Freedom beckoned beyond the walls, in the black of night. Sweet freedom. His luck had held again.

Morgan relaxed.

"*A las armas!*" Barba shouted suddenly and, snatching the reins from Morgan's hands, leaped from the carriage, tripped, and went sprawling in the street. "Here is Morgan the pirate. *Mátelo!* Kill him!"

Morgan leaped from the carriage as a musket roared and a tongue of flame spat toward him out of the gloom. The buccaneer hit the ground, rolled, scrambled to his feet, and charged toward the sentry who had fired upon him. Morgan heard a scramble of footsteps and realized a third sentry had been watching them from the shadows. Morgan fired in the direction of the soldier. The Spaniard yelped and stumbled away from the wall. A flash of priming powder preceded the roar of a musket and something white-hot grazed Morgan's side, glanced off a rib, passed through his torso, and ricocheted off a spoke of the carriage wheel. The impact sent the buccaneer reeling against the carriage harness. The mare shied and tossed its head. Morgan gritted his teeth, growled and charged his assailants. He drove in close and fired at the dimly seen figures in the mist. One of the soldiers groaned and sagged against a rain barrel, his musket clattered to the ground. He twisted and clutched at the rim before his strength gave way and he slumped to the ground.

Another shot stabbed through the mist. Morgan could hear Barba shouting for someone to come and untie his hands. The major continued to keep a tight grip on the reins to prevent the mare from bolting. Morgan touched his side. His hand came away sticky. He could feel the blood soaking into his shirt and woolen breeches. *I have to finish this, and soon.*

He closed in with the man who had wounded him. The grenadier dragged a saber from its sheath and lunged at the buccaneer. Morgan threw his empty pistol in his attacker's face and darted out of harm's way as the Spaniard attempted to decapitate him. The blade bit into the door.

Morgan kicked the soldier in the gut, drew the *miqulet*, checked the third sentry and saw the man was preoccupied with reloading his musket, swung back around and pulled the trigger. The small-bore pistol misfired.

"Damn!" Morgan the slashed the swordsman across the face with the pistol. The brass lock opened a gash in the soldier's cheek. Droplets of blood spattered in all directions. Morgan cast aside the pocket pistol. His hand closed around the hatchet in his belt. The Spaniard clutched his ravaged cheek and howled in pain as he wrenched the saber from the door. "Bastard. Now you will pay," he grumbled, and pressed the attack.

Morgan ducked beneath the slashing blade and sank the hatchet in the Spaniard's chest. The effort sent a wave of pain through the buccaneer. But the Spaniard only seemed to sigh and make a clumsy swipe with the saber. Morgan caught the man by the wrist and tore the saber from his weakened grasp.

"You have killed me," the soldier muttered and, turning, staggered off down the Via España, managing a few paces before toppling into the mist.

The third sentry brought his rifle to bear. He had no target, only the swirling tendrils of mist and the dark. "Show yourself!" He thought he saw something, turned, held his fire.

"Careful, *hombre*, he is the devil," Barba muttered. "Come, bring your knife and cut my hands free."

"*Sí,*" the grenadier replied. He wasn't afraid of any man, but *el diablo* was something else entirely. "Where are you, Major?"

"By the carriage. Hurry."

The sentry heard a noise off to his right. He tracked the sound with his musket, his finger poised on the trigger. He could make out the open gate, the brooding backdrop of the wall against which the fog swelled and settled, utterly blanketing some sections; in others, patchy at best.

"You'll have to do better than that," the Spaniard called out. Was that the crunch of a bootheel behind him?

Cold steel stung his thigh.

The grenadier twisted around and slashed wildly with his musket, clubbed the curling vapors, sensed movement and brought the musket to bear and almost shot the mare. He held his fire at the last second, received another cut and howled in pain, began to stumble around in an ever-tightening circle.

Morgan charged past the mare, and with the saber caught the end of the musket barrel and tilted it up as the Spaniard pulled the trigger. The musket discharged into the air. Morgan slashed the man across the chest, the back, the chest again. The Spaniard twisted and turned and writhed in agony as the steel blade carved him like a side of beef on a spit and left him sprawled and spilling his bodily fluids onto the hard-packed earth.

Morgan stumbled forward, braced himself on the saber, his strength momentarily spent, everything blurred for a few gut-wrenching seconds, and his legs turned watery. He experienced a few seconds of panic until his vision cleared. Then his sight returned, all was restored: the blackness of the road ahead, the ghostly tendrils of fog, the stench of powdersmoke, and Major Gilberto Barba. The Spaniard, gasping and kneeling, raised his hands in a futile attempt to shield himself from the buccaneer's retribution.

Morgan staggered toward him. Gilberto shrank back against the carriage. He scrambled to his feet, turned and broke for the street. The noise of the skirmish had alerted the inhabitants of the houses and shops a few blocks from the gate. Shutters were flung open and lanterns appeared in the windows, men with guns in the doorways. The major tripped over one of the dead grenadiers and fell on his face.

Morgan intercepted the officer, dragged him up onto his feet and back toward the entrance, forcing him against the outer wall of the small guardhouse from which two of the sentries had emerged.

The buccaneer jabbed the business end of the saber against the major's round belly, then dragged it up, severing the brass buttons from his jacket, until the pointed tip came to rest nestled in the hollow of the officer's throat.

"I will ask, and ask only once. If I think you are lying, I will pin you to the door and leave you for the carrion birds."

Barba recognized the desperation in the buccaneer's voice. And desperate men were capable of rash and dangerous acts. Gilberto tried to swallow. His Adam's apple bobbed against the pointed tip digging into his flesh. He coughed and nearly impaled himself.

"*Por favor, Señor.* You cannot blame a man for trying to escape," he blurted out, expecting each breath to be his last.

"Shut up!" Morgan hissed.

"*Sí.*"

"After I killed the governor, what then?"

Gilberto grew pale and stalled for time. "Señor, I don't understand . . ."

"I am not blind. I have seen the *Castille* from the waterfront. I asked among the other slaves and learned it has no crew but a token guard, and it is in no shape to depart. No water has been brought aboard, nor provisions of any sort. What were Doña Elena's plans for me?"

White-hot pain engulfed Morgan. He sucked in his breath to keep from screaming. Instead, he narrowed his focus, willed his hand steady; a loss of balance would prove fatal to the major.

"The señorita's plans?" Barba knew the altercation had not gone unnoticed. Help had to be on the way. If he could only stall for time, he might yet redeem himself.

"I have no more patience." Morgan seemed to read the officer's thoughts. He growled and forced the man to his knees yet again. "Join your compadres in hell."

"No, wait, I speak. I speak." Gilberto opted for the truth, hoping it would set him free. "After you were done with the governor, I was to . . . to . . ." Barba gulped. Words failed him.

"You were to see I never made it to the *Castille*. I was supposed to die along with Don Alonso."

Barba nodded glumly, accepting his fate. Morgan chuckled; he had suspected as much all along. But there was something in him that wanted to be proved wrong, a desire to believe that Elena Maria might have cared for him, at the end of the day, that at the moment of her triumph over this marriage of necessity, she might have felt something. Love? Perhaps.

"So be it," Morgan said. "You were to kill me?"

"*Sí.*"

Morgan slowly exhaled and straightened and lowered the saber. Then, with a sudden swipe that caught the major off guard, he severed the bonds and freed the major's wrists. "Get up." He turned and started toward the gate.

Barba glanced at his freed wrists, hardly daring to believe he was still alive. The dead grenadiers littered about the entrance bore mute testimony to how close the major's own demise was. Morgan turned his back on the officer, cut the mare free from its harness and led the animal to the main gate. Barba watched the man go about his escape, unwilling to press the matter further. He did not want to die this night.

"It is easy to take a life, harder to give it," Morgan said. And slowly, painfully, he eased himself astride the mare. "Carry my words to Don Alonso del Campo and to his new bride. And to all of Panama City. I charge you with this."

"I will do as you ask," Barba said. The major's blood turned cold. "What would you have me say?"

The buccaneer kept a tight grip on the reins. He held his mount in place, and raised the saber in his hand. Framed by the gateway, the sword resembled a scythe and the faintly discernible figure, an all-too-real resemblance of a Grim Reaper, terrible in his resolve.

"Tell them, Morgan is coming."

We are Brethren of Blood,
   we are sons of the sea.
   We are children of havoc
   and born to be free.
Sourge him and hang him and do what you will,
A man who won't break is a man you can't kill.
Screw your heart to your backbone, the Black Flag's anon,
Cry "Morgan is coming" and pity the Don.

20. A litany of the dead.

Morgan is coming."

Don Alonso softly repeated the message to himself as he sat astride a black charger, perspiration glistening in his close-cropped beard, his graying head shielded from the broken rays of sunlight by a broad-brimmed hat made of straw. The governor had personally assumed the responsibility of hunting down the escaped prisoner. It was a matter of honor. But Don Alonso took comfort in the fact that he was protected by a detachment of Spanish dragoons, hard men with a reputation for ruthless efficiency and courage in battle. Behind them, the walls of Panama City were a beckoning sight in the distance. But these men were not the kind to look back.

Skirmishers rode ahead of the column, ranging to either side of the road, searching the underbrush, their short-barreled muskets loaded, primed and ready to shoot. The tracks they followed led for a time down the road to Portobello, a passage that eventually would have brought the escaped prisoner into a confrontation with one or more of the many patrols ranging the mountain road.

Don Alonso assumed Morgan must have realized his dilemma, for the tracks showed he had altered his course after a couple of miles from the front gate, and backtracked, heading east through the tall grass and marshy ground toward the distant jungle and the forbidding-looking barrier of the great Darien swamp.

An hour passed, then two, and the heat began to rise and the excesses of the previous evening began to take their toll on the soldiers and the governor. The sun overhead seemed intent on purging the sins of the night before. The column of dragoons rode through the thick humid air, sweat seeping from their pores, heads throbbing; an errant step or a misunderstood remark exploded into quarrels and reckless threats.

Don Alonso slapped at his neck and crushed an annoying fly before it began to sting. Another buzzed his face, and he swatted the air with his gloved hand. *Curse Henry Morgan.* This was not the way the governor had planned to spend the morning after his wedding day. Curse the brigand. The miscreant should have been hanged back in Jamaica. Don Alonso rued the day he had ever listened to the counsel of a woman.

"Morgan is coming."

Indeed, well, Henry Morgan was a fool, and hardly in any position to offer threats. He was a man alone. What could he do, where could he go? And how had the pirate managed to escape in the first place? It was said the brigand lived a charmed life. Well, the jungle was more than a match for Morgan's luck.

While the governor was pondering the unanswerable, one of the skirmishers lost among the trees and tall reeds fired a shot that alerted the column and sent Don Alonso and the rest of the dragoons riding at a gallop toward the sound of the gun. The brutal effects of heat and humidity were shunted aside as adrenaline energized the entire column. These men were mean-tempered and ready for a fight. Don Alonso simply wanted this nightmare to end, to free him from this escalating madness.

Maybe it will finish this way, before the day is out, and I can return to my marriage bed, the governor thought as he drew his saber and held the weapon upright, the curved blade resting against his shoulder, brass hilt gleaming as he walked his mount along the edge of the swamp, taking care to avoid stumbling into the quagmire.

Don Alonso wanted to make a good impression. He was among veterans who had been honed by their war with the savage Kuna. These dragoons had fought pirates and thieves and jungle savages for the better part of three years. They deserved a leader they could respect and trust, whose courage was the equal of their own.

The column rounded the encroaching jungle and a thick stand of white-trunked trees that towered two hundred feet into the air, and caught sight of the skirmisher who had signaled them. The scout had ridden out across a shallow fork of the bayou and reached a knoll of firm ground where he had discovered the mare Morgan had stolen and apparently left behind to graze upon the reeds and fringe grass.

"Is it Morgan? Have you found him?" Don Alonso called out, plodding through the sultry air. He watched as the skirmisher caught up the trailing reins, turned the mare and guided his own mount back into the murky shallows. The sluggish water rose to his mount's belly as he carefully attempted to retrace his path to the knoll. Kiskdees and parakeets chattered in the surrounding treetops. Monkeys chattered and hurled from vine to branch in the treetops, their domain the canopy of trees beckoning inland. Suddenly one of the dragoons with the column snapped up his musket and fired. A geyser exploded a few yards to the rear of the skirmisher. Don Alonso, startled by the sound, searched in the direction of the marksman and saw a curious trail of ripples in the water.

"Es un crocodilo," the dragoon called back. And several of his companions shouldered their weapons, prepared to defend their companion belly-deep in bog should any other crocodiles take an interest in him. But the skirmisher managed to reach firm ground with the mare in tow. He immediately approached the governor and saluted before reporting what he had found.

"Your Excellency," the soldier began, "I saw marks in the mud that looked as if a *piraqua* has been shoved or dragged into the water. There was blood on some of the grass and more on the mare's flank. I think Señor Morgan is badly wounded. He may even be dead, adrift in the swamp. But wounded or dead, either way the crocodiles will have him, or the fer-de-lance, the jaguar, or maybe the Kuna will take his head for a prize. I saw signs they have passed this way."

The skirmisher shuddered and wagged his head. "I would prefer the gallows," he continued. "The rope is a clean death compared to what the Kuna will do. I have seen things . . ." His voice trailed off. From the expression on the man's face, it was clear the man had witnessed mutilations that continued to haunt his sleep.

Don Alonso dismounted and walked stiff-legged to the water's edge, till his boots began to sink into the marshy ground. He stood there, saber drawn, facing the vast swamp and the forbidding recesses of the Vierde Infierno, the Green Hell. He raised his saber and slashed at the water's edge then straightened, his eyes blazing as he searched the vine-draped trees, the dense undergrowth and the glassy surface of the bayou.

"Morgan!" he shouted.

The name reverberated through the emerald gloom, echoed like a litany of the dead, a single name, hurled into the jungle and drifting back toward him out of the wilderness that had claimed the pirate as its own.

"My lady . . . your tea." Consuelo set the tray down on a nearby table in the garden house. She pulled back the curtains and allowed the sunlight to flood into the garden house, illuminate the interior, lend a cheery brightness where there had been depression and doubt. The woman on the bed stirred and rolled over on her naked shoulder, one breast poking insolently from the covers. Elena Maria reached for her dressing gown. She pulled it on over her head and sat upright. Her eyes were puffy and dull-looking. An aura of defeat clung to her.

"Child . . ." Consuelo approached her, held out a hand. Elena Maria took and kissed it and clung to it and for one brief moment was like a small child to her mother, lost and frightened and seeking comfort. "Such a face and on one so newly married."

Elena Maria scowled. "What would you have me do? Be grateful? For what, that I am married to a man who already has plans to restore his family's estate, using my birthright? He intends to sell the sugar plantation in Paraiso to pay off his father's debts to the court." She brushed her black hair away from her face, tied it back with a ribbon, then rose from the bedcovers and began to pace the small room. She stood in the sunlight flooding in through the window and closed her eyes, allowing the molten gold warmth to seep into her. Her hands knotted into fists. Suddenly her body was wracked with sobs. Her shoulders sagged and she brought her hands to her face. She heard the rustle of Consuelo's skirt.

"No," she said. And the nurse halted in her tracks, arms outstretched but unable to embrace her charge. Elena Maria almost gave in to the pain. But her resolve was stronger. She was her father's daughter. And a daughter of the house of Saucedo did not simper or weep or dissolve into tears just because her world had come crashing down and all her plans come to naught because of some wily pirate whose presence of mind she had underestimated.

How had he known? What had given her away? If his escape hadn't brought her to ruin she might have found joy in his freedom. After all, she had arranged it. And the passion they had shared was a strong memory, heady as a rare wine, powerful and profane. Another time or place and she might have . . . no . . . the awful present must be dealt with.

She could still feel Don Alonso climbing atop her, sweating and reeking of wine and rum, his lust overpowering any thought of tenderness or consideration for her own enjoyment. Why, the fool even thought he was the first, but then again, she had played the part well and convinced him of everything he wanted to believe. And all the while she had wondered why and how her plans had come crashing down. Where were Morgan and Gilberto?

Come morning she had learned the truth, when the major had disturbed the governor's rest and reported what had happened. The news had been like a knife plunged into her breast, cold steel into her heart. She was the governor's lady now, she had the name that ensured her prominence. But what use the name if her husband was bent on squandering all her father had built, dismantling an empire to feed his own vices and those of his dissolute family? Elena Maria resisted the urge to surrender to her tears. And slowly her backbone stiffened.

"My lady, what can I do for you?" the half-breed said.

"Draw me a bath back in the house. I would wash his stink off me." Elena Maria glanced at the servant, her dark eyes the color of dead leaves. Fate and a clever bastard had dealt her a cruel blow. She was bowed but hardly broken. Elena Maria looked around as her servant started to leave.

"Consuelo, look beyond and tell me, will I see *mi boucanier* again?"

The nurse frowned; she looked troubled, plagued by her own inner demons perhaps. Her second sight was more a curse than a blessing. She would have traded it, gladly, for a life of peace and maybe, just maybe, another visit to Port Royal. But as pleasant as that memory was, the sweetness was overshadowed by a premonition of disaster. But the question had been asked and must be answered.

"I cannot tell for true," Consuela replied. "But he will see you."

"Another riddle, old woman. Is that all?"

"Such is life."

Maybe Don Alonso wanted a war, but Henry Morgan was in no shape to give him one. His keen sense of self-preservation overruled the fury in his heart. He was weak from loss of blood. At least the wound in his side had finally quit bleeding, and the last thing it needed was another melee. He had two rounds in his pistol, and Gilberto's saber, hardly the kind of force one needed to take on the Dons. So he lay on his belly on the bottom of the shallow dugout canoe he had found and paddled into a thicket of tall reeds a couple hundred feet from the knoll where he'd left the mare.

Peering through a covering of fronds with which he had covered the *piraqua* to further conceal it, Morgan watched Don Alonso flail away at the edge of the swamp, heard the governor call him by name, waited in silence until the governor grew weary of his display and led the column of dragoons away from the bayou and back onto the trail toward Panama City.

Morgan remained there in the heat until the thirst became unbearable. Then he fought free of the reeds and the fronds he had used to disguise himself and the boat. Groaning with the effort he forced himself to paddle to the closest dry ground he could find, a mound of thickly carpeted earth at the upper end of a winding creek, a sluggish tributary that grew narrower and narrower until it petered out.

The buccaneer climbed out of the dugout and dragged it up onto the creekbank. His exertions had started him bleeding again. He braced himself against the twisted trunk of a mangrove tree and removed the pistol from his belt, emptied the priming powder onto his wound, then, placing a branch between his jaws, struck the flint and ignited the charge. The powder flash cauterized the wound. Morgan bit clean through the stick, spat out the wood fragments, sank against his backrest, sighed and fainted dead away.

He is carrying several bolts of silk upon his shoulder as he cautiously makes his way along the pier. Morgan dutifully follows a line of Africans, all of them burdened by a wealth of goods they've spent the day unloading from the Santa Clara, *a merchant ship that has recently arrived from the Far East. Morgan is careful with the laboriously dyed silks, they are highly prized by the ladies of Panama, not to mention the women who attend the court of King Carlos. The silks would be a worthy prize in Jamaica as well. The prisoners wind their way along the waterfront and up the Avenida Balboa for a couple of blocks until they reach the governor's warehouse, a large stone-and-wood structure protected by a redoubt and a contingent of grenadiers.*

Henry Morgan works without complaint, for he is constantly studying the layout of the treasure district with its warehouses and defenses. Under the watchful glare of armed guards, Morgan carries his load into a storage hall, past ingots of gold, the pagan treasures of an empire, jeweled cups and statues of elder gods. He longs to run his hands through a chest of gems, catch the light with emeralds and rubies. Drink rum from topaz-encrusted goblets. Dance on a pile of doubloons by fire-light. He sweats and groans like any slave but in his mind's eye the for-tune belongs to el Tigre del Caribe. The Spanish are merely guarding it for him.

He pauses in the dim light and a guard immediately reproaches him for wasting time. Morgan nods subserviently and goes about his business, unloads the silk and retraces his steps. The guard returns to his place by a great mahogany desk where one of the officers remains seated, attempt-ing to make note of what goods are brought into the warehouse and dis-patching loads of timber, barrels of salt and sweet figs and bales of tea from the Orient on to other warehouses along the waterfront.

"*Get along now, back into the street,*" *the guard bellows.* "*The day is young yet.*"

And Morgan complies, seemingly immune to the insults of his captors. In his thoughts, he strides the burning streets of the conquered city, lays waste his enemies, and gathers in the wealth of kings. He can see it clearly. It will come to pass, if he lives.

An image of a man, a familiar face, only inexplicably saddened.

"*Father?*"

"*I shall wait here among the ashes.*"

"*Come away from the heat. I cannot bear it.*"

"*That's because of the wound. Infection is setting in. You won't last long.*"

The apparition fades. "*Just as well, Papa, if you are going to speak nonsense.*" *But he knows his father has spoken the truth. He wouldn't lie about something so important. But it wasn't all that hard, just the act of letting go. Forget revenge, forget the fabled treasures, the glory and greed. None of it seemed as important as just letting go. What is there to cling to?*

Doña Elena, now there is a woman for you, she'll put the fire in your belly. *He almost reaches out to her, then changes his mind.* No, thank you. *He will resist that temptation. And besides, she will not save him. He needs someone strong, someone who will stand with him in fair times or foul, a soul born free like his.*

Darkness surrounds him. He is sinking, clawing for the light and the light reaches down and the light is a face.

Nell Jolly comes to him then, with her eyes like blue sapphires, a pert nose and unruly auburn hair and sweet sad smile and she is good and she is true and she has always been at his side and carried him in her heart.

"Toto," he whispers.
"I am here."
"Do not leave me."
"Never."
And her love is stronger than death.

Water touches his lips, a cool compress of moist leaves, a poultice of jungle herbs and moss draws the poison from his wound. Morgan opens his eyes and finds himself staring at the thatched roof overhead. He stares at the interwoven branches, marveling at the skill necessary to make the roof tight enough to keep the rain off. He can hear the patter on the roof, the raindrops spilling from the rounded entrance.

A dark-skinned woman knelt at his side and removed the compress from his forehead. She cradled his head upon her lap and placed a gourd to his lips and gave him to drink of a particularly noxious brew. The bitter liquid was a hard go at first, but she seemed determined to make him swallow and chuckled at his distress, pinched his nose and refused to allow him to spit it out.

"Enough, good mistress," Morgan sputtered. The woman allowed him to recline and went about changing the poultice on his wound. "How did I get here?"

She ignored him.

"I found you. I brought you here, to Patria," said a voice from the entrance. Kintana ducked and entered the jacal. The muscular warrior squatted alongside the man on the pallet. "She told me your fever is broken. I think you will live now."

Morgan looked up into the Kuna native's implacable countenance. He had stolen away from the city without incident. Kintana brought out a small clay pipe, took a glowing coal from a nearby brazier, lit the tobacco and began to smoke.

Morgan asked, "How long have I been here?"

"Many days." The warrior had been presented with a curious dilemma. "My companions said I should kill you."

"They are fools. I did not drive you from your lands and sell your people into slavery and force them to work in the mines. Spain has done this. The soldiers behind their walls are your enemies." Morgan closed his eyes. The effort to speak taxed his strength.

"The Kuna are too few in number now." Kintana spoke softly to Patria and the woman nodded and crawled out of the jacal. "The walls are strong, the Spaniards have many guns, many soldiers. And all we have is . . ." Kintana exhaled a cloud of smoke and chuckled.

"Me," Morgan finished. The buccaneer closed his eyes and allowed himself to drift into sleep.

"*Sí.*" Kintana nodded ruefully and his eyes narrowed. "And what can you do, Anglais?" There followed a moment of silence. Kintana even began to suspect that the pirate had lost consciousness again, then Morgan spoke and the conviction in his voice could not be denied.

"I can take Panama City."

21. A chant for the dying.

Henry Morgan had been brought to Portobello in chains. Pity the Tiger, blinded by the sunlight, led down the pier in shackles, blinded by sunlight, led down the pier in shackles, unkempt and haggard and brought down by jackals, destined to be brought across the isthmus to Panama City, doomed to play a gallow's game and suffer an ignominious end as a slave.

Three weeks to the day, it was a far different man who emerged from a grove of windswept palms and walked out across the Caribbean strand to make his benediction to the star-flecked surf while the moon rose like a silver chariot to chase a lonely cloud across a jeweled sky.

"I am Henry Morgan," he called out. And he cupped water to his naked torso, washed his chest and the puckered white scar on his side. He was lean and hard as men must be who walk with the jaguar. His long hair hung to his shoulders, his black beard aged him, but his gray eyes that caught the moonlight, beheld the constellations, sparkled like the sea. He was alive and he had an adventure to live, vengeance to slake, a furious heart that only rivers of blood and chests of gold could appease. "I am Mad Morgan!" he roared.

Behind him, Kintana and two other warriors stood well back from the water, as if suspicious of the great expanse over which the Spanish conquerors had come. Kintana's companions were similiar in attire, they all wore cotton breeches, their muscular bare chests crisscrossed with straps for a powder flask and shot pouch. War axes with obsidian blades encased in crocodile skin hung between their shoulder blades.

"Morgan . . . come," Kintana called out.

And the buccaneer turned as if surprised to find his savage bene-factors still with him. He turned his back on a shooting star and walked out of the ocean's embrace and followed the three Kuna Indi-ans as they led him in the opposite direction of Portobello, which lay a two days' ride west.

The four men continued on in silence, Morgan lost in his thoughts; Kintana and the other two warriors, Chaua and Felipe, maintained their guard. Spanish troops had been known to patrol the coast, although not without provocation. An hour later Morgan caught sight of a wooded cove and correctly assumed this was to be their des-tination. However, Kintana had more in mind then a mere campsite for the night.

Night birds swept the sky, tree frogs chittered a merry chorus in the dark. Rodents scurried from underneath the safety of fronds whose leaves were large as elephant's ears, bobbing and flapping in the sea breeze. Morgan noted they had passed a couple of likely campsites, when Kintana halted in his tracks, spoke in his native tongue. Chaua and Felipe immediately tramped off into the tidal shallows and fell to work uncovering something large and long. Morgan could not make the object out in the darkness. But Kintana, on the shore, set about making a fire, using dry sea moss for kindling and a piece of flint scraped against the brass butt plate on his stolen musket. The sea moss burst into flames and was quickly nurtured into a warming blaze by the Kuna chieftain. He handed a burning brand to Morgan, who glanced around at the other two Indians and in the firelight discov-ered what they were hurrying to uncover.

The buccaneer's eyes widened and his heart leaped in his breast as Felipe brushed away the last of the woven reeds and Chaua, who was the youngest of the three natives, grinned broadly and stood off to the side to allow Morgan to see the fishing boat in its entirety. It was a twenty-foot craft, with a gaff-rigged sail on a single mast. Near the stern, by the rudder, someone had erected a small thatch screen to provide some shade and relief on a hot day. Morgan gingerly approached the craft as if fearful it might bolt from his grasp and make for open water like a frightened fish. He placed his hand on the side of the craft, stroked the wooded flank and iron oarlock. At the bottom of the boat, Morgan was overjoyed to discover a backstaff, used by the boat's former owner to measure latitude and navigate while at sea. With this instrument, and a couple of weeks' provisions and water, a man could sail this boat from Panama right into Port Royal, with a bit of luck and a madman's sense of pluck.

"Where did this come from?"

"Same place as the guns," Kintana said, slapping the musket's butt plate as he drew abreast of the buccaneer.

"And the owner of the boat?"

Kintana lifted a burning brand, climbed out of the water and began to kick around in the underbrush. "His head is around here somewhere."

"Never mind," Morgan said. "But I shall need supplies, food and drink for at least ten days. Fourteen days would be even better, in case I lose the wind."

"There is fruit. And we can kill a peccary and dry the meat. Smoke fish, too."

Morgan nodded. "Then so be it. I will leave."

Chaua broke into a chant, the bulk of which was unintelligible to Morgan although he had picked up a smattering of the native tongue during his stay with the Kuna and thought he recognized words for *journey* and *spirit* and *good fortune*.

"He knows you will make this journey," Kintana explained. "He asks the Spirit of the Great Water to bring you to your people. I, too, shall sing it when you have gone. It is a good song."

"I haven't had much acquaintance with prayer lately," said Morgan, his hand still caressing the boat. "I say it's good to hear one now and then, even if it isn't a proper Christian tongue. I am grateful."

"*Sí.*" Kintana nodded sagely, and then, with just a hint of a grin, added, "It is also a chant for the dying."

It took almost another week for Morgan to ready the fishing boat that he christened *Little Nell* for good luck. From dawn to dusk he repaired the mast, patched the sail, trimmed away any decay, and restored the hull. Chaua was sent back toward Portobello to watch for any sign of approaching dragoons, while Kintana and Felipe gathered provisions. The forest provided a rich bounty of mangoes and bananas, wild goats and peccary; turtle meat was a prized delicacy.

At last, with November a few days away, Morgan poled *Little Nell* out of the estuary and into the sea. The craft took to the rolling tides as if eager for what lay ahead. Morgan tacked across the wind, criss-crossed the inlet, spent the afternoon getting a feel for the craft, how it might handle in a storm. She proved sound and willing to accept him. Only then did Morgan return to shore, to spend his last night among his savage companions. They gathered by the campfire and feasted in silence on turtle meat and plantain. Later, at Morgan's insistence, they built a pyre of decayed wood. Kintana seemed particularly preoccupied though he worked tirelessly alongside the buccaneer. The Kunas' ability to conceal their emotions made it difficult to read his silence. With the pyre about chest-high, the three men quit for the evening and returned to their campfire and stretched out on their blankets. The Kuna had a knack for drifting off to sleep in a matter of minutes. Morgan envied them. His was a restless night.

The morning dawned gray and misty, a sobering omen but one Morgan took in stride. He'd be sailing north by northeast, charting his course by the sun and the stars, following the trade winds and trusting, when all else failed, in Morgan's luck. Kintana and Felipe rose with him and, with the new day barely an hour old, followed Morgan down to the water's edge.

"See you keep watch for my return," Morgan said.

"I will keep runners in the hills. They will watch for smoke from the fire and bring word," Kintana told him. He betrayed no emotion. The man had a center of calm that Morgan envied.

"What will you do until I return?"

Kintana shrugged. "Fight."

"Then fare you well." He held out a length of rawhide in which he had tied seventy knots, one for each day. He figured it would take him about two months to reach Jamaica, gather a force, repair, and ready enough ships. "*Un nudo para cada dia.* I will return before you get to this." Morgan indicated the last knot in the string. He held out his hand. "I will bring men to fight at your side. There will come a day when we walk the streets of Panama City together. It may not be the end for the Dons but it will be the beginning of the end."

Kintana stared down at the gesture of friendship. He had been fighting for so long, suffered too many losses to completely trust. "Until that day," he said and, turning, headed toward the palm trees. But at the edge of the undergrowth he looked back and raised his hand. "Mad Morgan!" he shouted.

"Good enough," Morgan muttered to himself, and waved farewell. He trotted down to the fishing boat and walked the craft out of the shallows with the tide's help. Gaining deeper water, he crawled aboard and lowered the sails. The canvas rippled and then caught the wind. *Little Nell* plunged forward as Morgan tacked into the mist.

Watching from the shore, Felipe glanced in Kintana's direction. "Do you think the Anglais will return?"

Kintana shook his head. "I think he will die."

"Then what should we do?" Felipe asked.

"Keep watch."

With the shore falling fast behind him, the sea ahead, gray like his eyes, like the color of gunmetal, Morgan felt his resolve waver. The waves were getting choppy. Perhaps he ought to turn back. He might be sailing into a storm. Jamaica was a far piece for a man alone. All alone . . .

"Damn, what's this, Henry Morgan, have you lost your backbone?" the buccaneer said aloud. He stood and drew his knife and reaching behind his head cut off a lock of his hair and threw it into the wind. "Have at me. See, I shall dare the devil. Do your worst, I charge you." Here in this mist, he faced his fear and, in a moment of weakness, discovered again his brave, proud heart. He was *el Tigre del Caribe*.

Morgan hurled the lock of hair upon the black waters before the coast of Panama was lost to his eyes. He had dared the devil and taken a solemn oath. "I will come again. Or ne'er will I rest in death, this is my pledge."

Now the pact was sealed.

Five days out, the devil did his worst and stole the wind. Left becalmed, Morgan dragged out the oars and began to row. All around him the sea was one great vast undulating plane. He felt small indeed, a mere speck upon the wide ocean, alone, but enduring.

He was thankful for the canvas screen he had erected to protect him from the sun's brutal glare. Morgan used his spyglass to study the surface of the waters, in hopes of catching a disturbance on the surface where a gust of wind might ruffle the glassy sea. After a few hours he lost his stomach for rowing and pulled in the oars and stretched out beneath his canvas tarp, propped his head on a bag of possibles and went to sleep. There was nothing to do but wait. And drift.

The gaff-rigged sail hung loose and lifeless, the boat's motion imperceptible, the stillness like being adrift in the mind of God. With nary a cloud to block the view, he watched the sun dip below the horizon, painting a path of gold across the sea. He could appreciate the sight now, but give him another week of calm, and the sight would lose its appeal when his tongue was stuck to the roof of his parched mouth.

Night, and still becalmed, and Morgan wrestled with the same fears any seaman has faced when the wind dies. But it was hard to despair in the face of so much beauty. The stars in the heavens, bright and gleaming swaths of diadems, stretched from horizon to horizon and reflected off the ocean so that it seemed as if the galaxies were above and below, and Morgan transfixed in the center of eternity. Perhaps that's how it was with all mankind, all of us hung between unpredictable nature and the whims of the gods.

Past and present merged. Images paraded through his mind, years of plunder, wild days and libertine nights, he had lived and fought and conquered, victories like tribute laid before his feet: Morgan the conqueror, Morgan the Tiger, Mad Morgan will harry you and not forget a slight. But guile could not help him. There was no tricking the tides and the trade winds. He watched himself, stood apart, marveled at the changes ten years had wrought; better yet, two months in Panama as Don Alonso's unwilling guest had given him a clearer look at himself. What a fool he had been to allow Elena Maria's poison beauty to dull his instincts.

Then Nell came to him once more, a voice heard in the silence of his heart in the spinning stars and she was calling him home. What could a man do in the face of such defining love but persevere?

How could he have been such a fool to overlook Nell, whose friendship meant more to him than any other man or woman? Now he saw her in a new light, starlight, and he knew she would be waiting.

Morning came and Morgan rationed out a cup of water and hungrily devoured a mango, scanned the surface of the water, and was about to retire to his canvas screen when he glimpsed a disturbance on the main. He hurried to fit the oars in the locks and began to pull toward the trace of breeze. More than an hour later he was about to admit his delusion and abandon his efforts when the canvas sail ruffled and snapped as the wind found it. The fishing boat sprang to life, the wooden hull trembled and cut through the sun-dappled sea. He was on his way again.

"I am Morgan, Henry Morgan!" he shouted, exultant, his eyes blazing. "Here I am, you bastards. I'm still here!"

22. "I heard you."

I built my house to catch the last light of day. Every sunset is mine," Morgan tells her, sweeping his hat from his head and bowing, inviting the sixteen-year-old girl to enter.

"I am told that is how you invite every woman into your house for the first time. I think you hope to charm them into your bed," Nell laughs. But there is a hint of anticipation in her voice.

Morgan feigns a wounded pride. "Why, I have never shared that with another. Only my little sister."

Nell fumes at being referred to as his sister. When will he realize how much of a woman she really is and that the desire she feels is hardly a child's fancy? But she is delighted to be alone with him, in his house overlooking the sea. And indeed the sunset is his. They sit together on the porch steps and witness a dazzling display as the clouds become tinged with gold then deepen in hue. She suspects Morgan is lying about all the women he has brought out from Port Royal or Kingston and romanced here to the siren call of the rolling tides and whirling gulls and whispering wind. But they will never love him like she can. One day he will see her for what she is and what he needs.

"I thought I would find you here," Sir William said, riding up in his carriage. There was an expression of kindness upon his thick homely features, and sympathy in his voice. If only he could spare his daughter this pain. Nell was sitting on the porch steps of Morgan's house, her mind ensnared by memories of three years past, the first time Henry Morgan had brought her to his house above the sea. She had been all of sixteen, a woman by most standards, but to his eyes, still a girl and worse, like a sister to him. Now, in his absence, the house had become her retreat from the rude streets and rough populace of Port Royal.

With Henry Morgan taken and more than likely executed by Don Alonso, a gloom had settled over the peninsula. In the aftermath of the Spanish visit and the broadsides from the *San Bartolomeo* that had crippled the sleek, shallow draft sloops and schooners favored by the freebooters, men like Thomas LeBishop and Calico Jack and a handful of others were left with but a couple seaworthy ships in which to ply their illicit trade. And even then they had to sneak from port under cover of night in hopes of avoiding the English authorities.

Alas, the Spanish Main offered a meager harvest. And to make matters worse, every merchant vessel the Brethren managed to catch sight of sailed under the protection of an armed escort, the likes of which only a fool would approach.

Returning to Port Royal after a brief foray into the Caribbean, the English governor had ordered the crews to remain in port. Captain Hastiler and his men confiscated the vessels and brought them over to the Kingston piers. It seemed the governor of Jamaica was more concerned with placating the Spaniards and their treaty and completing his fictitious memoirs than seeking justice for the denizens of Port Royal.

"Please, Father, you do not need to follow me about." Nell frowned at her father, displeased that he had shattered her reverie.

"I worry about you." The physician thought his daughter looked thinner. But she had to grieve in her own way.

"Worry for yourself and our good friends when the council meets tonight. See that the Black Cleric does not assume too much. I daresay he thinks his flag flies over all of us." Nell stood and stretched her legs. The resentment toward Sir Richard Purselley had been building for almost a month now, ever since Don Alonso's visit, when the Spaniard under Sir Richard's protection had fired on Port Royal. "No one can doubt his skills at sea, nor LeBishop's match with a blade, but dealing with the governor will take more craft than cutlass."

"The Black Cleric has many followers."

"As does Henry Morgan, far more than Thomas LeBishop."

"But Henry is de—"

Nell gave him a sharp glance. Her expression turned belligerent. "He is not dead."

"How can you say that? I doubt Don Alonso presented Henry with a nosegay."

"I would know if he had come to harm."

"You fool yourself, lass."

"I—would—know."

"Nevertheless, and I loved him like a son, Henry is not among us. And should Thomas LeBishop choose to march on the governor, I am not certain I would oppose him."

"And who would sit in the governor's chair—Thomas LeBishop, Calico Jack? Or perhaps the Portugee Devil. They'd kill half their number before nightfall." Nell scowled. "Tell them to wait a while longer. Father, they will listen to you. Henry Morgan will return. Then we can deal with Sir Richard Purselley."

The physician shook his head and sighed. "Ah, daughter, you have the faith of an angel. It is out of place among the hellions with whom I chose to cast my lot so long ago." Sir William took a kerchief from his coat pocket and dabbed at his bulbous nose, coughed and wiped his mouth. He mopped the perspiration from his high forehead. A sea breeze tugged at a few wispy strands of hair. His tone softened. "It troubles me. When days pass and I haven't seen you . . ."

"Then you should know I am here."

The physician had to admire his daughter's tenacity. Ever since Morgan's abduction by the Spaniards, Nell had made a point of visiting the house, lighting a lamp at night and placing it on one of the beams that framed the porch. She was determined to keep a signal burning, a pinprick of light against the great darkness, a beacon of hope. Who was he to dash her dreams and argue the futility of her efforts? Life would teach her that lesson in its own good time.

"Join us this night. I would have my daughter at my side."

"Very well. As you wish. I will remain here and see the sun down, then set my lamps and return to Port Royal."

"As you like it," said Sir William. He flicked the reins of the mare in harness. The animal ceased cropping grass and started forward. The physician trotted the animal back onto the road and toward the jumble of houses, shops, taverns, and warehouses that dominated the far end of the peninsula.

Nell leaned on one of the support poles and watched her father disappear around the corner of the house, following a well-worn path through the golden palms and tulip trees.

She breathed in the fragrant air, enjoying the peace, while a flock of bright green parakeets with jet-black wings dipped and dove and chased one another through the frangipani that grew in thick profusion to either side of the road. The woman returned her attention to the merging of the azure sea and sky, the oncoming waves that spilled their opalescent foam upon the shore. Then, sated for the moment with the natural beauty of this vista, she sauntered back inside the house.

Morgan takes her by the hand and brings her into a large front room furnished with the plunder of innumerable raids, a settee from Hispaniola, an armoire from Maracaibo, mahogany tables and velvet-cushioned chairs taken from a plantation house outside Santiago de Cuba.

"Remember, should some lad in town invite you to sit alone with him in his father's house, keep one hand on your knife, for men are hotspurs when it comes to beautiful women."

Nell picks up a jeweled hand mirror from a nearby table and holds it up to inspect her image, intrigue in her blue eyes as she studies her reflection, runs her fingers through her auburn hair. She is wearing a dress today, something her father stole from a contessa's wardrobe. The bodice is quite Parisian, revealing much of her bosom. She looks around at Morgan and flashes him a saucy smile.

"So you think I am beautiful?"

Morgan gulps and averts his gaze. Perhaps bringing her out from town wasn't such a good idea. Up until now he has been teasing her. Suddenly the tables are turned and he doesn't like it. He is too close to the girl and her father. They are like family. Although the way she looks right now makes him tempted to forget all that and risk Sir William's wrath.

"Toto . . . what are you doing?"

And she just laughs and skips across the room, slowly turns, as if in a dance. She senses her effect on him and revels in it. Nell Jolly, a pirate's daughter, has begun to realize that beauty is power. "Maybe there are some men I would not resist." She extends her hand to him.

"Oh, indeed." Then Morgan sweeps her into his arms and Nell tries to look wanton. He carries her outside, down the porch steps, through the palms. The sixteen-year-old is puzzled at first, then realization dawns. He is walking toward the shore about fifty yards from the house.

"No," she warns him. "Henry Morgan, don't you dare."

But of course he was born to dare, and marches out knee-deep into the surf and drops her into an incoming wave. "Best you cool off, Toto."

"Oh! You toad-spotted snipe!" She scrambles out of the sea; drenched and sputtering and ready to pin his hide to the wall. Her youthful lust is the last thing on her mind. Nell tries to chase him but the dress weighs her down and she trips over the soggy material that wraps about her legs. She falls forward into the mud, the incoming tide catches her again, she struggles to her feet spewing salt water. "Henry Morgan! I'll have you at sword's point for this."

"Not in that dress, you won't," Morgan laughs, and scrambles out of the surf. He makes a mad dash for his horse, vaults into the saddle and gallops off toward Port Royal. Tonight, the "wickedest place on earth" would be safer than anywhere near Nell Jolly.

Nell laughed now, the memory had lost its sting. Oh, but if she could have laid a hand on him then. Morgan and his teasing ways, that was how he resisted what was in his heart. He cared about her more than he dare allow himself to realize. Even then, in her anger, she had loved him.

She walked to the doorway that opened onto a bedroom, sat down on the edge of the feather bed, her hand upon the mahogany four-poster bedframe. Funny. She could no longer remember what had happened to that contessa's dress. Only that it never recovered from its seawater bath. She lay back upon the coverlet. "You'd be proud, Henry Morgan," she said to the stillness. As per his advice, she placed her hand on the hilt of her knife.

Staring at the thatch roof overhead she wondered what it would be like to hold him, to feel his flesh upon her, within her. His hands caressing her, slipping her shirt to her waist and covering her with kisses. She rolled on her side and placed her hand on the space beside her in the bed, admired the shadows and slanted sunlight and watched the patterns on the wall shift and lengthen as the sun dipped into the western quadrant.

She yawned.

The minutes slipped by, then the hours. Past memories collided with the present, the sound of the waves, the droning tides, ebbing and falling, like the ocean's heartbeat, unchanged since world began, when the great globe cooled and the rains fell and the first rains collected upon bleak and thirsty soil. Praise for the unceasing miracles, laud the hand that molded earth and sky and bound all living things to one another for better or ill.

The minutes slipped by, then the hours. The sun drifted on its golden course, the warmth that stirs as in the human breast where love dwells, the fire that spills like honey over hill and mountain and shore. Praise for the glory of the light. Yet the light must die that men might praise an infinite expanse of sky adorned with twinkling gems, the most precious of which is hope. Time and the woman glory in the velvet night to come, where dreams dwell and stars align to guide the sailor home.

The minutes slipped by, then the hours. Suddenly Nell sat upright upon the bed. She rose and hurried across the room, through the house and out onto the porch, drawn by something more powerful than reverie or illusions, a call that wakened deep in her soul. Not quite understanding, no matter. She heeded the call, took one of the hurricane lanterns, and plunged off through the grass and the palm trees and ran to the shore to stand in the fading light, shielding her eyes as the sun turned a vibrant peach-gold as it dipped to the water-line and cast a path of molten light across the waves from the edge of the earth to the woman on the strand.

And there against the setting sun she saw a blemish on the horizon and her heart leaped to her throat. A sail? It had to be a sail. A small craft was out there. Someone from Port Royal or Kingston? Perhaps. But her heart said no.

And she had learned to trust her heart.

Nell hurriedly began to gather driftwood while she could still see. She hurried back to the house and gathered kindling from the supply alongside the north wall, darted inside to help herself to a pistol and powder flask, then back down to the shore where she arranged the pyre, sprinkled gunpowder on the kindling, and fired into black powder, igniting the charge. Flames sprang up. She fed them more of the kindling, then some of his firewood, tearing her shirt in the process. She didn't care. Her heart was racing with the tides. She stood in the firelight facing the ebony sea and prayed. And waited . . . waited . . . waited.

And then, at last, a gaff-rigged sail loomed out of the dark. It was a fishing boat—despite ten days at sea, a craft still worthy, still ready to fight the elements, to rage against the night like the man who had defied all odds and piloted her to the shore.

The bow scraped sand and Henry Morgan leaped over the side and splashed through the surf to reach the strand. He was naked save for a pair of threadbare breeches and his hair was bound with a leather string and his burnished flesh looked as if forged in a crucible of wind and sun. But his stride was steady, if a bit stiff for having spent ten days at sea, and his limbs were corded with muscle and he looked for all the world like some ocean deity as he approached the woman framed by firelight. He stood before her, his gray eyes locked with hers. His neck and side were scarred, his features seamed from squinting into the sun, but he seemed remarkably steady and Nell could not help but marvel. And then he spoke.

"I heard you," he said.

And Morgan swept her into his arms and carried her up the beach and through the tender grass, beneath the palms whose leaves, heavy for lack of wind, trembled as he passed, and up the steps and into the house where love would dwell forever more.

23. "For honor . . ."

Henry Morgan woke to a new day and thought the sunlight on the wall had never seemed so bright and the breeze drifting in through the windows had a sweetness that had to rival the first gust of wind to stir the branches in Eden. He had dreamt of the crossing, of being alone upon the expanse of sea, a solitary man caught between the sea and the sky. The stars in their courses pointed the way, and when the heavens grew overcast, he listened in his heart and heard Nell's voice and he steered by the longing in his soul and the truth burning in his heart.

A man can be a blind fool for only so long. She had come to him as he lay wounded, come to him in his dreams, then at sea, come to him in the wind and the waves, whispered his name in the early hours before dawn when the waves were tinged with phosphorous and lightning shimmered on the far horizon.

Morgan grinned and reached across to stroke the naked back of the woman beside him and found the bed empty. He sat upright, then swung his legs over the side of the bed and pulled on a pair of black taffeta breeches and a linen shirt, and padded barefoot across the room, checked the interior of the house and frowned, wondering what had happened to her.

"Nell?" he said, breaking the stillness. But she was obviously gone. Oh, God, what would Sir William Jolly think once he learned what had happened with his daughter? It was going to be impossible to keep this from the physician.

Morgan had no choice but to confront his friend before he learned what had happened from someone else. And what had happened? Just about everything. Morgan grinned. Nell was a tigress. He walked to a basin and filled it with springwater from a nearby pitcher and washed his face, slicking back his mane of hair then drying himself on the hem of his loose-fitting shirt.

He frowned. Something was amiss. His senses had never failed him. He walked to the wall and chose a brace of pistols which he quickly checked and found loaded and primed. He tucked them in his waistband and then walked to the front door.

The silence, that was it. No birds chattering among themselves. Nothing. The palm grove sounded devoid of life. And yet he knew he was no longer alone. Steeling himself, he tugged on the latch, opened the door and stepped onto the porch. And stopped dead in his tracks, face-to-face with what appeared to be nearly the entire population of Port Royal, his own crew standing to the fore. A cheer erupted from the gathering that filled the clearing, and echoed down the slope to the sea. He recognized them all, Sir William Jolly, Rafiki Kogi, Israel Goodenough, Pierre Voisin, and more, even Calico Jack and Anne Bonney and surprisingly enough, the Black Cleric, wearing a glum expression as he stood at the rear of the crowd surrounded by his crew and the men loyal to him.

Nell Jolly came forward, a grin on her face. She had stolen from his bedside and raced to town to bring word to the council that Morgan was returned. At first no one believed her, but when she threatened to duel any man who called her a liar, the Brethren became convinced she spoke the truth. Word soon spread like wildfire through the settlement, emptying the shops and taverns and the waterfront as men, women, and children had to see for themselves if *el Tigre del Caribe* had indeed returned.

"They wanted to see you," Nell said, waving a hand in the direction of the crowd.

"What do they want?"

"To follow where you lead," Nell replied. "Speak to them."

Morgan coughed and cleared his throat while waiting for the noise to subside. He locked eyes with the Black Cleric. LeBishop remained defiant, cautious in appearance as if he expected to have to fight his way out of the clearing. "I see my friends here," Morgan said. "If I e'er had an issue with you, know I harbor no ill will."

"Tell us, *mon capitaine*, have you got religion?"

"Better than that, Pierre," Morgan said. He vanished inside the house and returned before the crowd became too restless. He held a pouch in his right hand and raised it aloft then emptied its contents on the earth. Gold doubloons rained forth upon the hard sand. A murmur of appreciation swept through the gathering. "The Dons are preparing their gold fleet. I have seen sea chests filled to the bursting point with gold and pieces of eight and jeweled scarabs, rubies, and emeralds. I have seen rare woods and the finest silks, crowns and rings and necklaces fit for a queen. Their warehouses in Panama City are filled to the bursting point. I intend to relieve them of their burden. There's plunder aplenty for each of us."

Morgan paused to allow his remarks to sink in.

"Don Alonso betrayed his flag of truce and left owing a debt that can only be paid in bone and blood. Who will go with me to avenge our brothers and sisters? We sail for gold and vengeance!"

Another great cry erupted from their throats. His enthusiasm was infectious. And the glitter on the wooden flooring had the desired effect. Calico Jack and Anne Bonney, Dutch Hannah Lee and the bulk of the crowd pressed forward, firing their pistols into the air.

"We're with you, Captain Morgan."

"Three cheers for *el Tigre del Caribe*."

"Panama City cannot be taken!" said a lone voice attempting to bring sanity to the crowd by shouting above the din. It was Thomas LeBishop, looking grave, his eyes full of suspicions. "Some things cannot be done. Better to accept what must be, than to attempt a feat that can only lead to destruction. Happy is the man who finds wisdom and the man who gets understanding." As he spoke, his right hand rested on the hilt of his cutlass. The Black Cleric was prepared for the worst, but it was up to Morgan to make the first move.

"I escaped from a Spanish prison, eluded the troops Don Alonso sent to capture me, crossed the Isthmus of Panama and sailed that fishing boat yonder across the Spanish Main," Morgan casually replied. He opened his shirt and tilted his head to reveal the rope burns that scarred his neck. "I have been hanged five times," he added with a grin. "And here I stand." His expression turned serious, his voice colder than the ages. "Panama City will be mine." But he wasn't talking about a Sunday stroll in the park. "However, I am wise enough to know I shall need all the Brethren, *every* man jack of you. So I say this for all to hear, I charge no man among you." He shifted his stance so he could look directly at the Black Cleric, a brooding figure against a backdrop of golden palms. "Any grievance between us is ended."

"I say there is no quarrel a handful of rubies and pearls won't settle," Calico Jack called out. "What say you, William Jolly? You are the physician here."

"Gold heals all wounds," Sir William replied, and the gathering cheered once more.

The energy in the crowd was a volatile mix of bravado and greed, fueled by a desire to avenge the attack on Port Royal. These sea rovers were not the kind to forget Don Alonso's visit, and more especially his departure.

"Then we are for Panama," Morgan told them. "Send word throughout the island. Any man with the will to join us is welcome."

With the accolades of the populace ringing in his ears, Henry Morgan reentered his house and quickly finished dressing. Nell followed him inside, her cheeks flushed with excitement.

"I am going with you." Although she stated a fact, the physician's daughter steeled herself for an argument.

"Of course," Morgan replied. "It is your right. We are all free here. And you shoot better than me."

"Don't try to talk me out of it," she added; then, "Oh"—realizing he had not tried to change her mind. "Well then . . ." she fumed. Nell had been prepared to argue her cause. Now, suddenly, it was unnecessary. Too bad. It would have been a stirring speech.

Morgan finished dressing, donning a russet-colored coat and burgundy waistcoat. His shoulder-length brown hair framed his craggy features. His beard was flecked with silver. Then, without warning, he pulled Nell to him and kissed her long and hard until her legs went weak.

"Sir Richard will never allow any of us to break the treaty with Spain," Nell said, managing to pull away, to catch her breath.

"He won't be able to stop us."

"Purselley has threatened to jail any and all of us should we take up our old ways."

"Enough," said Morgan. He turned toward Kingston and fixed his gaze on the hill overlooking the bay. "I think it's time the governor and I came to an understanding."

"More sausages, Captain?" Sir Richard asked, seated across from the officer in the warm glow of another morning in paradise. Joseph and the other house servants had brought a table out to the terrace over-looking the harbor. The governor enjoyed taking the first meal of the day in the soothing sunlight, bathed by the gentle breezes sweeping up the hillside from the bay.

From this vantage point Purselley could watch Kingston come to life, the empty streets dotted with the social intercourse of the early hours. A Maroon farmer made his rounds, going door to door, haul-ing a cart loaded with clay jugs of fresh goat's milk. A woman with a pushcart called a list of her wares, salted fish and ackee, herbs and poultices to cure the grippe or mend a broken heart. Fishermen made their way to shore, readied their nets then clambered into their single-masted boats, turned their sails to the wind and headed out to open waters to harvest the bounty of the aquamarine sea.

Purselley's gaze pointedly avoided the fire-gutted waterfront of Port Royal. Don Alonso's exit had left him in a bad light. The bloody Spaniard should have taken the damn pirate and been done with it. Firing on Port Royal had been an act of contempt. Purselley frowned, his mood darkening. He took a moment to gather his thoughts, focused on the officer seated across from him.

It galled the aristocrat that he should have to cultivate a close per-sonal bond with the captain. But Sir Richard needed friends and, what with the sentiment on the island turning against him, especially friends with guns. "I insist, Captain Hastiler. A man in your position is bound to have a hearty appetite. Joseph, serve the captain here."

"Don't mind if I do," said Hastiler. "You set a fine table, Gover-nor." It was far better than what the officer was accustomed to down in his quarters. Too bad he could not say the same for the company he was keeping. There was a time when this gesture of familiarity from the governor would have been welcomed. But that was before the abduction of Henry Morgan and the visit by that insolent Spaniard, Don Alonso, who had had the temerity to fire on Port Royal as he snuck out of the bay. The denizens of Port Royal might be bastards, but by God they were proper English bastards and kinsmen all the same.

Joseph, responding to the governor's command, stepped forward, bearing a silver platter of sausages sizzling in their own juices from a side table, and presented it to the officer. Hastiler used a pair of silver spoons to transfer a couple of links onto his plate and helped himself to a second serving of fried plantain while the opportunity presented itself.

A streamer-tailed hummingbird hovered near the table. Hastiler tossed the bird a piece of bread crust but the tiny little creature flitted away and lost itself among the vines and frangipani. The hummingbird preferred the company of its own kind. Hastiler considered the lesson nature was teaching him. Cleverer men than he had been invited to sit at the governor's table. The captain wasn't fooled, he understood Purselley's reasons. Despite the attack on Port Royal that had all but crippled the buccaneers, Sir Richard had refused to give chase in his English brig. It was as if nothing out of the ordinary had happened. Don Alonso had repaid Purselley's generosity by dishonoring his flag of truce. Even the plantation owners and well-to-do merchants of Kingston found the Spaniard's behavior detestable and an affront to the Crown. They were reminded just how vulnerable was their position.

Sir Richard knew he was treading on dangerous waters, dissatisfaction from Port Royal and Kingston were like an undertow threatening to drag him under. He needed all the support he could muster. His first priority was to placate the local troops. Hastiler and his marines offered the first line of defense should any insurrection arise against authority. Purselley was beginning to doubt the loyalty of the merchants and landowners. They had grown accustomed to a constant supply of Spanish goods, courtesy of the privateers and freebooters populating the port across the bay.

Purselley was attempting small talk and helping himself to the soursop, coconut, sliced mango, and pawpaw melons which Joseph had arranged as a centerpiece, when he glanced up and saw a ghost walking toward him from the drive.

"Morgan," he whispered in horror, his features suddenly pale. How? Where?

Hastiler half turned, rose from his chair, knocked over a teacup and spilled the contents on his scarlet coat. Morgan ambled on through the morning sunlight. He looked thinner, Purselley noted, taking heart, but he moved with the grace of a stalking tiger. The closer Morgan came to the table, the less confident Sir Richard became. A breeze stirred and ruffled Morgan's unbound hair. His deep-set gray eyes were hard and unyielding in his sun-burnished features. He bowed, never taking his eyes off either man. In the distance one could hear the cries of the gulls; close at hand, the hovering bees alighted on the fruit and stole nectar from the few wild blossoms that bordered the drive.

"Well met, Sir Richard," Morgan said with a rueful grin. "Don't let my resurrection spoil your morning meal."

"What are you doing here? Where did you come from?"

"Did you think the Don could hold me? Tell me, Sir Richard, had you washed your hands of me? Well, I'm the nettle in your garden and won't prune so easily."

"Now, see here, Morgan," said Hastiler, "I do not hold with what happened, but do not attempt to bring your troubles across the bay. I will not stand for it."

"Too late. Trouble is here," said Morgan.

"Have it your way," Hastiler said. His hand slipped beneath his coat pocket and produced a flintlock pistol which he aimed at Morgan's stomach.

"Well done, Captain Hastiler," Sir Richard exclaimed, beaming. His rouged cheeks and arched brows made him seem more foppish than usual. "Well now, you smug bastard, what do you have to say for yourself?"

Morgan raised one hand in a fist. At this signal more than two dozen men materialized out of the trees lining the road to Kingston. Another handful poked their heads and their weapons over the wall. Theirs had been the trickiest ascent, and Morgan had stalled his own efforts to see his men safely in place before he approached the terrace. Hastiler cleared his throat and looked around at the muskets and pistols trained on him.

"I may only get off one shot but it will be for you," Hastiler promised, hoping to keep the upper hand in what had become an unpleasant standoff.

"Of course," Morgan replied. "Rafiki!"

"Aye, Captain."

"Mister Hastiler intends to see me dead. As soon as he has killed me, blow off his head."

"With pleasure," the African said. "*Ku-jeruhi.* I will personally cut out his heart."

"And you lads, see that the governor is caught in the crossfire," Morgan said.

"Don't you worry, Monsieur Henri," the Frenchman, Voisin, called out. "He'll have so much lead in him we'll be able to cut him up and use him for grapeshot."

The governor shuddered. "For God's sake, Alan. Set down your gun."

Hastiler hesitated, then slowly lowered the pistol and placed it on the table. He slid it across to Morgan who slid the weapon right back to the officer. The marine looked puzzled.

"Why don't you put that to use elsewhere?" the buccaneer explained. "With me in Panama."

"My God, are you mad?" Sir Richard blurted out.

"You are a soldier," Morgan continued, ignoring the governor's outburst. "Will you serve as some Don's lap dog and take arms against your own? Don Alonso came here in peace but he left a trail of blood in his wake. The lads he chained and tossed over the side to drown might not have been gentlemen, but they were your countrymen, they were English and deserved to die like men, not dogs." Morgan lowered his voice and leaned toward the officer. "I say I know you, Alan Hastiler, that it sticks in your craw like a chunk of bone after a big feast. You cannot abide it. Join us. Sail with us—if not for gold or glory, then for honor."

Hastiler said nothing, nor did he move or indicate what he was thinking. One way of life confronted another—both of them important—where did duty lie? Morgan's words set his spirit ablaze like Greek fire. The truth burned but could not be denied. The minutes crawled past, then, to Purselley's astonishment, the soldier took up his pistol and returned it to his coat pocket. The captain tried to think of all the reasons why he should not listen to the likes of the notorious Henry Morgan. But the memory of Port Royal in flames and the bodies of English men and women floating in the black water were etched upon his soul.

"I should like to see Don Alonso's face when he sees our colors at his gate," the officer said. "For honor, then."

"No! You mustn't." Sir Richard rose from his chair and almost fell over backward. "This is madness," he sputtered, searching for an argument. How to reason with a man like Henry Morgan? "The treaty . . . you fools . . . there is a peace treaty. Try to understand. England is not at war with Spain."

"No," said Morgan. "But I am."

24. "The devil, I am."

In mid-December while bitter temperatures assailed the thirteen English Colonies along the east coast of North America and swept across the Atlantic to bury Britain beneath a blanket of forgetful snow, a warm trade wind rippled the blue-green surface of the Kingston bay and sent the gentle tides to rock the ships nestled along the piers of Port Royal.

In the six weeks since Morgan's return, the Brethren of the Coast had managed to salvage the *Glenmorran* and the *Jericho* and the plucky little sloop *Bluefields*, to the delight of its captain, Dutch Hannah. Stronger than most men, "the duchess" worked as hard as any man when it came to hauling her sloop onto the shore for tarring. By the time the *Bluefields* was seaworthy, the woman's hands were as callused and rope-burned as any man's among her crew.

Meanwhile Sir William Jolly tended the myriad hurts and injuries that beset the repairs. The physician was constantly being summoned, and kept too busy to keep from dwelling on the fact that his daughter and Henry Morgan seemed inseparable. Something had happened to change the buccaneer, his experience in Panama had marked him. He seemed driven by an almost desperate desire to return to Panama City. Sir William suspected that only by conquering the stronghold could Morgan purge whatever demons were plaguing his soul.

Henry Morgan, on the other hand, was merely bemused by the physician's diagnosis when he broached the subject near twilight, on a humid evening in mid-December. Sir William and Morgan were standing in the doorway of Edward Pastusek's carpenter's shop, a ramshackle stucture that could have passed for a barn. Pastusek, a Moravian, had come to Jamaica and found his skills as a woodworker and shipwright to be in immediate demand. The gregarious craftsman had converted the barn into a space suitable for his labors.

"Demons and plagues—Lord help us, Will, you're beginning to sound like the Black Cleric. Best dispatch you to the *Jericho* and unleash that long face of yours on LeBishop," Morgan told him while overseeing his own special project.

Two years ago he had raided an armory in Santiago de Cuba and made off with a shipment of *patereros*, Spanish mortars. The weapons had a barrel a few inches longer than a swivel gun's, were of a similar bore, but fired an explosive shell much like a grenade, a round spherical projectile with an inner fuse. If fitted with a crude but functional stock, under the supervision of Pastusek and old Israel Goodenough, the *patereros* could be handled and fired by a single individual. The weapons were light enough to be transported across the isthmus and would provide the pirates with a kind of artillery when they reached the walls of Panama City.

"Scoff all you may," Sir William drily observed. "But I see what I see."

Morgan tied a black bandanna around his head to keep the perspiration from his eyes. He was dressed for the expedition, in brown sleeveless waistcoat, plain linen shirt, dark brown breeches, and black boots. "Nothing escapes you, eh, old friend?"

"Nothing. More especially when it concerns my only daughter," said Sir William, lowering his voice. "Any man that would take advantage of Nell's . . . heart . . . and cause her pain, will have to answer to me."

"Then they'll answer to us both," Morgan said. "For I treasure her. And hold her in the highest esteem. And when I am done with Panama, I shall say more."

"So be it," the physician replied, satisfied. "Though I wish you would refuse to bring her along."

"Nell is one of us, old man. It is her right to come along. And besides, she can manage her own fate. She is no stranger to fire and sword. And I warrant she could shoot the eye out of a sandfly at twenty paces." Morgan returned his attention to the assembly of mortars. "Israel, keep the men working until all the *patereros* are completed and loaded aboard the *Glenmorran*."

"As you wish," Israel replied. "Hear that, lads, not a drop of jack iron for the lot of you until we're finished here." The half dozen men seated in a circle around a common room grumbled and cursed their fate but continued to work.

Morgan followed Sir William out from the warehouse and into the street where Nell approached them, marching down the street at the head of a ragged parade of British soldiers. Morgan recognized Sergeant Robert McCready just behind Nell, and with him several of the marines hauling pushcarts down the street to the recently repaired sloops.

"What have we here, Nell?" Morgan called out.

Nell grinned and indicated the pushcarts and the column of marines behind her. "Sergeant McCready remembered these recently-received stores, black powder and shot, that came in on the *Westerly* during your absence."

The homely little sergeant beamed with pleasure. He harbored no grudge at the manner in which Morgan had escaped his confinement weeks earlier. "I figure since you intend to make me as rich as a Saracen prince, robbing the governor's magazine is the least I could do."

"That, and lend your hand at the cookfires," Morgan said, waving the column past. Nell remained by his side, dressed as a young squire but smelling like a woman, all lilac water and pink hibiscus.

"Look at them," she said. "It has happened, just as you said." She was looking down the waterfront at the recently patched ships that comprised Morgan's armada.

Three sloops, the *Glenmorran*, *Jericho*, and *Bluefields*; a Dutch flute called the *Sea Spray*, the *Wolfbane*, a single-masted schooner; and the English brig, the *Westerly*, would transport the force Morgan had assembled. Throughout November and into December, his call had gone out across the island, far beyond the rum-soaked confines of Port Royal. Sons of shopkeepers and plantation owners abandoned their Kingston homes for a chance at adventure and Spanish treasure. Fierce Maroons, the dark-skinned descendants of slaves and former enemies of the Spaniards, drifted down from their well-guarded villages in the Blue Mountains and the Cockpit Country, and last, but hardly least, Captain Hastiler and his Royal Marines.

The column of soldiers led by McCready filed past some of the rowdy crew of the *Jericho*; they persisted in admonishing the men in uniform, who for the most part remained unperturbed by the louts. Morgan scowled and shook his head. "If I didn't need them . . ." he said aloud.

"But you do," said an icy-smooth voice behind them. Thomas LeBishop materialized out of a nearby alley. In his funeral garb, the Black Cleric blended into the deepening shadows. "My lads are a bit rough about the edges, but they've never backed away from a fight." LeBishop sauntered forward, peered in at the activity in the shop then rejoined Morgan in the street.

"I have business elsewhere," Sir William grumbled, and headed off down the waterfront. His business involved a visit to any number of taverns. He was welcome in them all.

"Nell, see those powderkegs are distributed among the ships. If we hit a storm I don't want one ship to have all the powder and shot."

The young woman nodded and hurried off to rejoin McCready's column. That left Morgan alone with LeBishop. The man in black quietly appraised Morgan.

"I don't trust you, Henry Morgan. I fear you may be leading us to a grim end."

"Then why come along?"

"The damn Spaniard betrayed me as well as you." LeBishop glanced aside at the buccaneer. "Why didn't you tell the others what happened out in the bay, that it were me and Tregoning that night in the johnnyboat?"

"To what end would it serve but to fuel division among us?" Morgan said. "Besides, I understand you, Thomas LeBishop."

"And you have made your peace, eh? Because you need me and my men for what lies ahead," LeBishop said, stroking his scarred cheek. "And I also have unfinished business in Panama City."

Morgan did not like the sound of that. "Be advised. You sail beneath my flag in this venture. I will not tolerate further treachery."

"A warning? You forget, no man is my equal with a blade," said LeBishop. "When we reach Panama City, if we haven't got ourselves lost in crossing the isthmus, stay out of my way." He removed his hat, wiped his bald, bony skull with a silk scarf, a cold smile on his face. "I am told Sir Richard Purselley is preparing to leave the island on the Dutch merchantman."

"I suggested he might come to harm if he remained," Morgan explained.

"Do not mistake me for Sir Richard," the Black Cleric warned, and stalked off toward the pier and his ship, the *Jericho*.

Morgan gave him a hard look. "LeBishop!" he snapped. The man in black spun on his heels, thinking he had been called out by *el Tigre del Caribe*. LeBishop prepared to defend himself. His long bony fingers clutched at his cutlass. Then he relaxed, realizing Morgan had not made a move toward him.

"I've read your Bible. I know you chapter and verse," Morgan said, his own, gunmetal-gray eyes promising a dire fate. "Do not cross me again."

"The devil you say."

"No," said Morgan in a voice smooth as silk on a sliver of steel, "the devil I *am*."

The Black Cleric frowned and swung about, lurched forward, and continued on his way.

Morgan sighed. And heard his father whisper in his ear.

"The lure of Spanish gold will keep Thomas LeBishop in line, my lad," the ghost cautioned—or was it the first night breeze stolen from the darkening bay? *"But once you take the city . . ."*

Morgan knew the rest.

"There'll be hell to pay."

25. "Before I die..."

They came from the sea, a congregation of tall ships with their
cruciform masts and wide sails bulging, they came on the trade
wind, easing along the coast until Henry Morgan recognized the inlet
from which he had set forth two months ago in the fishing boat he
christened *Little Nell*. Nell was with him now, standing at his side on
the main deck of the *Glenmorran*. She watched his face brighten with
recognition and heard him shout orders to Pierre Voisin at the wheel,
to turn the sloop to starboard and point the bow toward the narrow
entrance between two spits of land that opened onto pristine bay
ringed on three sides by dense forests.

Morgan issued orders to Israel Goodenough, who hurried amidships, cupped a hand to his mouth and shouted, "Mister Kogi! Captain Morgan requests you signal the others if you would be so
kind."

"At his pleasure," Kogi called out. The African riding on the main
top unfurled a crimson banner and hung it from a stay. Meanwhile,
Israel Goodenough instructed his gun crew to fire a signal round
from the only cannon aboard, to make sure they had the attention of
the other ships. The *Glenmorran*, like the other vessels, was virtually
unprotected. Morgan had ordered all the cannons to be removed
from the ships comprising his makeshift armada, and left back in Port
Royal, a gamble that allowed each vessel to carry more than its usual

complement of men. Each vessel had been permitted a single twelve-pounder for the purpose of signaling one another. Thomas LeBishop only grudgingly gave up the *Jericho*'s cannons. But in the end he relented, when Morgan threatened to leave him behind.

A shot rang out from the *Jericho*, the *Westerly* with its complement of Royal Marines, and the *Bluefields*, where Dutch Hannah and Calico Jack and Anne Bonney had taken up with each other and formed a consort the likes of which Morgan didn't even want to think about. The other ships, a pair of flutes captained by Six Toes Yaquereno and Cockade Tom Penmerry, also reported and followed the *Glenmorran* into the bay.

Nell sensed her father standing beside her. She turned and nodded in an unspoken greeting. Sir William tried to imagine the little girl he had taught to sail, the child he had bounced upon his lap. Who was this blue-eyed woman, dressed in canvas britches, a seaman's linen shirt and waist sash, her bosom crisscrossed with pistol belts, powder flask, and shot pouch? She'd vouchsafed a proper lady's nosegay for throwing daggers. Who was this vixen, her cheeks tan and tinged with windburn, her auburn hair concealed beneath a yellow bandanna? His daughter, a hellion? And keeping company with Henry Morgan? He suddenly felt old, assailed by every father's lament—where did the time go? When had the river reached the sea?

Morgan ordered the johnnyboats lowered away. He intended to be the first person ashore. Nell patted her father's arm then hurried to rejoin her paramour, wanting to be at his side when he set foot upon the coast of Panama. Morgan exhorted the crew to put their backs into the oars while he stood at the bow. Rafiki Kogi, who had scrambled down from his roost to take his seat at the stern, kept the oarsmen working in cadence with a singsong chant. He sang of hard work, of times long gone, words he had once labored to in the fields of those who had purchased him on the slave docks; a slave, but now free, the equal of any man in Port Royal, equal among the Brethren, for whom gold was the only color that mattered.

> "*Pull to the left*
> *Pull to the right*
> *Put the child to bed*
> *Put out the light.*
> *Break my back*
> *But I won't cry*

Break these chains
Before I die."

The boat scraped sand and Morgan leaped over the side and splashed the few remaining yards to shore, striding up onto the beach, ferocious as a storm that's blown ashore, grateful to feel solid earth beneath his legs after nine days at sea. He drew his cutlass and raised it aloft in his right hand, his left extended, fingers splayed. His eyes blazed and his limbs shuddered for a second and then he loosed a terrible cry that sent shivers coursing the length of Nell's spine, and had the same effect on the dozen men who leaped after her and slogged to shore.

"Henry?" she said, gingerly approaching, startled by the cry that had issued from somewhere deep within him, a place of rage and anguish and a fierce exultation. He frightened her, and she loved him.

Morgan turned and looked at her, returned the cutlass to his belt and held his out his arms, fists close together. "Break these chains before I die."

"What do you mean?"

"You will know, when Panama City lies at my feet."

Before long, johnnyboats from the other ships dotted the blue waters of the bay. Above the masts with their trimmed sails, the seabirds whirled and sang, wild gulls and terns, their garbled cries carried to shore and mingled with the sounds of the jungle, the high-pitched chatter of night monkeys, and the rasp of tree frogs—and all of it suspiciously like laughter, as if the creatures of earth and sky knew something Morgan and his men did not.

The signal pyre was where Morgan had left it, but taller by a third. No doubt Kintana and his men had added to it. Morgan wondered if the Kuna were still keeping their vigil somewhere inland. Or had they given up on him? *They might have come to the end of their string.* Morgan was late, overdue by nearly a week—or Kintana might be dead. In the jungles of Panama, there were no guarantees of tomorrow.

Morgan removed a brass flask from a pouch, uncorked the bottle and emptied the whale oil it contained onto the timber. He struck flint, using his pistol for a firestarter. Flames danced along the branches, grew ravenous, feasted on the taller logs, spread quickly, leaped skyward, sent a column of smoke and sparks spiraling toward the sky like spent prayers.

Then there was nothing to do but unload the ships and men. Morgan watched them come on and marveled at the mixture. Had there ever been an army as disparate as this? There was Captain Alan Hastiler, his ears no doubt still ringing from Sir Richard's admonishments, and the King's own Royal Marines. Farther along the beach, Nell Jolly and the crew of the *Glenmorran*, a salty bunch loyal to a fault. Maybe for a moment he had his doubts about Nell's presence, that he was placing her in jeopardy. But Nell was free to follow her heart. Indeed, Morgan did not rule by some decree. They called him Captain and followed him because they chose to, he had earned their trust. Freedom was the precious element. Nell chose to be at his side. And Henry Morgan was grateful. And as for her safety . . . well, now, she could take care of herself, and thinking any less would be an insult to her.

Morgan considered the rest of his force, aristocratic sons of Jamaica's landowners, the sons of shopkeepers and merchants anxious for adventure. Here were the men from a Maroon village, silent, dark-skinned warriors who had more in common with the Kuna than the men they sailed with. But the Maroons were welcome. Morgan knew they were relentless fighters. And then more freebooters, pirates of every size and shape, Calico Jack and Anne Bonney and the rest, and last but never least, the Black Cleric and his *Jericho* boys and every one a cutthroat. There wasn't one of the Cleric's "choirboys" whom Morgan would turn his back on.

LeBishop troubled him more than any of the others. The man had his own goals and Morgan suspected they would reach beyond the walls of Panama City. The Black Cleric was also driven by a thirst for vengeance, for the indignity he had suffered at the hands of Elena Maria and her new husband.

Doña Elena Maria troubled Morgan. She still mattered to him after all that had happened, even while he loved Nell, and yet though he continued to care, he also was keenly aware how she had betrayed him, plotted his death. Morgan intended to settle the matter one way or another. But he was not Thomas LeBishop, whose mind worked in devious ways. He did not hate like the Black Cleric.

Then again, no one did.

By nightfall, most of the force was ashore and the inlet was ringed with campfires as the watch was posted and men settled down for a well-deserved rest. Rum flowed and cookpots were filled with rice and beans and jerked beef. The men ate their fill and rolled into their blankets for a quiet rest beneath the stars. Morgan and a handful of hardy souls, among them Rafiki Kogi, Sergeant Robert McCready, and Dutch Hannah, who liked to prove she could outwork, outfight, outshoot, and outdrink any man, added timber to the pyre, brought the blaze back to its former glory, and then retired for the night.

Morgan and Nell managed to sneak away from the armed host. He brought her to a small clearing a dozen or so yards into the jungle. She looked with some misgiving at the thick stand of palm trees and the barrier of great leafy fronds that protected them from being seen. But Morgan's confidence inspired her. She relaxed, and reclined alongside him. Morgan produced a wheel of cheese, a bottle of port, dried fruit and biscuits. She was appropriately impressed.

They ate in silence, feeling comfortable with the proximity of his force and the journey that lay ahead. And when they had finished their meal, the two reclined beneath the stars. Nell's skin was cool to the touch, as if kissed by the moonlight. Together they surrendered to the hunger harbored in their hearts. They clung to each other in the timeless dance of desire. Their passion was a kind of prayer, a union made holy, a oneness that is the purpose of love, a yearning to be connected to the Divine.

In the morning, the sun rose over the ashes of the pyre. And with the dawn came gray skies, a warm downpour, then a damp mist that curled among the palms like the spirits of the dead. Morgan woke and lay quiet with Nell in his arms, enjoying the stillness until it was shattered by LeBishop haranguing several of the men about the foolishess of this venture. "The Cleric's picked a poor time and place to find a flaw in my plans," Morgan muttered.

"He'll talk himself out soon enough, like every big wind that blows hard." Nell sat upright and reached for her clothes, found herself staring up at Anne Bonney who had been enjoying her own nightly tryst with Calico Jack. Anne grinned and cocked a thumb in the direction of the beach.

"The Black Cleric's preaching poison. Best you face him down or you'll wind up handed a black spot and forced aside."

Morgan rose and pulled on his clothes, ignoring Anne Bonney, who only pretended not to watch. When he had left the clearing, Bonney chuckled. She noticed her shirt ribbons were untied and the folds parted to reveal her enormous bosom. "Well now, I see why you kept him in your gunsights all these years. A man like that needs more than one woman."

"Don't bet on it," Nell replied icily.

Anne Bonney was taken aback. Calico Jack's paramour chuckled and backed away; her heavyset frame rippled as she laughed. "These men of ours, bless 'em, says I. Keep your honest sods, I'll take a man with a little hot steel in his blood."

Out on the strand, where the longboats were drawn up on the shore, Thomas LeBishop had assembled his own crew and many of the men from the other boats as well. But the crowd fell quiet as Morgan entered their midst. However, the Black Cleric held his ground.

"What mischief are you conspiring now, LeBishop?"

"We are free men here, we can discuss what we will."

"Indeed. I would have it no other way. And if you choose to leave, so be it. I have no need for cowards."

LeBishop's expression grew mottled and his eyes blazed. "I say this is a fool's errand."

"Do you indeed," Morgan laconically observed.

"We have eyes. You did not tell us about the jungle. We thought you'd use the road out of Portobello."

"The road is well patrolled. Panama City would know of our coming long before we arrived," Morgan said. "But no one expects a force of any size to attempt to cross the isthmus through the lowlands and bayous."

"Of that I have no doubt!" LeBishop waved a hand toward the forbidding-looking wall of trees and vines. "Look at that green hell. You expect us to march through that all the way to Panama City."

"I do. And I expect us to fight like the devil when we arrive. I expect each of us to fight and maybe die, but to take the city and if we live, lay claim to the treasure of the Dons." Morgan folded his muscled arms across his solid chest as he searched the faces of the men around him. "We shall sack the city then return by the road. The patrols will retreat toward Portobello and warn that fort of our approach. However, we shall bypass the fort and march down the coast to our ships and return to Jamaica with the wealth of the Dons."

Let LeBishop appeal to their failing courage; Morgan would play to their greed.

"We'll never see Panama City," the Black Cleric said. He strode from the circle and walked toward the vast green barrier of vines and fronds and towering trees. LeBishop turned his back to the jungle and held up his hands in dismay, spreading the flaps of his coat until he resembled some overgrown, gangly raven as he confronted Morgan and the rest of the men. "And who will guide us across the isthmus?"

Morgan and the others continued to stare at him, then past him. Thomas LeBishop felt the hairs rise on the back of his neck and slowly turned on his heels as a ripple of awareness spread through the entire encampment.

A ragged line of fierce-looking Kuna warriors, armed with axes and muskets, materialized out of the ghostly mist and impenetrable-looking landscape.

Kintana had arrived.

26. Nowhere to run.

And this was Consuelo's dream . . .

First there was poetry, in nature, the moon round and draped with gossamer clouds, transformed into a milky-white orb, like her blind right eye. So that was it. The gods were blind! Perhaps this was the answer for all that had happened to her mother's people since the coming of the Spanish conquerors, whose descendants Consuelo had been raised to serve, while they hunted down her mother's people, sent them to work in the mines, had them hanged or drawn and quartered to serve as an example, to guard against insurrection.

Foolish savages. They only brought it on themselves. Shameful-shameful-shameful, they should have learned like her. Consuelo had survived. She had found a place, a crack in the colliding worlds, and had ridden out the storm tucked away in a protective niche of loyal service.

And now, here she was dreaming of blind gods. What kind of thanks was that?

The small-boned woman moaned in her bed, in her little room that she did not have to share with any other servant because she was mistress's favorite, her little room that was at the end of the upstairs hall instead of down below, in the barracks like servants' quarters off to the side of the hacienda. No, Consuelo was upstairs with the privileged, and it had served her well, this little room. But tonight it offered little comfort. Because of all the blood and the fire and the screams of the dying that filled her head.

First there was the moon, then the dawn, and the dying, and the blood. The blood was the most curious of all. It started at the front gate, a glassy crimson pool welling up out of the languishing earth at the entrance to the city, where the road to Portobello led off into the hills. The blood, imbued with a life of its own, followed a serpentine course through the outskirts of the city, flowed beneath water troughs and around the fountains bubbling in the centers of the smaller plazas, past brothels . . . Dogs lapped at the blood and trotted off, their jaws dripping ichor, past churches with their bells and carols and bones of the saints.

The blood lingered by the cathedrals, these monuments to a loving Creator whose people seemed bent on enslaving other races, a God who sent his priests into the jungles to convert the very people Spain had come to subjugate. The Kuna were only too happy to turn them into martyrs. It was hard work but someone had to do it.

But the blood flowed on, leaving a crimson trail through alleys, through streets where men and women went about their lives, dreaming, loving, trading goods and gossip, talking of the weather, downstreet where fishermen set out for the bay, and where merchants lined the shelves of their stalls with their wares, where a potter loaded the firebox of his wood kiln and prepared for a long day. But the river of blood marked him, soaked the reed moccasins on his feet, and continued on through his house and out the front door and down the city streets until it reached the Avenida Balboa. Buildings erupted into flames in the wake of the blood trail, as it seeped and creeped across thresholds and windowsills and into the house of Saucedo, through the door and up the stairs and down the hall . . .

Consuelo reached up and clawed at her blind eye, an act that brought her completely awake, gasping for breath. Her flesh the color of the potter's clay was streaked with perspiration, her bony fingers splayed before her as if to ward off a demon.

"Oh, O heaven save us, preserve us all." The Christian god was her god now, but she spoke in the tongue of her mother's people, for whom the world was alive with spirits and devilish animal tricksters, a people for whom the earth and the sea had many moods and must be appeased.

Consuelo sat upright, struggled for breath, terror an iron glove gripping her chest. She pulled the covers to her chin and stared at her bedroom door and imagined she could hear the crackling flames as the city burned around her, and waited for the blood to well beneath her door and ooze across her floor.

She reached out and caught her robe, heard a hammering in the hall and gasped anew, wondering if this was the end, the dream slowly receding from her thoughts, leaving her with the dread of all that she had witnessed. She rose from the bed, padded barefoot across the cool tile floor, steadied herself on the table that held her washbasin, reached and found the doorlatch and opened the door and stepped into a wide airy hall, the floor strewn with handwoven rugs from Chiloe. The walls were ablaze with *molas*, intricately stitched aprons from Kuna craftswomen, hung like works of art on either side of the hall. Elena's father had prized the garments with their colorful designs, swirls, and interlocking loops, peacocks and frogs and sea creatures rendered in the natural shades of the world around them: the yellow of trumpet-vine blossoms, the blue of sea and sky, the cardinal colors of the hibiscus flower, coconut-shell brown, and sun-gold.

Don Alonso del Campo stood outside his wife's bedroom door, his patrician features flush with the effects of too much drink. His fist hammered on the walnut-paneled door. "Woman!" he shouted. "Elena Maria . . . this is foolishness. I am your husband."

The strains of a Celtic harp drifted from the room. The woman within seemed wholly unconcerned, and continued to practice her Irish jig. The melody coaxed from the stringed instrument seemed to mock the man in the hall.

"As the governor of Panama I order you to receive me. Open this door." He slammed his fist against the heavy panel and winced and drew away, cradling his right hand. He shook his head and mimicked a silent scream, his silver-streaked hair tousled from his efforts. He pressed his forehead against the wood and sighed, glanced around and saw Consuelo watching him. He ignored her and spoke to the woman in the room.

"I will do what is best for my family, my parents and sisters. The monies I receive for the plantation will enable them to eliminate their debts, return the estates in Toledo to their former splendor. It is my right to do this. Your father would understand."

The harp continued. It seemed evident that once again, Don Alonso would not enjoy his wife's favors. He scowled. So be it. Let the little vixen sulk. She was a *criollas*, and without his good name, that was all she would ever be. He shoved clear of the wall and stumbled forward, slowly regained his footing as he approached the stairway. The governor could feel the old woman's baleful eye upon him.

"Get back, old witch," he said, drawing back his hand as if to strike her. Consuelo held her ground, refusing to budge; after what she had seen, she had no fear of Don Alonso. He sensed this, drew close, blinked, scrutinized her dark features, noticed for the first time a circular tattoo upon her neck, back behind her ear, a swirling vinelike pattern similar to those found on the *molas* I adorning the walls.

"What are you looking at?" he snarled, his eyes mere brown slits.

"La muerte," she whispered, the dreams still clinging to her thoughts, unable to rid herself of the horror.

"Bah!" he exclaimed, and shoved past, continuing down the stairway and out through the front door where a carriage waited to take him to his favorite bordello, a place where he knew he would be welcome, where the women never said no, where being el gobernador really meant something.

Back in the hall, Consuelo continued to Elena's bedroom and knocked upon the door and announced herself. The harp ceased. She heard footsteps, the latch slid back and the door opened. Elena's features appeared in the crack, a candle in her hand. "Consuelo, what is it? I am sorry, little mother, if Don Alonso disturbed your rest."

"No. But he does nothing to help it, either," said the nurse, with a doleful expression on her face. "But he did not wake me."

"Then what brings you to my door?" Elena stood aside and permitted her to enter. The bedroom was high-ceilinged, wide and airy, with a comfortable-looking canopy bed near one wall, a walnut wardrobe and cherrywood table and chair providing additional comforts. Her harp rested on its stand near the window. "Look at you, Consuelo. You are trembling." Elena Maria put her arm around her old nurse, revealing a tender side she had subjugated for the most part since the death of her father. "You must take care of yourself. Now that Don Alonso has chosen to punish Major Barba by ordering him to patrol the bayous, you are my only true friend in the city. How quickly the merchants and moneylenders forget all my father did for them. He protected their interests, and now there is none who I can trust, save Gilberto and you."

"And if you trust me, *pobrecita*, then you must do as I tell you."

Elena's green eyes narrowed. "What do you mean?"

Consuelo recounted her dream in vivid detail, everything she could remember, though some of the images had begun to fade. But there was enough to frighten her again. "We must leave Panama City. Go to the plantation down the coast. We cannot stay here."

"And run from a dream? Abandon everything here, the mines, the gold and silver in my father's warehouse? What of the coffee, the cacao, and sugar, ready for transport? I will not hand it over to Don Alonso. But there is no longer a place for us at the plantation to the south. My husband sold it yesterday."

"You were born there," Consuelo replied. She did not like the thought of strangers occupying the land.

"That does not matter as long as my husband can provide the means to rescue his family from their debts." Elena crossed the room and sat on the side of the bed. She had slept with Don Alonso in every bed but this one. Her room would never be open to him. This was the bed of her childhood. He would not soil it with his sweat or any other fluids. Two months of marriage had revealed some most unpleasant flaws in his character. Don Alonso had a brittle, vindictive temperament and a penchant for drink that would one day be his undoing if not brought under control. Unfortunately, all the wealth and power at his disposal merely accentuated his character flaws, gave him free rein to indulge his own peculiar vices.

Elena Maria handed a tortoiseshell brush to Consuelo who immediately began to stroke the doña's long black tresses. Old habits died hard. "Sometimes a dream is only just that, a dream and nothing more."

The daughter of the house of Saucedo winced as the brush fought its way through a tangle. "Gently," she chided her nurse, and turned her thoughts to the matter of Henry Morgan. Had the jungles really claimed him? More than likely. And yet there was a part of her that imagined him surviving, because she had lain with him, listened to his heart, and come to share the belief in his luck and his indomitable will. And if he lived, then one day he would exact vengeance. Panama City was a tempting plum, ripe for the plucking. She freed herself from Consuelo, stood and walked to the window, opening the shutters to catch a glimpse of the city at night. Lanterns gleamed in the windows of the haciendas. Light flooded the streets through open doorways. Music and laughter permeated the air, underscored by the *tramp, tramp, tramp* of soldiers filing past. For Don Alonso had all but gutted the garrison stations in the harbor, choosing to swell the ranks of the garrison defending the city. Barricades had been built throughout the city, turning walkways into fortresses and plazas into killing fields. But would these preparations stop a man like Henry Morgan?

Perhaps Consuelo was right after all. Elena Maria should leave, flee.

But thanks to the greed of her husband, Don Alonso del Campo, there was nowhere to run.

A ghostly glare briefly illuminated the Plaza de los Armas, outlined the gallows and the long stone buildings that housed the grenadiers, before draping them once more in shadow. In his carriage Don Alonso del Campo emerged from the Avenida Saucedo, reined in his gelding and paused to identify his surroundings. Earlier in the evening he would have found any number of soldiers lounging out-side their quarters, playing cards, sharing their wine and spirits, trad-ing the gossip of the city. But the governor had patronized several cantinas this night and the doe-eyed vixen at his side was keeping him occupied, pressing her hot, willing form against him, reminding him of all the unfulfilled passions she was prepared to accommodate. Her name was Felicia. At least, he thought it was. Not that her name mat-tered. She was dark and wild-eyed and had full lips and a plump, well-rounded derriere. *Who needs any woman's name, as long as her bed is warm and she is a willing partner?* he thought. *That's all any man requires.*

Don Alonso intended to spend the night at the governor's palace. If only he could find the Avenida Balboa. Every time he asked the lit-tle *puta* for directions she would merely laugh and tell him anyplace would do. The effects of the wine they had consumed at the brothel had left her worse off than the governor. She knew only the moment, that for tonight she was the consort of *el gobernador*—nothing else mattered; least of all, directions. Felicia laughed and draped one arm around his neck, placed her other hand on his thigh, ran her tongue along the inside of his ear, then whispered indecencies.

"Later," Don Alonso growled, and shoved her back against the seat. His patience was at an end. Anger added force to his gesture, more than he intended. The woman lost her balance, her arms flailed the night air as she tumbled from the carriage and landed on her back in the street, her head slapping the brick surface, cutting short her cry. "Woman!" Don Alonso closed his eyes and pinched the bridge of his nose, tried to clear the cobwebs from his brain. He locked the brake with his left foot, climbed out of the carriage and, steadying himself with his hand against the wheels and frame, walked around to the other side. "Get up or I will leave you here," he ordered.

A faint moan escaped her. Don Alonso knelt, wheezing as the walnut grip of his flintlock pistol dug into his gut. He removed the weapon and tucked it into his coat pocket. Then he bent forward and placed his head upon her chest and listened for her breath. Thankfully, he heard it. He examined her head and discovered an egg-sized lump on the back of her skull. Don Alonso cursed softly and then struggled to his feet. He swayed, the world careened, he felt he was striding the deck of a ship in the aftermath of a storm where the slate-green sea swells and pitches.

He shrugged off the sickening sensation and proceeded across the plaza toward the long houses. He was certain once the soldiers within were alerted he could count on them to see him safely to the palace—no, to the house of Saucedo. He would not permit himself to be the subject their idle talk. No matter if Elena Maria refused her favors.

Don Alonso scowled at the thought of her insolence. How dare she treat him this way! He was her husband. All that was hers belonged to him. This conduct must not stand. By right it was his responsibility to administer her fortune as he saw fit. Did she expect him to allow his own family's estate to fall into disrepute? Never. The little *criollos* had much to learn if she thought he was going to tolerate this situation any longer.

Lost in the city and in his thoughts, the governor was midway across the plaza when the moon cleared from behind a gossamer cloud and bathed the plaza in silver moonlight. Don Alonso stopped dead in his tracks and stared at the gallows. A solitary figure was standing astride the trap. The governor caught his breath, stifled a scream of horror. What specter was this? Ghost or man? Could it be Morgan? But he was lost to the jungles lo these many weeks, food for the cougar or slaughtered by Kuna rebels. What arcane force had roused him from the land of the dead and sent him back among the living?

"Well, then, I shall finish what I failed to do before," Don Alonso muttered, and pulled his pistol from his coat pocket. He lurched toward the gallows, his mind reeling from the sight of this apparition. His blood coursed like ice water through his veins, his steps were leaden as he approached the gallows steps, thirteen in all, and he paused, summoned his resolve, then charged up the steps.

"*Bastardo del infierno*, I will send you back to the devil!"

Don Alonso vaulted over the last couple of steps and landed on the deck and leveled the flintlock at the startled figure he had glimpsed from below. He squeezed the trigger. The flint struck the frizzen and sent a minute shower of sparks into the priming pan in which the governor had failed to measure a trace of gunpowder. The weapon misfired, fortunately for Father Estéban Pinzón.

The priest gasped and held up his arms as if to ward off the lead ball. Don Alonso blinked, his eyes grew wide as he recognized the priest who had been the celebrant at his wedding. The governor sheepishly lowered his weapon.

"I dare say, Señor, that I pray it is into the arms of the Father I shall send my soul when my time is ended."

"Your pardon, *mi padre*, I thought you were . . ." The governor's voice trailed off, as if he was loath to speak the name for fear of summoning the brigand from his place of torment.

"Morgan?" asked the priest. "No, I am not the man. But I fear I may have as much blood on my hands as that uncommon rogue." Father Estéban lifted his bony hands from the folds of his brown robe. The moonlight on his face gave him the appearance of a man carved from stone.

"What are you doing here at such an hour?" said the governor. The exertion and rush of energy had sobered him to some degree.

"Looking for answers."

"Seek them in the Cathedral de Santa Maria. If you cannot find them there, of what use to search the streets? And at such a late hour?"

"Late, yes, the hour may be too late for all of us, Excellency," Father Estéban replied. He placed a hand upon the timber frame from which the hangman's noose would dangle on a day of execution. "We have built an empire on suffering. Now and then it troubles me. I pray for guidance. I send the young priests to go among the slaves and speak to them of God, to teach them the way of truth. We save their souls even as we break their backs."

"It is the way of things. God chose us to be their masters. We have built an empire to the glory of God. It why we are blessed, padre. Those who do His Will, prosper."

"I wonder . . ." said the priest. "Perhaps I am getting old and think too much. Like some clever merchant, I have begun to weigh everything."

"Of course," Don Alonso assured him, mopping his sweat-beaded brow on the sleeve of his shirt. The warehouse of Elena Maria de

Saucedo was filled with gold and silver ore, silks and chests of jeweled trinkets, and gold doubloons, *reales*, and pieces of eight. That was all the assurance he needed that he had God's favor.

"And yet here we stand," the old priest said, "on a gallows in the middle of the night, fearing the retribution of Divine Providence." He sighed. "And the wrath of a ghost."

27. "... the dogs of war."

The waterfall spilled down from a jagged line cliffs over a hundred feet above the hillside trail that had brought the column of freebooters up from the valley floor. The waters cascaded down the moss-gray face of the cliff and plunged into a deep-green pool large enough for half the column to gather round and drink their fill.

After leaving a token force under Sir William Jolly's command, to guard the ships or pilot them out into open water if necessary, Morgan had lost no time in marching the remainder of his command away from the coast and into the rain forest. He assumed, and rightly so, once these sea rovers were good and lost beneath the canopy of towering white-trunked trees, the naysayers among them would cease their grumbling and complaints. His ploy worked. By the afternoon of the first day it became clear there was no turning back, not without a proper guide. The grousing and grumbling ceased. It was now a matter of Conquer or Die.

They'd pressed hard, walking from sunup to sundown, with only brief stops to rest and slake their thirst and gnaw a strip of jerked beef. Tightening their belts, the motley little army had managed to cross a good portion of the isthmus in less than a week. Eventually they filed out from beneath the canopy of guayacan trees and climbed into the highlands, where the waterfall was a welcome discovery. Morgan had permitted an early camp, fearing if he pushed them too hard, his force would arrive exhausted at the gates of Panama City.

Hastiler's Royal Marines, and the Maroons from the Jamaican highlands, were in the best shape. The soldiers were accustomed to being drilled and marching on parade. The Maroons, on the other hand, spent much of their lives crisscrossing the Jamaican highlands in search of game; walking mile after mile through vine-thick jungle was of little concern. The buccaneers and the Kingston men fared the worst, and were grateful for the opportunity to stack their muskets and take an early rest.

Morgan posted pickets along the trail in both directions and then returned to the pool to drink his fill. He worked his way to the water's edge through a thicket of birds of paradise, whose claw-shaped blossoms made a startling pattern of scarlet-and-pink splashes against a backdrop of emerald fronds.

The water was cool to the taste. Morgan removed his sleeveless brown waistcoat and cupped water to his face and splashed it over his head and neck. He promised himself he would return in the morning for a proper bath. Emerging from the thicket he saw that Rafiki Kogi had built a cookfire over which Nell began to prepare a meal of beans and rice and flatbread.

Morgan acknowledged them both, but instead of joining his friends, he continued through the encampment. He wanted to make his presence known, to gauge for himself how the men were holding up. It was a unique assortment, this force of brave souls who had followed him from Jamaica. And amazingly, save for the Kuna, the rest of the column intermingled. Royal Marines in their lobster-red coats and faded white breeches conversed with dusky-skinned Maroons in homespun garments. Young squires, the landed gentry of the island, hobnobbed with freebooters and pirates. A familiar voice called out from one fire as Morgan passed a circle of marines.

"Well, now, Captain Morgan, come by later and break bread with us," Sergeant McCready called out.

"I should be in your debt if you've a meat pasty among your possibles," Morgan grinned.

"Maybe when we reach the city. I'll serve you a proper feast on Spanish finery," said McCready, while the men around him cleaned and primed their muskets and sharpened their bayonets.

"You'll have your pick of gold plates and silver spoons," Morgan chuckled. He ambled past the good-natured soul and followed the line of redcoats until he came to Captain Hastiler. The officer looked haggard, like he'd been twisted and wrung out and hung to dry. He had been in discomfort and unable to keep anything in his stomach for the past couple of days.

"How do you fare, Captain?" Morgan asked.

"I've seen better days."

"It will be worth it when we take the city."

"The way I feel right now, it will be worth it if I get killed trying," Hastiler groaned, rubbing his abdomen. He leaned on his musket, using the weapon for a crutch.

"Another day and we'll be at the walls. Will you be able to command your men?"

"I did not come all this way to hand these good lads over to another. You point me to the Spaniards, my lads and I shall have at them," Hastiler replied, forcing himself to straighten up and put on a good face for his men. They derived their confidence from him. He was not about to let them down. "And should I survive this, perhaps your luck will shelter me from Purselley's wrath. He will have the admiralty convinced I have mutinied."

"Purselley is finished," Morgan replied. The confidence in his voice allayed the officer's fears. "I shall personally speak on your behalf. Those were Englishmen the Spaniards killed. You are merely acting on their behalf for King and Country."

"Still, the Dons might save you the trouble." Hastiler groaned and, pressing a hand to his belly, excused himself and darted off behind the bushes.

Morgan made his farewell and headed for Kintana's campsite. He had questions. It was time for answers. Their Kuna war party had settled down in a clearing apart from the buccaneers. The natives in the clearing studied Morgan as he approached. Felipe and Chaua, unlike their suspicious companions, shouted their greetings.

The two were hunched over a cookfire of their own. Felipe was turning a pair of plump lizards on a spit. Chaua waited patiently, his eyes on the searing meat. Several of their companions had killed, skinned, and butchered a capybara. Chunks of dark meat sizzled above the flames. Morgan was offered a place at the makeshift feast but politely declined. There had been days when he'd been hungry enough to eat rat, but this wasn't one of them. He searched the clearing and discovered Kintana standing in the shadow of a cluster of trees bedecked with orchids. The rebel leader was lost in an animated conversation with a squat, barrel-chested, tattooed native who had been waiting by the waterfall.

Kintana appeared upset, and grew more so the longer the inter-change continued. Eventually they noticed Morgan. Kintana dis-patched the warrior, who trotted off down the slope while the rebel leader continued along the hillside until he came to a bluff overlook-ing a path that wound across the ridge and dropped off in a steady decline to the emerald cloud forests in the valley below.

As the column behind him settled in for the night, Morgan kept Kin-tana in sight, and when the warrior paused on the overlook, Morgan chose that moment to approach him. The music from the cascading waters filled the air while a whole chorus of wildlife noises—parrots, parakeets, umbrellabirds, and motmots—created a symphony at sunset the likes of which Adam might have heard in Eden. Morgan was satis-fied that they were far enough removed from the main camp that Kin-tana could speak without anyone overhearing what he had to say.

Morgan waited, hooked his thumbs in his belt while the diminu-tive Indian leaned in toward him. "My brother Miguel," the warrior said, indicating the crushed trail the departing Kuna had left in the tall grass behind them—"he brings bad news, Anglais."

"I can guess," Morgan said.

Although Kintana had met them on the shore with about thirty men, he had promised just about every Kuna rebel in Panama would join the column here in the highlands. At the beginning of the march, Morgan had estimated the Kuna reinforcements might swell his ranks to more than a thousand men—an army still outnumbered by the Spaniards, but a force to be reckoned with all the same. From Kin-tana's sick expression and the lack of anyone to greet them here by the highland pool, it appeared Morgan had woefully overestimated the resolve of the Kuna people.

"Where are the others?" Morgan asked. "Will they not fight to free themselves?"

"They fight and they die," Kintana retorted, offended by the pirate's attitude. "But my people do not trust you. No matter what I tell them: Anglais, the Spaniards, all the same. My people will remain in the jungle, to watch, to wait, hoping you and the Dons kill one another off."

"Sounds like a good plan to me," Morgan replied glumly. He couldn't blame them. The Kuna had been invaded and subjugated and driven from their homeland. To them, this army of cutthroats and English soldiers was to be regarded with suspicion. "Maybe you and the others should join the rest of your people."

"I will fight at your side," Kintana said flatly.

"Are you certain this is wise?"

"No," Kintana conceded. The man was blunt if nothing else. "Last night, I saw a flaming light fall across the sky and burn itself out like an ember from my campfire. It was my death. Or perhaps, yours."

"Kintana, I have seen this before. It means nothing," Morgan protested.

The warrior shook his head in dismay. Then he shrugged and started back the way he had come. That was the trouble with Anglais and the Spaniards—all of them—they could not see the Great Circle of Life, they were blind to the fact that there was meaning and portent in the simplest act of beauty.

The buccaneers filled their water casks and devoured the last of the beans and rice, and with the evening, settled down for the last night's rest some of them would ever have. Calico Jack, Anne Bonney, and the Dutch Hannah Lee sprawled together on the same blanket, Calico Jack in the middle—and and there was not a man among the column who envied his position. Nell pointed them out with a grin as the sun settled beyond the hills and shadows lengthened across the landscape. Blue butterflies drifted down from the trees, attracted by the waterfall. Toucans and bellbirds announced the approach of night, and sang down the sunlight. A few of the pirates produced their concertinas and played a merry round but no one had the energy to dance. At last, the musicians wearied and the music died out.

Henry Morgan sat by the fire, with Nell at his side. The woman had a whetstone and was sharpening her daggers. She spat on the surface, used the coarse side to grind the steel, then the fine surface to give the blades the razor-edge she favored. Israel Goodnough, Rafiki Kogi, and Pierre Voisin, the little thief, were never far from the couple.

The world might brand them brigands, but Morgan knew them as good men, loyal and true, who could be counted on when things were at their darkest. They had sailed long and far together, through fair wind and foul, ridden out the storms, torn down the flags of Spain, and run up the Jolly Roger on a dozen ports and countless merchant ships, whenever they could pick one off from its well-armed escort. They'd roamed where they would, free men, bound by no code but their own. Morgan could ask for no better company.

"Take care, Toto, you'll make the edge too keen."

"A knife can't be too sharp," she said. "Nor a man too ardent."

"Is that so?"

"Yes. Ask any woman."

"Maybe I will," he grinned.

Nell scowled and decided to change the topic. The closer they came to Panama City, the more she sensed Elena Maria's "poison" still affected Morgan. "Best you worry about how to get us past the walls of Panama City."

"Perhaps the Spaniards will believe we are pilgrims and pass us through." Israel spoke up from his blanket. Their conversation had carried to the men around them.

"*Mai oui, mon frère*, and perhaps the next pigs we see will have wings," Voisin chided.

"And roost in the treetops," Kogi added. "In my village, I have seen many strange things. I have heard the dead moan from their graves. I have watched a demon pass from a snake to a man and then into a bird. In my village we know all things are possible."

"I heard a snake quote chapter and verse," Morgan said. "Just the other morning, as we broke camp."

"Be wary of that serpent, it has a deadly bite," Israel warned. Practically everyone had heard the Black Cleric, at one time or another, rant on about some biblical verse.

"I can handle LeBishop," Morgan said.

"That's what the blind man said when he caught the copperhead by the tail," Rafiki Kogi muttered.

"He and I have reached an understanding."

"That's what the shark said," Voisin chuckled.

"All the same, watch your back whenever LeBishop or that toad of his, Tregoning, is about," Nell told him, setting the whetstone aside. "Not all your enemies will be in front of you when we storm the city." She wiped the knife clean on the hem of his shirt and held the dagger aloft until it captured the last golden rays of sunlight. She glanced toward the water, glimpsed the blue butterflies, and marveled at the beauty of this place. Too bad a person could not find contentment among the simple things. The world was full of riches, if only there were time to notice.

The men around the fire grew quiet. The flames danced and fed along the surface of the timber, branches cracked and sizzled, moisture popped, and embers exploded, sending streamers of glowing sparks spiraling into the night. Then Nell asked the question that was on everyone's mind. "Can we do this?"

The Spaniards were bound to outnumber them two to one, perhaps three to one. The renegade army had no cannons, only the small-bore handheld mortars, the *patareros*. How were they to storm the walls? The closer they came to Panama City, the more daunting the task that lay before them.

Morgan continued to stare into the blaze . . .

"Captain?"

. . . drawn to the fire, to the heart of perdition . . .

"Captain? Can we do this?" Nell repeated.

This time he heard. He blinked and looked away from the blood-red coals and the dancing flames. And found his voice: Morgan was coming, with fire and sword, with justice in one hand and judgment in the other.

"Trust me," he replied.

28. The wall.

Morgan was one of the first to rise, and in the gray hours before the sun announced the new day. He lay with Nell nestled against him on the blankets, his steel-gray eyes searching the dimly seen canopy of branches overhead, catching a glimmer of color, the plumage of birds soaring and diving among the branches. His thoughts were not of nature, however, but human nature, the order of things, the tricks he must try, the lies, the patience, and the men he must face down, bend to his will—bend, but not break. Had he planned for every possible occurrence? No. But he was ready and willing to adapt. He'd have to.

The Spaniards were a tough and formidable foe. They would fight for their city. He would have to be ruthless to prevail. Put the fear of God into them. Break their spirit, and the entire garrison would surrender.

It was simple.

Send Hastiler and his marines, along with the Kingston boys, around the left flank. Depend on Calico Jack, Thomas LeBishop, and another third of his force to clear the right flank and turn any resistance back toward the waterfront. Morgan, Tom Penmerry, and Six Toes Yaquereño, the Portugee Devil, the remaining freebooters and the Maroons, along with the Kuna scouts, would cut straight through town, destroy the barracks and reach the waterfront where the pirates intended to free the prisoners, recruit as many as they could to serve the Black Flag, and drive the rest into the streets to cause havoc.

The lure of treasure and the force of his personality had held this diverse army together. They were so close now, and each man knew what was expected of him once they breached the walls: to fight, and die if need be, gain control of the battlements facing the bay, and be prepared fire upon any of the longboats coming over from the forts. Once the city had fallen and its battlements were under Morgan's command, the forts guarding the seaward approach would either surrender or witness the looting, but be unable to act.

For now, the buccaneers had the element of surprise. Once that was gone Henry Morgan and his men would have to rely on their boldness, their ruthless skills, and Morgan's luck to conquer the city. *"Morgan's luck"—so it was now and had always been. He believed in it, and in himself and his destiny* . . .

Morgan sensed the woman alongside him was awake. He glanced down and met Nell's gaze. For a brief moment he succumbed to emotions he dare not encourage. *Love her now, then put love aside.* Fear for her safety for one brief moment; but, with the dawn, he must set aside his concerns. When the shooting started, he'd need a heart of iron.

"What are you thinking?" she whispered.

"I think you know," he said. Then he patted her arm, leaned down and kissed her forehead with all tenderness, then he stole away from the remains of his fire.

He moved carefully past the huddled forms of sleeping men, chose his path wisely, and made his way back to the pool. Morgan stripped away his clothes, set his pistols and cutlass aside, and walked out into the shallows to stand beneath the waterfall. It was an invigorating experience. The cascading waters pounded his flesh and set the blood flowing through his limbs.

He emerged a quarter of an hour later, gingerly stepped across a shelf of table rock and returned to edge of the pool where he had left his clothes. As he dressed there beneath the cliff, Morgan noticed for the first time a faded display of petroglyphs, images drawn upon the rust-colored stone face in black and faded chalk-white clay. Some of the images had been etched into the surface and then filled in with tints from a variety of pastes made from minerals and jungle plants.

He recognized one image which appeared to be a man standing near the falls; there was the depiction of game, symbols he did not recognize. Other scenarios showed men locked in mortal combat, wielding axes or crude bows; there were severed limbs and headless torsos. Morgan was drawn to the images, reached up, placed his hand upon them, as if attempting to make a connection with an ancient past.

"Nothing changes," a voice said behind him.

Morgan, startled, turned, ready to fight, only his weapons were on the ground out of reach. The same could not be said for the Black Cleric's. Thomas LeBishop grinned and held out the cutlass in his hand and jabbed at the pistols and cutlass Morgan had left on the ground.

"You should be more careful."

"Why? I am among friends, am I not? Look, even you have come to protect me while I bathe."

"And yet, the great *Tigre del Caribe* would be a tempting prize for most men."

"Not as tempting as the riches that await us in Panama City."

"Hmm, you have a point." LeBishop flashed a devilish grin. He walked past Morgan and exaimined the petroglyphs on the cliff face. Behind him, Morgan finished dressing, pulled on his boots and then tucked his pistols in his belt and draped his cutlass and baldric across his shoulder. "It never changes," LeBishop said, his sunken features looking ashen in the gray dawn.

It had begun to rain, a fine, faint shower that spattered off his black cloak until he moved beneath an overhanging ledge that protected the ancient-looking depictions. He indicated the artfully rendered carnage with the point of his cutlass.

"Men struggle, men die. 'The Lord is a man of war,'" LeBishop solemnly intoned.

"Exodus," said Morgan, identifying the quote as he joined LeBishop beneath the ledge. "Don't look surprised. I had parents, before the Spaniards came."

"Indeed. But did their lessons take?"

"I follow my own charts," Morgan said. "Always have. Always will."

"Of course, of course," LeBishop replied, dragging the tip of his blade across one of the drawings, leaving his own mark upon the work of ancient hands. Morgan reached up and batted the blade away.

"Don't."

"And a man of sentiment. Most impressive. Laudable. But it can get you killed." LeBishop returned the cutlass to his belt. "How much farther?"

"We'll be at the gates of Panama sometime tonight."

"Then we'll unleash the dogs of war, eh? Well then, let us spend this last moment in truth."

"I would have it no other way."

The Black Cleric stroked his bony chin, his tapered fingers looking pale and bloodless. He fixed his cold blue eyes upon the younger man. "We must be ruthless if we are to carry the day. And even then, many of us may fall—I think, perhaps, even you."

Is this a veiled threat? And poorly concealed at that. A man should expect no less when he makes a pact with perdition. But LeBishop and his men will fight like berserkers, and if we are not to perish in the streets of Panama, then I must give the devil his due.

"It may be as you say." Morgan studied the petroglyphs, these ancient drawings of men in battle. Whose hand had left such a legacy for an age-old curse, that men must wage war, must struggle and die for game or gold? He felt a connection with those who had come before, who had left their mark as tribute or warning. "I may fall, or you, Thomas, or the both of us. But no matter. Men like us are destined for the same place."

"And where's that?" LeBishop warily asked.

Morgan flashed a wicked smile. "Upon the wall."

29. The devil at dawn.

W hat day is it?" Morgan whispered, standing in the darkness at the edge of the Darien swamp, from which he had recently emerged along with the hungry, bone-tired army of rogues and adventurers who had followed him into this green hell. Only now, among this dissimilar collection of pirates and soldiers, noblemen and Indians, only now with the walls of Panama City a bold slash of shadow against the night, did the enormity of their undertaking strike home. The stygian reaches of the swamp offered a perilous route of escape at best. The words *Conquer or Die* began to mean something more than a brave man's rhetoric.

"It is the twenty-ninth day of January in the year 1671," said Nell, touching his hand. She could see his face, with its growth of beard, the grime-stained purple coat he wore, the linen shirt stained from swamp water, his mudspattered breeches and boots. She knew even in the darkness, his weapons were clean, from musket and pistols to the blade of his cutlass, the tools of his bloody trade. This was not a man to take lightly.

"The Dons will talk about this day," he muttered, wearing the burden of command as lightly as the scarlet scarf about his head that was holding back his unruly hair and keeping the sweat from his eyes.

"And frighten their children to sleep," Nell said. " 'The day Mad Morgan came to play.' "

"From your lips to God's ears," Morgan replied, his gray eyes burning. "Israel Goodenough . . ."

"Aye sir," a voice called from farther down the column.

"If you and Mister Kogi will be so kind as to bring your powder monkeys along with me."

"As you wish, Captain," Israel called back, and softly issued orders to half a dozen men to join him.

"*Mahali gani*, my captain," said Rafiki Kogi. "What sort of place is this?" The deep-set eyes in his coal-black face peered at the walled city a few hundred yards from them.

"It is the place of blood and thunder," Morgan told him, but his voice carried along the line of men, from Sergeant McCready to Calico Jack and past him; Morgan's words were repeated the length of the column, by the Duchess and the Portugee Devil, Kintana and Captain Hastiler and his marines, to the end of the line and the crew of the *Jericho*, who owed allegiance to only one man here, the Black Cleric. "Screw your hearts to your backbones, lads, for I am taking you in harm's way." Morgan started forward, leading the powder crew away from the column. The rest of the men would pursue them from a distance. Morgan sensed Nell walking at his side.

"I thought you would remain with Pierre and the others."

"My place is with you."

"Toto, I would not have you take undue risk."

"I chanced worse than this when I took you to my bed," she scoffed.

"It was my bed," Morgan reminded her. "My house."

"So you say. That only proves you are not as clever as you think."

"I had better be," Morgan grimly reminded her as they neared the main gate.

Nell sensed his change of mood. She had her own worries. "And what will you do when you find her? For no doubt Elena Maria de Saucedo awaits within." She was under no illusions concerning the hold the Doña had on him, Morgan with his dreams of nobility and his weakness for a pretty face and the sultry wiles of a sensuous woman.

Her question was fairly put. And Morgan wasn't sure he had the answer, at least not at first. Elena had used him in an attempt to free herself from the grasp of her new husband, to win his name and title but not his hand. But for all Elena's pretenses, their passion had been real. Of that he was certain. But it was Nell who had come to him and walked in his soul and saved him, Nell Jolly, his friend, his consort, his woman.

"I am for you," he whispered.

But that was the last endearment. Talk was at an end. It was time to get down to business. Gold and glory would not be won by romance, but with cold steel and hot lead.

By dawn's first blush, Major Gilberto Barba led a column of sixty-four mounted dragoons along the Via España toward the front gate of the city. Barba noticed at a glance the empty walkways stretching off to either side of the main gate. El gobernador had left strict orders that the sentries were to be posted on those walls both day and night. But from the look of the huddled shapes clustered around their cookfire beneath the thatch-roofed lean-to, the soldiers were lax in caring out the orders of issued by Don Alonso. Then again, these same men had once been loyal to Barba, whose own fortune had suffered since Don Alonso's arrival.

The major halted his mount, a gray charger he had raised from a colt and gentled to the sound of his voice. The men behind him also reined in their mounts as a small herd of goats followed by a pair of *criollo* goatherds and their dogs guided the animals down the thoroughfare. One of the lads walked beside a mule-drawn pushcart loaded with clay jugs of goat's milk. He called out, "Fresh milk. Fresh milk today!" in a reed-thin voice that carried along the street and soon brought a variety of inhabitants out from their adobe houses to wave him down and purchase his wares. Other carts were loaded with caged birds, poultices, woven baskets, trinkets, and fresh eggs.

Barba ordered his men to continue on without him while he delayed his own progress by a small but well-kept house and front garden protected by a low wall barely a foot high. Barba straightened his uniform, sucked in his bay window of a gut, and tried to look as if he had arrived at the house by accident. He dismounted and began to check his mount's leg for a nonexistent injury. As his men filed past, the owner of the house, a comely widow by the name of Mimi Sanchez, emerged and hurried out to greet the goatherds as they passed. The wooden wheels of the milk wagon creaked and groaned like a pair of chained banshees.

"One jug!" the widow called out, her plump womanly shape wrapped in a shawl and cotton smock. It seemed as if her bedclothes were always in danger of falling off her body. Especially whenever Major Barba was nearby. As per the woman's instructions, the young *criollo* left his cart and started to carry a jug of milk up to the widow's house. Barba intercepted the younger man at the gate. He had been planning this move for several days now, ever since the widow had flashed him a smile in church and sat by his side on the wooden bench nearest the statue of Our Lady during the mysteries of consecration. Whatever guilt he felt for such sacrilege paled at the prospect of having a relationship with such a delightful creature as the widow Sanchez.

"I will take that from here," Barba told the younger man. "If it is your pleasure, Señora."

"By all means, you are too kind, Señor Barba," Mimi said, flashing a toothsome smile. Her dark hair was gathered back from her features by a scarf. Her round cheeks seemed to have a natural blush. The aroma of woodsmoke and flour and roasted coffee beans clung to her like a warm invitation for a man to abandon his solitary life and enjoy the pleasures of domesticity. A man had to wonder, just who was baiting whom?

The jug was heavier than it looked and Barba almost regretted his decision to meet her this way. Plus it was difficult to keep from spilling the contents of the jug as he made his way through the garden. And the saber in its scabbard seemed to have a mind of its own this morning and tried to tangle itself about his ankles. Barba gave a kick and almost lost his hold on the jug, clutched at it and splashed the front of his uniform, soaking the green tunic. Barba cursed and then noticed the señora was none too pleased to see her goat's milk wasted on the ground and the soldier's coat. The major flashed her an innocent grin and shrugged his shoulders.

"It is not the weight of this clay jug but the proximity to such beauty as yours that makes me awkward, Señora Sanchez." Barba knew he had salvaged the situation the minute the words left his lips. The widow beamed and motioned for him to watch his step and follow her.

"You are most gallant," she said. "Such conduct deserves a reward."

"Alas, I must not tarry," the major said. "My men await."

"It would be a shame to hurry things along, Señor. After all, I fear you will be gone all day. It will be a lonely time for us both. But we could have something warm to remember," the widow suggested. She peered through the burgeoning light at the column that had begun to bunch in the middle of the street in front of the gate. "They are grown men. Let them wait. What harm can they come to?"

Before Barba could answer, the gate and a portion of the surrounding wall exploded with a deafening boom that obliterated the wooden panels, sent a column of dust and mortar billowing into the air, collapsed the front walls of the nearby houses and storefronts, buried the sentries in the lean-to beneath a mound of rubble, and knocked Barba and the widow to the ground. The air was filled with jagged splinters and fist-sized chunks of stone that sprayed the dragoons and their mounts and felled almost every man.

Barba gasped and cried out for God's mercy as he felt a warm liquid spread across his chest. *Madre de Dios!* His chest had been blown open and he was bleeding to death! He rolled over on his side and winced as jagged shards of pottery dug into his side. He had landed on the jug of goat's milk. It was this liquid he had felt, not blood.

"Señora Sanchez!" he gasped, spitting out the name as he crawled to his feet. The widow was lying right where a projectile of brick-and-mortar had clipped her temple, giving her a mottled purple bruise and knocking her unconcious. One look over the low wall and Major Barba envied the woman. His blood turned to ice and his grimy features could not mask his astonishment as a lone figure, an image of terrible dread, materialized out of the swirling gray smoke and white dust, came like a wraith on the wings of the wind to blot out the sun and all hope.

"No," the major groaned, momentarily transfixed by the horror. Cringing behind the wall, Barba watched the scattered remnants of his patrol gamely try to repel the howling brigands hurtling through the shattered entrance. Barba blessed himself with the sign of the cross, and crept away. He had to save himself. The major had to reach Doña Elena and warn her of what he had seen.

It was the devil at dawn.

It was Morgan!

30. "Let them remember this day."

Morgan felt a musket ball tear at the sleeve of his purple coat, another fanned his ear, just below the scarlet silk scarf keeping his long brown hair away from his face. He squeezed off a shot from the double-barreled pistol in his left hand, saw a Spanish dragoon clutch at his chest and stagger out of sight. Morgan parried a second attack with his cutlass, shoved the desperate defender aside and into the path of Kintana. The Kuna rebel wielded his ax and crushed the Spaniard's skull, leaped over the fallen man and charged off through the rubble in search of another victim. The screams of the dying and the war cries of the pirates and Indians could be heard above the din.

A figure in black shoved past. Morgan turned as the Black Cleric drew abreast of him. LeBishop's scarred pale features split with a grin. He resembled a cadaver come to life, death's own angel in the garb of a minister, gold cross twinkling from his earlobe, a freshly blooded sword in the Cleric's hand.

" 'O our God, wilt thou not execute judgment upon them!' " he bellowed. The brigand was jubilant. He fixed Morgan in his wild-eyed stare. "I do not think we will meet again, *Tigre del Caribe*. I suspect it is your last day upon this earth." He laughed, flung himself into the melee and led his men off toward another section of the city.

Morgan ignored LeBishop's admonition and pressed on through the smoke and the fire, kicked aside the splintered timbers and smoldering ruins that blocked his path, while all around him a battle raged, fighting and dying overwhelming the senses. Morgan was in no hurry. Men rushed past him, men he knew and recognized: Hastiler and his marines, more of the Kuna rebels, then another company of buccaneers, Calico Jack and Anne Bonney, Israel Goodenough, Pierre Voisin, eager for plunder; Rafiki Kogi, an ebony flash of movement and destruction with his dagger and pike.

Morgan loosed his own war whoop, the violence of the moment fueling him. Once he had been paraded through these gates, a prize captive pelted with stones and refuse by the populace, strung up and hanged for their amusement. Where were they now? Was there no one to greet him?

Suddenly Morgan heard his name called out.

Nell's voice!

He whirled about, sensing danger, fearing she was in trouble, only to find himself the target of an assassin's blade. He felt a dagger sting his side, heard a pistol roar close behind him. Morgan grimaced with the pain and retreated, a trace of blood seeping from a superficial gash a few inches above his hip. Peter Tregoning, LeBishop's man, his ugly pockmarked face contorted in pain, staggered forward. The Cornishman brandished a jeweled dagger in his hand, the very weapon LeBishop had taken from Elena in Maracaibo, a lifetime ago.

The dagger slipped from Tregoning's grasp and he sank to the ground, a look of surprise upon his face. LeBishop's henchman had not expected to die. Few men do. Nell stood behind Tregoning; smoke curled from the pistol in her left hand. As quickly as she had acted the first time, her right hand raised up and she snapped off a second shot. A Spaniard emptied his musket into the air instead of Morgan's back, and fell dead.

"Am I going to have to save your life all day?" she shouted angrily, reloading her guns. " 'Morgan's luck,' indeed."

"You are my luck, Toto," he grinned, and turned back to the city. Then his gaze hardened, stung by the swirling smoke and dust. He stood for a moment as if in rapture, while his army poured through the streets. The unnerved populace near the front gate abandoned their homes and shops, their cries swelled like a tide of terror to engulf the city of gold.

There was terror in his name: "Morgan! Mad Morgan!" The outnumbered remnants of the dragoons broke and fled before the onslaught of the buccaneers, who surged through the shattered entrance like blood spurting from an open wound.

"Let them remember this day." Morgan turned, thought he glimpsed his father's silhouette shrouded in the settling dust. "I swear it," Morgan called out. The specter dissolved into the haze of burning timbers, perhaps it never was. Reassured by the sound of his own voice amid the gunfire and the shouting and the crackle of spreading flames, Morgan paused to inspect the gash along his side, a flesh wound, then knelt down and retrieved the jeweled dagger. This was the Black Cleric's doing. There were two enemies within these walls, the Dons and the Black Cleric. So that was the game. Morgan frowned. So be it. Morgan would play. But by his own rules.

From her balcony, Elena Maria de Saucedo del Campo watched Panama City convulse like a wounded beast. The city seemed to writhe and shudder as flames spread along one perimeter, a series of explosions rocked another district, as panic ensued and rumors quick as wildfire swept through the ranks of the defenders. She had heard the terrified populace choking the streets as they sought to escape the invaders. An army of bloodthirsty freebooters had stormed the gates accompanied by hordes of howling savages. Where were the troops? Where was the new governor?

Elena clutched her dressing gown about her shoulders as she listened to the church bells peal their warnings then fall silent one after the other as cathedral doors were battered down and the sanctuaries looted. Homes and shops were abandoned as the frightened inhabitants trampled one another in a frenzied attempt to reach the waterfront and escape along the coast.

She reentered her room and crossed to another window that offered her a glimpse of the distant waterfront. Townspeople crammed themselves into fishing boats and set out for the relative safety of the forts in the bay, whose garrisons could do nothing to stem the assault. The forts had been built to defend against an approach from the sea. There weren't enough longboats to ferry reinforcements to shore. The soldiers out in the bay were prisoners behind their own walls and could do nothing but wait and watch— and ask themselves the same question as the citizenry: Where was the governor?

Elena could tell them. With Consuelo's assistance, she quickly dressed in a simple gown of heavy cotton, a cloak, and buttoned boots. Consuelo's fingers fumbled with the fastenings. She was understandably unnerved by the sounds of explosions and gunfire that drifted through the open window. When her curiosity got the better of her, Elena returned to the balcony. She gasped at the black pall that hung like some mantle of despair over the north end of the city. Several houses, stables, and shops were ablaze. Skirmishes seemed to be occurring throughout the streets. Behind her, Consuelo began to chant in her native tongue. Elena turned to scold her but her admonition died at the look on the half-breed's face. Consuelo's mouth was a straight slash, her dark gaze guarded, blind eye a bleak milky-white orb. Her movements were jerky and tense.

"What is it?!" Elena asked.

Consuelo fled from the balcony and sought the safety of the room. She shook her head and began to chant beneath her breath. Elena shivered and caught her by the shoulders.

"Old nurse, what is it? What do you see?"

"Nothing. Only darkness." Consuelo, locked in her own gloomy thoughts, shook her head then continued to chant in a monotone her unsettling prayer-song. Even after all these years and the efforts of the padres, the old ways were still alive within her. The blood of the Kuna that coursed through her veins called out to her, beyond the din of destruction, beyond the fire and death. In her mind she saw the great swamp, the hidden bayous, the secluded villages of the people her own mother had been taken from. The Dons and their gold were none of the half-breed's business. Besides, Elena Maria had changed since her father's death. The girl Consuelo had nurtured had vanished long ago down a dark path the old nurse no longer wished to follow.

Elena Maria sighed in exasperation at Consuelo and left the nurse alone in the room. Proceeding down the hall, she paused at the open door to the bedroom Don Alonso had taken to using when he chose to spend the night within the house of Saucedo. She heard the sound of a heated conversation drift up from the lower reaches of the hall. She hurried downstairs and followed the voices to their source, her father's library, where Don Alonso was busy issuing orders to a number of subordinates, a trio of handsome young lieutenants with sun-bronzed features dark as coffee. They doffed their tricorn hats and bowed as Elena entered. The officers barely took time to speak before they scurried from the room and departed through the front door.

Elena entered the study as Don Alonso, behind her father's desk, finished loading a brace of pistols and shoved them in his belt. He brushed a hand through his sliver hair. His brown eyes darted to the desk and the ledgers he had been putting together in a stack before she came in. Elena recognized the transcripts of her father's holdings, the entries from mines and plantations and the shipping manifests that listed the contents of her father's warehouse. She frowned and started to speak, then noticed a familiar figure with powder-burned features slumped against the wall behind her.

"Gilberto . . ."

Major Gilberto Barba waved weakly. His tunic was torn, his trousers spattered with dirt and bloodstained from a slit above his thigh. She had hardly recognized him at first. He smiled wanly; seeing the daughter of the house of Saucedo helped to restore his strength. The brandy she quickly poured for him was of immeasurable help.

"The major brings disturbing news," Don Alonso said, trying to sound calm. But his voice carried a brittle edge.

"It's Morgan," Barba rasped. He drained the contents of his glass, wiped the droplets from his thick moustache on the sleeve of his rumpled green coat. The brandy burned going down but the warmth that spread through his limbs was a blessing. "Morgan and an army of brigands and savages," he added, already sounding stronger. "They've breached the walls of the city."

Elena Maria hid her reaction, her surprise betrayed by the merest flutter at the corner of her mouth and the subtle widening of her eyes. Morgan . . . here? Back from the dead? An incredible feat . . . She glanced at her husband, the governor, and immediately began planning how she might exploit this situation to her own advantage. There was a good chance Don Alonso might fall in battle. She longed to be a grieving widow and in charge of her fortune once again.

"We are ready for this cutthroat. I will have him on the scaffold yet, and this time"—his gaze hardened, he was looking right at Elena Maria—"he shall hang, once and for all." Don Alonso slid a rapier into its scabbard and draped the baldric over his shoulder.

"No one is ready for the likes of Morgan," Barba said. "The brigands came at us through the dust and the rubble, like some kind of great and terrible storm. My men could not stand against him. I barely escaped with my life. It wasn't easy getting here. I was nearly captured several times. Just a couple of streets over I narrowly avoided a band of butchering cutthroats. *Madre de Dios*. The rogues are close at hand."

"Major Barba has behaved like a coward and we shall not forget his example," said Don Alonso. "I have dispatched troops throughout the city. Should Morgan fight his way past them, he will find me waiting with over five hundred men in the Plaza de las Armas. Let him break his attack against us. These pirates are an untrained rabble and no match for regular troops. We will stop him in the plaza and drive the remnants back into the swamp." He lifted his attention back to Elena. "As for Major Barba's warning, if indeed the pirates are close, I suggest you come with me. For I have no men to leave here with you, Señora. And this coward will be of little use."

"I will take my chances," Elena replied.

Don Alonso frowned. Disobedience did not sit well with him.

"I have my own defenses against a man like Henry Morgan." Elena Maria did not enumerate the other weapons she could bring to bear. Her considerable charms, sultry beauty, and feminine wiles had worked in the past on *el Tigre del Caribe*. She saw no reason they wouldn't succeed again, if need be.

"Suit yourself," Don Alonso replied. "But these accounts will go with me. I shall place them in the armory by the Plaza de las Armas."

"They are my father's, you have no right to them."

Don Alonso stacked them and placed them under his arm. "They will be safe with me."

"Nothing of my father's is safe with you, Señor."

Don Alonso ignored the verbal dagger. He glanced at the wounded officer. "Major Barba, I suggest you see to your injuries and then make your way to the stockade. I expect you to keep an iron hand on the slaves. No telling what mischief they may attempt this day."

"As you wish, Señor."

Don Alonso tucked the ledgers under his arm and started toward the door. Elena Maria moved to block his departure. Their eyes met, the governor and his bride locked in a silent struggle of wills while all around them their world was coming to an end: fire-gutted buildings came crashing down and others burst into flames, while the streets ran red with blood.

"Señora, you plucked a pretty tune when first we met," Don Alonso said bluntly, "but the music soured once you had my good name." He forced his way past her and was gone through the front door before she had a chance to reply. The governor walked briskly into the broad, tree-lined avenue where a column of dragoons, astride their nervous mounts, waited to escort him to the Plaza de las Armas.

Elena watched him leave with the ledger books. There was nothing she could say. And words were a waste of time. Action was called for. She turned, brushed her long black hair back from her face, and fixed her gaze on her father's old friend. Elena's lustrous green eyes held him bound as she spoke in a warm and seductive tone. "Gilberto, you will come with me. You have always been the one friend I could count on. I shall need men to empty what I can of my father's warehouse and ferry the goods and gold out to one of the merchant ships in the bay. If we hurry we can save a good portion of it. But I need your help, now more than ever, my dear and trusted *aliado*."

Barba considered her request. It meant disobeying the governor's orders. Don Alonso wanted him back at the prison stockade, back guarding slaves and prisoners. But Gilberto Barba's allegiance had always been to the house of Saucedo. And he had never been able to refuse Doña Elena anything. If Morgan and his men got past the Plaza de las Armas, there would be no stopping them. Let the prisoners fend for themselves. The major ambled forward, galvanized into action. "Come, Señora, I will find you men," said the portly officer. The cutthroats he had avoided could find them at any moment. "We will do what we can."

"Harness the mare to the carriage," Elena said. "I shall bring Consuelo and join you at the garden gate." She leaned forward and kissed his grizzled cheek, then hurried from the room.

Barba blushed at the endearment and followed her out into the hall but proceeded past the stairway and moved quickly toward the rear door of the house. The rest of the servants were nowhere to be seen. It was obvious they were keeping close to their homes or had already fled the city. With no one about to report him, Barba lingered in the kitchen long enough to help himself to a bottle of wine left by chance on an oaken table near the cooking hearth. He drank as much as he could hold, barely pausing for a breath. He didn't know when he'd have such luck again. And when he had finished, the major tossed the empty bottle into the hearth and resumed his course.

Outside, the garden was devoid of life, sun-washed, with paths of crushed shell and stone that wound among patches of brittle weeds and dying shrubs. A flock of parakeets, their bright yellow-and-green plumage dazzling in the drooping limbs of a forlorn-looking willow, scolded the intruder as he crossed their domain. The air was thick with the stench of powdersmoke. Barba began to cough and had to pause to catch his wind, his great bulk rising and falling with the effort. He stared at the wrought-iron gate and beyond to the barn and carriage house. *Hurry!* an inner voice commanded.

"*Sí,*" he replied aloud, answering his own thoughts. He lumbered down the garden walk, favoring his wounded leg with every other step. His large hand caught the gate and shoved it open. He stepped into the alley.

To his immediate left, a pistol boomed. Something struck his skull with enough impact to twist him about so he could see his own skull fragments, blood, and gray matter smear the garden wall. Mercifully, the light in his eyes faded as Barba toppled like a felled oak, slid down the wall, his legs splayed behind him as the weight of his body dragged him to earth. His arm caught in a vine and kept him from slumping completely to the ground, but left him kneeling, his ruined face pressed to the garden wall.

Thomas LeBishop grinned in satisfaction, reloaded his pistol, stepped over Barba's garishly positioned corpse, and entered the garden just as Elena Maria emerged from the back door and hurried down the steps, oblivious to the major's fate. "I cannot find—" she said, and halted dead in her tracks.

She recognized the Black Cleric swooping toward her. She turned and made a break for the house. Her left foot found a large stone among the crushed seashells. Her ankle turned and she lost her balance, fell to her hands and knees, lost precious seconds, scrambled to her feet and tried to reach the back door in time. Too late. The man in black descended on her like a raven to its prey.

31. "I have seen your heart."

The red-haired Scot was dead. Poor Sergeant McCready, a damn good cook and a jolly soul. No prisoner could have asked for a better jailor. *Mother McCready... what have you done to yourself? Gone with your dreams.* Morgan knelt and closed the dead man's eyes, stepped past him and a half dozen other fallen English marines who had attacked a troop of Spaniards defending the Cathedral de Santa Maria.

Captain Hastiler had fought all the way to the top step before being bayoneted by a dying grenadier. Now a strange calm settled over the street and the church, although the bell in the tower overhead continued to ring ominously, to sound an alarm no longer needed. The citizenry, already routed from their complacent lives, had been sent through the streets.

Hastiler was sitting on the top step surrounded by dead Spaniards, his back to the pockmarked stone wall, his legs outstretched. The captain's powder-burned features held a vacant stare. The grenadiers had outnumbered the marines three to one. The corpses littering the church steps like discarded rag dolls testified to the furious melee that had transpired.

"Well met, Captain Morgan," Hastiler said, blood trickling from his lips, spreading across the lower three buttons of his waistcoat.

"I would wish for a better meeting," Morgan softly replied, kneeling by the officer. "Your men fought well."

"The same cannot be said for your kind," Hastiler muttered bitterly. "LeBishop had been at my side. But when we struck the Dons, the Cleric held his men back and let us take the first volley."

Morgan frowned, regretting now he had ever brought LeBishop along. The man was as treacherous as a barrelful of black snakes. "I shall read the Black Cleric from his own book when next we meet."

Hastiler nodded, taking comfort in Morgan's tone. "The devil and I will be listening."

"I need to get into the church," Morgan added. "The belltower will give me a good view of what awaits us in the plaza."

"Knock and it shall be opened unto you," Hastiler chuckled, then coughed pink froth. He looked at the remnants of his command standing among Morgan's buccaneers, then lowered his gaze to the Spanish dead. "It was a grand little fight. They outnumbered the lads but we took their measure and taught them something about the price of English honor."

"That you did, Captain Hastiler," Morgan told him.

The Englishman grimaced. "I leave a wife, Beatrice, in Kent. She's a good lass who deserved better than the likes of me."

"She shall have your share of all we gain. You have my word on it."

"That'll do," the marine said, and closed his eyes. "That'll do." His breath slowly escaped. And his chin sank to his chest.

Morgan felt Nell's hand upon his shoulder. He shrugged her aside. He had no time for tenderness. Morgan stood and crossed to the cathedral door and began to hammer on the wooden panel with the butt of his pistol.

"Open this door, or by heaven I shall burn the church and everyone in it!"

A series of protests could be heard within. Then he heard an iron latch slide back on the opposite side of the door. The heavy oaken panel creaked open. Morgan caught Nell by the arm and dragged her out of the open doorway as a ragged volley blasted the sunlight and wounded a pair of Kingston lads who were foolish enough to try and be the first into the church.

Morgan scowled and charged into the shadows. He glimpsed movement, emptied both pistols, heard screaming, saw a man stagger into the light, clutching his abdomen. Behind Morgan his crew arrived. Nell Jolly, Pierre Voisin, and Rafiki Kogi dashed into the shadowy interior. More gunfire ensued, followed by the clash of swords. The remaining grenadiers were no match for the buccaneers.

Morgan parried a bayonet thrust, escaped disembowelment, and

clubbed his assailant across the face. The man fell backward, unconscious, and knocked over a holy-water font. His companions met
more violent ends, perishing by gun or blade or speared by pike. As
the last of the defenders lay dying, Father Estéban hurried forward.

"Enough! Enough! Have you no shame? This is the house of
God!"

Morgan blocked the priest's progress by stepping directly into his
path. "It's my house now, padre." Morgan took the priest by the arm
and led him back toward the cluster of men, women, and children
who had gathered around the altar in fear for their lives. "But God
can have it back when I'm done with it."

"Mercy, for heaven's sake," cried the priest, placing himself in front
of the families who had sought sanctuary in the church.

"You ask for what was never shown me," Morgan snarled, his gray
eyes cold as mist on a grave. "But a brigand will grant what your flock
would not, padre. Keep them out of my way and none shall be
harmed."

Morgan turned away from the priest and the families under his protection, and stalked across the church to the ladder built into the
tower alcove that led up to the bell. Evidently one of the Spaniards
had been sounding the alarm, for the noise had ceased. With Nell and
his crew looking on, Morgan borrowed a spyglass from Kogi then
proceeded to scale the ladder up to the top of the tower.

Pierre Voisin took that moment to refresh himself. Fighting was
hot, dirty, thirsty work. He walked down the aisle to the baptismal
font, flashed a gap-toothed grin and winked at the cowering families
who, despite Father Estéban's assurances, expected the worst at any
moment. Then Voisin dunked his head into the pool of water. The little thief drank his fill, splashed the holy water over his neck and face,
and emerged from his "bath" dripping and refreshed.

"Bastard," one of the Spaniards hissed, an arrogant-looking merchant, his round belly pressed against the folds of his sleeping gown,
his white hose fallen around his ankles.

"Mais oui," the Frenchman lamented. "With me, an unfortunate
accident of birth." He stepped up to the merchant and poked the tip
of his dagger against the well-fed merchant's stomach. "But I see you
are a self-made man." The thief turned away from the altar and swaggered back down the center aisle of the church. Nell had finished
reloading her weapons and was anxiously awaiting Morgan's return.
The gunfire seemed distant now. Rafiki Kogi was standing in the

doorway, watching the street and the gathering force of buccaneers awaiting Morgan's orders. The African stepped aside and glanced toward the tower room as he permitted Israel Goodenough to enter and directed him to the tower alcove. The lanky gunner joined Nell at the base of the ladder.

"Kintana's here, and what's left of his men," Goodenough reported, shouting up to the man above. "He said that the stockades have been opened. Most of the slaves and prisoners have taken to the hills but there are some who've joined us." Goodenough cradled one of the bulky mortars. It was an ugly-looking weapon with a short barrel mounted to a stout-looking stock. The missiles themselves were fist-sized iron spheres, larger and heavier than grenades and packed with black powder and a fuse that ignited when the mortar was fired. It was a frightful weapon when fired into a group of men, and was capable of inflicting terrible damage both from the explosion and the iron splinters that would tear through flesh. "Calico Jack has showed up with the *patareros*."

"Good." Morgan's voice drifted down from the tower. His boots scraped the rungs as he descended to the alcove floor. He removed the spyglass from his belt and returned it to Kogi. "Don Alonso has prepared a warm welcome for anyone attempting to storm the plaza," the buccaneer informed his companions. He glanced at the grimed, powder-burned faces surrounding him. "This is it." His voice had a hollow ring in the confines of the alcove. The painted visages of saints surrounded them, peering out from the whitewashed stucco walls. Well now, here were his disciples: no band of angels, but every one a true heart. "The city stands or falls in the next few minutes. How do you fare, my pretties?"

"I'm fresh as a daisy," Voisin remarked, still dripping holy water. And everyone laughed, defusing the tension.

"I say we run out the guns," Goodenough remarked. "Give 'em a broadside and board 'em Captain."

"*Wakashambuliana!*" Kogi cried out. "We attack like wolves!" He leaped and slashed the air with his pike.

Morgan turned toward Nell Jolly, her beauty hidden beneath soot-streaked cheeks and a face of battle. The young woman might have counseled caution, but there was no way she would hold back now. She knew as well as anyone, they must conquer or die. "We don't have to accept Don Alonso's invitation," Nell began. No one liked the idea of walking into a trap. But like the men around her, she would follow Henry Morgan to hell and back if need be. "Then again, it would be a shame to disappoint the Dons after they've gone to so much trouble for us."

The men around her murmured in agreement and closed around Morgan, who slipped the jeweled dagger from his belt. "I've a plan," he said, and drew a rough diagram of the Plaza de las Armas upon the stucco wall, scratching his plan of battle across one of the more colorful frescoes, disfiguring poor St. Francis of Assisi as he communed with the doves.

Don Alonso paced the gallows like a captain on the deck of his ship. From the scaffold he could take in the entire plaza and the battle square his troops had formed. On two sides, north and south, the grenadiers in tricorn hats stood in firing ranks, their bayonets fixed. The dragoons and lancers, the feathers of their plumed caps aflutter, had been ordered to dismount, and defended the east and west flanks. The lancers had traded their ten-foot spears for muskets from the armory. The dragoons felt incomplete and only grudgingly agreed to fight afoot. The north and south flanks each had a nine-pounder artillery piece loaded with grapeshot. The artillery crews had stacked powder and shot behind each of the cannon. The field pieces were light enough to be brought around to protect whichever flank came under attack.

"Come on, then, show yourselves," the governor shouted, intending to bolster the courage of his troops. "Stand at the ready, men of Spain. We shall carry the morning and Morgan will rue the day!" The sunlight struggled to break through a soot-colored haze that hung above the Plaza de los Armas and the waiting troops like a layer of ghosts. Men shifted nervously, their eyes began to sting. The officers moved among the troops, cautioning the men to check the priming pans of the muskets they carried. The weapons seemed to grow heavier with every passing minute.

Don Alonso struggled to breathe as the haze settled over the plaza. His men needed a clear field of fire. Not this damnable smoke. Why here? Why now? Was the Almighty conspiring against him?

Already, reports had reached him that the prison stockades had been attacked and the prisoners and slaves released to wreak havoc on the populace. So much for Major Barba. Worse news swiftly followed. The troops in other parts of the city had broken and joined the frightened populace in their efforts to escape the freebooters who pursued them out onto the shore, killing them as they fled, chasing them to their boats or back into the forested coastline.

But Panama City could still be saved, here in the Plaza de las Armas. The governor tried to lick the inside of his mouth. Funny, the palms of his hands were wet with sweat, but his mouth was dry as sand. He stared at the low-roofed stucco barracks surrounding the plaza. The men he had stationed on the rooftops crouched low and tried not to reveal their presence. An eerie quiet descended over the plaza and the streets beyond. The calm lasted but a few seconds yet seemed an eternity, a stillness building in unbearable intensity.

And then it ended. Muffled blasts sounded from all sides as Israel Goodenough directed the fire from the *patereros*. Black iron spheres sailed in graceful arcs through the choking haze to land among the troops in their battle formation. Don Alonso recognized the sound of the mortars and flung himself to the gallows deck. Before his soldiers could scramble out of the way, the missiles exploded, gouging holes in the earth and showering the men with slivers of burning iron. Grenadiers and dragoons and lancers by the dozens fell writhing on the ground. Worse, one of the mortar rounds dropped next to one of the nine-pounder cannons among the powderkegs. A terrible blast sent men sprawling, and rattled the gallows frame so hard it nearly collapsed.

Then, in the wake of the explosions, came the blaring sea horns and the savage cries of the Brethren of the Black Flag. Don Alonso struggled to his feet, his ears ringing from the blast. He wiped a forearm across his eyes to clear his vision and watched in horror as his troops buckled and caved in toward the center of the square, firing as they retreated.

Morgan had instructed his men to use the drifting smoke for concealment, and massed his men behind the acrid haze. The explosions were the signal. He glanced at Nell, her features flush with excitement, then shouted for his men to follow him. "Do you want to live forever? Come on, you brine-soaked scalawags, steel your hearts for bloodshed and follow me." A roar of approval erupted from the men around him; it was a cry that swept around the plaza. This was the moment of truth.

Morgan plunged through the drifting shrouds of gunsmoke and dust, ordered his men to loose a volley and hurry before the Spaniards could regroup and form their square. Faces and silhouettes loomed out of the gray. A lieutenant was desperately exhorting his men to return to their ranks. He whirled about in time to see Morgan bearing down on him. The young officer slashed with his saber. Morgan blocked the attack, kicked his opponent between the legs, and bludgeoned him as he doubled over. Pierre leaped astride two grenadiers and knocked them to the ground. His dagger rose and fell twice in quick succession. The Frenchman scrambled to his feet, his knife blooded, and dashed off to help Kogi who had impaled one dragoon on his pike. Kogi didn't need his help. A breeze stirred the smoke.

Morgan glanced up and spied the gallows. He started toward the steps. Men in uniform rose to contest his advance. They were no match for his blade, or the cold fury in his iron eyes.

The other nine-pounder got off a single round before its crew was overrun by a host of ax-wielding Kuna rebels. Kintana, one arm blown away by grapeshot, was the first to reach the cannon and with his dying breath shattered the skulls of the first two soldiers he reached. Then, with a loud, anguished moan, the warrior collapsed, his body draping the corpses of his enemies, his blood mingling with theirs.

Morgan fought his way past the cannon, slashing and parrying with his cutlass. A grenadier tried to skewer him with a bayonet. Morgan head-butted his attacker and knocked him senseless. The buccaneers, attacking from all four sides, had closed fast with the troops so the musketeers on the surrounding buildings could not shoot for fear of hitting their own. Before long a few well-placed rounds from the hand mortars cleared the roofs.

Within minutes the Plaza de los Armas had been transformed into a butcher's yard. The discipline of the Spanish troops crumbled before the onslaught of the buccaneers. Pistols and muskets were fired at point-blank range; cutlass and knife, pike and club slaked their fill till the ground ran red from the carnage.

To his horror, Don Alonso saw his command lose heart, panic, and break for the adjoining streets. "No, you cowards! No! You must stand. Stand and fight for your King, for your governor, for your own honor!"

"What do you know of honor?"

Don Alonso recognized the voice. His veins filled with ice. He tried to swallow and nearly choked. Then he slowly reached for his rapier, removed it with thumb and forefinger and allowed the weapon to drop to the gallows floor. "Señor Morgan, I am unarmed."

"That's too bad," Morgan replied, climbing the steps to stand upon the deck, gray smoke swirling about his torn shirt and the wounds that streaked his torso. "It won't stop me from killing you."

Don Alonso had only one chance, and took it. His hand dropped to the pistol tucked in his belt. He spun and stepped to the side, saw Morgan with a pistol. From below, Nell Jolly emerged from the haze in time to see the two men fire as one. She cried out in alarm.

Don Alonso staggered, stumbled forward, and sank to his knees. "No," he groaned, clutching at his chest. "I am the governor," he protested, as if his position protected him from death. "I am *the governor.*"

Morgan shrugged. "You're just dead now." He tripped the latch, the trap door dropped open, and Don Alonso, no longer in the world, disappeared through the center of the floor. He landed with a loud thump on the hard-packed earth below.

Henry Morgan crossed to the steps and halted to survey the carnage. *Well, Father, we are avenged,* he thought. He watched the remnants of the Spanish troops scatter, with many of the buccaneers spurring them on. A breeze sprang up, parting the haze, revealing the dead—most of them Spanish troops, but enough familiar faces to make the victory a costly one. Dutch Hannah and Six Toes Yaquereño, the Portugee Devil, lay among the dead, and others he recognized and some he hardly knew, but his crew had come through unscathed save for a few flesh wounds. Kogi's black face split with a grin. Voisin looked anxious to head for the warehouses, to see for himself the wealth of the city. Nell was unharmed, but grim-faced. So much death unsettled her. Israel Goodenough made his way forward with his crew of men with their hand mortars. They had proved invaluable. Several minutes passed in the aftermath of the fight. Morgan issued no orders, but allowed himself and his men a moment to gather their strength. There was more to be done.

Calico Jack and Anne Bonney picked their way across the plaza, escorting an old woman Morgan instantly recognized. Jack and his notorious paramour had somehow come across Consuelo, Elena's nurse. Morgan glanced about to see if the noblewoman was with them.

"Now, that was a fight, Captain Morgan," said Calico Jack. He seemed remarkably unscathed. But Anne Bonney had certainly been in the thick of things, from the look of her. "Worth marching through the swamp for." He motioned for Anne to bring Consuelo forward. "And look who Annie found."

"She found me," Bonney corrected, tying a strip of cloth about a slash on her forearm. The heavyset woman had been nearly disrobed in the fight; her checkered shirt did little to hide her ample bosom. She motioned for Consuelo to approach Morgan.

The half-breed's eyes widened at the sight of Don Alonso's lifeless form crumpled beneath the gallows. "I followed the sound of battle. I came to see you, Señor Morgan."

"Where is your mistress?" Morgan said, his gray eyes searching the woman's face for a any sign of treachery. He read only fear and a sense of resignation. But his request caught Nell's attention.

"The man in black, Captain LeBishop, has taken her. He would have killed her. But she offered to take him to the waterfront, to show him the wealth of her father's house." Consuelo shook her head. "I am leaving this place. I shall try to find my own people. Tell my mistress I am gone."

"Me?"

"When you save her, Morgan. You will go to Doña Elena." Consuelo had said her piece. She inured herself to the sight of all the wounded and dying, and disappeared through the swirling, acrid-smelling haze. "I have seen your heart, Mad Morgan," she called back to him. "You will go to her."

The buccaneer shook his head—*Thomas LeBishop*—and then, unable to meet Nell's stare, Morgan took up his cutlass, leaped from the gallows, landing lithe as a cat, and stalked off toward the waterfront. He knew the way, he'd walked it often enough in chains. Morgan did not look back to see if anyone was following. Because at the moment, he didn't give a damn.

32. Dead men's eyes.

Morgan had never seen the piers and the waterfront so deserted. News of his arrival had sent many of the townspeople scurrying out along the coastline. The sun-dappled blue bay was dotted with all manner of boats: skiffs, johnnyboats, fishing boats, dinghies—anything that would float. But those who could not make good their escape had retired to their homes, resigned to their fates. Morgan would leave them there. They had nothing he wanted.

El Tigre del Caribe had come for treasure and a reckoning, and both could be found only here on the waterfront. He could not have one without the other. And what of Elena? Did he really want to see her again. Yes, for the last time. To prove something to himself. And there was the matter of Thomas LeBishop.

He sucked in a lungful of air, relishing the scent of the cleansing breeze that blew the gray-black haze landward toward the hills but left the waterfront bright with the sweet light of dawn. The fire and noise of battle had disturbed the gulls and sent them farther along the coast away from the storm and the fury that had swept through the city.

He caught sight of the crew of the *Jericho* making their way along a pier after they had secured but one longboat. When they saw Morgan waiting for them, the men balked then came sheepishly forward.

"The sun will set on only one flag today. *My* flag," he told them. "You must decide for yourselves . . . who will you serve."

One of the men indicated a massive wooden building with the name

Saucedo emblazoned above massive twin doors. "Captain LeBishop may have something to say about that."

"Fair enough," Morgan replied. He turned and glanced toward Nell, Israel Goodenough, and the rest of his ragtag army. "Wait here with these good men. Kill them if they try to come to their master's aid."

"He'll need no help from us," another of the Black Cleric's men called out.

"The seadog speaks the truth," Nell said, catching Morgan by the arm. "LeBishop is a dangerous man. Don't let your honor lead you to ruin. We can face him together."

"Stay here, Toto."

"Nell speaks the truth, *mon ami*," said Voisin. "Let us deal with him together. It is our right to go with you."

"No," Morgan exclaimed flatly. "It is your right to avenge me."

Gold. Silks. Pieces of eight. The treasure of kings glittered in the Black Cleric's eyes. He was alone with Elena Maria. But he wouldn't be for long. He'd dispatched his men to find some johnnyboats and bring them around to the pier nearest the warehouse. He intended to take what he could and sail from the port. And no one was going to stop him.

He gazed in awe at the contents of the warehouse. Except for the open center of the building with its tables and bench seats, aisles led off past trunks of gold ore and chests of rough gems that caught the lantern light and twinkled back at him like stars, only blood red and ice blue and sea green, and opal white like dead men's eyes. He was rich. No, not rich—a king.

He sensed movement, caught a glimpse out of the corner of his eye and sprang to the left. He caught Elena Maria by the arm as she tried to make a break for the entrance. The woman grimaced but would not cry out as he twisted her wrist. The more she struggled, the greater the pain. At last she surrendered, knowing he had the advantage of strength.

"I don't think so, my pretty," LeBishop purred, dragging her back and forcing her down upon a bed of silk. His scarred features glistened with sweat. Lust was the gleam in his eyes. "Perhaps I shall have a taste of the treasure you denied me in Maracaibo. I don't have your pretty dagger, pity, but I gave it to a man who has no doubt put it to better use." He placed her hand between his legs so she could feel his arousal. "See here, lass, I've saved a different dagger for you. My unsheathed flesh, eh? What say you?"

"I say that when you load my father's treasure aboard my ship, best you take me with you or you will never sail past the forts," Elena blurted out, her cheeks flushed. Strands of her unbound black hair clung to the corners of her mouth, slick with sweat. "Allow the garrisons to see me on deck and you will not be fired upon. But I will have to be alive and well. Touch me now and I will resist until death."

"You are a clever girl," LeBishop purred. Lust was one thing. Treasure another. The Black Cleric had his priorities. The pirate shoved clear of the woman, rose from his makeshift bed and allowed her a brief moment of freedom. "But my time will come. Now or at sea. Mark you, my time will come."

"Indeed, LeBishop, well said," Morgan called out as he shoved open the doors to the warehouse and stood in the entranceway, allowing a bright shaft of sunlight to bathe him in gold. "For your hour is at hand."

LeBishop shielded his eyes and retreated from the glare. "Morgan . . . still alive?"

"Henry, thank God!" Elena darted out of the reach of the LeBishop, putting as much distance as possible between LeBishop and herself. Morgan was the man to defend her. She could think of no better ally. The woman quickly made her way to his side.

Morgan tossed the jeweled dagger at the Black Cleric's feet. LeBishop scowled. Tregoning, the clumsy fool, must have bungled the assassination and gotten himself killed. There was no accounting for Morgan's luck. But it would end today.

"Mother always said if you want something done, better do it yourself."

"You had no mother, only the fen-sucked flotsam that spawned you."

"Bold talk for a man about to die," LeBishop said, drawing his cutlass. "We both know I am the better man. I have no equal with a blade. I will carve you like a beef and have my treasure loaded by noon."

"Kill me if you can," Morgan replied.

LeBishop charged. His black coat flapped as he bore down on his victim, his cutlass a blur as he chopped and hacked and stabbed from side to side then tried for the head. Morgan retreated, parried what he could, then dodged most of the other blows, yet suffered another gash along the ribs and lost a bit of scalp. LeBishop pressed his attack, unrelenting, his blade whistling through the air as it sought flesh and blood.

Both men began to breathe hard. The clang of steel on steel echoed through the warehouse. Their boots scraped across the floor. Morgan almost lost his footing more than once. His arm was weary and he began to doubt himself. For years the two men had been heading for this confrontation. It was long overdue.

With a clash and a clatter, Morgan's blade snapped, the blade spun off into the shadows. LeBishop lunged for the kill. Morgan tossed the hilt in the Cleric's face and dashed out of harm's way. He retreated, searching the area around him for another weapon, noticed the jeweled dagger out of reach and instantly regretted tossing it out like a challenge.

He kicked over a chest of spices, tossed another box of gems at LeBishop, who ducked and danced away, laughing. Hurling anything he could get his hands on into the Black Cleric's path, Morgan fell back to the depths of the warehouse, back where the riches gave way to the produce of the plantations, barrels of salted pork, grain, and cut cane. And there among the shadows he spied a leather-wrapped wooden grip and he smiled grimly in recognition as his hand closed round it, remembering a youth spent in captivity and the years of labor in the fields of Santiago. Morgan knew in that moment he would not die this day.

"What are you waiting for, LeBishop? Come and finish it."

The Black Cleric paused, caught his breath. The man was unarmed, wounded. No longer a threat, but still insolent to the end. And indeed this was the end.

"What is this? Are you afraid?" Morgan called out. "Come on. One good cut deserves another."

LeBishop raised his cutlass and charged, bearing down like the wrath of the God Almighty. Twenty feet, fifteen, ten . . . "Morgaaaannnnn!" Kill him. Kill him. Kill . . .

Morgan stepped aside and as the Black Cleric rushed past, swung the weapon he had found, the tool that once had been like an extension of his arm. The cane-cutter rose and fell. Lantern light flickered off its broad hooked blade and caught LeBishop along the back of the neck. The Black Cleric's body collided with the back wall and flopped atop a stack of hides. Elena Maria cried out and averted her gaze as

LeBishop's head rolled into the light and came to rest against an overturned box of pearls.

Morgan emerged from the shadows, he paused by the gruesome remains of the Cleric, lifted the cane-cutter—the symbol of his servitude had been his salvation. He laid it gently by LeBishop's remains and crossed the warehouse to Elena's side. She turned to him, pressed her face against his chest and began to sob.

"You're a widow now," he said.

Elena Maria stifled a gasp, tried to conceal the joy surging through her spirit. Her fortune was safe. And she had del Campo's name. Everything had worked out. Morgan was here. They could be together again, at least for a while, and she would have his protection. This was her hour of triumph.

"Thanks be to heaven, my love. My own true love." She wrapped her arms around his neck, her chest crushed against him. She ignored the blood that stained her dress, and covered his face with kisses. "I knew you would come for me. I knew I could count on you, that you would not forget what we once shared. It can be that way again now. You will grant me your protection as you once did not so long ago. I know you will, my beloved." She sensed they weren't alone and peered past his shoulder and noticed Nell Jolly standing in the doorway, and behind her, Pierre Voisin, Rafiki Kogi, Israel Goodenough, and a crowd of buccaneers, all of them awaiting Morgan's orders.

"Sacre bleu," Voisin muttered, in awe at the treasures. The others could not even manage an oath. They were struck dumb in the presence of such wealth.

"Panama is yours, Captain Morgan," said Israel. "What are your orders?"

Morgan gently freed himself from Elena Maria's grasp and faced his companions, this time meeting Nell's gaze, seeing the question in her eyes, and answering it the only way he knew how.

"Leave the pearls, LeBishop sort of has his eye on them."

Elena Maria's features turned ashen. She couldn't believe what she had just heard. His protection, he must spare her, because he loved her, because . . . "No."

"Take it!" Morgan called out. Yes, Panama was his! Morgan's great heart swelled to near bursting as he indicated the gathered wealth of the house of Saucedo. "Take it!"

"Wait!" Elena wailed, and collapsed to her knees in horror and buried her face in her hands. "No!"

"Yes!" Nell Jolly shouted. She dashed across the room to leap into Morgan's waiting embrace.

Henry Morgan raised his arms aloft and raised the roof beams with his thunderous cry.

"Take it all!"

We are Brethren of Blood,
we are sons of the sea.
We are children of havoc
and born to be free.
Draw up the gangway and come take a stand,
We'll have prize money aplenty, when next we spy land.
So here's to the Black Flag we follow with pride,
Here's to Morgan, Mad Morgan who sails on the tide.

Author's Note

Panama City and indeed the might of Spain and its presence in the Caribbean never recovered from Morgan's raid. The buccaneers remained long enough to empty every warehouse and pilfer every private strongbox and chest of valuables to be found. Henry Morgan, with his army strengthened by a number of freed prisoners and slaves, crossed the isthmus by the high road and returned to his ships. The remaining Spanish forces around Portobello had no wish to confront *el Tigre del Caribe*, and allowed him to escape without so much as a challenge.

Sir Richard Purselley returned to London where he abandoned a political career but achieved some notoriety as the author of a colorful but unexceptional memoir based upon his many "adventures" in the islands.

Doña Elena Maria de Saucedo del Campo, her fortunes lost and Panama City in ruins, attempted to rebuild her family's estate. Changes in the Spanish court further undermined the influence she had struggled so desperately to attain. History does not record her fate, only that she set off into the heart of the isthmus to reestablish her father's sugar plantation and was never heard from again.

Henry Morgan returned to Jamaica, and after a brief stay sailed for England. By then the peace with Spain had already unraveled and

Morgan's exploits, not to mention some well-placed gifts of Spanish gold, won him favor with the English court. He was knighted Sir Henry Morgan and appointed governor of Jamaica. He returned to that island, took Nell Jolly to wife, and lived out his days a man of power and influence.